Denyse Woods, who sometimes writes as Denyse Devlin, is an Irish novelist based in Cork. Born in Boston and raised all over the place, her novels include the critically-acclaimed *Overnight to Innsbruck* and the bestselling *The Catalpa Tree*. Reflecting a long-held interest in the Arab world, three of her books are based in the Middle East. Her work has been translated into six languages. *Of Sea and Sand* is her sixth novel.

Of Sea and Sand

Denyse Woods

First published in 2018 by
Hoopoe
113 Sharia Kasr el Aini, Cairo, Egypt
420 Fifth Avenue, New York, 10018
www.hoopoefiction.com

Hoopoe is an imprint of the American University in Cairo Press
www.aucpress.com

The translation of the quotation from Imru' al-Qays on page vii is by A.J. Arberry, from *The Seven Odes: The First Chapter in Arabic Literature* (London, George Allen & Unwin; New York, Macmillan).

Exclusive distribution outside Egypt and North America by I.B.Tauris & Co Ltd., 6 Salem Road, London, W2 4BU

Dar el Kutub No. 11388/17
ISBN 978 977 416 803 1

Dar el Kutub Cataloging-in-Publication Data

Woods, Denyse
Of Sea and Sand / Denyse Woods.—Cairo: The American University in Cairo Press, 2018.
p. cm.
ISBN: 978 977 416 803 1
1. English fiction
832

1 2 3 4 5 22 21 20 19 18

Designed by Adam el-Sehemy
Printed in the United States of America

To Henry, Lauren, Diana, and Sebastian
To Jonathan Williams
In Memory of Aingeal Ní Murchú

قِفا نَبْكِ من ذكرى حبيبٍ ومنزلِ   بسَقْطِ اللوى بين الدَخول فحَوْمَلِ

Let us weep, recalling a love and a lodging
by the rim of the twisted sands

—Imru' al-Qays, *al-Mu'allaqat*

In the dark of night I believe
And sometimes in the day;
Maybe they're not there at all
But still I believe.

—"The Good People" by Vincent Woods

I

Dear Prudence

IN THEORY, GABRIEL HAD COME for a month; in practice, he knew he would never go back. Glancing out, and seeing jagged black mountains appear on the right of the aircraft, he gasped. He had thought he was beyond any such reaction, believing himself to be numb and numbed, too detached for wonder of any sort. Awe, he thought, was a luxury enjoyed by the emotionally alert, by those of enhanced perception, whereas he was dulled, blunted, now and forever, amen. And yet he had gasped when he had looked through the aircraft window and seen those magnificent angry edges scraping the blue-blue sky. It looked to be an inhospitable environment down there, but it could hardly be worse than the environment from which he had come.

He had been dispatched to stay with his sister in order to recover—not from a breakdown or a bout of serious illness (although he felt as if he'd had both) but from guilt. Shame, too. Pointless, he thought. What cure for shame? A change of scenery could hardly be expected to wipe it out. No, the only thing that could repair the damage was for time to go into reverse, to undo his steps and allow him another direction. Unfortunately, air travel could not offer the same facilities as time travel but, still, he had come away; although he could not undo the remorse, he could at least escape his parents' wordless agony.

His heart burned. This was the beginning of an odyssey, one that had already failed, because it could not do otherwise, but he would nonetheless trudge along its way, going wherever it took him, never, ever, turning back. He would not even look over his shoulder. He would not return to Ireland, or see again her lumpen skies, her slate headlands or creamy beaches. It was a heavy price, yet no price at all.

His brother-in-law met him at the airport with a cursory handshake—scarcely a welcome; more an acknowledgment of his arrival. Gabriel, it seemed, had traveled three thousand miles to receive the same chilling treatment he'd been enduring at home. The airport building was small, dusty. Men wearing long white dishdashas and skullcaps stood around chatting, but offered a nod and a greeting, "Welcome to Muscat. Ahlan," as Rolf led the way out into the sunshine and across to the parking lot.

As they drove into town, Gabriel noticed, along the shoreline, bundles of white boxy houses, like a crowd that had rushed to the coast and been brought to a halt by the sea. Muscat looked like an outpost, a place on the edge. The edge of the sea, of the land, of Arabia. An ideal place to cower.

"This is Muttrah, actually," Rolf said. "The town is spread out, and old Muscat is farther along, beyond those hills." He pulled in behind some buildings. "We have to walk the last bit of the way."

The March heat was manageable. Gabriel welcomed the sun on his shoulders—some warmth at last—as he followed Rolf along narrow, scrappy streets, where small shops were opening their shutters to the day and shopkeepers nodded as they passed. Space nudged itself between the compacted thoughts in Gabriel's head, spreading their density, making elbow room. For weeks he had felt compressed, as if the air were tightening around him and would go on doing so until he was unable to think at all; a kind of mental suffocation.

They turned up to the right and followed a curved lane, with houses pulled tight on either side, until they came to a corner house. "This is it," said Rolf. "We won't be here much longer. Our new place will be ready soon, but for now . . ." He pushed open the low wooden door and stood back.

Gabriel dipped his head and stepped straight into a white living room. Immediately he saw Annie, and felt relief. She came through a doorway at the back, wiping her hands on a tea towel. They embraced. "How are you?" she asked.

"Wrecked."

They were close, Annie and Gabriel. No better person, he thought. No other person. If there was any hope for him at all, it lay in the understanding and soothing ministrations of his sister. At least he could bear to be with her.

"Come, come," Rolf said, trying to get past them.

"Nice," Gabriel said, looking around. The whitewashed room was sparsely furnished, with bench seating, draped in fabrics the colors of sunsets, along two sides, and a narrow window allowed one beam of sunlight to target the floor. A breakfast table and chairs stood near an entrance that led into a small kitchen, beside which another opening led to the rest of the house. They had impeccable taste. Annie was a stylish bird, he used to tell his friends—and Rolf was Swiss, a perfectionist in all things esthetic; and they had money, which helped. Rolf had been working for an oil company for years and had accrued his wealth on a fat expat, tax-free salary, which he generally referred to as "grocery money." His only real interest was painting.

Annie stood, watching her brother.

Gabriel smiled. There was something in her he adored. Simplicity, perhaps; the way she got things right. He liked Rolf too, a pragmatic artist twelve years her senior.

She did not return his smile. She said, "Funny, you look like the same person you were two months ago."

It cut right through. So this was how it was going to be.

She went into the kitchen. "Tea?"

"Great, thanks. Mam gave me some for you. Tea, I mean. Bags and . . . well, leaves."

"Rolf, would you show Gabriel his room?"

Gabriel followed his brother-in-law up a narrow whitewashed stairwell to a room that stood alone on the top floor. "A little tight," said Rolf, "but cooler in the hot weather. It gets the sea breeze."

"It's perfect. Thanks."

Rolf seemed on the point of saying something. Gabriel hoped he wouldn't. He was only just off the plane, for Christ's sake. Couldn't they keep the recriminations until later? With a blink, Rolf seemed to reach the same conclusion. "Bathroom one floor down, I'm afraid. Come down when you're ready."

Gabriel moved backward to the bed and sat on its hard surface. His hands were trembling. In his own sister's house, he was shaking. What had he hoped for? Compassion? Yes, a little. He scratched his forehead, entertained, almost, by his own narcissism, because only undiluted ego could have allowed him to expect open arms and a shoulder to lean on. And he was fearful now, because if Annie could not forgive him, no one ever would.

He had a quick shower, changed into lighter clothes, and went downstairs. Rolf and Annie were in another room—long and quite formal, with a blood-red hue about it, set off by dark red rugs and drapes. The seating, which ran along the wall, was low and soft and covered in cushions and bolsters.

"Nice," he said.

"This is the diwan," said Annie. "We use it all the time, but in traditional houses it's like the reception room, used for special occasions."

"Ah, like the Sunday room at home. Never used except when the priest calls."

They were sitting rather stiffly in front of a tray (thermos jug, three glasses, bread and fruit—he was hungry suddenly), looking like stern parents who had discovered their teenager had been smoking pot in his room.

Gabriel tried to lighten the mood. "You two look like you're about to give me a major telling-off."

Annie leaned forward to pour. "What good would that do?"

"Might make you feel better." He sat down.

"You think so?" she said, one eyebrow arched, her eyes on the stream of urine-colored liquid flowing from the jug.

They sipped their tea as Gabriel looked around at their accumulated artifacts: Eastern rugs, heavy timber chests, daggers with adorned silver hilts. How easily Annie wore this life, he thought. He envied her. He wished he'd done it. Got out. Away. Before he'd had to.

The tea was served in the small glasses and bitter without milk. He was a man who enjoyed a great wallop of milk in his tea, but he would get used to it, just as he must get used to other things. Like the light—so very bright, white almost, and cheering, as it shone through windows high in the wall. Gabriel felt the change of air, of country and continent, in his blood, which already seemed to be flowing thinner through his veins. "So this is an old-fashioned sultanate, yeah?" he asked. "And the sultan deposed his own father?"

Rolf nodded. "Twelve years ago, in 1970."

"Sounds pretty cheeky. There's no dissent?"

"He's doing a lot for the country," said Rolf. "There were nine schools in 1970, but schools and hospitals are opening every week now, and transport is improving, with new roads heading out in every direction. So of course he's popular, but he's low-key."

Annie was nibbling on a corner of bread—nervously, Gabriel realized. *Christ.*

Rolf cleared his throat and grasped at conversational straws. "So, umm, you've escaped the deep freeze."

Gabriel nodded. "That's long over."

Annie's curiosity dived around her rectitude, like a rugby player getting over the line. "What was it like?"

"Bloody cold is what it was like. We didn't have the snow they had in Dublin, but even in Cork people struggled to get about. Ice everywhere." He wanted to add, Just like there is right here.

"Sandra wrote and said there was a lovely atmosphere, everyone helping out and being cheerful and stuff."

"Yeah, I cleared quite a few driveways."

And that was all it took for Annie to swerve right back into disapproval. "I should hope so. But doing good deeds for the neighbors won't change anything."

"Annie," Rolf said quietly.

Gabriel turned to him with a sheepish glance. "Thanks, Rolf, for . . . fixing this. I hope it wasn't too much hassle getting me that certificate thing."

His brother-in-law lifted, then dropped one shoulder in a half-shrug.

"What does it mean—a 'No Objection Certificate'?"

"It's a type of visa. Oman is loosening up a bit, but you still have to be sponsored by an employer to get in."

"So how did you pull it off? Do I have to work for someone?"

Rolf shook his head. "I explained your—our—circumstances to a well-connected friend of mine, Rashid al-Suwaidi. He owns an import–export company and has other interests. He organized the paperwork."

"Did you have to . . ."

Rolf gave him the hard eye.

"You know—baksheesh, or whatever it's called."

"Bribe him, you mean? He's a friend, Gabriel. He did it for us. So for God's sake don't make any trouble for him."

Gabriel raised his hands in apology.

Rolf stood up. "Baksheesh! Is that the extent of your understanding of this part of the world? The Arabs understand friendship better than any nation. Don't forget that. I must go to work, Annie."

"Don't be late," she said anxiously, as if she feared being left alone with her younger brother.

After he left, silence settled on them, like sepia over a print. Although it had been ages since they had had any proper time alone together, Annie had little to say, it seemed, and Gabriel even less. "So, you like it here?"

"You know I do." With one finger, she pushed a corner of flatbread, smeared with honey, across her plate. "Even more than I expected, in fact. I've made great friends." She put down her glass. "It's a pretty good life, all in all."

Annie was the only remaining person whom Gabriel could look straight in the eye, but it pained him to do so now, because there was only sadness there, and he could see a weight around her, as if the dense atmosphere that had been strangling him was also hugging her, curbing her movements. And that was him. *He* was the very density that restricted her.

She cleared her throat. "So, what do you want to do while you're here?" she asked, as if he were some kind of tourist.

"What is there to do?"

"Well, there's loads to see—mountains, desert, sea. People go fishing and snorkeling, but Rolf paints when he's off work, which might be a bit dull for you."

She made it sound like a personal reproach, which was another low blow. It had been Gabriel, after all, who had picked Rolf out of the crowd in a pub and had engaged him in conversation at the bar. Introductions were made, drinks were bought, and Annie was unobtrusively proffered. "Come and join us," Gabriel had said to the visitor. "I'm with my sister." With a formal nod and almost a click of his heels, Rolf declared himself to be enchanted when they were introduced at the small round table in the corner, though Annie was less impressed. He'd looked like an old bloke to her, but Gabriel had persevered, inviting him back to their home for supper, after which Rolf took over, wooing Annie in a quiet, discreet sort of way. Gabriel knew, instinctively, that he was the perfect life partner for his adored second self, and when the time had come for Rolf to leave Ireland, Annie found it inexplicably difficult to let him go. She had become accustomed to his presence, to the quiet fuss he made of her, to his curious English and his solid, attractive frame, so Gabriel told her to follow, even though that meant going to Oman, where Rolf had been working for some years. To her own surprise, she was easily persuaded. Her job in the bank was dull, the news always bad, with one or another atrocity reported daily from Northern Ireland, and the Republic was gray, grim, and sinking deeper into recession. The Arabian Gulf and the twinkling white town of Muscat, which Rolf had described, were, in contrast, attractive propositions.

They had married after a short courtship—it was the only way for her to reside in Oman, and now, two years later, she was hoping to become pregnant.

"You should get some rest," she said suddenly. "You look exhausted. Aren't you sleeping?"

A sliver of concern shows through at last, Gabriel thought. "Are any of us sleeping?"

"We've been invited out this evening. Dinner with friends," she said. "I accepted on your behalf."

Annie was slight, always had been. Pale of complexion, with short brown hair and livid blue eyes (unlike either of her brown-eyed brothers), she looked younger than she was—gamine; more like twenty-two than twenty-eight. Her long spindly fingers, like spiders' legs, were never still—as now—rolling bits of torn-off bread between her fingertips. She kept her eyes on her hands when she went on, "There isn't much in the way of nightlife. The Intercontinental, mostly. So we socialize a lot in one another's houses. . . . Anyway, our friends are keen to meet you."

"I'll bet."

She looked up. "You don't think I've *told* them? Good God, why would I do that?"

"You haven't said anything?"

"No. I didn't feel I had much choice. Anyway, it's bad enough that my friends at home are gossiping about us over their coffee-breaks." She rubbed her hands together in an abstracted way. "Still, the story's losing its legs now."

"Who told you that?"

"Aunt Gertie. She's been great. Writing every week. She's the only person who seems to realize what it's like for me over here, out of the loop."

"You're far better off."

"Oh, am I? Away from Mam, at a time like this? Have you any idea how hard it was to come back last month? Only I had no choice, had I? Because *you* needed somewhere to run away to!"

This was not it, not it at all. Gabriel had believed he was coming to Muscat to be comforted by someone who loved him unconditionally, and therefore forgave him. Instead, she was hissing and spitting and twisted with hurt. There would be no reprieve here.

"It's so hard at times like this," she said, her voice breaking, "being away."

"I suppose." It seemed fair that she too should be allowed to believe that this was worse for her than for anyone else in the family. There had been a lot of that going on.

"But as far as our friends here are concerned," she continued, "you're on holiday, so perk up. Make an effort, *please*."

Dinner with friends, Gabriel thought, going upstairs to rest. The prospect made him sweat, but at least they wouldn't have to sit across a dining table, just the three of them, trying to duck the elephant.

It was difficult for Annie. She loved Gabriel; adored him. Sometimes she wondered about that, about whom she loved most and to whom she owed the greatest loyalty. Gabriel was a part of her, an extension. He had come the same way with her; they had come the same way together until he'd delivered her into Rolf's safe hands. Into contentment. Initially, she had worried about finding love enough for both men, but had discovered room in her heart to accommodate her brother and her husband in comfort. Neither pushed the other aside; they could remain shoulder to shoulder, it seemed, and her loyalties need never be truly strained. As for their older brother, Max, well, everyone loved Max, and so did she, but when they were growing up, he wasn't affectionate, cuddly, or approachable, and he'd always had work to do. By the time she was a teenager, she'd found him irritating, even embarrassing, and he was no fun; the grooves in his forehead were deep by the time he'd turned thirteen. Gabriel was the soft one, amenable. He and Annie looked out at the world from the same point of reference.

Annie had suspected, when she was younger, that it was on account of her partiality toward Gabriel that she believed him to be so much more talented than Max, but this was fact, not affection. Everyone knew it. Gabriel was hugely, instinctively gifted. He never had to work as hard as Max, but because his focus could meander, the gift eventually became limp. Where Max had passion, Gabriel had fun. Where Max was competitive, Gabriel was laissez-faire. If his big brother had outperformed him, if he had achieved greater things, it would have been because Gabriel allowed it. But for all his work, all his hours on the piano stool, Max's playing had none of the edge of Gabriel's sharp, intuitive expression. *His* interpretation, one teacher had said, was close to perfection. And yet, although applause and admiration were heaped upon him, he had had enough by the time he turned sixteen. He wanted a life, he had told his devastated parents, not the career of the concert pianist for which they, and the School of Music, had been grooming him since he was four. And so Max went after the laurels that everyone—teachers, examiners, and relatives—knew were rightfully Gabriel's. But Gabriel, Annie used to tell her frustrated parents, had another gift—for living and giving, for friendship and humor.

They valued that not at all. Perhaps they were right.

Max had only his work, and they all admired him for it. They loved his peculiarities, his stooped frame hanging over the keyboard come what may, and the way he forgot to eat, sometimes even to wash. They loved him for his poor attempts at telling jokes, though he had no timing, except when he played, of course, and even that had been acquired through hard work. Perfection was the only mistress Max had ever sought.

Recently he had almost, almost, found her.

"This is my brother, Gabriel."

Annie waved in his direction as they stepped into a square hallway, and a tall, dark-haired Frenchwoman reached out. "Gabriel, how lovely," she said, shaking his hand. She looked like a long black pencil. "I'm Stéphanie. Come and meet the others."

In a broad living room, two other couples stood up as they came in. He didn't take in their names, but tried hard, for Annie, to adopt some kind of great-to-be-here expression. Keen. He had to seem keen, to appear as though he had come of his own volition, but the assembled guests, it turned out, weren't particularly interested in him. Small talk rushed in behind the introductions. Expat gossip. He sat mute, feeling like a prize idiot. Baksheesh. Ignorant bastard. Books about Oman had been thin on the ground in Cork, but Annie had left a couple behind, which Gabriel had read while waiting to leave, so he knew about the Portuguese, the British, and the battle of Dhofar. He knew to expect desert and mountains and longed to learn something of Bedouin ways. These had been his expectations of Oman—rudimentary, perhaps, but not unreasonable—and yet the first word he had assigned to this culture was "baksheesh," which came from he knew not what preconceived notion. He still felt the sharp sting of his worldly brother-in-law's rebuke.

He turned his attention to the assembled company: Stéphanie's husband, Mark, was a dapper Englishman, even sporting a silk cravat; Joan, a woman in her forties probably, wore a long skirt and cheesecloth top, and looked as if she had fallen off the hippie wagon, keeping the clothes, but rejecting the lifestyle, to live in air-conditioned comfort in the Gulf. Her husband wore pristine whites and had such highly arched eyebrows that he looked like he was about to take off. Marie, clearly a good friend of Annie, and her husband, Jasper, also English, were warm and engaging.

It wasn't until they were seated at the dining-table that they turned their attention to Gabriel, with a rush of questions. How long would he be staying? What did he hope to do during his holiday? How was he finding Muscat? He had little to say on that score—all he had seen of Muscat was a small airport with two huge sabers over the entrance, some gray-gold hills and a short stretch of seafront, where he had walked with Annie in the late afternoon.

Joan, leaning her forearms on the edge of the table, said, "Annie was telling us that you're a musician."

"A teacher, actually. I teach piano." They all looked at him, expecting more. "At the School of Music in Cork."

"So are you in between terms right now?" Stéphanie asked, perplexed.

Fair question, since it was mid-March, but how was it, he wondered, that people sniffed out the holes in any story without even knowing there were any to be filled? "No," he said. "I've taken a leave of absence."

That silenced them, but a change of topic only made things worse when Joan said, in a pert, determined tone, "Annie, I haven't seen you since before Christmas! How was your brother's wedding?"

"Not *this* brother, I hope," Jasper quipped. "Unless you've run away from your new wife already?"

Gabriel smiled.

Joan persisted: "Did you find something to wear? You were fretting, I seem to remember, about finding something elegant but warm."

Annie chewed a mouthful of lamb at length, as if hoping for inspiration, then swallowed, reaching for her glass, and said, "We stopped off in Rome and I got a dress there."

That at least was not a lie, Gabriel thought.

"It must have been a *wonderful* day," Joan went on. "I always think winter weddings must be so romantic. Did it snow? Winter Wonderland and all that?"

Annie turned her glass between her fingers before saying, "Mmm. It was lovely. No snow, but a great day."

Gabriel frowned at her. Rolf frowned at him.

"I don't think it's romantic at all," said Marie. "I've never understood why anyone could possibly want to get married in the winter. The bride must have been perishing, poor thing."

"Oh, she was," Annie said, turning her eyes to Gabriel. "*Perishing.*"

Pressed for more details, Annie got off to a halting start, but then the words, the fables, began to flow out: she described the wedding, related key moments and amusing anecdotes, and even made Rolf and Gabriel smile indulgently when she looked to them for confirmation that this or that had been the funniest, most touching moment. It was altogether bizarre: a conspiracy of invention.

The wedding chat exhausted, the guests turned their attention back to Gabriel, pushing forth suggestions of how he should use his time and telling him he must see this and this, and mustn't miss that.

Mesmerized, exhausted, he had never worked so hard to be courteous to people who meant nothing to him, but he would have feigned interest in a babbling parrot if it would help him regain his sister's respect. Looking at her face now was like gazing up from within a deep pit to see her peering over the rim, down at him.

❋

"Why did you say all that about the wedding?" he asked her from the back of the car after they'd left. "You don't have to protect me, you know."

"I'm not protecting you. I'm protecting myself. Besides, one lie is much the same as the next. I went with the happy lie."

"But how can you sustain it? Isn't Marie a close friend of yours?"

"Yes, and I'll tell her . . . in my own time." After a moment she said, "I mean, they'll think we're a very odd family." Rolf put his hand on her lap. "But we're not . . . or we weren't, or at least I didn't think we were."

Gabriel knew better than to speak, since he was the one who had given the family this new perception of itself. He looked out. The night lights of Muscat told him little about the town, but when they continued on foot, after parking the car, the dark, quiet alleys that led to the house spoke louder. This was a secretive place; much was held in behind the thick walls. Probing deeper into the warren of back streets, Muttrah felt like a den. His den. He and his shame could hide out there, he thought, for quite a while, undisturbed.

When they came into the house Annie went to the kitchen; Rolf followed her, while Gabriel, near-blind with exhaustion, said goodnight and went up the stairs, but stopped when he heard Annie say to Rolf, "I wanted to tell them. I wanted to say, '*This* is why he is here. *This* is what he has done.'"

"But you didn't," Rolf said, in his most pragmatic tone, "and you mustn't. He didn't come here to be judged, and you, my darling, you of all people, must not judge him."

"Why not? Why should I not? Everyone else does!"

Gabriel could not move without revealing that he was still on the stairs.

"This is how we change," Annie went on. "I turned my head and he became someone else. Do you think I should try to save what's left of him? Of *my* Gabriel?"

"I think it's best you let that Gabriel go."

"I wish I could. And I wish I could leave. Get away. If I don't, I'm afraid I might hurl a glass across the room and cut his face. I want to cut his beautiful archangel face!"

Gabriel went on up. Short of breath, he passed his bedroom and climbed to the top of the house, where a wooden door led onto a small rooftop balcony. He stepped out and stood, fingers in hip pockets. In spite of stars aplenty, galaxies crowding, and a glow coming off the streetlights on the seafront, it was still, somehow, a dark night. Between the stars, the sky was black as oil and deep. Perhaps all Arabian nights were this black.

He tried to root himself in place, not time, to blot out why he came to be there. It took quite an effort to strip away the circumstances, but a slow intake of warm night air and the sight of a minaret along the bay brought him properly to Oman. He thought about the invaders and the traders sailing into this cozy cove over the centuries. Arriving in their long wake, he felt the history in the soles of his feet and saw it in the towers that overlooked the town from the surrounding hills. The three Muscat forts, Rolf had said, were built in the sixteenth century when the Portuguese, alarmed by the size of Oman's navy, occupied this coast to protect their route to the Indian Ocean. Now it was one of the busiest waterways in the world, and the lights Gabriel could see on the blinking horizon were oil tankers, no doubt, plying back and forth.

The dinner party had been the first social event he had attended in months, the first time he had been part of light conversation, had eaten a meal in lively company. It was a relief that nobody had known anything about anything. He had been prepared to face further reprobation, and even though a bunch of strangers could inflict no greater humiliation than he had endured in his own tight neighborhood at home, he was grateful for his sister's discretion. In Muscat he could breathe, was breathing already, in spite of Annie's froideur. How deeply aggrieved she must be, he thought, to go to such lengths to disguise the events that had brought him here. She had almost convinced Gabriel that Max's wedding *had* been a grand shindig, so much so that, listening to her describe it in fantastical detail, he had vicariously enjoyed what had not happened, and never would.

"Max, Max, Max," he said out loud, and the warm Muscat wind curved around him, like a longed-for embrace.

A shuffle of bare feet in the stairwell made him turn: Annie, coming to join him. Good. Perhaps they could talk here, with only the sky to eavesdrop. But no one emerged. He had heard her, he was sure of it. Stepping toward the door, he put his head inside. No Annie.

It was Geraldine who kept Annie awake, not Max. Geraldine, the perishing non-bride.

She had been, in Annie's view, an entirely predictable event. Ten years earlier, she could have described to a T the woman who would one day drag Max away from his piano for just long enough to get him to the altar. Geraldine had made herself indispensable from the start, as if she had seen too many films in which able, slightly frumpy but frightfully sensible women take on those men who are not quite tuned in to the diurnal workings of a life and manage to make them function by reminding them to eat, show up for appointments, and change out of their pyjamas before leaving the house. Geraldine almost certainly seduced Max first—it would not have occurred to him to do so, and if she did not exactly propose to him, he most likely proposed under nifty direction. Everyone rejoiced: the family now had less cause to worry about Max because, with Geraldine's help, the world made more sense to him, and he to it.

She had been endearingly excited about getting married and went for the full hoopla. This otherwise sensible woman in sensible clothes became altogether giddy when talking wedding dresses, bridesmaids, and banquets. Her dull purposefulness was lost in the romanticism of the event, and she even counted the days, she coyly admitted, from ten months out. When Annie had gone home for the summer, to avoid the murderous Omani heat, she shared in Geraldine's excitement—somebody had to, since her brother frequently forgot that they were getting married at all and seemed bewildered whenever his fiancée mentioned entrées or invitations. So Annie became fellow plotter and even helped Geraldine select her dress. It was at least elegant, which could not be said of any other item of her clothing.

What of Geraldine now? she wondered, sitting up in her bed.

She got up, as had become her habit, and went to the kitchen, where she sat, desolate, pretending to wait for the kettle to boil. For all his oddities, Max was never a caricature; he wasn't a nerd, quite, though his eyes were round and protruding, and his smile vaguely goofy. He was thin and gangly, and always wore drab V-neck sweaters (dirty gray and dull olive), with check shirts, inoffensive corduroys, and heavily rimmed glasses. He enjoyed watching soccer (he supported Liverpool, because his younger brother did), had few friends, and he liked for everything to be nice and for the people around him to be happy, so that he didn't have to expend energy on their concerns. Most of the time, he simply wanted to think about musical scores.

He was an unassuming person and Annie liked him, but she loved Gabriel more. She still hoped that nobody would ever find this out. When she was little, having a favorite brother felt like a sin; as an adult, it felt unfair. But Gabriel was so much more accessible than Max and he knew her so well.

Until recently she had always believed that she knew him too. Now she had learned that there was something in Gabriel that none of them had known or seen, not even himself. She wanted to pretend that it had nothing to do with him, that he too was a victim, an innocent. It didn't work. What he had done was part of him, was in him. It had come out. He could not disown it any more than Annie could, because there it was—out, for all to see, and *horrible*. She could not swallow when she thought of it, and often woke at night sweating, waving her hands over her head until Rolf took them and calmed her.

She felt ashamed: guilty by association. The truth was, she hadn't wanted to be the one to put Gabriel back on his feet, but there was no one else to do it, and she owed it to their parents. Her job, and Rolf's, was to gather him in, as only family could, and reconstitute him. Not punish him, but fix him, then put him back into the world with the fervent hope that he would never do anything like it again. The black patch that had shaded all their lives would surely pass over, having dumped its storm upon them.

But this visit—Gabriel coming for an indeterminate stay—was difficult before he had even arrived. Her anger with him bordered on disgust, tinged with hatred. That was it. That was why it had been so hard to smile when he had come in, looking forlorn, from the airport. She had wanted to shake him, but she had hugged him instead, saying, "How are you?" when she meant, How could you? Oh, she'd already said it, many times, in Ireland. It had become the broken record, an unspoken mantra, a plea. Even when she held him against her, feeling the steady embrace of the brother who had protected her, comforted her, seen her through bullying schoolgirls and broken hearts, all she could hear in her head was, *How could you, how could you, how could you?*

In her dreams, she hit Gabriel. In her dreams, night after night, she hit him, over and over, and woke exhausted from all the slapping. It never served to reduce him, or what he had done.

"We must take you to Nakhal," Rolf said to Gabriel over breakfast the next morning. "It's a beautiful spot, with hot springs and a fort. I like to paint there."

Whenever he wasn't ordering spare parts for heavy plant machinery down at the refinery, Rolf was painting. Self-taught, and good, he was neither immensely successful nor struggling, but he was generally preoccupied with his canvases and colors, and Annie knew how to live with that. She had come well prepared for life with an obsessive.

"Great, yeah," said Gabriel. Tone of voice was everything, he was learning. In Cork, he hadn't spoken much of late. No one had wanted to hear what he had to say, and they had had nothing to say to him, so he had been getting the silent treatment, far and wide. But not *this* far, he hoped. Here, he would surely find his voice again.

"So what will you do today?" Rolf asked him.

"I have to go to the house." Annie wiped some crumbs off the table and into her palm. "Check on the painters."

"I'll go with you, so," Gabriel said, looking around the neat front room. "I don't know how you can leave this place, though."

"It's too small," said Rolf. "The villa is very nice. You'll like it."

Gabriel didn't like it. It was in a new suburb made up of low houses with high walls, big gates, and yards too young to have sprouted so much as a weed. The house was spacious, open-plan, and had a huge window overlooking an uncultivated space, the kitchen was wall-to-wall with dapper American units, and the three square bedrooms each had their own bathrooms.

"But this is the best bit," Annie said, flicking a switch in the hall. "Air-conditioning! It'll make such a difference. It's pleasant now, but the summers are . . . well, they don't call this 'hellish Muscat' for nothing."

"How do you cope?"

"By leaving. I'll get away again this year, for the hottest months. Go to Switzerland and then home. Poor Rolf has to stick it out, though. It's like a furnace." She led him down a corridor to one of the bedrooms, where easels were stacked against the walls, and canvases, used and unused, stood in clumps. "And, look, Rolf can have his own studio now. Honestly, I cannot wait to get out of Muttrah."

"But it's lovely there. Authentic."

"Maybe, but that house never felt right to me."

When they got back home, Annie went to the kitchen to make lunch, while Gabriel stood in the front room facing the wide, narrow window, hands in his pockets. Annie was right. There was something odd about this place. He had come indoors, yet felt as though he was still outside. Warmth permeated his bones, like the heat of direct sunlight, even though he was in the cool indoor umbra. Someone passed through the room behind him. He glanced over his shoulder. Whoever it was had gone to the kitchen, but all he could hear was Annie banging about.

Gabriel shivered.

There was something odd about this house.

They were invited out again that night, to a party in the home of soon-to-be-neighbors. Gabriel played it Annie's way—he chatted and flattered, laughed at jokes he didn't altogether understand, and frowned in concentration when the conversation turned to the atrocities just north of them, across the Strait of Hormuz.

"Saddam Hussein is as much of a tyrant as the Ayatollah," said Thomas, a Dutchman, standing with a small group by the outdoor buffet. "They should both be wiped out."

"I thought he was the good guy," said Gabriel. It hadn't impinged much on his existence, the Iran–Iraq war, but now he was a lot closer to it—uncomfortably so—and he realized the only thing he knew about it was that the Ayatollah was a raving madman.

"Hussein—a good guy?" Thomas exclaimed.

Embarrassment drenched Gabriel; he had said "bak-sheesh" again.

"He took power in a coup, wiped out his own cohorts, and now the West is throwing him garlands!"

"No, no," said Jasper, all earnest, "America is *neutral*! Just like the Soviets."

Everyone laughed.

"Hussein's tanks are Soviet," Thomas explained to Gabriel, "but his intelligence is American."

"The West has no choice," Mark said flatly. "If Saddam doesn't win this war, the Ayatollah's fundamentalism will flow out of Iran, and God knows where that will lead."

Gabriel glanced around the walled-in, paved yard, with a solitary tree in the corner, and noticed how the men were all standing together, while the women were chatting indoors, draped across the living room. Voluntary segregation.

"This is propaganda," said Thomas. "America should not be assisting this dictator. If he's still in power when this war is done, his own people will pay."

"They are already paying," said Jasper, "with their young men."

"And he's building a nuclear reactor," said Thomas. "*And* using chemical weapons, according to the Iranians."

Gabriel was aghast. "Chemical weapons?"

"Yes," said Thomas. "We seem to be going backward, not forward."

"World War One rolled up with a nuclear threat," Jasper said grimly. "Something for everyone."

That night, as the night before, Gabriel remained trapped in restless sleep, his dreams intrusive, his consciousness too close to the surface. This was the very state he feared—the wretched half-sleep that suspended and exposed him. That was when blackness came. . . . *Live burial, coffin closed, closed on the living, sinking into quicksand, drowning in sand, in water, mud, like Flanders,*

Flanders-like mud. . . . Every type of burial. Always burial, always alive. It rushed at him from the depths whenever he was off his guard and had lost grasp of his own thoughts. Couldn't control it. Couldn't contain his thinking.

He opened his eyes. Turned. Threw off the sheet. Silence hummed in the background, in this quiet, quiet town. He wanted to switch it off. Silent Night Effect: Off.

Several times he shook himself, like a dog, head to tail, to throw off the sleeplessness. It will wear itself out, he thought. All I can do is wait. Time, Time, the Medicine Man. . . . He trusted in it, waited for it to do its thing. He would let time bleed him, imagine the blood flowing into the tin dish, like in the Elizabethan era, believing it would make him better, while in truth every hour was making him worse. Still, he would go on hoping for a lighter day. An easier day. He was, had always been, an optimist.

He closed his eyes and thought of Sandra, of making love to her . . . and of never making love to her again.

When the first shades of daylight pushed slowly across his walls, opening out the night, it brought some relief. Gabriel slept for an hour and woke again in a sunlit, breathless house. He got up and went downstairs, glancing into the diwan, where beams of sunlight slid in from high windows, slanted across the air, and landed, like children's slides, on the red rugs.

The kettle was burbling in the kitchen, so he walked in, saying, "Sleep any better?" And as quickly realized that he was talking to a stranger.

"I didn't know there was someone else staying here," he said to Annie, when she came down some hours later, poorly slept and cranky.

"Huh?"

"Your friend. She was in the kitchen earlier." She had been leaning against the sink, wearing a long blue kaftan.

Annie blinked at him. "What?"

"You could've told me you had another guest."

"We don't."

"Well, she sure as hell wasn't the maid. Not in a kaftan that was slit up to here."

"You been dreaming, Gabe?"

"No. Tawny hair. Long legs, knobbly toes. Went upstairs. At least, I think she went upstairs."

Annie picked up the coffee pot, took off the lid and inhaled, as if the aroma alone would keep her going until fresh coffee brewed. "You need to wake up, Gabriel. Red hair, long legs? Dream on."

Perhaps she was right, he thought. Bad night, early sun, dazzling. . . . Maybe he *had* dreamed her. If so, he must do so again.

He helped Annie set up breakfast on the glass table in the front room. "I don't know how you two can leave this house, I really don't."

"I told you. I don't like it."

"But why not?"

She shrugged. "Dunno. It has a kind of atmosphere, I suppose."

Rolf joined them in ebullient mood. As he sliced a mushy peach with meticulous care, he told Gabriel about a particular spot near Nakhal where he liked to paint.

Gabriel watched him fuss over the fruit, then suck its gooey slices into his mouth, disintegrating on his lips. She—the woman in the kitchen—had been holding an apple and, with her eyes fast on him, had bitten into it. Silently. No crunching. It confused him that he could not hear her munch in the dead quiet, but then she had dipped her head, walked past him and out of the room.

Annie was right. Must have been a dream, since dreams have no sound.

"Over and over," Rolf was saying, with his forceful enthusiasm, "I'll paint the Ghubrah Bowl until I catch its light and pin it down. You will see, this weekend, how it changes."

After he had hurried off to work, Annie and Gabriel sat in silence. Annie turned her engagement ring around her finger with her thumb. Voices and screeches filtered in from the street.

"Well," she said eventually, "I've a lot to do, packing and so on."

"I can help."

"It's fine. You should go out, explore the town. You'll only get under my feet otherwise."

So Gabriel took himself through the suq where, for the first time, he properly opened his eyes to the Middle East. The narrow alleys, mostly shaded by corrugated-iron sheeting hanging over the shops, were busy enough, though nobody seemed to be in much of a hurry to get anywhere. There were scarcely any women about, and those he glimpsed were shrouded in black, so it was mostly the men who were buying the groceries, and sitting on the steps of their own shops—Indians, Arabs, Africans—calling out to Gabriel, some of them, in unintelligible Arabic. When he came to the seafront, the Corniche, he set off toward the old town, expecting to find it around the bend. The hills, which hugged Muttrah like a protective ring of friends, glowed in the morning sun, and below them white buildings—old merchants' houses mostly, with roofed balconies and intricately latticed railings—curved along the sea in a graceful arc. Dhows bobbed about in the port, their prows raised and their back-ends boxy, like grand old dames wearing bustles. Gabriel stopped by the railing and, for a moment, could almost feel Max beside him, leaning on the railing also, his spectacles on the end of his long sweaty nose. He would have loved these beautiful boats. As kids, they had messed around in dinghies and talked of sailing the world together when they grew up.

On the horizon, oil tankers were waiting offshore. Muttrah formed a perfect natural harbor, a horseshoe of sea pressing into the coast. As Gabriel walked on, Muttrah Tower looked down on him from its perch on one of the hills.

Old Muscat was not where he'd thought it would be. He went around another bend, and another, until finally he skirted a hill and saw a gathering of houses tucked into the mouth of a ravine. A fort perched over it—al-Jalali Fort, perhaps, which had once looked out for the little town and its inhabitants. Gabriel's legs were beginning to feel the walk, but he wandered between the low houses, climbing back streets, lifted by every minute of solitude and by every face that passed him wearing no expression of condemnation.

That evening, when they were all in the diwan—Rolf reading, Annie and Gabriel playing cards at a low table—Gabriel nudged Annie's knee with his foot and nodded toward the door.

She glanced over her shoulder. "What?"

"Your mysterious guest."

Annie looked around again, and back at him.

Gabriel spread out his hand. "Don't you think we should be introduced?"

"What are you on about?"

"I just saw her go into the kitchen."

"Gabriel," she said wearily.

"Oh, I'm sorry. Dreaming again, am I?"

His sister's shoulders seemed to retract, come closer to her body. "There's nobody here except us."

"In this room, maybe, but there is somebody in the kitchen."

Annie put down her cards, pushed herself up from the floor and went through to the kitchen. Gabriel followed. "Nobody in here either."

Perplexed, he leaned over her shoulder.

Annie gave him a sharp, steady look. "Don't start having visions, Gabriel. We have quite enough on our plates at the moment without you going doolally." She went back to the diwan and, as she sat down, Gabriel caught her rolling her eyes at her husband, which forced him to acknowledge the other dialog that was going on—the one between the two of them to which he was not party, the one about him. That look of impatience and irritation accentuated his exclusion.

Isolation shook him. There was little difference between this and home. He might as well have stayed in Cork, enduring ignominy until people lost interest, because to come this far and still find himself alone was proving equally hard.

He wondered what his mates were doing right now. Having a pint, perhaps, while at the School of Music the evening students would be coming in, scales up, scales down; the sonorous moan of a cello would be escaping the old walls; the river outside would be black and cheerless, but the city would be humming with traffic and the pubs filling with customers, as pints were poured and lined along the counters. All this he had denied himself.

Welcome to exile.

"Are you playing or not?" his snappy sister asked. The one he didn't recognize.

He ambled back to the table and picked up his cards. It might have been a shadow, he supposed; shadows, after all, tended toward blue, and she wore blue. Loneliness *could* make you mad. His own self-respect and the respect of others had gone forever. Perhaps he should go help starving kids in Africa. Or work in a Romanian orphanage. Live a life of contrition. Contrition—that strange Catholic concept. It was all coming back to him, the Catholic stuff. Had the schools, against the odds, managed to instill such a belief in sin that now, now he had really committed one, he grappled and clung to that discarded morality?

It wasn't a sin, a voice said, it was a mistake. A voice. *Her* voice—the woman who had not yet spoken.

Rolf was standing over them. "You two," he was saying, "this is enough now. You must stop this tiptoeing. It's like living with paper shapes."

Annie threw down her hand.

"So talk now," Rolf went on. "Courtesy serves no purpose here."

Gabriel glanced at his hand, and also put down his cards. It was a good hand. A pianist's hand. His thin sister, her eyes bigger than they used to be—the rest of her had shrunk—was staring past his shoulder. He swung around, expecting to see the other woman, but Annie was looking at the wall.

"I don't know how you can imagine I have anything to say," he said to Rolf. "I'm deeply sorry, but I've already told you that, told everyone that, and it isn't good enough, so what's the point of repeating it?"

"But Annie has plenty to say, haven't you, Annie?"

She held her fist against her mouth. Take away the enforced normality and there it was, right there, dead close. Behind a very thin veil.

"She wants to say," Rolf began, "or perhaps it is me who wants to say, that she doesn't eat or sleep enough, and we have to resolve that."

"How?" Gabriel looked up at him again. "I can't undo it."

"No, but we have to get better. We must somehow get better, and Annie needs to tell you something."

It was her turn to look up at Rolf. "Go on," he said.

"Which bit?" she asked quietly.

"Any bit will do. Tell him about your dreams maybe."

Gabriel could hear the wind outside, but nothing rattled in this stone house. There was no sound at all inside while Annie sat, her arachnid fingers playing with the hem of her skirt. Then, suddenly, she reached across and, with a swift swipe, struck Gabriel.

His jaw jerked. He had expected it, yet could never have expected it.

She sat back. "Feels slightly better than it does in my sleep."

His hand went to his cheekbone.

"What Rolf means," said Annie, "is that I'm so angry that sometimes I can barely speak. I love you, and hate you, and I hate myself. Mam and Dad blame themselves—did you know that? Do you know they feel such shame they won't walk down the street?"

I'll just sit here, Gabriel thought, and wait until it's over. Let her have her release.

So Annie talked. He'd heard it all before—that is, he'd seen it in her eyes and heard it in his head—but if it would help her, he'd sit it out. His mind wandered—not to pianos or pubs, but to the woman, gone upstairs. Was she listening to this, learning things he would prefer she didn't know?

"And now I've spluttered and ranted and I feel no better," Annie was saying, with a depleted sob. "No matter how much I rage at you, awake or asleep, it doesn't help. It doesn't help, Rolf."

From the start, Annie's friends were determined to show her brother a good time, so Gabriel was invited everywhere: barbecues, garden parties, swimming parties at a beach club. These people seemed to have no cares and were enjoying themselves mightily. The women, unable to work, had little to do beyond child-minding and entertaining, so Gabriel quickly became the focus of their attention. Handsome, tall, and sad, he was a glorious distraction from the usual run of social events. They cooed at Annie. She was well used to it. Her good-looking brother had always drawn appreciation from her own sex and now, in his midtwenties, he looked better than ever. His expression, at once distracted and concentrated, and the ill-concealed distress behind his eyes, only added to his appeal.

Keeping pace with the hospitality offered by others, Annie also entertained him, taking him out and about in a company car. It was a question of keeping up. When asked, socially, where they had been and what they had done, she had to have answers. She couldn't say, "No, I haven't taken him to

Bimmah yet," and "No, we haven't done the wadis," because then they would ask why and she was all out of lies. Creating a convincing wedding scenario had left her exposed. Sooner or later she would let something slip or contradict herself, and someone would say, "But you said . . ." She longed to be honest, to say, "I'm not taking him anywhere because I can't bear to be with him, because he has let me down more thoroughly than anyone could imagine."

Yes, that was the weight on her shoulders: disappointment. The one person who should never have disappointed her had rocked their shared foundations to the point where she could no longer look down. So she took Gabriel first to the Bimmah Sinkhole, some way along the coast, where a comma-shaped pool of sparkling green-blue water reflected the layered limestone walls of its deep crater. Wiry Bedouin boys jumped off a protruding rock on the edge and dropped like stones into the water below, throwing out a great splash, while their friends cheered.

"Tempting," said Gabriel. "What a way to cool down."

Annie peered over the rocky ledge. "Don't be stupid. Those kids know what they're doing."

"How deep is it?"

"No one knows for sure. Divers haven't even got to the bottom yet."

"Maybe there is no bottom." Gabriel couldn't take his eyes off the pool, still and mysterious, a dazzling eye on the orange landscape. "It's like liquid emerald."

"That's because the water is both salty and fresh apparently." Annie pointed to where it disappeared into a low cave. "The channel leads out to the sea. The boys swim through it sometimes. Not to be recommended."

The sea, behind them, made for a bland horizon.

Gabriel was still staring into the sinkhole. "She'll be here."

"Who?"

"Hmm?"

"You said someone will be here," Annie said.

The sun was burning a hole through his scalp, the sweat soaking into his shirt. He couldn't remember how to speak.

"Gabriel?"

He pulled back his shoulders and looked up at the harsh brown hills. "I . . . tourists. They'd come in their hordes if they could only get into the country."

"Oman doesn't need a tourist industry, and it doesn't want one either."

"You mean *you* don't want it to have one."

"Exactly. The fewer people who know about it, the better. And you'll agree after we've had lunch in Wadi Shab."

Gabriel did agree. Jutting ridges, brown and bare, followed the stone riverbed on either side, like spirit guides. On a sandy patch in a grove of date palms, they stopped for a picnic, and sat with Abid, the driver, enjoying flatbread stuffed with cold lamb.

Gabriel squinted up at the fronds that were giving them shade. "I could really get to like this place," he said, thinking about the little house in Muttrah that would soon be seeking a tenant.

"Well, don't."

A few months earlier, Annie had longed to share this with him—her letters had been full of what they could do if he ever managed to visit—but now they were merely in cahoots. Playing roles; playing at being on holiday. Lying to each other every day, every minute from the moment they got up.

"Sleep well?"

"Yeah, not bad," one or the other would say, though both had tossed and fretted.

"Hungry?"

"Umm, starving."

And they would sit over a nice Omani breakfast, which Annie would force down and Gabriel would eat, though the void in his belly could never be met. He had thought it would be easier with Annie, but it was hardest, because he loved her the most. There was so much he could not say. He could not ask, as he would once have done, about the other emptiness—the baby that would not come—because that too was his fault. He could see it, clear as day. Annie had not yet conceived because she was so thin. She had lost a lot of weight. Skin and bones were no home for a baby, Nature knew that, and Annie was not eating properly because of him. He imagined sometimes that he would come down one morning and she would be standing there, holding down the news with rosy cheeks and a sucked-in grin, until it burst out of its own accord: "We've done it!" The whole family could then rejoice. Good news. New life, new birth; a fresh start for all of them. Meanwhile, Gabriel could not mention the thing that wasn't happening.

They couldn't even admit that they were haunted by the same thoughts and no longer knew enough of each other to discover that their very nightmares were moving up and down the house, from one restless mind to the other, changing very little along the way.

Stag nights. Max hated stag nights. He had no stomach for all those relentlessly slopping pints, the forced conviviality, the putrid jokes and mandatory inebriation, but even that was nothing compared with the humiliation that the mob, the groom's own friends, inflicted on their helpless prey. Never having been part of a pack, he couldn't understand the pack instinct, the inherent, irrepressible violence of men, one to another. Neither could he grasp the point of initiation ceremonies seen the world over, from sailors inflicting Neptune's sadistic pleasure on every innocent who crossed the Equator, to the Japanese delight in televisual abasement, and the cruel rituals with which Western men initiated boys into gangs and men into marriage.

Max didn't get it. Gabriel and Annie knew this, and tossed and turned and wondered.

Annie wondered, often, what had become of the wedding dress that had been hanging on the back of a bedroom door, pristine, glittering, ready for the excited bride to lift her arms and dive upward into its silk on her wedding day. Whatever had Geraldine done with it?

She came into the room, swiftly and with purpose, like a wave racing to the shore. Rolf was kneeling over photographs spread on the floor of the diwan, but Gabriel's eyes followed her as she came across the room, barefoot, silent, wearing the same blue kaftan with a silvery panel of embroidery down the front. She was about his age, he reckoned, but she didn't look in his direction when she took an apple from the fruit bowl on the dining-table and bit into it.

"Rolf, introduce us, would you?" Gabriel hissed at Rolf who, with half-moon spectacles on the end of his nose and tilted forward over his pictures, reminded him of a mole in a children's story. No sooner had he spoken than she had left the room.

"I'm sorry?" Rolf didn't look up from his work.

Gabriel was stretched across the cushions, reading. "Who's yer woman?"

"What woman?"

"The one who just came in."

Rolf lifted his chin. "Someone came in?"

"She walked right past you," Gabriel whispered.

"I didn't see anyone."

Gabriel looked at him deadpan. "That's wearing a little thin."

His brother-in-law went back to his photos. "This again? There is no woman, Gabriel, apart from your sister."

"You sure about that?" Once again, he went through to the kitchen: empty. So he took the stairs four at a time and checked the two bedrooms on the second floor and the bathroom. Rolf was right. There was no woman, and yet there was. All the time. Even when Gabriel couldn't see her, he was aware of her. Yet he could hear no footfall, no sound. Odd, how she made no noise.

In subsequent days, the swift passes by their unmentioned guest became unnerving and increasingly perplexing. She wandered about, coming in and out of rooms, but Gabriel's were the only eyes that followed her if she moved, and noticed if she did not. That the others failed to acknowledge her was not a little disconcerting. In fact, they were remarkably adept at turning their heads a fraction too late to see her. He couldn't fathom their reasoning. This was no time for practical jokes and Annie looked no more in the mood for games than Rolf did. So what then? Why the denials? It seemed too deliberately cruel to be some kind of retribution. Since Annie had derived no satisfaction from slapping him, perhaps this was her way of making him suffer—tantalizing him with visions, trying to make him crazy with sightings of an apple-eating beauty, like throwing poisoned cheese at a hapless mouse.

This, however, was not the way to hurt him. On the contrary, he was gaining strength, somehow, from the woman's presence. Her un-present presence. Instead of feeling more adrift, less attuned to reality, he was beginning to feel connected, if not to the world or to his sister, at least to himself.

He felt bolstered, and for the first time in weeks he had something fresh to think about: a new preoccupation. It was a delightful conundrum to ponder during those wakeful nights, wondering about their motivation, where they had found her, what she would sound like if she spoke and feel like if he touched her. He thought about touching her, about calling her bluff, since she too was playing a role, teasing him with glimpses—there again, gone again, real and not-so-real. By arrangement or whimsy, she was messing with his head and that too was flirtation; a delectable flirtation. He wanted to respond; he wanted *in*. Annie and Rolf meant to humiliate him, perhaps, but their motivation was of less interest than the woman herself. She was in the house, and they were lying.

During another bad night, he went downstairs, treading quietly to avoid disturbing Rolf and Annie, but also hoping to disturb the secluded guest—to catch her out. He might steal upon her munching cornflakes in the kitchen, making up for all the meals she missed during the day when she was hiding in whichever cupboard they kept her. By the window in the small kitchen, he poured himself a glass of water and stood looking out into nothing. He didn't hear her coming; he didn't need to.

A flush of desire seeped through him. It had been too long. Nothing Sandra could do, tried to do, had brought back the comforting rush of heat. His impotence was simply another by-product. He could not allow himself any release. He had to live his brother's life, depriving himself of the joys Max no longer knew and even striving on his behalf. Before he'd left Ireland, he had been playing himself ragged to perfect Bartók's Second, which Max had been working on, as if he could somehow finish it for him. But for whom, he wondered vaguely, as he turned to the woman, had he intended to play it?

They made eye contact at last. Sitting on one of the high stools by the counter, legs crossed, one foot bouncing slightly, she looked at him steadily. The kaftan, slit to her thighs, fell over her knees. Her hand rested around a glass of water. This was no trick of his troubled mind—she was as real as he was. Absolutely solid. Her toenails showed the remains of brown nail polish. Gabriel was thinking fast. He needed to provoke a reaction, to shock her into revealing the game, but if he grilled her too harshly, she might take flight or raise her voice, causing a showdown that would bring Annie from her bed. He would then, at least, get some sort of explanation from this deceiving trio. Trouble was, he didn't much want Annie to come.

There was an exchange, short and inconsequential: "You don't say much," he said.

No need to, she replied.

So she did, it turned out, have a voice, a language. In fact, a few languages, he discovered, when she came across to where he was leaning against the sink, and kissed him. It was so sudden that he was the one to pull away, but she followed, leaning into his mouth so that their contact wasn't broken, and from within the closed box, the tomb in which he had been living, he stepped into warmth. He closed his eyes to reconfigure this, and when he opened them—she was gone. In the blink of a kiss, she had vanished.

Sleepwalking. Damn it all if he wasn't sleepwalking. Annie was right, again. Trauma had shocked his body into altered states of mind and turned him into a sleepwalker. There was no arguing it: he was standing alone in the kitchen by the sink in the middle of the night, with an erection sticking out of his shorts—all dressed up and nowhere to go.

It might be revenge, he thought. Max's revenge.

Desire was still there when he woke, his bedroom stagnant with late-morning airlessness. Restive and horny, he kicked off the tangled sheet, her kiss dragging off him still, squeezing him with frustration. Sleepwalking could not account for its lingering taste.

Annie and Rolf were sitting at the glass table, drinking coffee and eating dates.

"I wish you'd eat something substantial," Gabriel said to Annie, sitting down.

"You look tired," she said. "Didn't you sleep? I thought you were taking pills."

"I should leave. It's not doing you any good, my being here."

"You're not here for my good, or yours. You're here so that our parents don't have to look at you all day long. Anyway, where would you go?"

"Africa, maybe? I've been thinking about volunteering for an aid agency."

She snorted. The loving, tender Annie he'd always known was drifting farther into the distance. "You won't find atonement in Africa looking after little children," she said. "You won't find it anywhere," she added, more to herself than to him, and she sounded so aggrieved that a surge of despair rose in his gut.

He went into the kitchen, hoping to find at least a sense, if not a sighting, of their other guest. Though she might be nothing—a wisp, a non-dimensional fantasy working of its own accord on his sad little mind—he sought her out. The glass from which she had been drinking was no longer on the counter, but Annie could have moved it.

He sought her out again when they had left—Rolf to work, Annie to her villa—but this time he was looking for hard evidence, scrabbling around in search of shoes, toiletries, underwear, signs of a hidden life. There were none. Nothing. It came as a relief. It gave him ownership. Any signs of ordinary living on her part would mean that she was just another woman—and not a very nice one at that, if she conspired with Annie to toy with someone she didn't even know. That would be a particularly nasty trick, one that became nastier with every showing, and he could not believe that Annie wished him such ill. That the woman should also be a mystery to Annie and Rolf was a far more attractive proposition, but the mystery made no sense. They *had* to see her. No one was damn well invisible.

The next time she came among them, he tried honesty.

"Listen, lads," he said, with a glance toward the end of the room where she was actually sitting among the cushions her legs curled around her, gripping her ugly toes with her fingers, as if to hide them. "You should call this off, whatever it's about. It isn't very fair to her, or to me."

Neither of them responded. It was as if he hadn't spoken. Perhaps he hadn't.

All right, he thought. I'll play along. They couldn't ignore her forever. Poor girl would starve. Levity might work. "Don't you think you should give the ghost some breakfast?" he asked.

"Oh, don't start," said Annie.

"You don't want her going hungry, do you?"

Annie and Rolf glanced at one another. He hated the way they kept doing that but, undeterred, he kept up the banter. "At the very least a cup of coffee, no? Here, let me get her one." He turned to speak to the woman, "Hi, I'm—Oh, shucks, gone again!"

"Gabriel . . ."

"Now, where the hell did she get to?" he asked, looking at them wide-eyed. "Darn it all if she doesn't keep doing that!"

Rolf stood up, saying, "*Non, non*, she must be somewhere." He looked under the table. "No one. Ah," he stepped across the room and opened a closet, "she must be in here. . . . No again. What a mystery!" He poked his head into the corridor. "Perhaps she went through the wall?"

His antics made Annie smile. "Honestly, you two."

Gabriel smiled also. If he could assuage Annie, engage her with talk of their wandering friend, that would do for now. "I swear to God," he said, "there's a woman in this house who loves apples."

"Apples?"

"Yeah. Noticed your supply dwindling recently?"

"I eat apples," said Rolf.

"Careful, Gabriel." That flicker of a smile was still on Annie's lips. "We don't want the men in white coats coming to take you away, now, do we?"

For a moment they were there, back in their old relationship, when they had nothing between them beyond uncluttered affection. So their vanishing friend was at least serving a purpose, creating light relief, if nothing else.

❃

When Rolf suggested, the following week, that he and Gabriel should take an excursion that Friday, Gabriel was torn. He wanted to see the country but he liked staying put too, enclosed behind the walls of the house, where he could take the air from his tiny stretch of roof, looking across Muttrah's skyline. The town was laying claim to him, and he to it, as it became his quarter. Most mornings he wandered through the suq, acknowledging calls from traders who had come to know him, as he passed on his way to the Corniche, then walked out to old Muscat and back again, sidestepping cars and goats. As the district grew more familiar, so his surroundings embraced him.

Still, it was time to go farther afield and Rolf was restless, fed up with to-ing and fro-ing between town and their new villa, and desperate to get out to his waiting panoramas. Gabriel embodied a good excuse. So they set off early and headed up the coast. The mountains were reticent, as if shy of the very sea from which they had emerged.

"These are ophiolites." Rolf waved at the craggy lumps that passed for hills along the road. They had a curious composition—tubes of rock compressed in and around one another.

"Looks like intestines," said Gabriel.

"Well, yes. 'Ophio' is Greek for 'snake,' so this serpentine formation gives them their name. Oman is unique," he went on, "in its geology. It used to be at the bottom of the sea. When the continental plates moved, the oceanic crust was pushed up and the land buckled, like a carpet rippling. So we have this extraordinary mountain range—the Hajar—and at the edge here, the Tethyan ophiolites."

"Tethyan?"

"The Tethys Ocean separated Laurasia from Gondwanaland during the Triassic."

"Gondwanaland and Laurasia?"

Rolf smiled. "Asia and Europe to you."

They turned inland at Barka Fort and crossed the plain to reach the foothills. Children dallied by the roadside, sometimes waving, sometimes scowling, at the passing jeep, the girls in flowing patterned dresses, the boys big-eyed and curious.

"Where are we headed?"

"The Ghubrah Bowl. You'll see. It's quite amazing."

The countryside dipped and humped as they made their way into a wadi—the Wadi Mistal—with foothills closing in until they were in a narrow gray gorge. Gabriel went with the sway as Rolf negotiated boulders and steep ridges along the zigzagging watercourse, but suddenly the limestone walls fell back to reveal a vast natural amphitheater.

"Wow." Gabriel gaped at the surrounding rim of mountains and mishmash of hills. "I understand why you get so fidgety to come up here."

"This is nothing. The view from Jebel Shams, now *that*—that view belongs to God."

They headed out across the plain. Already Gabriel was impatient to stray between those bare ridges, where the creases, plump with greenery, were flush with goodness: streams and fruits and flowering trees. A small village was perched on the flank of the southern mountain, but Rolf parked before they got there and began to prepare for a hike.

They followed tracks, scrambling over scree and sliding rocks, while Rolf looked for his spot and Gabriel, in his wake, breathless and unfit, tried to keep up. Whenever Rolf stopped to photograph or sketch, Gabriel perched on a rock to rest, then dragged his feet when his grumbling brother-in-law scurried on in search of a more suitable viewpoint. He was a grumpy, irritable companion on this and other outings they would make over subsequent weeks, but Gabriel liked this Rolf—the one who was not in control; the one who had to be cared for, babied almost. He liked to make him tea on their burner and persuade him to put down his tools and his frustration. It was easier man-to-man, with no Annie, confusing the fact that they were friends as well as brothers-in-law. Out here, in Oman's best wilderness, they were pals again. It was like going fishing together as they had in Ireland—Rolf hissing and fussing as he failed to get his catch; Gabriel calm, flinging his fly forward, absorbing the scenery, the feel of his boots in the cold river, while the trout, caught or not, were incidental to the day's pleasures.

But that first afternoon, when they were trekking up a shambling hillside, Gabriel made one last stab at the subject that preoccupied him. "About the girl, Rolf," he said, panting. "What's the story?"

Rolf threw out his free hand in an irritated flurry. "Why do you keep on about this? There is no one coming into the house! I don't know why you insist, but I wish you would leave it. Annie is worried already about you and this talk only makes her worse."

"But I've spoken to her."

Tapping his camel stick—the short hooked stick that many Omani men carried—against his thigh, Rolf turned. "Gabriel—"

"Look, I'm not kidding and I'm not thick either. There's a woman in that house, Rolf, and you bloody well know there is."

"There *cannot* be!"

"Why not? No one locks the doors—she could come in from the street any time."

"But the women of this country would never do such a thing."

"She isn't Omani, she's a Westerner, who parades around me like some kind of marauding prostitute, and I don't understand why you allow it. What's the point? Am I supposed to be learning something? I mean, is she there to tantalize me, like in some Hitchcock film?"

Rolf was looking down at him from a few meters up the track. "You're dreaming, that's all. Sleepwalking."

"In the middle of the day?" Gabriel wiped sweat from his neck. "You'll have to do better than that, Rolf. Sleepwalking, my arse."

"What else can I say when we are only three of us at home?"

"Most of the time, yes, but you have a regular visitor. I've spoken to her. For Christ's sake, I've even kissed her! So won't you tell me, please, who it is that I've kissed?"

After a moment, Rolf turned away with a dismissive "She must be a jinniya then."

"What?"

"This is jinn country." Rolf hiked on up the track.

"You mean . . . some kind of ghost?"

"Jinn are not ghosts."

"Well, do they have knobbly toes and legs as long as—?"

"You are exasperating me, Gabriel! It was a good joke for a day or two, but enough now."

The slate-like hills threw back the dazzling light and the only sound—of stones rolling away from Rolf's tread—scraped against the still air. Some of the rocks had faces like grinning gargoyles.

As they scrambled on, Gabriel had to wonder: *Jinn country*?

The journey back to Muscat seemed interminable. Gabriel couldn't wait to get to the house. He hoped she would come and he hoped there would be no hint of her, and when finally they stepped into the dimly lit front room, he knew she was there already, ahead of him.

The following evening Annie's tone had quite changed when she asked him if he had seen his jinn lady that day.

He never knew from which direction she might come, or when. At night, he lay on his back facing the door, nervous and expectant, like a virgin bride, or if he stood on the roof he faced the stairwell, because he wanted to see her coming.

She never did it that way, though—creeping up like some kind of spook: she was either there or she was not, and yet he grew fidgety for fear of missing out, missing even her fleeting passage across a room. He wanted to see her, any time, every time.

Annie, noticing his distraction, became irritable one evening when they were having dinner in the diwan. "Gabriel, what is it with you? Even when I'm speaking to you, your eyes are jumping around and you keep wandering from room to room. You're hardly ever still!"

"Just trying to keep track of your occasional guest."

Annie stared. "You still think there's someone here?"

"I know there is."

Rolf tore up some bread. "So where is she now?"

"Excellent question."

His sister shook her head. "You really think there's some woman coming in and out of our house without us knowing about it?"

"Either that or you *do* know about it."

"But it isn't even possible! I mean, who is she? I've asked around, you know. No one knows anything about an expat on the loose, and she can't be in Muscat on her own. She'd either have to be working or married to someone, or she'd never have got into the country."

"I'm neither working nor married and I got in."

"Yeah, and it wasn't easy either. Sometimes I wish we hadn't bothered!"

"Hey, don't get miffed with me, Annie. How the fuck am I supposed to know what gives? This is your town, your house. *You* tell *me* what's going on."

"I don't know." She screwed up her paper napkin and threw it onto her plate.

Stalemate.

"I don't like this," Annie said quietly. "It's this bloody house."

"How do you mean?"

"There might be something here . . . a presence or . . ."

"Oh, not the jinn thing again! Look," said Gabriel, "she didn't come out of any bottle, all right? And if she had, it'd be pretty damn hard to get her back in again."

"Don't confuse jinn with pantomime genies." Annie's voice was still low. "People believe in them. There are loads of stories."

"What kind of stories?"

"It's folklore." Rolf spoke, waving his hand. "Local folklore."

Annie shot a look at him, "It's part of Islam," then turned to Gabriel. "They're in the Quran—part of the religion. It simply depends on where you're from, doesn't it? I mean, we have our ghosts, but Muslims don't believe in ghosts. When they die, they go to Paradise. They don't hang about like our lot can. Jinn, on the other hand, are around us all the time."

"*Us?*"

"Yes. I mean, what about fairies? Irish folklore—the serious stuff—they're exactly like jinn. Living alongside us. Our world and their world and never the twain shall meet, and yet they do. They cross over."

Gabriel looked at her with a mix of astonishment and ridicule. "Fairies? Are you serious?"

"Not sprites with wings. That's rubbish."

"Oh, please don't mention the Little People!"

"I'm just saying—a girl in my class in secondary school did a whole project on fairy lore and it was chilling. I didn't sleep for two nights. It's all the same stuff, you know."

Rolf was lining watermelon seeds along the rim of his plate, equally spaced.

"And as for jinn, well, they're like a third being," Annie went on. "God made angels and jinn and humans. Angels from the air, humans from the earth, jinn from fire. But we can't see them, unless they want us to."

"Annie," Gabriel said gently, "forget jinn and fairies. On the level—you haven't asked some friend of yours to mess with my head, have you? Because I swear to Christ, if you don't know who she is, then what's she doing in your house?"

Annie held his eye. "Is she in the room now?"

Gabriel could see, beyond her listlessness, a longing to buy into this. "If she was, you'd see her—*obviously*. Like you must have done when she came down this morning and went into the kitchen while we were having breakfast."

Still she held his eye, biting the side of her lip. "If this is some kind of joke, I want you to drop it."

"You think I'd be up for joking?"

"Rolf," she said, "maybe there is—"

"What, Annie? Maybe there is what?"

"Maybe this place has its own resident jinn. Some houses do. We should ask around."

A droplet of cold sweat ran down Gabriel's spine.

"That's all nonsense," said Rolf.

"Well, *you*'d think so, wouldn't you?" his wife snapped. "But lots of people don't."

"What people?" asked Gabriel.

"It's part of the scenery here. Good jinn. Bad jinn."

"Do *you* believe in it?"

"About as much as I believed in that ghost at O'Mahony's farm."

Gabriel chuckled. "God, I hadn't thought about him in years."

"Which ghost is this?" Rolf asked.

"Why would you be interested?" Annie retorted. "You don't believe in that stuff."

"I like the stories."

Gabriel and Annie exchanged glances. "It wasn't so much a ghost as—"

"His foot," said Gabriel.

Annie smiled. "On one of the landings of this old house we were sent off to every summer to learn Irish."

"Everyone said the house was haunted," Gabriel explained. "On certain nights, so the legend went, you could see the ghost's foot glowing on the landing. Lots of people claimed to have seen it."

"But you never did?" Rolf asked, with a supercilious smile. He turned to Annie. "Or you?"

"Don't be so patronizing!"

"Ghost stories are always the same." He shrugged. "Someone else sees something. Never the person who tells the story, the person right in front of you. Always second- or third- or tenth-hand. I have never met anyone who had this kind of experience directly."

"Except Gabriel."

Another drop of cold sweat slithered down Gabriel's back.

He walked. Through Muttrah and Muscat and on up into the hills. Usually he could read Annie, because she allowed him to. He would have said that her curiosity about the woman was genuine, especially since there was a touch of fear in it. He wasn't sure how well Annie could dissemble, but she was doing a persuasive job with this talk of jinn, and he had to be on his guard. This too could be part of the charade.

Over subsequent days, it became clear that Annie's interest was indeed sincere, though she wouldn't let on in front of Rolf. One afternoon when she was ironing, she asked Gabriel again, with faux-nonchalance, if his jinn lady was about.

"Nope."

"You know, jinn are often good. Sometimes they help humans."

Behind her eyes, Gabriel could see something akin to envy, as if she suspected he had touched on something that was denied her. "They say? Who says?"

"Oh—you hear stories. Sometimes at these women's parties I go to, the Omanis tell stories. Exactly like we do at home. It's just a different context."

"What kind of stories?"

"They're all, you know, quite touching." She laid out the sleeve of Rolf's shirt and ironed. "There was a nice one I heard about an old man in the hills who was injured in a fall, in a gully, and ended up with his arm broken and his leg crushed, but somehow he got back to his house, outside a remote village. No one knew how he'd made it. He said he walked, but he couldn't have—his foot was smashed—so they said that a jinn must have carried him home. Then his leg got worse. They didn't know what to do with it—it was suppurating and gangrenous—and he was getting sicker, and after a while, the villagers stopped going to visit him. Then one night he heard a voice calling him, so he crawled to the door, where he found a pot on the step with a sort of paste in it. He rubbed it into his leg, day after day, and it started to get better. He kept applying it until his foot was healed, and that was when a jinn woman appeared and said she had been looking after him, but that he must never tell anyone." Annie shook out the shirt, flattened another sleeve and ironed the cuff. "When the villagers saw that he was cured, they hounded him until he told them how it had happened. The jinn was very angry with him then and said he would never see her again, and he never did, but he was able to go back into the hills with his goats. So you see—a well-meaning jinn, come to save him."

Gabriel smiled. "Pure bollocks."

"Maybe." She held up the shirt, gave it a shake and put its shoulders around a hanger. "Every culture finds a way to explain the inexplicable."

"Like Rolf said—folklore."

"Oh, you know that, do you? You're so worldly-wise, so all-knowing, that you can dismiss it just like that? Centuries and centuries of belief?"

"Centuries and centuries of storytelling. That's where all the Irish fables come from."

"Be careful, Gabriel. You wouldn't want to be so scornful about something you don't understand."

Sometimes she was there; sometimes she wasn't. She chose her moments; Gabriel chose to believe. He chose, also, to stay with her rather than with his sister.

The night before they moved to the new house, he told Annie he wanted to stay in Muttrah.

She was packing a suitcase, putting in the last of their belongings. "How do you mean?"

"I'll pay the rent and hang on for a bit."

"But why?"

"It's central, which is handy when I don't have transport, and you shouldn't have to put up with me every single day."

"I don't mind that."

"Really?"—

She rolled some socks one into the other. "I don't . . . I haven't exactly been good company, I know, or maybe as welcoming as I should have been but—"

He stood up and put his hands on her shoulders. "You've been everything you should have been, but I'm not really in the right frame of mind for lounging around the suburbs in between dinner parties and barbecues, and you need space. Us being on top of each other every hour of the day is proving counter-productive, wouldn't you say?"

"Being on your own could also be counter-productive. Too much time to think."

She believed, no doubt, that he thought a lot about Max and, if left alone, would do so even more as he tried to come to terms with what had happened—a laughable concept. None of them would ever come to terms with it, least of all Gabriel, and although he could have grieved for Max—that much at least, in his empty time—he did not. Even when he walked under that high, light sky, with seagulls coasting overhead and goats wandering about, even then he didn't think much about Max any more, or of his parents, or his spoiled prospects and the prominent stain on his character. But he did want more time alone to think. To think and delight in this intriguing woman.

Annie resumed her packing, piling in clothes way beyond the capacity of the suitcase. "I suppose, if you're going to stay for a while, it makes sense to have your own place," she looked up, "but how long are you planning to stay?"

"A bit longer, if I can, but I don't want to tread on your toes."

"Don't be stupid. I don't own Muscat." The suitcase lid, as she pulled it over the mound of clothes, was like a glutton's jaw closing over a greedy mouthful. "What about money?"

They leaned on the suitcase. "I could get a job."

"You'll have to talk to Rolf about that. We can't ask Rashid for too many favors."

"Let's sit on it."

They sat on the case. "We've paid the rent until the end of next month," said Annie, "so you might as well stay. But I hope this doesn't have anything to do with that specter of yours."

After they had made the final move the next day, Rolf dropped Gabriel back to Muttrah in the early evening. Walking toward his house was like walking from one world into another. He had longed for solitude these many weeks, and the dark alleys were like a squiggled path leading out of his head. When the time was right, he planned to make his way back into it by another route.

In the empty house, he sat in the dim light of an inadequate lamp and waited.

He had left the front door unlocked when he went to bed, then lay, listening, and staring across the darkness toward the doorway.

He didn't see her come. When the mattress dipped by his hips, his eyes struggled to fix on her outline, but her warmth spread over to him like a low mist. He found her wrist and gripped it in an uncompromising hold. "How much are they paying you?"

It was the first of many questions; she answered none.

And yet she lay like this in a stranger's bed. . . . What were the limits, he wondered, and the rules? What would she allow? With a restraint just short of painful, he contained the urge to make love to her, because he would have done so with neither tenderness nor affection, only with the desperation that had festered over months of enforced celibacy. In all that time he had enjoyed not one shared spasm of pleasure, no intimate release, and yet turned on, again, at last, by the woman lying alongside him, he managed to hold back.

The drip-drop of conversation became as tantalizing, over the next few days, as her body. It wasn't that she didn't speak—she did, in short, neat sentences, although when he thought about it after she'd left, he was aware more of her having spoken than of having heard her voice. There was no substance to any of it. She answered questions with questions and spoke in vague terms about little of consequence, which explained nothing about anything. She was there and that was all; she didn't know much else. Not even her own name. Apparently.

When he said one day, "They say you might be a jinn," she put her hand on his thigh. This was more dangerous than ice on the roads. If someone was trying to frame him, this was the way to go: one accusation of rape or assault and he'd never see the light of day again. But even that didn't stand up. His family hated him, for sure, but not forever. They couldn't wish to have him jailed for a long spell in some distant outpost.

"Why do you keep coming here?"

She needed to be away from somewhere else, she said.

"Like me," he muttered.

She could hear the sea, she said.

"Not possible." He ran the backs of his fingers along her neck. "The sea is as languid as jelly out there."

Her eyes lost focus, as if she were listening to something on a frequency unavailable to him, and she insisted that she could hear the sea.

"I wish *I* could." A snapshot of the Irish coast followed the thought—the white of the Atlantic throwing itself against the last rocks of Ireland. "I remember standing on a walkway near Mizen Head when I was a kid, near the lighthouse there. A small bridge crossed a gully and we'd been told—me and my brother and sister—that you could see seals frolicking in the surf far below so, heads hanging over the railings, we watched and watched, the waves breaking up in this gash in the rocks, sending up bubbles of foam, until finally we saw a flash of silvery brown slithering around down there. The sea was throwing itself about, deadly dangerous, but the seal was having a lark, diving into the gush of nasty-looking waves, like a kid in snow."

Don't talk, she said. Listen.

Gabriel held himself still, eyes closed, until he heard in the far-off faraway the sound of the sea battering his island.

He woke alone. He could barely move, such was the depth of the sleep from which he was emerging, as if he was swimming up from the fathoms. He hadn't slept so well since the last time he'd got drunk.

He had thought she meant to seduce him; instead, she had brought him sleep. Solid, fretless sleep.

In the wake of a dream about home, he had the impression that he had just walked from one room into another—from their family room in Cork to this bare bedroom in Muscat. His mother was right there, beyond his reach yet still close, still loving, as she had been in the dream. Restored by one good night, Gabriel allowed himself to think about his mother. He was able now to look into her face, the face that had turned to him when he had arrived home that morning, disoriented, inebriated, and found her sitting at the table against the wall, one elbow leaning on the patterned plastic tablecloth, her quilted robe buttoned to the neck. Her eyes had been hanging on something he couldn't see, because he did not yet know. Fearing his father had died, he asked her what was the matter, and she had lifted her eyes and tried, but failed, to say his name.

The family room—with its aging green couch and brown-tiled fireplace, and a large television in the corner with a plant on top, the fronds of which were pushed sideways, like a comb-over, to stop them flowing across the screen—that room had been the hearth of his life. There, on the day of his Confirmation, spruced up in his school uniform, he had retreated to watch television, until his mother had scolded him for not playing with his cousins. There, he had lost his virginity, on the floor between the couch and the fireplace, when his parents were at the pub and his girlfriend's body was hot along one side where the flames had warmed her skin. There, his home had dissolved forever when he returned hung-over from his pals' flat and found his mother destroyed. "In God's name," she had said, "what have you done?"

Later that day, in the same room, his father had pushed him, shaken him, shouted until Gabriel feared they would both burst into flames.

They had breakfast together, he and the woman. After a walk along the Corniche, he had returned to the house, where she soon joined him as he lay curled on the bench in the front room, sobbing. Limp, he was, with self-pity. His life, wreckage. He missed his work, the pub, his parents, but missing Max was another form of branding. Sometimes he fancied he could smell his own flesh burning. The abyss beneath him—the only thing he could see—was a huge thing, empty and dark. He felt himself floating into it, limbs outstretched; it was the only place for him, this great hole into which his soul tumbled.

And then she was there, holding him back, as if by his shirt-tails.

"Can't buckle," he said, sitting up. "Have to get Annie through."

Recovered, he had made coffee and heated bread, while she sat at the counter feeding him slices of watermelon. Her lack of appetite, in food as in conversation, meant she ate only apples and sipped warm water. Gabriel, for now, appreciated being in a room without words. Most words, when it came to it, were superfluous. All the language that had poured out of Annie had done her no good, but in silence her anger had been truly chilling. This was better—a few chosen, necessary words. And touch. He pushed his companion's kaftan back over her knees to stroke her thigh. They kissed. His resolve weakened. Let them frame me, he thought. There could be no stopping this when she was creeping inside his clothes, and into his heart.

He told her, afterward, that she was the most beautiful creature he had ever beheld. Then he laughed. "*Beheld?* What's with the virginal language? I'm coming on all Catholic again. *Behold the Angel of the Lord. Behold the Virgin Mary!*" Gabriel chuckled. "Mind you . . ." His lover was hardly virginal, but in some respects she shared characteristics with apparitions of the Virgin, from Lourdes to Fatima: she was an incontrovertible fact to a chosen few, air to others, and deeply controversial.

Light on his feet, he wandered through Muttrah, knowing no malevolent eyes were upon him, no whispers breaking out behind. He went every morning to buy bread and came back to eat in the bare kitchen, listening to the voices in the alley—the woman next door, with her tendency to screech, the boys running along the lane, the bleat of goats. It was cozy. Tight. No prying eyes. No bloody foreigners.

He was, by all accounts, having an affair with a woman no one else could see. A woman who had coasted into his life, into the room in which he stood, and, just like that, had saved him and doomed him all at once. Had he been at home, he would have assumed that he had fallen into a liaison with a high-class call girl, set up as an elaborate joke at his expense or even as some kind of punishment, but who would have any motive to tease or torment him beyond his own shores? Either way, he went with it. It took some time to get used to her selective invisibility, but when he came to grasp her occasional nature, he embraced it. That no one else believed in her became an abstraction, a curiosity, because the woman in question was clearly defined in his eyes, and her flesh was quite, quite solid. To him, she was real to the point of distraction.

Since his lover had no known name, he called her Prudence, after the woman who wouldn't come out to play. She liked it, especially when he explained he'd taken it from a great song by a great man. "She was a real person, Prudence was," he said. "Mia Farrow's sister. Lennon wrote it when they were in India with the Maharishi, because Prudence wouldn't leave her hut and he was worried about her. Thought she must be depressed because she wouldn't come outside, so he penned "Dear Prudence." Brilliant song. *Inspired.*"

His appreciation of silent companionship had been short-lived. Her reticence, a few days in, was giving him a new respect for conversation, enunciation, and indeed his own voice. He had taken to rambling—the inevitable result of spending time with someone who had little to say—and his capacity for drivel astounded him. He had never realized he knew so much about nothing in particular or that he was quite handy at impersonations. One afternoon when he was telling Prudence about his most peculiar student, he began imitating him—rather accurately, he thought. The humor, however, was lost on her.

He spent most of the week in the house, venturing out only to get food. He even lied to Annie, saying he had a stomach bug and could not go over to see them. "Stay in bed," she said. "It'll pass."

He stayed in bed. They made love, a lot, and Prudence slept a lot, and Gabriel feared leaving the room because sometimes when he did she was no longer there when he came back, and then he would have to kill the shapeless hours until her return. Boredom set in. He had no work, no friends, and the house had been stripped of all but necessary utensils. All books, games, and magazines had moved to the suburbs. Walking was the only thing to do when she was gone, and it used up the energy, the pent-up desire that made him jittery. Sometimes he would dive into the suq to make contact with living, working people, and chat to the shopkeepers in the shaded alleys. They would talk to him in their limited English and taught him to say "Hello, how are you?" in Arabic. Other times he would go farther afield, out of town and into the hills, hiking for hours until, suddenly panicked that he'd been gone too long, he would hurry home, passing shrouded women and floppy-eared goats, arriving back, hot and frazzled, to find that Prudence was there, or not.

One afternoon Annie called over, and sat on the rampart of the roof with him, the sea breeze ruffling her spiky hair.

"How are you?" he asked.

"Still not pregnant. How's your stomach?"

"Still rumbly."

"I hope you kept yourself hydrated."

"I kept myself hydrated."

Prudence stepped out of the house and moved to another corner of the roof.

Annie did not react, not in any flickering way Gabriel could detect. Instead she looked at her toes, dusty in her sandals. "I'm getting desperate, Gabriel. Rolf is pushing forty."

"Yeah, but you're only twenty-eight. You've loads of time," he said, unsettled by her desperation, since he could do nothing about it. "And there are so many likely causes right now. You're stressed and unhappy, but it *will* happen."

"I wish I had the luxury of that kind of certainty."

"Putting pressure on yourself isn't going to help, is it?" Gabriel glanced sideways at Prudence, willing her to go away. This was family stuff, private.

"How can I not stress about it?" Annie's eyes were brimming. "Rolf longs for a family and it just . . . it isn't happening and I'm worn out with all the trying, and the disappointment that comes back every time. It's crushing. I'm even sick of having sex!"

Gabriel flinched. Prudence was sitting on a low wall, her face to the sun, well within earshot. He hadn't given the logistics of her mysterious comings and goings much thought—how she got in and out of the house, that kind of thing—because he didn't care, but Annie would never speak of something so personal in front of a stranger. So either she knew Prudence, very well, or she was genuinely oblivious of her presence.

"Sometimes I worry that our marriage won't survive the strain," Annie went on, staring straight past Prudence.

There were limits even to Gabriel's skepticism.

He had to find out more about jinn.

Chocolate-colored mountains rimmed Muscat—a wall encasing him. His own chosen prison wall. Sea on one side, mountains on the other. Beyond, he knew, was desert. Space. Anonymity. He would see it soon. These arrogant hills would not contain him for long. In the desert, he might find his real thoughts, the ones concealed by the disdain of others. There, he might shake off the weight of shame and meet himself. Find the person who had destroyed his own brother. Even discover the why of it. Envy, they said. In Cork, it was widely peddled that Gabriel had resented Max's success, modest though it was, which he had achieved by overcoming mediocrity with sheer hard work, while Gabriel let his talent dribble away, boozing and fucking. That was what they said, what even his parents thought, though they would not have used those terms, and it was true that beneath the blasé veneer, Gabriel did care about his so-called gift. Of course he did. He cared that he had ditched it when still too young to value it. So perhaps he *had* wanted to make Max pay. How else to explain what he had done, three days before the wedding? Under the broad blue sky of the desert, in solitude and silence, he might find out what had sparked that one warped, thwarted idea, so ghastly to him now that he hesitated to look over his shoulder in case it was right behind him. Like a devil on his back. It *was* a devil—something nobody could look at, face on. His own sister seemed wary of being alone with him in case it popped up, joined them, his disgusting idea. *We all have them*, he wanted to say, *we all have putrid imaginings, beyond our control*. The difference was that he, and some others, had carried it out. Perhaps, in the wilderness, he would have a biblical encounter with himself and slay his own sins, like Jesus had done.

He snorted. Where *was* this religious stuff coming from?

Abid, their driver, was a tall man with a thin mustache and a glint in his eyes. He glanced over, smiling and curious, while he drove. He had offered to take him out for the day. Annie had probably engineered it, concerned that Gabriel was becoming too reclusive, so now they were on the Nakhal road, heading into the grooves of landscape.

"Nakhal is a nice place," Abid told him. "The fort is two hundred and fifty years old. It is built on a big rock, to keep them safe."

There were forts in a state of collapse everywhere. On every excuse for a hill, there stood at least one tower, looking all around over the humps of its own ruins.

"One of the ways they pushed back the enemy," Abid gesticulated, "at Nakhal is—they poured down boiling date honey over them."

"Agh, Jesus!" Gabriel grimaced. "Talk about sweet torture."

Nakhal was surrounded by an ocean of date palms, fed by the falaj, Abid explained—an ancient irrigation system of channels bringing water from al-Hajar. The fort curled around its own rock base, like a creeper climbing a tree, until the main tower sat up on its perch with a 360-degree view of al-Batinah Plain on one side and al-Hajar Mountains on the other. A purple cloud had gathered over their peaks.

"It will rain," Abid said, frowning.

"Have we time to check out the hot springs before it does?"

"Of course. Yes."

Down by the river, Gabriel pulled on his trunks and fell backward into the water. His body exulted. He was getting used to the contrasts in this country—the way crevassed slopes of gray rock were suddenly interrupted by a bulge of green, and blinding white gravel riverbeds invariably led toward a suburb of Paradise hidden in an S-bend.

Abid sat on the bank, munching hard-boiled eggs and bread. It took only one prompt from Gabriel: "My sister has been trying to explain to me about jinn," he said, lying in the shallows, and Abid was off, one story hurrying after another, flowing out in his imperfect English.

"There is a house in Muttrah," he began, "a house like any other, where no one lives any more. The family who owned it, they tried to live in there, but every time they brought their things and put them inside the house, the jinn removed them."

"How do you mean?"

"The family would come home and find their belongings outside. On the street, on the roof. So they would bring them back in again, but whenever they went out, they came home and even the furniture was outside the house. They said, 'No more!' and left, but another man, he came and said he would live there. He did not mind about jinn. Jinn, you see, are weaker than men. They cannot control us. We have the stronger soul. So he moved into the house and he brought some things, and for two days everything was fine. Until one night, he was thrown from his bed. The wall pushed him out. He was very frightened, but he stayed another night. And the same thing—something pushed from behind and he fell on the floor. Still he would not leave. He did not want to be weaker than the jinn, but he had no sleep and was afraid of being hurt, and he was becoming crazy. His sister, she say, 'Come to my house, and you will sleep like a baby.' So he went with her and slept for two days and then he went back to his house—and, ya Allah! All his belongings were in the street. He left then and that house is still empty. The jinn have it now. They wanted it. They have it."

"So . . . in this case, they *were* stronger than the humans?"

"This man had a weak soul."

He had another story, and then another, in which jinn were angels of mercy.

The warm waters of the spring were tingling on Gabriel's skin. "So they're not evil? I mean, dangerous?"

Abid wobbled his head. "Sometimes yes. Sometimes no. Men are stronger, so bad men can use jinn to do bad things to their enemies."

"You mean like casting a spell on someone?"

"A spell, yes."

"And you believe in them?"

"God made man and jinn to worship Him. They are like us—Muslim and Jew and non-believer."

"Have you ever seen one?"

Abid looked down along the gurgling river. "Yes."

"And?"

But Abid got up, wiping the dust off the back of his dishdasha.

"So humans *can* see jinn, yeah?"

"If the jinni wants you to see him, you can see him. We must hurry." Abid was heading back to the car. "It will rain soon."

A black cloud had darkened the river, which no longer seemed so tame; in the gloaming, it looked very much like a hideaway for spooks and specters. Gabriel felt edgy as they set off for Rustaq to see another fort, especially when a few drops of water on the windscreen suddenly became slashing rain that thundered down onto the jeep.

With a glance at the sky, Abid invoked Allah as the vehicle bumped off the stones and back up to the track. "This is not good. It has been raining in the mountains. The wadis will flood."

"Flash floods? Really?"

"Don't worry. It will be fine."

They managed to get across one wadi, where the river was rising, before coming to another just as a great torrent of brown water came roiling past. Abid drove back to a more elevated spot and parked. They could go neither forward nor back. "We have to wait."

"So this is a flash flood?" Gabriel asked, raising his voice to be heard above the lashing on the roof and watching the slow flow of sludge. "Not exactly flashy, is it?"

"But it is very strong."

Raindrops bounced around the bonnet, furious.

"How long will we be here?"

"A few hours maybe."

"How many hours?"

Abid shrugged. "Five. Six."

"Jesus." They might be there all night. Omanis were loose with time. It was an elastic concept: five, six hours could mean ten, or two, and Gabriel loved it. He'd be happy to get into the groove of a time-loose existence—but this flood was keeping him from her.

From her, his jinniya. No way. For one thing, she had an Irish accent. She wasn't Eastern in any respect. Irish jinn—now there's a concept.

The water, thick as mud and full of debris, pushed past, with sporadic rushes, as if upstream someone was sweeping out a lake.

Unprompted, Abid began to talk again. His uncle, he said, had married a jinn and had a jinn family—female jinniya, he explained, always gave birth to jinn children—and they lived alongside his human family in another house beyond the orchard, but no one knew about them until his uncle died. He had divided his estate between his jinn family and his human family, since the Quran insists that all wives and children should be equally cared for, but his mortal children could not accept this. His eldest son even moved his own family into the house where the jinn lived. Abid shrugged. "For the jinn wife, it's punishment time. After the funeral—fourteen days—any time the family has a meal, huge dust comes and spoils it. And then the house, the windows are rattling, shaking, showing her anger. Still they won't recognize her, so she sends her boys to cry outside the door and the human family couldn't do anything to stop this, so his sons went to find out what was the problem and she came to meet them. 'I came only for one reason,' she told them. 'My children they have human brothers and if you don't recognize them, I will make sure you will disappear from this world. One by one.' The dead man's sons laughed and told her that jinn are not strong enough to do that, but she said, 'I have the power. My husband made me that promise, that my family would be recognized, and if a human promises something, he should do it.'"

Abid looked up and down the watercourse a little uneasily. "Jinn live sometimes near riverbeds. Places where not many people come. Like this. They come at the end of the day."

He seemed a little spooked; Gabriel was fairly spooked himself.

"Very soon after that," Abid went on, "one of the sons, his little baby disappeared. Two months old. The whole village went searching, looking, until finally, when it was almost dark, a young girl heard a baby crying deep in the oasis and found him on the ground beside a tree. The son's wife, she took her children and moved back to her mother, saying she would never again go near that place, but the husband, he stayed, until one night he woke and there was a fire burning in his room. It happened many nights—fire burning, like that. So he left also, and the jinn family stayed, undisturbed until today. Still now, nobody goes there. It is full of jinn.'

"So humans can marry jinn?"

"Yes."

And have children, Gabriel thought, and therefore have sex.

Back in Muscat, late that night, Gabriel checked every room in the house, and the first-floor windows, before locking the front door and the door to the roof. Then he waited, more apprehensive than usual, his chest tight, his bedsheets cold and crinkling. He thought about Annie, her longing to conceive, and shivered.

He didn't want a jinn-child roaming the earth, the issue of this beautiful creature and his mangled conscience, and he fell asleep wondering what kind of a jinn he might create—evil or good?

When he woke, Prudence was lying with him. He went downstairs—the door was still bolted from the inside. Doubts pricked at him, but not enough to stop him going back upstairs to do what they did best.

"Come out with me," he said to her afterward. "You always speak of the sea. Let's get a blast of sea air."

There was no moving her. She couldn't go from where she was, she said, and it made sense that she didn't want to be seen around town with him. It would be all over the expat community within hours.

She had to stay, she insisted, where she could hear the sea.

"You'd hear the sea a whole lot better if you were walking beside it," Gabriel insisted, and with a faint sense of irritation he got up and left the house before she did.

On Yiti Beach, Annie stood by the water, loose waves fussing over her feet. Marie and Jasper's pretty daughter was playing in the sea with Thomas and Margarethe's trio of blond babes and Rashid's moon-eyed sons.

"Gabriel was almost washed away in a flash flood last week," Rolf said behind her, to their gathered friends.

"Oh, you have to be so careful!" Marie was sitting in the deckchair next to Gabriel's. "It can be dangerous. You shouldn't go driving around the country, especially when the weather isn't good."

"It was fine. I was with Abid. We sat it out."

The children's high-pitched screeches, their simple joy, held Annie there, adrift from the reclining adults who, apart from Rashid and his wife, Sabah, were oiling themselves against the blistering sun. Annie tried not to mind. She and Rolf were the only couple she knew in Oman who had no children, but she tried not to mind.

Yiti Beach, east of Muscat, was accessible only by 4x4, but worth every jolt of the physical shake-up that had to be endured before getting there. At one end, two huge rocks lifted out of the shallow waters and Annie stood gazing at them, her hands on her haunches, her toes sinking into the sand.

"Walk?" Gabriel asked, coming alongside her.

They paddled toward the jagged humps of rock.

"It's nice to meet Rashid at last," he said. "I owe him."

"He's a lovely man, and Sabah is a good friend of mine. She's teaching me Arabic. Or trying to." Annie raised her chin. "They're called the Sama'un Rocks. Sabah told me they were inhabited by a jinni called Sama'un and that people used to leave gifts at the base at low tide."

"Like an Irish shrine. A few pennies for a miracle."

"I suppose."

"So what does Sama'un have to offer? Sight for the blind? Cash for the strapped?"

"Fertility for the barren."

Even through sunglasses, she could feel Gabriel's eyes shoot over to hers. "So that's why you organized this little expedition."

"Don't tell Rolf."

The rocks were turning to a shade of burnt orange in the late-afternoon sun. "Do you know what gifts he likes, your Sama'un?"

"Dead goat, probably. Anyway, he's gone now. Legend has it he took off after the British tried to bomb his rocks in the fifties."

They paddled all the way to the rocks, where some fishermen were sitting on the sand mending their nets, then returned to the party. Rolf pointed toward the muddy lagoon farther along the strand and told Gabriel it was good for waders. "Fantastic bird-watching."

"Fantastic everything," said Gabriel. "Is Sultan Qaboos ever going to let tourists in?"

"I hope not," said Marie.

"Give him time," said Jasper. "There's no infrastructure yet for tourism."

"I do love your name," Stéphanie said, out of the blue, looking at Gabriel with her fox-like eyes. "Were you named after the angel?"

Gabriel threw Annie a weary look. The question of his life. "Remember to put that on my tombstone, won't you?" he said to her. "'P.S. He was *not* named after the angel.'" He turned back to Stéphanie. "An uncle," he said. "Sort of." He sat on a towel and perched a sunhat on his head.

"Sort of?" said Marie, as Jasper handed her flatbread, stuffed with lamb and salad. "Thanks, darling. How do you mean 'sort of'?"

"In that he wasn't actually called Gabriel himself. My uncle. Our uncle."

"How then can you be named after him?" Stéphanie asked in her tetchy French accent.

Rashid wandered back from where he had been playing with his younger son and sat on the sand near Sabah who, in spite of the heat, remained cloaked in her abaya.

"Go on, Gabriel," said Annie. "It's a nice story."

"Oh, do," said Marie.

Clearly unsettled at finding himself the center of attention, Gabriel hesitated.

Annie felt a pull of compassion. He had probably grown accustomed to averted eyes in recent months, but now these people were staring, waiting, as if asking him to account for himself, not simply for his name.

"Our mother's brother, Jack, died with the name 'Gabriel' on his lips."

"He said it over and over, during his last days," Annie put in.

"But no one knew who Gabriel was," Gabriel went on. "Jack's wife was called Helen, their sons were Declan and Paul, and nobody in the family knew anything about a Gabriel, so they had no idea how to fetch him. Still, he kept asking for this Gabriel. Even years later, my mother couldn't speak of it without welling up, because she couldn't forget the way he had looked at her, pleading. She asked him where he was, this person, but Jack could barely speak.

"So, determined to find this man, she went through all Jack's papers, his address books, his desk, and one day she even pulled every single book he owned off the shelves and looked through them for a note or a name on the flyleaf, anything."

"That's one of my earliest memories," said Annie. "I must have been about four, and I remember all these books falling off the shelves at Jack's house, raining down on us, with Mam leafing through them, like a madwoman."

"What about his wife?" asked Stéphanie. "Did she not know?"

"She'd left him years before," Annie explained, "so it was just Mam nursing him through his illness. He was only forty-nine."

"And all the time she was looking for Gabriel," said Gabriel, "it turned out she was expecting me."

"Did she ever find him?"

Gabriel shook his head. "No. My namesake has never been tracked down or been found lurking in old papers. Not one clue. The family concluded that there must have been a son. Our cousins, Declan and Paul, still wonder if some bloke will one day roll up on their doorstep claiming to be their brother, but Mam has her own theory."

Marie swallowed a large mouthful of food. "Which is?"

"A love affair," said Annie.

"Ah," said Stéphanie, "of course."

Annie nodded. "It wasn't spoken about, but it was fairly obvious why his marriage had failed."

"When I was born," Gabriel went on, "she wanted to pay homage to the love she had witnessed for the unknown Gabriel."

"So you were named after a stranger," said Stéphanie.

"Yes, and the only thing Mam knew about him was that somebody loved him, a lot, and that's good enough for me. Better than being the namesake of some twerp with wings."

"In the Quran," Rashid said, vaguely, gazing down the strand, "the angel Gabriel is called Jibril."

By day, Prudence stayed around more often, wandering about the house, eating the apples or lying on the cushioned bench, sleeping, staring, smiling if he passed. She even read, or at any rate flicked the pages of his few magazines, leafing through them again and again. He suspected she didn't see what she was looking at; it was a movement, something for her hands to do.

"How does it work for you?" he asked one afternoon. "Do you decide, 'I've had enough now, I'm going home?' Do you call it home, wherever it is that you go?"

When she was with him, she said, she knew of nowhere else, and she came because she wanted to be in that quiet place, where she could listen to the sea and lie with him.

Dutifully, Gabriel phoned his parents every few weeks, the calls coming toward him, days out, like a slow-moving storm that could not be avoided. His parents' voices would echo and bounce along the line and only the expense of the call saved him from anything more than fleeting inquiries. His father's anger had not subsided. He said each time, "I'll get your mother," and she would say each time, "Is it very hot?"

Dutifully, he visited Annie as often as he could bear to leave the house, because he wanted to see her and to work on her. One weekend she intimated that, come the end of their lease in Muttrah, he would be moving in with them.

"Actually," he said carefully, "I'd like to take on the lease myself. It's working out so well."

"In what way is it working out well? You have no friends, no music. No work. What do you do all day?"

"The solitude is good for me. It's helping."

"Helping with what? You're not ill."

"Christ, Annie, I'm ill as a dog!"

Her dead eyes turned back to the dishcloth she was running across the table. "Then you should be here, where I can look after you."

"No."

She looked up.

"I mean—no, thanks. I'm better alone. Really."

"Your jinn lady keeping you busy, is she?"

He was not so dutiful, however, toward Max, whom he betrayed on a daily, sometimes hourly, basis. Irrational though it was to be in love with a woman he knew nothing about—who claimed, indeed, to know very little about herself—Gabriel was nonetheless gliding through the days in happiness. Prudence soaked through his pores and flowed through his limbs. Every time they made love, he betrayed his brother with exultation and oblivion. He delighted in her presence, quiet though it was, and relished her ignorance. She knew him not at all. There was scarcely a person in Ireland who didn't know what he'd done. Even the nation's favorite broadcaster had churned it over with his listeners, many of whom rang in to the show to express their heartfelt outrage that he escaped with only a warning. It must truly have been a living nightmare for his parents. He had crippled them. The depravity had been momentary, perhaps, but its gruesome consequences would be lifelong. His every relationship had been compromised, damaged or destroyed, and any future relationship would feel it also. But Prudence knew nothing. He asked her. He said, "If I told you I'd done something despicable, would you still come?"

It was nothing to her, she said.

"I could be dangerous."

She pointed out that she could leave any time.

"You leave too often."

When she lay with her back to him, letting his hand curve over the hill of her hip toward the dip of her belly, he felt good, rich, *lucky*. Luckier than he had any right to be. When he pressed into her, he reached his own hearth, that safe place where no one could touch his conscience. And then the fucking took over. He loved the way she twisted, stretched, coiled herself around him; he liked the power of giving her pleasure, and denying it, enjoyed her soft gutturals when he succeeded and when he desisted. Although she was generous, bringing him off in the kitchen, in the stairwell, in the diwan, he gave more than he took, because he had to hold her attention; he had to keep her coming.

Even so, the walls were moving in. "Come and get some sun on your face," he said, more than once. "You're so pale."

Her reply never varied. She could not go from there.

The mantra repeated itself softly in his mind when she was with him and when she was not. *I cannot go from here.*

In her soft company, he only loved, he never thought. But when he was alone, he thought a lot—about how long this could go on and, increasingly, about how to get beyond the impasse where she would go nowhere and see no one else. Prudence was . . . *wispy*. Wispy, yet firm. He could neither understand her, nor influence her, but outside their cozy playhouse reality knocked. He had to make a living, one way or another. His salary would soon be stopped—he would inevitably be fired from the School of Music—but if he went out to work every day, she might wander off, never to return. Somehow he had to tear her from the anchor of the house and anchor her instead in his life, and if she was indeed a jinniya, he would have to consult with those who could tell him how man and jinn could live together.

For that, he needed to talk to the men in the suq, who could tell him everything he needed to know—if only he could speak their language. Without Arabic, their knowledge was locked away. He could learn it, but not quickly enough to be able to grasp subtleties. How to inquire about the insubstantial with an insubstantial grasp of the language? He needed an interpreter, not only of Arabic but also of folklore, and he had to find one without involving his sister.

His best bet was Ali, a trader who spoke fairly good English and made very good tea. Gabriel had often stopped for a chat on his perambulations, although more recently he had been too eager to be home and passed Ali with a dismissive wave and a long stride. Now, again, he ambled into the suq and stopped at Ali's stall, where he sold scarves and garments, and accepted a glass of tea and a smoke. They sat for a time, chatting, but it was toward the end of the evening, when night was spreading in and the suq was emptying, that Gabriel asked Ali about jinn.

Ali, it turned out, had many jinn stories, but then so did everyone, and as he told that first tale, with the shops closing around them, others gathered, a few old boys with decayed teeth and sad eyes, who didn't understand, but nodded and praised God and sometimes added their own wisdom. The stories were convoluted, tangential, but Gabriel got the gist, and in any case enjoyed the throwback to those times, as a child, when he had sat around fireplaces, listening to old folk tell tales of the unsettled dead.

"There was a man, Abdullah," Ali began, that first time, "from Zanzibar, and he was suffering from illness, but nobody knew what this illness was. He felt sick all the time and he get very thin. His mother, she knew jinn had came into his body and after a few months, she found out who cast that spell—a woman who lived in the town, so they went to see her. When he saw that woman, he said, 'I know her.' She used to come to his bed, until he sent her away one day, and this makes her very angry. She cast the spell on him and sent a jinniya to make him suffer. When they got the spirit out of him and Abdullah felt well again, he left to come to Oman to get away from this jinniya. Long journey, but he was okay, until the day the boat is approaching Oman, and there is no one to say he has a job there." Ali's watery eyes looked down the alley. "In Muscat, nobody can come out of the boat until he knows someone. Someone who says, 'I know this man.'"

"Like a sponsor."

"Yes, but Abdullah, he is left in the fishing boat. . . . He didn't understand what is happening. He speak Swahili, not Arabic. He didn't know why they wouldn't let him get out of the boat and he's very scared that he has to go back again. But suddenly he is speaking in Arabic. He could not believe it! How he is doing that? So one of the fisherman invited Abdullah to come work with him and stay with his family.

"Until today he does not know how he spoke Arabic, except that it was the jinniya made him do it so that he would like her. And he stayed here. He's still alive, got kids, good job. Sometimes he used to dream and call the jinniya to come to him."

"The Zanzibar jinn?"

"Yes. After she helped him know Arabic, he wanted her to come back in his life. He wanted to feel safe. So he called her."

"Did she come?"

"Sometimes," Ali said, with a deep nod, looking at the ground. "Sometimes."

Sometimes, Gabriel thought. A powerful word.

Prudence didn't show up for several days. Perhaps his insistence that they should go out had bothered her. More likely, she was enjoying a normal existence of proper clothes, plentiful food and regular showers—none of this lying about, being mysterious. But in her absence, the fables that skirted around his reason kept trying to stake a claim. The parallels between Eastern and Western mysticism were comforting—the sudden command of an unknown language equated to the Christian belief of speaking in tongues. Comfort and evil, ghosts and ghouls, devils and spells, the effects were much the same; only the explanations were different. By day, he liked to toy and think about it; tease himself with the paranormal. Only in fear's natural habitat—the deep hours of night—did true apprehension shake him. He, Gabriel Sherlock, was having an affair with a woman no one else had seen, and he wished to God they could.

Rolf and Annie, he increasingly believed, had genuinely not seen Prudence. Before they moved out, she had been quick to pass through a room, usually behind them. She almost always moved behind their backs. Why? Annie appeared to be truly perplexed by his affair, which only perplexed him further, because if she did not know this woman, who the hell did? Who had planted her there, on his life?

Annie was also more unsettled, less in control, than she had been when he had arrived, as if she were seeking the ghost within him for her own reasons.

"You know," she said one afternoon, when they were taking a walk along the beach west of Muttrah, "they can cure things."

"Who?" The hot wind was beating through his shirt.

"Jinn."

A fleshy body lay farther along the shore by the waterline. As the waves came in, it shifted lazily, like someone turning in their sleep. Annie curved away from the shiny gray heap, but Gabriel stopped to look down at the dead dolphin. "So you reckon I should prevail upon the jinn to cure me of my jinniya?"

"I wasn't thinking about you. I was thinking about me."

He looked up. "You? How so?"

"There are jinn, Sabah says—special ones for different things, like . . . infertility."

"But you aren't infertile!"

"Who says?"

"It's far too soon to reach that conclusion."

"I've been trying to conceive for over a year."

"A very tough year."

"I was thinking," she said, moving on, her feet in the water, her thoughts farther out, "I could go to one of these ceremonies."

"Ceremonies?"

"You know, like . . . not quite séances, but you can go to see people who invoke certain jinn who have particular powers. Like when there's a bad jinni, it's because somebody has given the evil eye to whoever they're peeved with, so that the jinn will create problems or illness for them, but then there are good jinn too, who can also intervene through a kind of holy person, or sorcerer."

"Oh, Annie, don't buy into all that! Far better you see some specialist in Berne. Don't mess with that ritualistic stuff. From what I understand, a lot of it comes from Zanzibar and it's . . ."

"What?"

"A bit too close to black magic for comfort."

"This, from a man who sees an invisible woman?"

"She is not invisible. She is simply shy, careful about *who* sees her."

"Prove it then. Introduce us."

"But that's the thing—she won't meet anyone or go anywhere. It's not what she wants."

Annie shook her head. "What a choice—either I believe that you're going slightly mad or that you're being visited by jinn. Frankly, the latter option is less scary. I need you sane, Gabriel."

"I am sane and she is real, Annie."

"How can you be so sure when I look at the same place as you do and see nothing?"

"Because I'm sleeping with her, that's how."

Annie stopped, her arms hanging by her sides, the corpse of the dead dolphin twisting about behind her.

"And now you're going to call me depraved, I suppose, as well as delusional?"

"Humans *can* sleep with jinn," she said. "They even marry them. Every village in the country has that story: the man who married a jinniya."

"Listen to you. You're talking about them as if they're real."

"Maybe they are. What do we know?"

Gabriel put out his arm. She hesitated, then moved into him and he held her against him. "We'll laugh about this one day," he said. "When we're sitting around with our kids, yours and mine, Prudence'll tease us about how we thought she was a jinniya."

"That's her name? Prudence?"

"That's what I call her, yeah."

"From your favorite song." Annie looked up at him with what might have been a flicker of forgiveness in her eyes.

❁

Prudence asked him, one day, as they lay spent on the bench in the front room, why he was there.

There—where? Muscat? Oman? That particular house? There were so few specifics in her conversation.

Gabriel ran his finger along her breastbone, skiing through the sweat that lingered between her breasts. "I've run away," he said, coasting toward her navel.

A woman, she immediately presumed.

He had yet to speak of it to anyone. There had been deluges of earnest, but rhetorical, questions: "Why would you do something like that?"; "Did you not think?" But he had been given no right of reply, ever, since no one really wanted any answers or excuses. Here was his chance to speak, with this woman, who would not judge him. He could release it into the air, into sound and words, and see where it went.

"I'm running from what the French would call 'honte,'" he began. "A more haunting word than 'shame,' wouldn't you say? Being ashamed, that's what a child feels, that's . . . standing with your feet turned in, your hands behind your back, and your eyelids lowered. But 'avoir honte' is something else, something that has to be carried, much heavier than shame. It sounds like an unpleasant disease, doesn't it? And in most respects, it is."

She turned her gray eyes on him.

Did she see him at all? Did she see anything?

"Are you a jinniya?" he asked, without expecting her to respond.

Nor did she.

Back in her fresh new house in Muscat, Annie was sitting with Stéphanie outside the French windows, staring across her soulless unplanted yard. Their voices were heavy, the conversation low. Annie was smoking—which was stupid, since she wanted to conceive—but when Stéphanie had expressed concern for her, she'd reached for the fags.

". . . and I wondered," Stéphanie was saying, "if you and Rolf maybe—"

"No, no, of course not."

"So is it Gabriel?"

Annie released a long stream of smoke. Then she leaned forward to place the packet of cigarettes and a lighter on the table, and sat back. "I thought I could be the peacemaker, you know? That I would heal everyone. Instead, I can't heal myself and I don't even want to heal Gabriel. He's like . . . ants in the cupboard."

Stéphanie chortled. "Like what?"

"No, really—when I see him, it's like opening a kitchen cupboard and finding thousands of ants crawling all over my food, so I just slam the door shut, rather than deal with it. If I don't look, I'll forget I've been infested."

"Infested? Why such language? He is a nice man, and a good brother, and you love him very much, I think."

"More than myself. More sometimes than Rolf. I also dislike him now and that's what's so difficult. Every day when I get up . . . this new feeling. This *dislike*."

"But what has he done to deserve it?"

Holding it in was doing Annie no good. That much was clear. She was constipated with anger. And Stéphanie could be trusted not to spread it across the colony, so she picked up her cup to drink, saying very quickly and matter-of-factly, "He nearly killed our brother Max and in all other respects has destroyed him."

Stéphanie's head swung around, her jaw falling.

Leaning forward to flick ash off her cigarette, Annie felt like a schoolgirl divulging her brother's misdemeanors, but she had earned the right to unburden herself.

"He was to be married, Max," she went on. "He'd met a lovely girl. Someone to look after him, you know? He wasn't really made for this world, my big brother. To him, it was all so *confounding*. The one thing that made sense to him, the thing he loved most and could do well, was music. He played the piano—really very well, but then Gabriel came along and he was, from day one, a natural. Profusely talented. God, he could play. We were blessed, really, to live in a home resonating with sonatas and fugues, toccatas and concertos. I can still remember those pieces wafting up through the floorboards. A couple of times—I mean, I was young, I didn't know what I was saying, but sometimes I shushed Max, when he was speaking, so I could listen to Gabriel." She paused, smoked. "Max didn't mind. He was very proud of Gabriel too. Frequently he moved aside to let Gabriel practice. That's when he became really awkward in himself, in his late teens, like he no longer knew where to sit, but he didn't give up. He worked harder. He had no other life, you see. He'd sacrificed everything to the piano, so he took his music degree, ended up teaching in the School of Music, and sometimes gave recitals. He played . . . earnestly, I suppose, as if determined to subjugate the piano, because he couldn't really do it justice."

"And Gabriel?"

"Oh, he flourished. The piano owns him, so he sailed through every exam, got scholarships, won prizes, traveled to Europe to perform in junior competitions, but . . . I dunno, maybe the parents pushed him too much, because when he was sixteen, he ceased to care. He lost all sense of application. Wouldn't practice enough, refused to enter competitions, and eventually stopped performing. Like Max, he took a degree in music, since there wasn't much else he was good at, he said, but still, whenever he sat down to play, you'd almost wish that Max wouldn't . . . *bother*." She let out the word in a whisper. "Yet on he went, slamming those keys as if Gabriel's slump was his second chance. It was painful, hearing him practice. *Striving*. Never quite . . .

"Anyway, we were relieved when Geraldine came along—she showed him there was more to life than work and music, albeit with limited success."

"Aie," said Stéphanie. "And Gabriel took her?"

"I suppose that *is* what happened," Annie said, after exhaling and inhaling and exhaling again, "but not as you imagine it. He never laid a finger on her."

"She fell in love with him?"

"Oh, no. No, Max was the love of her life."

"Go on."

"Gabriel got very drunk one night and . . . he got very, very drunk. There was an accident."

"Car accident?"

With another sharp intake of smoke, Annie said, "Yes."

"My God."

"Actually, that's a lie," Annie went on quickly. "I wish it wasn't. I mean, young men drink and drive and people get hurt. Max could have broken an arm, or some fingers, and never have played again for that reason. That would be endurable, I think." Her voice slowed, the words losing their hurry. "Because he doesn't play anymore."

A door banged and Gabriel came through the living room toward them.

Later that evening, after Stéphanie had left, they sat on the terrace, while Rolf barbecued.

Gabriel stared at the ice in his glass as if looking for his reflection. "So she knows now?"

"Hmm?"

"Stéphanie."

A flush of red climbed Annie's face. "You were eavesdropping?"

"No."

"Well, don't worry. I didn't tell on you."

"I'm only worried about you," he said. "Once word gets out, it'll travel, fast, with varying degrees of accuracy and malice. People have little enough to do here. It'll attach itself to you and I don't want you paying more than you already are."

"We need a story," Rolf interjected, barbecue fork in his hand. "Me too, I'm asked about you. Are you here on holiday? Drifting? Looking for work? No one gets into Oman unless for a job."

"I'd love a job," Gabriel said, over his shoulder.

Rolf grimaced. "There isn't much call for a pianist."

"I'm no longer a pianist."

"Aren't you confusing yourself with Max?" Annie said tersely. "You at least can play if you want to."

"If you want to work," said Rolf, "I can ask Rashid. But you would have to take whatever is offered."

"Fine."

"Driving, that is one thing you might do. You have an international license?"

"Yeah."

"Rashid might be able to find something with one of the companies."

"Thanks. A job would put an end to awkward questions."

"We need a story," Rolf said again, "even so. People are curious, and I don't want to expose Rashid to gossip."

"You're getting over a broken heart," Annie said to Gabriel. "You were about to propose to her when she told you she'd fallen in love with someone else. You couldn't stay in Cork any longer, because . . . because—"

"You worked with her lover," Rolf interjected. "He was your boss."

"Or your friend."

"Your boss *and* your friend," Rolf went on, shaking his head. "Everyone knew." He turned a steak. "Everyone in the office. Except you."

Gabriel looked over his shoulder. "Did *you*?"

Rolf glanced at Annie, who nodded and said, "We didn't know how to tell you."

Morning. The inside of his eyelids glowing with early light. Before he could stir, Prudence put her mouth to his ear and asked him to find her.

There was little to go on, since she had no name that she knew of. Neither did it help that she had no memory, no sense of her past, nothing to tap into that could point him in any direction. No memory either of recent events, not even of Annie and Rolf. She knew only Gabriel. She remembered so little, in fact, that she sometimes came looking for love five minutes after she had worn him out.

He stood her in front of the mirror, gently bit into the flesh on her wrist, tasteless but chunky, and said, "There you are. I've found you."

That's not me, she said.

"Then we must go out. Someone might recognize you, or you might see something that has meaning for you. If you honestly don't know where you go to when you leave this house, then the only possible explanation is that you've been hypnotized."

Hypnotized, she repeated.

"Yes—you do what you're told to do and remember none of it afterwards. It isn't impossible, but it *would* mean that I've been set up and I've drawn a blank with that. Most of the people I know have no clue where I am."

I do, she said.

The Intercontinental Hotel needed pool attendants who could swim well enough to assist any patrons who might get into trouble in the water. Gabriel had laughed when Rolf put it to him: "I'm no lifeguard!"

"You can swim, you need a job and they need you. Thursdays and Fridays."

And so, on those days, Gabriel spent his time poolside, tidying and handing out towels while club members and businessmen lay around gossiping and making deals. Embarrassed by his weedy legs and shapeless arms, he was tempted to say to the sunbathing women who flirted with him, "I'm a pianist. The muscles are all in my fingers." Friends of Annie tried to poach from him the story of his broken heart, but he wasn't as good at invention as his sister, which appeared to leave them all the more intrigued.

One afternoon Annie turned up at the pool, when Rolf was off painting mountains, and stayed until the evening, lying in the dimming sun. "I can't bear to see you do this," she said, watching him stack lounger mattresses. "There's a grand piano in the bar, you know. Maybe you could play in the evenings?"

"Cabaret?"

"You mustn't forget how to play."

"I'll never forget."

"You don't come over anymore," she said.

"Well, I have work and—"

"The woman? So bring her with you. God knows we'd all like to meet her."

Gabriel folded a damp towel instead of dropping it into the basket. The sun beat down on the back of his neck. "I've tried, I really have. I've tried to get her to come out with me, but it's like she's been brainwashed. She won't budge."

"That fits. They don't move about much," Annie said vaguely. "They tend to stay in one place."

"They?" he asked sharply. "Who's behind this? Because if you know, Annie, own up. I want it wound up, finished. Let's call a halt to the whole charade so Prudence and I can be together properly."

"I meant jinn. They tend to be shy. They're usually found in isolated spots, and they certainly don't go around socializing and bumping shoulders with expats at swimming parties."

"Christ, not this again. In all the stories I've heard—and I've heard a few—I've never come across an Irish jinni."

Annie looked at her freshly manicured nails and said quietly, "Have you been told that they can make themselves look like anything and anyone? That they can make mortals see exactly what they want to see?"

He threw another mattress onto the growing stack. "Yeah, and that they eat feces and bones, and live in shitholes and outhouses. Give it up, Annie, for Christ's sake."

Whenever he didn't have to work, he stayed in. Waiting. At night he barely slept, fearing that if she came upon him oblivious, he would be oblivious of her coming. He usually became aware of her before he saw her, but as for actually watching her coming into the room—hardly ever. He no longer questioned it. On the nights she didn't show up, he would eventually fall into a half-sleep, a world of busy images and fretful dreams, a strange tormenting place in which he found no rest, because Max always made an appearance, looking young and well, seated at a piano, his hands dropped between his knees, his shoulders hunched, rounded, his head hanging over the keys as if they were familiar to him in some unfathomable way. He never looked up. Gabriel was grateful for that. In his dreams, Max never looked at him. But Geraldine did. She came to him also—a gray figure in a gray coat, standing in a doorway, her face uncertain, her hair lank, her staring eyes forcing Gabriel to wake in order to avoid them, only to find himself waiting for a woman in whom nobody else believed.

When she was with him, the nightmares, the accusations and scorn, withered into retreat, where they lay vigilant, ready for their next opportunity. He lived like a man walking down a dark alley, expecting its ghouls to jump him.

And jump they did. As the affair crystallized, Prudence added to the layers of torment a layer all of her own.

One morning, early, his ankle was vibrating when he woke from a deep post-Prudence sleep. Unable yet to open his eyes, he concentrated on the sensation, trying to identify it. Pins and needles? There was a weight on his foot, holding it down, and then he heard the sound that kept time with the vibration: *purring*. A cat was lying on his ankle. One of the street cats had got in, quite a heavy one by Omani standards, and it occurred to him that he would love to have a pet, especially a cat—so soothing, like this, first thing in the morning—and he hoped, as he raised his head, that it would be a pretty one.

He looked down at his feet. No cat.

Gabriel leaped into sitting and pushed himself against the bedstead.

The purring grew louder.

He jumped from the bed into the solid silence of his Muscati house. No cat, anywhere, and no purring, now, either. But the blue kaftan was on the floor. Prudence had left behind her only piece of clothing. That had never happened before. He picked it up and brushed chalky dust off its sleeve. She must have put on his clothes. He lurched toward the cupboard—he had only four shirts and two T-shirts—and counted those that were hanging: two short-sleeved shirts and the heavy one he would never wear made three; his T-shirts were chucked on the chair. Where was the other shirt? He pulled on shorts, went downstairs, and found it lying crumpled on the cushions where he and Prudence had pulled it off him the night before.

His heartbeat tripped into a run. What had she worn going out? He crumpled her kaftan in his fist, smelled it. Desire, fulfillment, abstraction. This woman was killing him. Unless, of course, that was the whole point.

He hated going to work, not because he was afraid to miss Prudence, as before, but because he was determined to catch her out. She *would* slip up. There was no magic in this; she was a woman in a dress. There was nothing ethereal about her breath on his face or the mess of sex. He had tried every which way to contain her. He locked the doors; she got out anyway. He locked them both in without food; it didn't bother her; she could live without sustenance. It was his own hunger that drove him to the market, where he gorged on watermelon until he'd had his fill. In the house, he searched for trapdoors, hidden passages, amused by his role in this B-movie, and he spent hours watching her—a long woman on a long bench, flicking through a magazine. Jesus, he thought, does she know no boredom?

He loved her. In spite of everything, she had become the skin on his skin, the eyes in his eyes, the heart in his heart. Yet he had to hold firm. Reason was making too many compromises and skepticism taking too many hits. He had to bring Prudence from the closed world they inhabited and out into the day. How lovely it would be to walk together on the Corniche, to see the sunlight on her hair and speak of normal things, because as long as they did not live like others, and among others, they had nothing on which to build their relationship, because he too had become an empty thing, with little to say and no comment to make. There was no air in their cell and yet she would not quit it—not with him, at any rate.

He decided to follow her: to leave the house ahead of her, lurk in a doorway and keep one firm eye on his own front door. She moved quickly; she could zip past him in such a swish that he would have to be sharp, wily. It brought a vile taste to his mouth. Spying on his own lover would break even the wishy-washy rules of their game, whereby Prudence could toy with him all she liked, offering in return sexual ecstasy and a nibble on the carrot of love.

Nonetheless, he *would* follow her when she left the house, tail her through the suq and when, as expected, she hailed a cab on the Corniche, he would catch up and confront her. He would be careful not to frighten her—harm was something he would never do again—but he would demand the truth. Other truths, meanwhile, were thwarting the plan: Prudence had no cash for a cab and she wasn't taking his, so either someone was collecting her nearby or she didn't need wheels where she was going. Good. He would either follow her all the way to her destination or, at the very least, get a car's license-plate number.

There was an alcove along the alley—the entrance to another house, which, to his knowledge, was empty. He chose this as his spot and picked the moment to slip out, one afternoon when Prudence was lying on the cushioned bench against the wall. For an hour he stood in the shade, his eyes on his door until his sight started shimmering. Eyes are like fish: they need to move. His neighbor passed, gave him a look, but in the absence of a mutual language, nothing could be said. It was hot, breathless. No breeze came in from the coast, no air. Only the heat, radiating off the ground, frying his concentration and his eyeballs.

Ninety minutes into his vigil, Prudence had yet to emerge. Trust me, he thought, to try this on the one day she decides not to leave. His lids wanted to close. The soles of his feet burned through his sandals. His throat was parched. Should have brought water. . . . Young boys began to point and tease, as their parents became suspicious, looking toward him and shouting back at one another, no doubt about why he might be standing there, in the full heat, watching his own front door. They didn't know him well enough to allow this loitering, and even with a good grasp of Arabic, he would have struggled to explain it, so he gave up. His vision was blurring, his head throbbing, and he couldn't afford to fall foul of his neighbors, so he crossed back to his house, glancing through the window as he reached the door. Prudence was no longer in the front room, as she had been when he'd left.

He opened the door; she was lying on her side on the bench, leafing through the *National Geographic*.

Gabriel couldn't move. He could neither step forward nor back, because that would have meant quitting this spot, this certainty. He didn't wish to leave the realm in which she existed in simple terms.

And yet, dizzy with apprehension, he forced himself to step outside again and leaned into the window until his nose touched the pane, straining against the reflected glare of the white building behind him.

Prudence was not in the room.

He swung back to the open door: she was lying there reading.

Again and again he moved from the door, where he could see her, to the window, where he could not. He strained against the glass, cupping his hands around his eyes, shutting out all other light, and could see the bench, with its cover creased from their earlier fumbling and his empty mug on the white stone shelf. No one. Nothing.

Back to the doorway.

There.

Gone.

There.

Gone.

They had left the realm of the explicable.

Officially spooked, Gabriel became fretful, watchful, and tensed whenever Prudence came into sight. With his senses on high alert, he became more focused. She had no odor; at night, she lay as still as a stone, her breath so quiet he had to lean over to make sure she was alive. He heard things, in the house and out of it. Those waves crashing against rocks. Heavy waves, ocean waves. Memory. Had to be. These were sounds streaming from his childhood days on the Irish coast. Could Prudence also be coming at him from behind—an acquaintance back along the way whom he no longer recognized? Memory made flesh. A gentle reminder. Had he retreated into some comfortable pocket of his own mind where he stored happier times? This, he knew, was what most concerned Annie—that the delusion was entirely of his own creation, for his protection from his misdeeds.

Because although that rumbling ocean was distant, he could have sworn it was getting louder.

Reason was sitting on the edge of his control, as if waiting for a chance to leap beyond his grasp. Where there is no logic, reason falters. He woke one night, hot. A strange kind of heat covering him, neither clammy—he wasn't sweating—nor dry, more like lying in the direct path of a beam, as under a sunlamp or the sun. The heat of the sun—yes. All over him, though the room was as dark as Hades.

Alarmed, he sat up. The heat vanished. He reached for water, trembling, but the glass was empty, and he longed for those other dark nights when Max's hunched figure and limp fingers haunted him. *That* he could explain. He could unclench it. But what kind of dreams were these—the weight of a purring cat and dark heat burning him—and what had they to do with Prudence?

More sounds came, filtering through his attempts to keep them out. Alert in the course of another unquiet night, he heard someone coming along the corridor—a woman—nylons rubbing together. He leaped from the bed, again, and stood naked halfway across the room, his panting breaking the silence. Heart thundering, he turned on the landing light, fearful of confronting some woman with large thighs, but no one stood on the whitewashed landing, even though he could not have dreamed it, since he had not been asleep, and when he turned, Prudence was no longer in the bed.

The lady in the stockings had taken her away.

In the broad light of morning—and this place was very bright—Gabriel rationalized. He wanted Annie to come but didn't want to scare her more than he already had, and there was no one else to talk to, except Prudence, who was rather short on commentary and opinion. She was not unintelligent. There was more to her than flesh—he could see it, behind her eyes, a life of some sort, hurt, pain, even wisdom. But all she needed from him, it seemed, was to be physically close. And water. The glass of water he left on the bedside table at night was always empty in the morning, whether he had seen her or not, and he found empty glasses all over the house, which he had not put there. This was a thirsty phantasm.

Prudence was dream and nightmare entwined. No way to reject the ecstasy, no way of escaping the fear. All in, it was beginning to cost him.

"What kind of family do you hail from?"

Prudence didn't reply.

"Don't want to talk about it?"

Still nothing.

"Nah, me neither. I never mention the parents, if I can help it. Don't think about them either. If I did, I'd see them. I'd see them as they were when I left. Did I tell you about that? About the day I left?" He dipped his chin toward the head on his shoulder. Her fingers were dallying on his chest, her eyelids lowered, but she showed no inclination to respond. "Not much to tell, as it happens," he went on. "I went into the living room, said, 'Bye, I'm off to Muscat,' and Dad didn't even look up from the newspaper. Thin. Got very thin, he had, like my sister. Mam, though, she came to the door and wished me Godspeed, her face hollow. Dead inside. It could be her fault. Parents blame themselves for everything, apparently, and maybe that's right. Maybe mine didn't handle it well, having, you know, the gifted son and the grinder. Max, he was a grinder. He didn't accept his limitations. I hated the way he kept on trying, wanting to be as good as me. 'Don't bother,' I felt like saying. 'It's not so great up here on the pedestal.' I felt like St. Simeon on his column, but Max never got that. He thought he could work himself into being me, as if my so-called talent could be earned. Deserved. How mad is that? I didn't earn it and I certainly didn't deserve it. *He* did, though. . . . He probably did."

Prudence rolled onto her back. She was listening, maybe.

"Mam used to weed a lot," he went on, regardless. "I'd watch her, from the window by the piano, kneeling on a kind of mat in her tweed skirt and woolly tights, and her knees would be muddy when she stood up, with the trowel in one hand, and she'd be calling at the back of the house—at me. 'Why have you stopped, Gabriel? Carry on or you won't know the movement by Thursday. Play on, Gabriel.' That's all I ever heard. 'Oh, do play for us, Gabriel. Play for the Joneses/the Murphys/the Looneys! They *so* want to hear you play, and even if they don't, they're going to anyway. Go on, now, we're all ready, dying for a performance, so don't be silly/shy/mean/selfish/contrary, *play*, you damn stubborn boy, and make us look good, because we did shit-all ourselves and we're living this tiny life where we look like everyone else and act like everyone else and do dull jobs and have no talents—so perform, Gabriel! Make us look bigger than our unremarkable lives. . . .'"

Rain falling, falling on a roof, some other, slated, roof—a steady stream, soft yet determined, like whispers behind the wall. He was becoming accustomed to this other soundtrack, but he didn't mind the shush of the rain so much. It calmed him. He could even hear it slashing on to broad green leaves, as if he were surrounded by woodland, and since he was homesick, he stepped out into it and felt the soft Irish rain on his shoulders, smelled it, tasted it, almost became it, until the Gulf heat drew him back, like a possessive lover.

Some other world had become entwined in theirs. The stockinged legs, they came again and again. Often when he dozed during the day, he heard the scrape of nyloned thigh against nyloned thigh. *Swish, swish.* And sometimes the low murmur of a radio, muttering voices and a jangle of jingles. He narrowed his concentration, pulled it in tight, like focusing on the eye of a needle, to properly hear what was being said—was it an English station? Arabic? Straining toward another existence—his? Hers? He was almost certain that the muffled banter was coming in an Irish voice. A jolly, smug housewives' presenter. The static he was listening to sounded very much to him like Radio Éireann.

The slop and slime of love distracted him. Touching her, feeling her, insinuating himself upon her, he heard only her cries and his grunts and saw nothing beyond the undulations of her body, the small of her back, the incline of her breasts, the peak of hipbone and lull of waist. He needed more fingers, another mouth, better lips to fully appreciate her because, no matter how heightened the pleasure, he now reached the end of every coupling short of absolute fulfillment. There remained always a part of him untouched, a gap left empty. Next time, he always thought, next time they would hit the greater height.

"You have to come swimming with me," he said to her, one warm afternoon in the front room when he wanted to be on the beach. "I'm not doing so well, being indoors so much, and if it's getting to me, it must be getting to you."

No. No, I'm fine like this. I don't mind.

"*I* mind. I'm sleeping badly, seeing things. The honeymoon period—all sex and no living—has gone on long enough. We have to begin a normal life. You could get a job, if you don't already have one."

You're tired of me.

"I'm tired of the way we live, Prudence. I came to Muscat to escape confinement, only to build my own prison around us. When I wake up every morning I have no idea where my mind is or in which direction I should reach to retrieve it. Is that what you want—that I should live in a permanent state of mystification?"

No.

"So let's go for a swim."

The water would be too cold.

"Cold? Here? Ha! This isn't Ireland, you know. But we don't have to swim. Let's go for a wander. Just to the corner and back."

No.

"Yes." He gripped her elbow and tried to hustle her toward the front door, but Prudence wriggled and struggled, insisting that he could not make her leave. He couldn't even get her near the threshold, let alone beyond it, and he came off worse for trying. Anger took him. He grabbed her by the waist and hauled her across the room until, near the door, she bit his arm and he dropped her, and when they both fell to the floor he found that he was crying.

Saturated with love and terror, Gabriel began making inquiries about the house. With Ali and his friends, he had tea in the suq, where the air, trapped under the makeshift roofing all day, was like a warm soup that had solidified as it cooled. The house he lived in, he learned, had been built by a wealthy merchant and had once incorporated the building next door. No one knew of any jinn ever taking up residence there, and it owned no stories, beyond that of the owner, who had fallen on hard times and gone to Abu Dhabi to work. His sister now rented it out. "Talk to her," they said. "She will know more." So, later that week, Gabriel asked the man who collected the rent if there had ever been jinn around the place, but people, he had noticed, didn't like to speak of jinn too specifically, and this man also shied away from the question.

His landlady, however, showed up without warning the following evening in the company of a man, Juma, who spoke English and introduced himself as her nephew. Gabriel invited them in; she pulled her abaya around her, strode in and perched on the end of the bench against the wall. Her name was Farida. She had heard reports, Juma explained, of jinn in her brother's house.

Farida's eyes wandered around the walls.

"You have questions," Juma said. He was as thin as a board, had high pointy cheekbones, and wore tiny round spectacles.

"I, umm . . ." If his landlady suspected that he was entertaining loose women, she could have him arrested, but this fragile opportunity could not be wasted. "Things happen," he mumbled.

"Like what?"

"Glasses of water emptied. Fruit disappearing. A sense, a strong sense, of someone else in the house. Noises."

Farida's eyes stopped on him.

"Noises like what?" Juma asked.

"The sea."

"But the sea—" Juma raised his chin toward the coast.

"No, no—big seas. An ocean. I can hear waves crashing, and voices."

"Your neighbors," he suggested.

"It isn't Arabic I'm hearing. I can't say for sure what language it is, except that it isn't Arabic."

Juma looked skeptical. How could Gabriel explain that he too was entirely skeptical? He stood like a man at an interview while Juma talked to Farida.

"Why are you asking about jinn?"

"I've heard that, sometimes, certain houses can have a presence. In Ireland also we have houses that have spirits and others . . . others with a history of strange happenings. I thought maybe this house had some such history."

The landlady rattled away at her nephew. Good, thought Gabriel. Finally he was getting somewhere. She was agitated. Her brother had perhaps married a jinniya and the jinniya had stayed on. In fact, might that not be why the landlord had gone away—to escape her?

Why was he thinking like this?

They were gabbling. Standing up, Farida announced that she would look around the house and made for the stairwell.

Gabriel died a death—the house was a complete tip. She would throw him out for untidiness if nothing else.

"Maybe," Juma said to him, "it will be necessary to bring someone here to . . . make go away the jinn."

"You think there is one?"

"We will see."

"Look, Juma, I don't really need anything to be done or anyone . . ." *interfering*, he thought, ". . . getting involved. I'm simply curious about this place."

"My aunt says there were no jinn in this house before."

"What about new ones? Can that happen?"

Juma sighed. Probably not much of a believer, Gabriel reckoned. "Yes, they say jinn can come in a house or yard."

"Why? Why would they come?"

"Sometimes they will come where there is something empty."

"Empty."

"Yes."

Juma's eyes were cloudy, so it was impossible to tell whether he was very intelligent, but embarrassed by it, or dim, like his eyes. Either way, he was an English speaker and Gabriel would have liked to talk to him more, but Farida came back then, her face wrinkled with . . . something. She spoke to Juma, but her eyes never left Gabriel's face.

"Your aunt looks concerned," he said.

"She is worried for your safety."

Gabriel glanced at his arm. There was no mark where Prudence had bitten him. "She thinks I might come to harm?"

Juma responded with a sort of a sweep of his dishdasha, his body twisting, his hands deep in his pockets.

"Please reassure her that I'll be fine. I'm interested, that's all, in the way things work here. I have so much to learn."

Farida smiled suddenly, a coy, teasing smile, and addressed Gabriel, the language slipping off her tongue like a spell.

"She says, Aisha Qandisha has you by the forelock!"

"Excuse me? Aisha . . . ?"

"Qandisha." Juma also smiled. "This is a Moroccan jinniya. She makes men go mad."

"Oh. . . . Great."

"The men, they go, you know, wandering, always searching for her and hoping she'll return. Whenever they catch sight of her, they have to have relations with her."

Farida rattled on some more. "Um, um," Juma said, nodding. "My aunt says love is possession."

But I didn't mention love, Gabriel thought. Or speak of any woman.

"You see," Juma was warming to the subject, "when men fall in love with a jinniya—if he is struck, mdrub, by a beautiful jinniya, he will lose interest in human women."

"I see. And what then?"

Juma was matter-of-fact. "These men, they may suffer psychological effects, or even physical."

Farida pulled her veil closer to her face and moved toward the door, saying with a chuckle, "Aisha Qandisha!"

Closing the door behind them, Gabriel turned. The room was tidy, which it had not been when they had arrived. He went upstairs to see what his landlady would have seen: order, everywhere. His dirty clothes were no longer on the floor of his bedroom, the junk he had dropped around the place had been tidied away; in the kitchen, mugs were upturned on the draining board.

This was the kind of poltergeist he could live with.

Pity, he thought, about the other stuff.

What you say about your parents isn't quite true, is it?

Gabriel started. He had been asleep, alone, and he woke to hear her say this, or something like it. He was wary of Prudence now. It was no longer a question of who she was but of what she was. Jinn were often capricious. But, then, so was he.

You are angry with them, but you long for their forgiveness.

Perhaps it was his own voice that had woken him. He no longer knew whose thoughts were in his head.

The weather turned up its thermostat. March had given way to April and April was behaving like May. Gabriel swam at work, when he wasn't meant to, wiped down lavatories, collected empty glasses, and got his fingers sticky with discarded ice-cream wrappers. He meandered between loungers, looking at people snoozing, their skin burning, and didn't warn them. Later, scorched, they handed in their towels. I could've told you, he almost said. He ate as much as he could at the bar, but wasn't fired. They offered him more hours. He needed the money. He said thanks, declined, and cabled his father for more cash.

Annie came and sometimes didn't, like Prudence. She turned up more often at the pool than the house. Checking up on him. One afternoon, she shaded her eyes and said, "Gabe, I want you to come to an exorcism with me."

He gave her a look. "You think I need to be exorcized?"

"No. I mean—yes, you probably do, but this is, well, about the baby thing. It's some kind of ceremony. It won't be much different from going to a Catholic shrine that promises babies to barren women."

"Of course it's different!"

"How do you know? Have you been to one?"

"There's a lot more to that business than throwing pennies in the shrine, Annie."

A dip of frown indented her brow. "You've been informing yourself, I see."

"Talking to people, yeah. People go into trances at these things."

"So it'll be interesting. I've always been fascinated by this stuff."

He gave her another wry look. "You don't need me. You have Rolf."

"He won't come."

"Why not?"

"Well, he . . ."

"You haven't told him."

"No."

"They call it 'sihr,' Annie. Witchcraft. Are you really so desperate?"

"And some call it 'ruqya'—healing."

"Only when it's done in the proper Quranic way by the right person. Like priests doing exorcisms."

"We need some joy in our lives, Gabriel. All of us."

"That's not your responsibility. You don't have to get pregnant to save the rest of us."

"I'm trying to save myself."

"It could unhinge you, something like this."

"Remaining barren is unhinging me. Will you take me?"

"I'd really rather not."

"You'd really rather not, would you? You'd really rather not."

The nights continued into darkness. Howling Atlantic winds raged across the tranquil Gulf of Oman and bits of sentences tiptoed across Gabriel's hearing, like actors muttering their lines backstage: ". . . maybe later?" and ". . . so much the better," and intriguing snippets like ". . . say that because it's time to look the other way." He even heard a woman say, "What the mind can . . ."

"Am I tuning into the jinn world?" he asked Ali. "And if I am, how come they're speaking English?"

Ali discussed it with the other men, who leaned over their camel sticks, stroked their white beards, and concluded, as they had before, that he had been put under a spell. Someone was angry with him and had brought the evil eye upon him. They waited while he considered this, more seriously now than he had before. For sure, people were angry with him, but Max was not a vengeful man; he would scarcely know the meaning of the word. Geraldine, on the other hand. . . . She would never forgive him, she had told him so, and no doubt she wanted him to suffer as she now suffered. Perhaps this was the spell she had cast: an evil fairy sent to torment him.

No. *No.* He was losing grip. Geraldine—casting spells? That meek woman sending purring cats and radio shows? Hearing voices, in any creed, was a common infliction.

And yet revenge was being sought, and found, and Gabriel was shrinking. "But she's very beautiful, my jinn," he said, feeling forlorn, "and kind to me."

"That is all part of the trick." Behind the beauty, they agreed, there could be a foul-looking jinn—an old hag who meant him harm—and they shunted about so uneasily in their plastic seats that he didn't like to query them further.

"You should go home to Ireland," one of the old men said.

Ali translated, retorted, then translated his retort. "Don't go home. Jinn travel. She can go with you, and in your country there is no one to subdue her. You must go to the holy man and he will send her out."

They all nodded sagely.

Gabriel walked back to the house, sticking to the shade where possible, and found Prudence waiting, ready to shoo all the riddles away. They had a shower, giggling when shampoo froth slid down her face and she blew through the bubbles. The very idea that she was anything other than a delectable woman standing in a shower made him smile all the more and come like a bull elephant.

There would be no exorcisms.

Afterward, wrapped in a towel, she sat on his bed, leaning against the wall, her hands clasped around her raised knee, and said, Your parents will forgive you. Your sister already has.

"Forgive me? For what?"

The night in the music school.

He stroked her ankle. "Who told you?"

Prudence talked, that day, as she never had before.

The self-loathing, she told him, would never dissipate. In years to come, he would still stink of it and parts of him would grow rotten and wither, but he should expect that. Such were the consequences. And although he would spend a lifetime trying to understand his motivation, that lost moment would never make sense. Such were capricious mortals. His bitterness toward his parents was a dead end; he went there only because he had nowhere else to go. In truth, he blamed only himself, which was as it should be, she said, since he was to blame. There would be no relief. Time intermingles. The past cannot be revisited, she said, because it continues with us, embedded in a network of capillaries in our hearts and minds. That night in the music school happened every day, over and over; it had been rooted in all their lives forever, and so he confused things, couldn't see through it. His mind could never be quite clear, because what he did was not behind him. It walked alongside him.

Gabriel rolled from his stomach onto his back. "Might as well just slice my wrists, so."

Enough with cowardice and self-regard, she said, and he looked up because, for a moment, her voice was much lower than usual.

"And I thought you'd come to save me."

Later, she said.

"But I need saving right now."

Again soft-spoken, she went on, What's left of you is for others. Your sister needs you.

"And you need to stop talking. You know nothing about anything."

You buried him. That's what I know.

As they came around a bend in the road from Nizwa, the huge fort at Bahla came fully into view, standing proud of its oasis against a backdrop of copper mountains. Annie was quiet, and when Bahla's ancient wall came out to meet them, curving around the plantations, Gabriel could feel her anxiety. He squeezed her forearm. She stared ahead. Sabah and Marie were chattering in the back. They had told Rolf they were taking a picnic and had left for Nizwa, on the other side of the Hajar, then headed out toward Bahla, known for sorcery, magic, and jinn.

"In Bahla," Sabah said, "you should keep your head lowered and not look at anyone. They might give you the evil eye."

"What will happen, exactly?" Annie asked. "At this thing. I won't be the main act, will I?"

Sabah patted her shoulder. "Don't worry. There will be others. She will recite verses over you, from the Holy Quran, and give you a little stone or something."

"A stone? Like a talisman?"

"Or an amulet," said Marie, fanning herself. "Golly, it's warm for April. Turn up the air-con, Gabriel."

In the village, Sabah asked for directions, first from a man on a donkey, then from two Bedouin, in crinkly calf-length dishdashas wearing belts and turbans and carrying rifles, who were themselves looking for a bus stop.

"Getting to these places is the easy bit," said Marie. "Actually finding the right spot takes much longer."

Gabriel did his best to follow Sabah's directions: "We have to go down that road."

"Which road?"

"Back that way."

They were looking for the home of a woman who performed exorcisms and would be holding court for three days. She had a good hit rate with infertility. There were two types of exorcism, Gabriel had learned: legitimate, carried out according to correct Islamic practice by holy men, and the rest, performed by anyone who had a reputation for cures and magic. This was a magic woman; a witch, in his view.

He had to get out of the jeep several times to knock on doors so that Sabah could ask for directions from the back seat, only to be sent off in another direction, but Sabah seemed confident that they were homing in on their target.

When, finally, she instructed Gabriel to stop, they parked in a back street and followed Sabah, her narrow ankles and dusty sandals hurrying along under her abaya, down a dusty track to a mud-brick house. The door opened onto a courtyard where a woman, swathed in blue and black and wearing the most intimidating, and alluring, burqa—beak-like leather strips masking her face—immediately screeched at Gabriel and shooed him away. This was women's business. His gut tightened when Annie stepped into the courtyard where, beyond the heavy wooden door, he glimpsed clay pots and baskets stacked against a wall. The door closed behind his sister and her friends.

He was adrift, alone in this place. He grabbed a bottle of water from the jeep and set off along a path with a high mud wall on one side, which took him into the palm grove, where he followed the falaj. It whispered with a thin stream of water. The shade was calming. There was something soft about this country, he thought. The landscape was harsh, by and large, but these oases, the cover of palms and the trickle of water, and the kindness of the people, in town and out of it, made him increasingly reluctant to leave. So much was happening in Oman: Qaboos was educating and modernizing, and while there were slim pickings for a piano teacher, Gabriel was sure he could find work. Proper work. The life Annie and Rolf led—beach parties, barbecues, and lunches—held little appeal, but his own lifestyle did: sitting in the suq with Ali, waking to the call to prayer, watching dhows bob in the harbor. Oman, he realized, as he wandered among the trees, had brought him a kind of contentment, which he had believed he would never experience again.

And he had yet to see the desert, learn the language, know the people.

The high ramparts of the fort loomed above the gaps in the palmtops, so he headed in that direction and emerged at the foot of the promontory on which it stood. It looked like a Crusader stronghold, perched on its hill, but it was being watered down, year by year, during the rainy season, and its walls were melting into one another, so that the whole edifice was doomed to collapse. Gabriel found the best approach and scrambled up to the base, climbing over rocks and sliding on scree, followed for a time by a set of children, who slithered away before he reached the point where lumpy stone became a smooth mud-brick wall rising to battlements. High above, windows that had lost the rooms from which to appraise their view stood bravely in an unsupported wall, like a mask held away from a face. Gabriel's ankles strained at an angle. Steadying himself, with one hand on the hot brick, he reached the tower on the corner. What a lovely old wreck, he thought, falling apart like a rotting galleon on a bay.

Sweat soaked into his shirt, cooling him. Below, the palm groves concealed houses and alleys, and as he slid and stepped down, he wondered how the hell he would find Annie again.

Back in the shade, the trees were at first like a crowd gathering around to protect him from the sun's hitman-aim, but then he began to feel increasingly small, shrunken, and the palms no longer appeared kindly. They didn't seem to acknowledge his vulnerability, and if they rushed at him, as he felt they might, he would be trampled. His imagination moved. It dawdled behind him, like a shadow stretching out from his footfall, a part of him, but with a will of its own. He looked back along the rows of palms that seemed to be closing in. Ifrit and jinn, he imagined, were dancing around him like fairies, probably darting between tree trunks whenever he turned. He thought he heard their sing-song voices calling to one another, mocking him. Jinn often mocked mortals, and ifrit were horrible beings, a tribe of jinn who liked to torment. Bahla's reputation had caught him; the evil eye was on his back. His thoughts, watchful and wary, scurried after him, rattled.

It was stuffy under the canopy but, more by accident than intent, he reached the track by the mud wall, breathless, and came across an old man sitting outside a small home, the ubiquitous camel stick between his knees. He called Gabriel over. It was good to hunker down beside a solid person, a tangible presence, who talked away at him, with one very long tooth protruding. Gabriel had no means to respond, but he crouched and listened, trying to pick out some of the words he'd learned in the suq. The man called out to a small boy and in time coffee was brought, with a plate of plump dates on an old tin tray. Relieved not to be alone, Gabriel sat cross-legged on the ground, slurped his coffee—not too loud, as was polite—and made appreciative sounds about the dates. The man smiled and pointed at the palms, nodding with obvious satisfaction at the greenery that flourished all about them, thanks to the falaj.

Quiet, they allowed the thirsty heat to drink their thoughts until the old man looked past Gabriel into the grove. He did it a few times, his eyes narrowing and his lips closing over that dental protrusion, and then he spoke.

Gabriel recognized one word and swung around.

Trees, silence, filtered light.

The man went on, repeating the word "sayyida" and pointing.

The blood turned in Gabriel's veins. "La. La sayyida," he insisted, opening his mouth to Arabic and hoping he was saying, No. No lady.

The man blinked, moved his jaw around, as if chewing his bottom lip, then called out, over Gabriel's shoulder, what sounded like verses. Quranic verses.

"And all that food!" Annie exclaimed.

"Food?"

"Yes, egg, beans, halva . . . honey. It's part of the krama—is that the word, Sabah? Like offerings, you know? And saffron, henna—"

"And clothes," said Marie.

"Money."

"All offered up?" Gabriel pulled onto the main road.

Annie was giddy, full-on, relieved that she'd gone through with it and that it was over. "But the drumming and the chanting!" She widened her eyes, threw up her hands. "Oh, I'll never forget it. There are different rhythms, beats, for different jinn. It's unbelievable. It goes on for days."

"So it wasn't scary?"

"Well . . ."

"There was some kind of exorcism," Marie said. "That was quite alarming."

"That lady, she had a bad jinniya," Sabah explained.

"She was only a girl," Annie said, "no more than eighteen, and she was moaning and calling out, but she sounded like a man."

"Or some kind of beast." Marie looked out. "Horrible, really."

Gabriel feigned nonchalance. "That's what I've heard—that in the course of an exorcism the person has a low growl, a devilish voice. Same with Christian exorcisms."

"And afterwards," Marie said, and Gabriel could see in the mirror that she was pale, "afterwards she was fine." She shook her head. "I don't know what to do, now, with all my disbelief."

"What did the witch do for you?" he asked Annie.

"Don't call her that. At home she'd be called a healer."

"Amounts to the same thing, doesn't it?"

"She gave me stuff—some kind of gemstone, amulet thing, and recited verses over me, but just being there, the chanting and, oh, it was powerful, Gabriel. *Powerful.*" She turned to him. "You should go—get rid of your jinn."

He didn't know how to tell her that he might have picked up another.

Something had changed. Often Prudence teased, but left him wanting; pulled away when he was close to coming, so that he cried out in frustration. The sweetness had faded. Her reticence had become grating and the sex unpredictable, and her beauty, her indifference, were harder to endure. She knew too much about him now. He still loved the sense of her and yet increasingly felt an inclination to be cruel, which alarmed him, because he knew how to be cruel. Perhaps he wanted to punish her for breaking her own silence.

It was academic. He could neither leave her nor ask her to leave.

The sound of a siren broke into the night and came closer until, when it was nearby, it stopped. Gabriel listened for the follow-up—voices outside, urgency in the streets—but the night was as lifeless as a dead rat. He got up and went down to Annie and Rolf's empty bedroom to look out. The ambulance, its blue lights still flashing, had parked on the corner. Concerned for his neighbors, he hurried downstairs and went outside, but the alley was empty. He went to the end. No ambulance.

Fuck's sake, he thought. More creepy stuff.

With a skip in his step, and a sense of something rushing at his back, he hurried back to the house, still spooked by the story one of the traders had told of a man who was going through his oasis one night when a jinniya jumped on him from a tree, attaching herself to him, and although he swung around to shake her off, she hung on, saying she wanted him, had to have him, until he pressed against a tree trunk and scraped her off his back.

Gabriel slammed the door behind him and leaned into it, shaking so hard his legs barely held him.

Dreaming about ghost ambulances now. Always fucking dreaming.

His heart was getting some bloody workout in this country, he thought, but as he made his way to the stairwell, he stopped. Blue lights were flashing in the diwan. He went in and across to the window and, looking out, saw the ambulance on the corner of the street. No one was getting out; no one was rushing over. No people at all. Just a white ambulance, lights spinning, throwing blue beams across his walls.

He went back to the front door where, after a moment's hesitation, he steeled himself to look out. Sure enough, the only thing standing on the street was the night.

He had one foot in each of two different worlds.

Prudence was standing across the room by the entrance to the kitchen, her face lit by the flashing light—blue, gone, blue, gone.

Gabriel backed away, and out. Out! And he walked the coast until morning slid under the dark, its light under his feet.

Annie knocked timidly and let herself in. Gabriel was in the breathless diwan, stretched out, half asleep.

"Are you sick?" she asked, standing over him.

"Could be." He wasn't quite sure when he had last seen her, given the weeks were passing in a muddle of slothful days and wretched nights.

"You haven't been to work in ages. They asked me about you. I've tried to ring, but you won't pick up."

"Sorry."

"You had me worried."

Gabriel kicked out his legs and sat up, leaning back against cushions.

Annie sat beside him, her feet tucked under her rump on the edge of the mattress. "Have you been eating?"

"I'm fine."

"If you're planning to stay, you need to go back to work. We can't support you."

"You don't have to."

"What I mean is, we won't be here. To help."

He forced his eyes to focus on her. The mist was clearing.

"We're leaving," she said. "Rolf wants the baby to be born in Switzerland, where I'll be closer to Mam and Dad."

"Baby?" His voice thickened. "Annie—" Her smile lit up the inside of his head. He reached out to her. "Really? Are you sure?"

"Yes." She bit her bottom lip as if to stop the grin spreading too far.

"God, that's excellent. Fecking brilliant! Congratulations! That's just so . . ." Suddenly overcome, he started to weep.

"Don't," she said, touching his face. "We've done enough crying. I was so completely convinced it was never going to happen, until—"

"No way," he said, regaining composure. "Don't put this down to Bahla."

"Something unblocked that day. I felt it, Gabe."

He smiled. "Okay. Whatever. Who cares?"

She nodded. All giddy.

Who is this beautiful, delighted woman, he wondered, and where has she been all this time? "So, umm, you're off?"

"Rolf's contract is up in July. He won't be renewing. I'll leave in a few weeks. End of May, maybe."

"So you needn't have bothered making that whole move out to the villa."

"Oh, I think we did." She glanced around. "This place is stagnant. Made *me* stagnant. Anyway, now we want to be where we want to be and do what we want to do."

"Rolf is finally going to paint?"

"Yup." She widened her cheerful eyes. "No more plant machinery!"

Gabriel wanted to say, That's excellent. Bloody great. But another slice of his heart was being chipped off as she sat there, glowing.

"Don't look at me like that, Gabriel. You can leave too. You've been skittering about in that stupid job long enough. It's time you got back to the real world."

"Wherever that is."

"You could come to Europe with us. Work in France. Play again."

"Thanks, but I'm not going anywhere."

Her expression stiffened and her shoulders suddenly seemed pointed. "Not because of that woman? Or that spell, I should say—because that's all she is, Gabriel. Some apparition you've conjured up."

"And this from the woman who believes she conceived as a result of sihr?"

"That's different."

"How?"

Looking around again, Annie said, "This place is disgusting."

"Yeah, my poltergeist cleaning lady is really letting things go."

"Is she here? Now?" She said it warily, as if there might be another person in the room.

He fell back on the cushions. "I haven't seen her in a while."

"What? But . . . that's good."

He turned his sadness on her, though it threw no shade on the deep contentment that poured from all her features. "If you say so."

Annie got up and wandered up and down, stopping in a shaft of light, where dust particles sparkled. "The air is dustier than usual. Dead. It's as if no one moves or breathes in this house." She looked over at him. "You absolutely must leave with us. At best that woman was a trickster. At worst, a devil. A shaytan."

"The devil was in me in Ireland, Annie."

"I know."

She stood; he lay; the air didn't move.

"So?"

". . . There was an ambulance," he said. "Lights. Flashing. Outside—no ambulance. Inside, lights. Flashing. There. Gone. There."

Annie kneeled in front of him. "Ambulance?"

"Flashing."

"Where?"

"Nowhere. That's the thing."

For the first time in months, his sister properly looked at him. "You're not well. You probably haven't been well for . . . maybe for a long time. Which is good. What you did," she looked to the side, talking to herself, comforting herself, "that would have been diminished responsibility. It explains everything." She took his hand. "You must come with us and be treated, made well again. There's no need to live in exile like this."

"I'm not leaving."

"You have to! The authorities will throw you out."

"I'll get around that."

"Come to Switzerland. This child, Gabriel, this baby is going to fix things. Make us all better. Mam sounds like a different person alr—"

"I have to be here. She'll come back."

Annie stood up. "This really isn't what I want to talk about right now!" And just as swiftly she softened again. "Why did she leave, anyway?"

"You see, I tried to . . ." Gabriel stared at his bare feet ". . . *remove* her. Called her bluff, and she called mine."

"What do you mean?"

He wondered about telling her; he even wondered if Annie was really there and if he was actually lying in the diwan or only thought he was. He spent his days and nights wondering.

❃

Prudence had said, the night after the blue lights, when he was in the kitchen and she was standing in the doorway, that she would be going now. She had never said that before.

"We'll go together," he insisted.

She had leaned against the doorjamb, watching him. I love you, she said, whoever you are, but I'm better now. Thank you for being here.

As she turned to go, he lurched toward her and grabbed her wrist. "Yes, let's do that. Let's leave. But where shall we go, Prudence?"

Not together, she said, wincing.

He was hurting her and didn't care. "It's late. There's no one about. We'll walk by the sea."

No.

"You want to see the sea, don't you? I'll take you. I'll take you right now."

No. Her voice had rumbled then, reached into his chest like a quake deep in the earth. It frightened him, but when he tightened his hold, Prudence whipped, lashed, spun out of his grasp, and made across the room. He lurched again, got hold of her elbow, but she fought dirty, scratching, spitting, a cat gone wild. Still, he managed to pick her up, though the twisting creature he carried was no longer a beautiful woman, erotic and supine, but an evil grunting thing with foul breath, and when, near the threshold, he reached for the door handle, he was suddenly overcome, knocked down by a cacophony of voices—his father's, his mother's, his aunts', even his brother's—and a hologram of faces, all of them hissing at him, cursing and berating him, and he wished it was Max in his arms, that he might carry him away from the place in which he had left him, but the clatter of condemnation grew louder until he pulled his arms around his head and begged them for quiet.

By the time they fell silent, Prudence had slithered away, like water into a drain, steam into the air.

Since then, he had tried to conjure up an alternative departure—Prudence walking out of the door with a fond farewell and a backward glance, as lovers do—and he could almost see it, just as he had almost heard the scrape of stockings and the sea moaning and the rain falling on broad green leaves.

All imagined, perhaps. All imagined.

Annie was still there, seated right by him. "Come with me, Gabriel. Please. This is over now."

II

Into Temptation

RED DOUBLE-DECKERS CROSSING THE bridge in the post-dawn gloom; palm trees and minarets; low white buildings in mud-brick enclosures, and the river, lazy blue in the early light. . . . Thea stepped onto the balcony, into the cool morning air. How peculiar, she thought, that this should be her first sight of the East: London buses.

Rush-hour in Baghdad.

Reggie, her new boss, had unruly light brown hair and a shaggy beard to match, and had seemed on first impression to be genial, a bon vivant Englishman who loved Iraq. When he had picked her up at the airport the night before, he had told her that, jetlag notwithstanding, she would have to be in the lobby at ten to seven the following morning.

"Because of the intense heat in the summertime," he had explained, "everyone starts work at seven and finishes at three."

But this was not the summer: it was cold and still dark when her breakfast was brought by a young waiter wearing a gray jacket and white gloves. Hotel living had its advantages, she would discover, such as breakfast in bed every day, which was just as well, since her team was likely to be there for some time. The company intended to find apartments for them, but nothing happened fast in Iraq, Reggie had warned her, and finding suitable accommodation would be a laborious process, so this dim hotel bedroom, with its narrow windows (to keep out the heat) and the balcony shaded by another balcony overhead (to keep out the heat), with its single beds and limited leg-space, was home for the foreseeable future.

She made it to the lobby before seven and met up with the rest of her cadre—Kim, an American girl who had been living in London, and an English surveyor, Geoffrey. They set off in a jeep to drive the short distance to the office. Kim was slim, pretty—blond hair in a tight curly perm, light brown eyes—and lively. *So* lively, and unspeakably chatty at that ungodly hour. She had been in Baghdad for a month and liked it, she said, but she longed to get out of the hotel and into proper housing. "I feel as if I'm passing through, you know? Like a tourist. Not someone who's going to be living here for a few years."

Thea found it difficult to look out without being rude, but she wanted to see the city rather than hear about it, especially since Baghdad was standing there, like a debutante in her ball gown, waiting to be noticed and admired.

Or pitied. The war was on every corner. Sandbags, piled high, concealed the soldiers but not the barrels of their protruding guns. Thea was more interested than alarmed, which was curious, since it *was* alarming—the Iranians might invade and then she'd be done for, caught, trapped, unable to get home, but what of it? She had made the decision to come; she had arrived. If the war should go badly for Saddam Hussein, there was nothing she could do about it now. Saddam was everywhere: posters, flyers, graffiti, photos dangling in the rear windows of cars. The cult of personality was doing its work. No space in Iraq could be left bare of his image.

The first thing she noticed about their otherwise unremarkable office building was the cold. It was freezing. There was no heating, even in the middle of winter, and that, Thea realized too late, was why Kim and Geoffrey looked conspicuously bulky. "Layers," Kim explained. "It's the only way to keep warm."

"Jayzus, I only brought a couple of sweaters. I never imagined it could be so cold."

"Me too. They should have warned us."

Their offices, on the fifth floor at the top of the building, were bright and a little chaotic—the desks sprinkled around large rooms in no particular order. Thea's desk was a wobbly table pressed against the wall beside a ceiling-high set of shelves. Her typewriter was electric, but only just: it was old and clunky, in contrast to the nippy, whispering golf-ball IBM she had used in Dublin. Her work was undemanding—typing reports and correspondence, filing, sending the occasional telex. Brainless stuff, but brainless stuff in stimulating surroundings. Reggie took her around, introducing her to their Iraqi colleagues; the women wore navy suits, mostly, and had come into work gripping their black abayas, pulled over their heads and clutched with one hand at their chests. The men were quite slight in build, had sharper features, and all wore the mean Saddam mustache, without which they would have invited suspicion. They were all professionals—architects and engineers—and, although welcoming, only a handful had enough English to make any degree of communication possible.

Reggie shared a large room at the end of the corridor with two other managers. The project director, Tariq, worked alone in his long, bare office. A thin man, who held his elegant frame like a pole, he was anti-regime, or so Reggie had said in the car, but his professional acumen was apparently such that the government needed him for this job—supervising the design and construction of state-of-the-art bus stations; his rigidity suggested that he, as much as his masters, had accepted the appointment with bad grace.

Within half an hour of arriving at her desk, Thea was craving coffee, tea, even another breakfast—anything to warm her up. The office boy, one of the women told her, could fetch her tea, so he was dispatched and returned with a glass of milkless tea so strong and sweet she couldn't drink it. That was the first shock to the system: no ready supply of coffee, no standing around a communal kitchen waiting for the kettle to boil while catching up with friends; no opportunity to stop, stretch, breathe a little. The second shock was that there was no lunch break. In Saddam's Iraq, nobody, it seemed, dared to stop working. They had to go right through until three o'clock—and Thea had brought no food. Their Iraqi colleagues produced their own lunches and ate at their desks, bread stuffed with beef and salad, the tantalizing aroma of unfamiliar spices wafting around the room.

"You'll get used to it," Kim said. "We'll eat something back at the hotel."

"What time will that be?"

"Only another three hours."

The first day was long. Thea's fingers were so frozen they could barely bang the sticky keys, and she knew that if she caught a cold, she would still have to show up to work in this icebox, because her contract allowed so few sick days per year. In search of warmth, she stood in the sunlight by the window, but the effect was minimal, so she retreated to her dark corner and Reggie's letters. Kim, along the corridor, worked mostly for Geoffrey.

When three o'clock came, they escaped into the brisk afternoon and their warm jeep, and Geoffrey delivered them back to the hotel, where they tumbled gratefully into the sunny lobby, which buzzed with businessmen. At one end there was a cozy alcove, with silky red cushions and bolsters, urns and copper lights, and a low table, so Thea and Kim spread out across the couches, and ordered tea and cakes. From where she sat, Thea could see, through the curved opening, the reception desk at the far end of the lobby, and the receptionist who had greeted her the night before.

"Who are you looking at?" Kim leaned to the side. "Oh, that's Sachiv. He's one of the managers."

"He seemed nice, when I was checking in."

"He's great. Really helpful—goes out of his way for us since we're gonna be here long-term. Cool guy. And married. I thought I'd just throw that in. Married with three small kids."

"Pity."

"Uh-huh."

His hands had been the first thing she had noticed, when she had arrived the night before. He was writing up the register, taking her details, wearing a black jacket and starched white shirt. His fingers were long and slender, his nails neat. A good start, she had thought mischievously, catching a flicker of those dark eyes, as she leaned wearily into the desk. It had been a long day, and a disconcerting one, not least when the jet had come in to land and all the aircraft's lights had been turned off—inside and out—so that they couldn't be fired at. It was reassuring that such a calm, attractive man should receive her on the other side of the bridge.

After tea with Kim, Thea went back to her room to unpack, and every time she took an item from her suitcase to place it on the shelves, her trajectory took her to the window. Baghdad. It was hard to grasp. Her mother had already decreed that it was her unattractive inclination to be impetuously reckless that had driven her there; her friends said she was like Amelia Earhart, always needing to reach higher altitudes; but she thought of herself more as a grasshopper. There didn't seem to be much she could do about it, this tendency to make snap decisions and leap above the tall grasses to see what lay beyond. For months on end, it seemed, she could live unobtrusively, happy with her lot, until, feeling suddenly crushed by normalcy and expectation, she would do something wild, even dangerous. In such a mood she had climbed the "In Pin"—the Inaccessible Pinnacle—on the Isle of Skye with her brother when she was nineteen, though she had only hill-walking experience. At such moments she was fearless, but the payoff was considerable. Reaching the top of the In Pin was like stepping onto Heaven's doorstep, where all she had to do was ring the bell for God to open the clouds and say, with a glance at His mountains, "Yes, I did rather well that day, didn't I?" At twenty-two, she had learned to surf in the dull, peeved seas off Strandhill, even though the words "surfing" and "Ireland" were infrequent bedfellows, and years before that, at the annual school concert, she had barged onto the stage and made a plea for a new school uniform because their skirts were so tight, most of them couldn't breathe. "Like women in corsets," she had declared, to the consternation of dignitaries and her own headmistress, who suspended her from school for three days and soon afterward redesigned the skirts. Thea's tendency to break out, like a whale coming up for air, gave her mother sleepless nights and was frequently embarrassing to herself. She regretted, bitterly, some of her devil-may-care impulses, particularly those involving men, which was possibly why she usually retreated into neutrality until she needed that rush again, that bit of chaos—the sliver of chili tossed into unremarkable food.

And so, when she had seen the ad on an unremarkable day in November, her personal Richter scale had flickered. She was having tea and toast at the time, at a counter by the window of a café at the end of Dublin's Leeson Street. Breakfast in the café was her morning yoga, a slice of peace before the slog that lay ahead—she was a commuter, a worker, part of the flow and throng into town, to desks and phone calls and whining shredders. Holding a half-eaten piece of toast, smeared with jam from a plastic packet, she read the ad and blinked. It was an alert, a call from the deep vein of unpredictability that ran through her, like a seam of ore, invisible, but rich.

Before she had even put down the newspaper, she knew the job would be hers. She was sharp and efficient, a mean typist, and had an excellent manner with clients. Her reference would glow like a red hot coal, making the envelope smolder. She bit into her toast, startled by this hitherto unseen confidence in her own abilities. It suggested that she was underperforming. In her twenty-fourth year, at a counter in a window, the *Irish Times* had thrown down its cape—all she had to do was step out.

Her confidence had hit the mark: within weeks, the job was hers.

One day Leeson Street, the next Baghdad.

The days were long in the office, and so were the six-day weeks, with only Fridays off. Thea adapted slowly, wearing layers of spring clothes and wrapping half her breakfast in a paper napkin so she could eat it in the cold office midmorning. The rest she could deal with because the rest she loved. Kim, in particular. Perhaps it was their situation that created a depth of understanding they might not have enjoyed anywhere else, but they believed they would have been close in any situation. Different enough to be compatible, they shared the same curiosity and a tendency to long-jump when small steps would do. It couldn't be long before they discovered one another's irritating foibles—how could they not, when they shared their hotel, workplace, transport, and social life, but the prospect didn't worry them. Kim was smart and gutsy and great company; emerging from a bruising relationship in London, she had come to Iraq because it was about the only place to which her obsessive ex-boyfriend wouldn't follow.

In the late afternoons they took to walking on the other side of the river, braving the erratic traffic and one of Baghdad's busiest bridges to reach the quiet stretch of its bank. Here, where their conversations were unfettered by colleagues and hotel staff, they found their common ground, the yin and yang of their immediate friendship, and they discovered that both had been accused, back home, of profiting from another man's war. Each felt guilty as charged.

"But if I am profiting from being here," Kim said, "the salary is only a very small part of what I have to gain."

Thea agreed. "So many people said to me that it must be for the money—why else would anyone come to a war zone except for the cash? Well, maybe because even a humble secretary can do more than work in a lawyer's office or a travel agency, and for my part, I just desperately wanted to see beyond the carriage return of a typewriter. I know that's greed too, especially given what's going on, but it might as well be me standing here on this riverbank as anyone else."

The evening sun was low. Kim stopped on the sandy track and shaded her eyes. The Tigris had turned pink. "I can sure live with being greedy if this is where it takes me."

Reggie was also easy to like. An expatriate of long standing, he couldn't remember when he had last lived in England, and his contributions to any conversation usually began, "When I was in the Congo/Argentina/Bratislava. . . ." His enthusiasm worked like a battery on his team, and his penchant for overly large yellow and orange shirts, hanging from his narrow shoulders, with contrasting orange and yellow ties made for quite a startling wake-up call every morning. Geoffrey, in contrast, tended toward the maudlin. He was there only and unapologetically for the money, but even that didn't satisfy him: he moaned tunefully about overbearing bureaucracy, inadequate leave and missing his friends. Their contracts *were* tough on the homesick—no holidays for twelve months, and then only ten days' leave before embarking on another year. It felt like self-imposed exile to Geoffrey, but Thea felt no draw, no pull for home—at least, not until one night, very shortly after she'd arrived, when the city started popping outside. Gunfire.

A zip of fear rushed over her, even as her friend knocked at her door. Kim hurtled in and made for the window. "What the hell's going on out there?"

The sky was flashing, the air banging. They turned off the lights and stood to the side of the window, flinching with every bang and watching arcs of light flying skyward. It was the oddest feeling—helpless, nothing to be done, nowhere to go.

Another knock: Reggie come to reassure them. "I thought you two might be anxious."

Kim turned. "Are we under attack?"

"No, no—it isn't the Iranians, it's a celebration. Those are tracer bullets. Usually means the troops have done well at the front. Probably won some battle or other, so they're letting everyone know about it."

"Oh, man," said Kim, hand on chest. "Scaring me half to death because they've killed more guys than the other side?"

"Where was the battle?" Thea asked. "Not too close, I hope?"

"We'll never know. There won't be any details in the papers tomorrow—or no details worth noting. The only thing the people of Baghdad need to know, those families who have brothers, fathers, and husbands at the front, is that some undefined battle has been won in some undefined place. Keeps morale up."

"So can we go outside and watch the fireworks?"

"Yeah."

They stepped onto the small balcony. A moment's homesickness glanced over Thea, as she thought about Dublin's peaceful streets and imagined what her mother would say if she could see her now: standing on a balcony watching tracer bullets fly across the night sky as a nearby-faraway war landed on her windowsill.

Dublin touched her again a few nights later when she heard that its streets had been, for several days, even more peaceful than she had imagined; that they had, in fact, been deserted. Every month an Irish colleague, Mic, came out from the London branch (usually carrying their mail) to do a few days' work with Reggie, and it was he who brought the news that Ireland had suffered blizzards and a historic freeze soon after Thea had left, with temperatures dropping, in some places, to minus fifteen. Over dinner, he captivated them with his account of his own experience of the storm: he had landed in Dublin on the last flight before the airport closed down under the weight of twenty-six centimeters of snow, and had been forced to walk to his mother's home, making the long trek into town in deep snow, along a deserted O'Connell Street and on out to the suburbs. It had taken him seven hours to reach his mother, but at least he'd got there, he said. Hundreds of passengers had been trapped at the airport for days. The image stayed with Thea, all that night and beyond: a white O'Connell Street, hardly a car or person in sight. It was in the letters she received too, this blizzard. Her mother had written of frozen pipes and snowdrifts two meters high, of ice floating down the rivers and of a strange quiet. The quiet of snow. It had gone on for ten days, the freeze, and Thea felt lonely for this disaster, this national emergency: she would have liked to have seen her city reduced to a whisper.

Homesickness never lasted long. There were too many distractions, even right there, in their hotel.

Her eye had been caught, and her heart was following. It was hard to ignore Mr. Sachiv Nair, impossible not to see him, center-stage behind the reception desk, when she hauled herself from the elevator every morning and made her way across the white marble lobby. He was also the first person she saw, most days, standing tall and straight, in his black suit and silver tie, when she came back from work. She found every excuse to speak to him: were there any telexes from home? Was the weather going to warm up any time soon? When could she hope to get her laundry back?

Hotel living meant they had no choice but to use the laundry service for all their clothing—even panties and bras had to be put into the plastic bags provided and noted on a list. They started off by handwashing their underwear, but soon tired of having it hanging off the shower rail and draped around the bedroom. Relinquishing privacy, they stuffed everything into the see-through bags, duly filling out the forms, and watched as they were taken away by young boys wearing white gloves. There was no knowing exactly where their clothing went—somewhere into the bowels of the building—but it was washed, dried, and ironed, then returned to the rooms in carefully packed parcels, each item ticked off the list. The system sometimes broke down, but when Kim lost a bra, she was too embarrassed to inquire as to its whereabouts. "Can you imagine describing my white, lacy bra to Mr. Nair?"

"I can just see him, down in the basement," Thea laughed, "rooting through piles of men's shirts in search of it! He does so like to provide a good service."

They spared themselves the embarrassment of sending him in pursuit of intimate clothing, but he was always particularly courteous to them, since they were usually the only women guests in the hotel, and whenever they came back from an evening stroll, he smiled and asked how their walk had been. Thea would veer toward the desk for a chat, like a speedboat changing direction, if he wasn't too busy. One day when she came in, he was standing in front of the desk in jeans and a blue shirt. It didn't help, seeing him in civvies. It eroded the barrier between them—the hotel manager behind the counter handing out telexes—and her attraction to him climbed a notch, becoming a more solid thing, an indisputable thing. It was his day off, he explained. He had been about to take his family to the park when he was called to the hotel to sort out a problem. He had now resolved it and was about to join his waiting wife . . . except that he stayed on, chatting with Thea.

She went to her bedroom, lay on her bed and stared at the ceiling.

It was said that the rooms were bugged. They were all working for Saddam Hussein. He was ultimately their employer, this great friend of the West. Build up Iraq, the reasoning went, and there'll be no hope for those raging fundamentalists in Iran. But Thea had been warned. One of her colleagues in Dublin had an Iraqi friend, a student doctor, who had agreed to meet her before she left for Baghdad. In an Irish pub, in an Irish city, he had been reticent, nervous. His eyes jumped toward the doors whenever someone came in, and when he asked her why she was going to work in Iraq, her naivety shone through. Oh, it wasn't the money, she had blurted, but then she had muttered and fumbled about with words like "adventure" and "experience" and felt ashamed. Looking for personal thrills in the mayhem sounded even crasser than being motivated by a tax-free salary, and it was an insult, she realized, to a man whose country was in despair. He was anti-regime, hence his nervousness, and he would have no option, he explained, once his studies were finished, but to disappear into a corner of Europe or America, where the Secret Service wouldn't find him. He would not work for Saddam—could not—so he could not return home, and yet he was polite to Thea, who was off to her high-paid job in the very city where his own family lived, the family he could not hope to see for years. He didn't seem to begrudge her, that quiet Iraqi man, who wore no mustache. Instead he had warned her, in the cozy pub, to trust no one in Iraq. To be very careful what she said and where she said it. He told her that the walls had ears and the elevators had eyes, but left unsaid that adventure might be better sought elsewhere.

Humbled, she had returned home that night feeling the first twinges of apprehension, and a little tawdry besides.

Weeks later, staring at her Baghdad ceiling, it still bothered her to think that his family were only a few miles from where she lay, while he remained so far away from them, but she liked the city too much to be nervous, even though the student doctor had been right. Reggie had warned them—when they were in the jeep (the only place where they could speak freely)—not to be critical of any aspect of Iraqi life at work or even in their bedrooms among themselves, and to be extremely careful about what they said on the phone. Whatever about the rooms being bugged, the phones certainly were.

But she endured the ubiquitous security and the giant poster eyes that followed her everywhere, because she loved the way it met *her* eyes, this city, with its fractured skyline—its modern monuments and the few high-rise buildings sprouting haphazardly from the low-roofed town. The Martyrs' Monument, which they drove past often, was like a huge blue onion carved through the heart, one half dancing with the other, and it glittered at sunset with deep pink flashes of light. She loved the slow flow of the Tigris, the dusty palm trees scattered along its banks, the resonating call to prayer and the honking traffic. Every morning she woke elated, knowing that when she pulled back the curtain, her eyes would fall upon one of the great cities of antiquity and legend.

And yet it wasn't all about the magnificent East. Thea loved Baghdad because it had already marked her, aged her. Already she knew that she could never recover from the Friday-evening scenes at bus stops, where huddles of soldiers gathered, young and scared, with their distraught families, who had come to wave them off, knowing they might never see them again. Those goodbyes gave her sight of other lives, of the crisp pain of war. She worked with people who had relatives at the front, and she saw, daily, the anguish in their eyes. *Her* brothers, back home at college, were safe from conscription, and her opinionated mother could speak her mind, whatever her views. In Baghdad, Thea watched her tongue, and grew up.

For the same reasons, their plans to integrate with Iraqis were largely doomed. The women at work were friendly, but wary. Most subjects were off-limits—travel, politics, what they had done at the weekend even—and any attempt to speak their language met with a studied bemusement. Those colleagues who spoke English insisted on doing so, even for the slightest pleasantries. There was no encouragement if Kim or Thea tried to say "Good morning," or "How are you?" in

Arabic. "No, no," their colleagues insisted, "we must practice English!" Perhaps they knew it might one day be their means of escape, but it was frustrating. Thea and Kim liked the women, wanted to know them better, but when, one day, they invited those who had a little English to join them for tea at the hotel the following Thursday afternoon, the invitation, though graciously received, was neither accepted nor declined. It was only toward the end of the week that excuses started coming: Alia had to help her mother; Rabia was expected by her grandparents; and Najma was vague—thank you, but she could not come. There were no reciprocal invitations.

"What happened to hospitality being the cornerstone of Arab life?" Kim grumbled over dinner. "I thought inviting strangers into your tent was part of the culture. What gives?"

"What gives," Reggie said, "is that it's against the law to fraternize with foreigners, except in very restricted circumstances."

"But we work with them!" said Thea.

"Yes, but all that is monitored. I'm sorry," he went on, dropping his voice, "I should have told you. They have to be very careful whom they speak to."

"Even a couple of harmless women like us?"

"Yes, because they might find out stuff Saddam doesn't want them to know. They might get hungry for a different kind of life."

"But they can't leave the country," Kim said, exasperated.

"Except to study," said Thea. "What about Iraqi students abroad—paid for by the government? They're out, mixing with people."

"That's a risk the government has to take. They need the expertise. Besides, those students are closely watched. They scarcely go anywhere without someone on their tail."

Thea remembered then how the Iraqi doctor had left the pub in Dublin as soon as a couple of fellow Iraqi students appeared.

"They were probably working for security," Reggie said, "and he knew that."

"Other students?"

"Sure. Regime and anti-regime. Everyone is on one side or the other. The same with our colleagues. One side or the other, and don't ever believe you can tell which. They don't know who's watching them, they only know they're being watched, so you two rather put the women on the spot. If they'd expressed any pleasure at being invited, that could have been taken as courting foreigners, even if they said no."

"Which explains the flatness of their refusal?"

"I imagine so."

An oblong platter of hummus, tabbouleh, and beetroot was placed on their table. The war had closed most of the city's restaurants, so the team usually ate in the hotel and they enjoyed their evening meal together, often retreating afterward to Reggie's spacious corner bedroom, where they were frequently reduced to helpless laughter by silly jokes and pointless anecdotes, amusing only to the blended mentality of a small group living closely in restricted circumstances. Thea loved it all—from the hummus to the hilarity. These were good times. Good times in Iraq.

Gently, swiftly, Sachiv Nair became a preoccupation, and as those early weeks passed, Thea had reason to believe that he knew it, maybe even reflected it. Increasingly, whenever she stepped into the lobby at that miserable hour of the morning, his eyes were already turned toward the elevators. As she emerged, he dropped his moon-like lids, and then, when her heels clipped across the marble, he looked up with a greeting, a hand reaching out for her key, and she would go her way while he stayed at his post. She began to wonder if the day would be as long for him as it was for her until she pushed those revolving glass doors and emerged into his world again.

It was harmless. A crush. He was married, in his early thirties. She passed by a few times a day. Pleasantries were exchanged, like the keys. A few flirtatious smiles, some eye contact, but there would always be that desk between them. That marble barrier. In spite of it, the longing—to talk to him, to linger and dally without attracting attention—grew more persistent.

There was very little they could talk about at Reception, with everyone milling around and military personnel coming and going, but she often watched him from the alcove, where she read and drank tea, raising her eyes when discretion allowed. Whenever an advance party of soldiers swarmed into the lobby, Sachiv managed to maintain about the place a distinctively civilian bustle, and Thea noticed how he even maneuvered the overdecorated generals and their eager underlings with a cold efficiency. He pulled the necessary strings, but showed no deference. In contrast, when wedding parties bundled into the hotel, he gathered a cheerful staff around him and allowed no missed detail to spoil the spectacle as the newlyweds arrived in their chariots—huge white Cadillacs—and families crowded into the lobby, the women ululating and waving their arms, while the bride came in under a swarm of hair and lace, broad with gown and grinning past her scarlet lipstick. On Fridays, the one day Thea could hang about, Sachiv was rushed off his feet, what with the martial and the marital, so it made no odds when Reggie started taking them out on day-trips. The kitchen provided picnics wrapped in foil, slabs of unleavened bread and cans of soft drinks, and they would head off to whatever sites of interest had grabbed Reggie's attention.

Thea was reluctant to leave the sphere in which she could catch even brief glimpses of Sachiv, but Reggie's excursions were to leave an indelible mark, because Iraq too could give her a look, could stand still and yet tinker with the heart. It brought out her other self—the one who was curious, daring, who could no longer see her horizon, since it was now so far away. In her room at night, she gazed at maps and made plans, and read of the Marshes, of Ctesiphon and Babylon, and the holy towns of Karbala and Najaf.

One day, in the western desert, things turned for Thea, on two counts. Removed from Sachiv for longer than she liked, she guessed herself to be in trouble, love kind of trouble, though she scarcely knew the man, and driving through Karbala, past its celestial golden mosque, she became further entranced by Iraq, though she scarcely knew the place.

Beyond Karbala, across the steppes, they approached al-Ukhaidir, a great rectangular fortress, miles from anywhere. At a distance, it looked like a shoebox, but as they pulled up, its remote elegance silenced them. Its long external walls, intact, were indented with bricked-in arches and stocky towers, while the upper part had crumbled away. It was all aglow; a golden place. They went in, reverently, through the arch and under a fluted dome, past stocky columns and architraves, and emerged into the main courtyard.

Reggie muttered facts and figures—built during the Abbasid Caliphate, eighth century; 165 rooms, mosque, guest quarters, bath with heated bricks; secret tunnels; forty-eight towers on the external walls; innovative architecture, including pointed arches and a new way to build vaults, which had later made its way to Europe with the returning Crusaders.

Shaded cloisters led to brilliant, sun-filled rooms, the light filtering down from above. It was like a sandy cathedral, with no town of its own, shining from the inside out. Two young boys, one in a leather jacket, led them up closed stairways and open steps until they emerged on another level, where they sat on a dome in the barely warm sun.

Kim pointed to a far-off tail of dust, thrown up by a pickup truck on the plain. Her arm and hand made an undulating curve against the flat, almost savage landscape. "We can see for miles," she said, "but there's nothing to see."

On the way back to Baghdad, they had to contend with road checks near every bridge and were careful to conceal their cameras beneath the seats. Photographs of any military installation would warrant immediate arrest, and since the military were everywhere, taking even the most harmless photograph was risky. Bridges were nerve-racking. The soldiers were edgy and bewildered, uncertain what to do with a bunch of foreigners who had scraps of paper allowing them to move about the country, but after frowning and trying to appear aggressive, they waved them on every time. So they drove on along the dead straight road to Baghdad that evening, watching a red sun sinking into the darkened desert. When Iraq wooed Thea, she offered no resistance.

Ireland, though, could still pull her strings, especially when history was in the making. On a cold February afternoon, Reggie, Thea, and Geoffrey huddled around a tiny transistor radio in Geoffrey's room, struggling to hear, through the scratch and screech of poor reception, the Ireland versus Scotland rugby match that would determine who won the Triple Crown tournament. Having already beaten Wales and England, the Irish had only to beat Scotland to claim a prize that had not been theirs for thirty-three years. That was why this decider had the whole country sitting on the edge of its seat, and around the world, among the Irish diaspora, many an émigré was glued to a transistor radio like this one. Thirty-three years. Thea was moved when she heard the crowd roar—the familiar distant din of Lansdowne Road—she could even feel the hum of the fans' expectation. The low voice of a commentator and the sharp pierce of a whistle meandered out of the radio with neither urgency nor compassion, yet they grappled with every sound, sucking in the aural crumbs that inadequate radio waves threw their way. Straining to hear the score, Geoffrey had leaned ever closer, as if his proximity to the plastic transistor would increase his proximity to this there-again gone-again match, while Thea and Reggie, who was also supporting Ireland, sat on the edge of the twin beds, twisting their hands, waiting for history to deliver.

In Baghdad, where the only contact with home was infrequent deliveries of mail brought in the bags of rare travelers from London, the agonized cries of Ireland were like a bittersweet illusion. Perhaps they weren't winning at all.

The commentary eventually faded as hissing interference took over the airwaves, destroyed the tenuous link with Dublin and swallowed the Triple Crown decider with a gulp.

It was much later that evening when Reggie, after running into a Scot at Reception, hurried up to Thea's room and banged on her door, yelling that they had done it! Ireland had indeed beaten Scotland and won the tournament. She squealed as they leaped about and a rugby party was hastily convened in her room, where they celebrated as late as a working night allowed. After the others had left, Thea pulled her curtains closed against the city lights and had a sudden vision of her father, so clear that she might have walked into their sitting room the moment the final whistle blew. Not for him great leaps into the air and roars of delight, no: he was sitting in his green easy chair, his fingers around a bottle of Guinness, eyes brimming.

"I hear," Sachiv teased her the next morning, "that congratulations are in order, Miss Kerrigan?"

"They certainly are, Mr. Nair."

Temptation was a toy, a plaything, and although she told herself she was no marriage-wrecker, she could not quit those significant glances, which soon mattered more to her than tea and cakes after work. She wanted to gush like a teenager, but Kim revealed a puritanical streak. A girlish crush on the manager, Kim could apparently accept, but open flirtation met with open disapproval, so she wasn't told about the subtle smiles that were exchanged at every opportunity. Neither did she notice that one day, when they passed through the lobby, Sachiv did not smile or say hello, but shook his head at Thea, as if defeated.

It moved her. They had had no more than three conversations on their own, and although those had been openly cordial, there was an undercurrent, accepted by both, referred to by neither. There were so few opportunities to speak to one another alone that Thea began to lose heart. She simply wanted to know him, a little, to find out if he was indeed the man she thought she saw. Perhaps they would have nothing to say, given the chance, but that chance never seemed to come and conversation continued to elude them.

Until, one night, Thea's phone rang, shaking her from deep sleep.

"I want to make sex with you."

She had turned on the light, picked up the receiver and heard the words before becoming properly conscious. "Huh?"

And the voice said again, "I want to make sex with you."

She slammed down the phone, her heart thudding. *What the hell?*

It was two a.m. A prank call. Fine, she thought, but an *in-house* prank call. Someone in the kitchen, perhaps, or another guest, even, killing the small hours, that was all. That was all. She turned out the light and rolled over. Most nights, she and Kim were the only women guests in the hotel, so it wasn't surprising that they should be targeted like this.

Fifteen minutes later, the phone rang again. Thea sat up, cursing. With every ring, fear climbed a notch. She waited, rigid, until it stopped. Her mind hurled itself around her brain until it became snared on one ghastly thought: those boys—the waiters—had keys to the rooms. They let themselves in every morning when they brought breakfast. . . .

They let themselves *in.*

Out of bed in a blink, she flew to the door, double-locked it and put on the chain. Then she sat up against her pillows, barely breathing so that she might hear every sound in the corridor. Half past two. Locked in fright, she waited, wanting to be asleep, feeling every minute pass until, in the deep silence of the building, she heard a key slip gently, quietly, into the door handle. Her eyes stared across the dark toward the alcove, where her ears were pinned to the door. Lungs jammed, heart whacking against her ribs, she thought she heard the handle turn, but the double-lock held. The key slipped out.

Thea pulled in what air she could. Her banging heart was hurting her chest, so she tried to take deep, even breaths, like her aunt always told her to do, to help her body relax, let go, but fear had better tricks. She hated to be afraid, to be squeezed until her faculties—movement, logic, control—were disabled, as when she had once gamely stepped out across an Incan suspension bridge made of grass and, a few meters in, felt a shaking in its fibers and forgot how to move. Paralysis. Fifteen minutes of it, during which terror held her so tightly that she couldn't even hear the voices urging her forward, or back, because she knew with certainty that if she stepped either way, she would slip between the ropes and tumble into the gully.

Fear, again, in the wild seas off county Clare, when, lying on the surfboard and gripping its waxy rails, she realized she couldn't read the waves. They were contrary, slapping about, bullying, like a battalion of grubby soldiers, white steam coming off their shoulders. The lads had told her not to go in: it was too gnarly for the likes of her, and when the sheer, clean slate face of one determined sucker reared over her head, it was only the nose of her board that got her over the top of its razor-sharp lip. And so she continued, flat on her belly, gripping for dear life, unable to make a clear decision, any decision, until an Australian had to come to shepherd her back to the foamy slop by the shore. "Properly clucked, eh?"

"Clucked?"

"Scared of the waves. Never go in when you're scared."

She was properly clucked now, too. Rigid, she lay in her hotel bed, every sinew alert. Her door was locked, secure;

there was no way her caller could get into the room, and yet . . . *he might get in*. Fear: that most unreasonable of reasonable emotions.

There were no more disturbances and, just after dawn, she fell asleep.

It was Friday, so breakfast came late, and when the knock woke her, she pulled her robe firmly around her before opening the door. There would be no more lying in bed when breakfast was delivered. She stood by the door while the waiter—he might or might not have been the prankster—put the tray on the table by the window, gave her the docket to sign, and left.

Kim was appalled. "You need to tell Reggie," she said, in the lift.

"Nah, it was a prank. His mates probably put him up to it. He won't try it again."

That day they drove to Babylon. Thea, tired, stared out as Reggie took them along the Euphrates, through Hillah, and out to the mound that was all that remained of the fabled Babylon. Its Hanging Gardens, had they ever existed, had long been surrendered to earthquakes and time, but the brick outlines of old homes and streets gave a strong sense of the distant past. As she wandered, Thea could hear voices—those of the women who had once stood gossiping by this doorway, perhaps, or the merchants who had hurried toward the grand ziggurat, making deals, or the people crossing the moat. . . . She could hear voices.

She turned. It must be a group. Tourists? But there were only a few meandering couples. "Reggie?" He was a few steps behind her. "Who is that?"

"Who?"

"Can't you—can you hear them?"

He listened, shook his head.

"It's like a kind of muttering."

As she spoke, a column of dust swirled up before them in a sudden twist. They shielded their faces and kept their eyes tight shut until it dropped to the ground.

"Ha," said Reggie. "You summoned a jinn!"

She wiped dust from her face. "I did what?"

"Dust devils the world over," he coughed, "are seen as spiritual manifestations of one sort or another. Here, they say they're jinn. You know, earthbound beings made from fire that we can't see. You heard voices and then, *whoop*, a dust devil whirls."

"I really don't want to hear this right now. I'd like to be able to sleep tonight, if that's not too much to ask. Ugh, my hair is full of sand!"

"So this is Babylon," Geoffrey declared, in his trombone voice. His hair was greasy, his eyebrows bushy. "A little underwhelming, wouldn't you say?"

"What did you expect?" Kim asked, bringing up the rear. "Fresh vines hanging down from the ziggurat three millennia on?"

"Apparently there's a considerable body of evidence that suggests the Hanging Gardens were in Nineveh," said Reggie. "Not here." He enjoyed being a fount of information, but in a gentle, unprepossessing way; he wasn't showing off, and what he knew, Kim and Thea wanted to learn. Potted history, as they took their Friday outings, was as much as they could absorb, in view of the extraordinary heritage of this country. As Reggie rattled on about Nebuchadnezzar, who had built the gardens for his queen, Amytis, because she was homesick for Iran's green slopes, Thea felt embarrassed. She had been ridiculous during the night—she had probably imagined the whole key-in-the-door scenario, and in the blue light of day, here at Babylon, it all struck her as very silly. Bored staff, playing up.

The Ishtar Gate was newly built, its blue tiles studded with frescos of golden lions, but the Lion of Babylon had survived in crumbling basalt. Kim and Thea stood quietly. "Are you thinking what I'm thinking?"

Thea looked over Kim's shoulder. "You mean that the man under the lion is the Iraqi people, and the lion," she dropped her voice, "is . . . ho-hum?"

Kim threw a squinting glance toward the hovering guides.

"Don't be mean to lions," Thea went on. "They kill only to survive. And look—the man is fighting back."

"Yeah. Resistance, in spite of overwhelming odds. We never see it, but it must be going on all around us. We don't know who's who or what's what, but . . ." Kim looked at the lion again and at the disintegrating figure trapped beneath it, ". . . this is a reminder. They will prevail and then," she turned, "hordes of tourists will come here, not one of whom will say, 'A little underwhelming, isn't it?'"

"I want to make sex with you."

Same voice, same words. The next night.

Another state of alert gripped Thea, stayed with her, as she waited out the hours, listening fretfully to every sound in the corridor, but once again, in the light of day, when nighttime felt a long time ago and a long way ahead, her anxiety seemed overblown. "It's ironic," she said to Kim. "A few hundred miles from the front, I'm fretting about a randy waiter."

There were no calls that night or the next. The test had run its course. Thea slept again and, as she walked through the lobby, she was able to smile at the fine man standing at his desk, but when the calls resumed the following week, Kim concluded that the caller had simply come back on night duty. They were both wary, now, of the waiters who brought room service, but only one made Thea uneasy. Younger than the others, and shifty, he had a flicker in his eyes that she didn't much like, yet she could not risk his livelihood—and that of his family, wherever he came from—unless she was sure.

Still, enough was enough.

Reggie's reaction, when she told him, was muted, but fierce. The hotel management, in turn, were alarmed, apologetic, and insisted that Thea should immediately be moved to another room. No one could know—only Sachiv, Reggie, Kim, and the general manager. That evening, two years' worth of clothes and six weeks of living in one room had to be squashed into suitcases, and when it was done, Sachiv and Reggie came to move her. No porters were called. Laden, the four of them hurried along the corridor and scrambled into the lift with suitcases, bags, sunhat, tape recorder, a heavy portable typewriter in its ungainly box and a pile of books. Thea could feel Sachiv's breath on the side of her neck.

He had found her a room on the same floor as Reggie. When the doors of the lift opened, he poked his head out, looked left and right, causing splutters of giggling behind him, and gave the nod. They scurried once more along a hushed corridor, sniggering, stumbling over their loads and peeking around corners. In his hurry, Sachiv had trouble with the key, but when the door opened, they crashed into the room, laughing.

Sachiv now had a legitimate reason to single out Thea. Special care was due to her, in view of the inconvenience she had suffered at the hands of hotel staff, and he addressed himself to the task with alacrity. He was not on duty the morning after she moved, but he phoned her room that afternoon.

"Have you had any more trouble, Miss Thea?"

"No, it's been fine, thank you."

"I'm very glad. . . . So everything is okay now?"

"Yes. Thanks so much for sorting it out. And this room is lovely." It was much larger than the last, with a seated area and a double bed.

"No, no," he said. "We are very sorry about this. Please call me if you are disturbed again."

But it was he who called again the next day, and the day after that—to check that she had passed an undisturbed night. She liked the sound of his voice, hesitant, coming from his office, not Reception, and soon they no longer referred to the nocturnal incidents. They chatted. He asked what had brought her to Iraq and if she was missing her family; she asked about his work, the career that had taken him from Bombay to Baghdad, but neither ever mentioned his children or his wife. It was supportive and companionable, but when, a few weeks later, a shrill ring shook her from oblivion in the dead end of night and that loathsome voice breathed, "I want to make sex with you," she was still alone.

Whoever he was, he had found her.

The circus repeated itself: Sachiv insisting again on subterfuge, to narrow down the suspects, since the only way the caller could know her room number was by bringing her room service. They didn't laugh so much this time, as they squashed into lifts, reached yet another room, and dumped her stuff; dumped her, she felt. She hated sleeping in the hotel now, but even though Reggie and Geoffrey were soon moving to a bungalow in the suburbs, Reggie's endless remonstrating with the company had yet to yield accommodation for the girls.

They were therefore relieved when, later that week, they were told an apartment had been found for them and set off to have a look with Reggie. It was after dark when they drove up to what looked like a vast shopping mall, a great hulk of cement looming out of a parking lot. There would soon be shops, Reggie had been told, businesses and tenants. Kim and Thea glanced at one another as he led them up a back staircase to the second floor, then followed him along an outdoor corridor and across a vast open concrete space. He unlocked a door and they all stepped in. Their apartment had a spacious kitchen, large rooms and a balcony, but it was all tiled, like a bathroom.

Kim said, "The only things missing here are a pathologist and a corpse."

Reggie looked about. "It'll be done up."

"Yeah? Are they gonna relocate that shopping mall downstairs?"

"It isn't safe," said Thea. "It's dark and deserted, and we'll have no transport."

"Hmm," said Reggie. "It isn't appropriate at all. I had no idea."

"You guys get a lovely house in the suburbs," said Thea, "and we get a changing room."

"Hey," Kim nudged her, "we're just secretaries."

Back at the hotel, Sachiv came into the restaurant while they were eating and stopped by their table. Thea, who had launched into her usual starter, tried to munch demurely.

Sachiv lifted his chin. "So—it is a nice place, your new apartment?"

"Disaster," said Kim.

Reggie shook his head. "A few rooms over a car park. It won't do."

"I'm very sorry to hear that." He sat on the bench next to Thea. "Tell me, the boy you were not sure about, have you seen him recently?"

She swallowed her mouthful. "Yes, but I've also seen three or four others."

"You didn't note his name? You know, on the. . . ." He gestured toward his own name tag.

"I've been trying not to look at them."

"Next time you see this one, the one you suspect, try to read his name."

"All right, but—"

"We won't do anything until we are sure. In the meantime, if he phones, call Reception immediately." He stood up. "Have a good evening."

"Night, Sachiv, thanks," said Reggie.

"Call Reception?" Thea hissed. "What are they going to do? Rush up to my room, grab the phone and tell him he's a very naughty boy?"

"Still." Reggie put down his napkin. "You have to be careful. He might take the next step and come up to the room."

"He already has."

Iraq, like the night caller, remained aloof. They worked in the midst of a silent population, among fearful colleagues. A friendly people, gagged. Though they smiled at one another, the foreign cadre and the local employees, though they leaned over the same desks and documents, consulted and considered, said "Good morning," and "Bye, now," they never really talked; they simply operated in the same space. To live in a war zone was one thing; to live in a zone where no one could speak, quite another. The only Iraqi who spoke to them fluidly, fearlessly, was Saddam Hussein—on their television screens every night, relentless, ranting and raging to his soldiers at the front or opening public lavatories in bleak villages, surrounded like a rock star by an exhibition of ululating women.

But, for one day in March, the barriers came down. Arriving at the office that morning, Kim and Thea made their way past the security man, who sat on a kitchen chair in the entrance, and the cleaning woman in the hallway who, every day, was hunkered to the ground with a bunch of twigs, sweeping the dust from one place to another. As soon as they got upstairs, they noticed a change. The women were not only made up, but dressed up. They looked at Thea's office clothes—skirt, panty hose, V-neck jumper—perplexed, yet with a degree of sympathy.

"You are not celebrating?" Najma, the chief engineer, asked her.

"Celebrating?"

"Yes. International Women's Day. We will have a small party later."

And party they did. At lunchtime, in the large office where Thea worked, desks were pushed aside, trays of canned drinks and snacks were set on a table, the men were kicked out, and the women gathered. There was chatter, laughter—lots of laughter—and talk of family, as the women opened up about their mothers and grandmothers, in turn asking Kim and Thea, who were feeling more than usually dowdy in the midst of glamor, about their homes in Dublin and Philadelphia. This soon gave way to singing and dancing until, as the party wound down, they all formed a circle, holding hands, and turned around the room, then broke off, kissed one another three times and repeated a blessing.

"What does it mean?" Thea asked Alia.

"We are wishing for one another healthy children, nice homes, and husbands."

"I love the husband bit," Kim said, sotto voce, to Thea. "Like an afterthought. A necessary accoutrement, like a good vacuum cleaner."

"Alia couldn't understand why we hadn't dressed up." Thea shook her head. "I was too ashamed to admit I'd never heard of International Women's Day before."

"Me neither."

"We should know these things."

"We do now."

For that one afternoon, the invisible film that surrounded their colleagues dissolved. For a few hours they were neither Irish nor American nor Iraqi; neither spies nor spied upon. They were women all. But when the party ended, their colleagues went back to their desks, the men were granted access, and the shutters came down.

"We caught a glimpse," Thea said, on the way back to the hotel, glancing at two women on a street corner gripping their abayas at the chest. "A glimpse of who they might be. The repression is paralyzing."

"After the war," Reggie said, "things will relax."

"And if he loses the war?"

"Iraq won't lose. The West can't let that happen. Why do you think we're all here, building up the place? Not to hand it over to the mullahs, that's for sure."

Back in her room, Thea took up her spot beside the window for her daily feed of muddy Tigris. Although those waters had come a long way, it was hard to see any flow or movement. The Tigris and the Euphrates had their sources in the same mountain range—the Taurus Mountains in Turkey—and, like siblings born of the same womb who kept their distance, they ran from north to south, sometimes quite close, sometimes far apart, before finally joining up to create the great delta of the Shatt al-Arab. The Euphrates was mentioned in the Bible and so too was the Tigris, although it was referred to by its ancient name, Hiddekel, because these, it was generally believed, were two of the four rivers of the Garden of Eden. This was Thea's day-to-day now: gazing down at the waters of Eden, no less. Whenever she stared at her map, her eyes always followed the rivers south and settled on the Marshes, highlighted by the blue dashes that symbolized wetlands, and she knew she would have to be patient, since such a trip would need planning and time off. Just as she could not wait to see more desert, so she longed to see this rare habitat, where people lived in reed houses and whole villages floated on water. These would be sights to tuck away in her little book of notes and memoranda. It didn't exist, yet, her wallet-diary. She had still to find the right-sized notebook, which must have a solid spine and lots of pages to accommodate her scribblings. There had been no time, before leaving Dublin, to go browsing in Easons, and at Heathrow airport every conceivable format of diary had been on display, except the one she sought. She could visualize it, see it tucked into her bag or sitting on the desk in this very room: it had a leather jacket, mottled brown, and wasn't much bigger than her hand, or wouldn't be when she eventually found it. She could even hear the snap of the rubber band that she would loop around it to hold in her bits and pieces. At home she had shoeboxes crammed with memos going back as far as primary school, and here, already, on the bedside table under a novel, a small stack of random papers was accumulating: hand-scribbled notes to herself capturing a scene, a smell, the sounds of this city; receipts; a scrap of paper on which one of her colleagues had written her name in Arabic; a map drawn by Sachiv on hotel letterhead showing the quickest route to the park.

Her Iraqi experience would be recorded in jottings and tangibles—she would flatten its petals, note its peculiarities, allow its dust to get between her pages. There would be no considered essays, well crafted letters or articles, such as her father had suggested. No. She would be no good at that. But memory, keeping it and controlling it, that was a job worth doing. Thea liked to be reminded, and she intended to capture this country, and hold it, in its minutiae.

The morning's celebrations had set her on edge. She wondered, possibly for the first time, why she had not attended university. At eighteen it had been a straightforward choice, to her, even though it didn't quite make sense. She was a reader, inquisitive, open-minded. Her parents' expectations had been disguised as suggestions: a degree in history or literature? French, perhaps? Their thoughtful, considered child—her occasional outbursts of inanity notwithstanding—was surely bound for study? And they held this opinion even though her father had told her frequently that she spent too much time thinking. "Tell me how to stop," she had teased him one day, "and I'll tell you how to stop dreaming."

There was, though, some truth in what he said—back then she spent a good deal of time inside her own head—but she wasn't pondering Jungian psychology or planning a rewrite of *The Great Gatsby*. She was scheming, dreaming, fashioning plans to give her restless, reckless thoughts something to do. So when a summer job in an office had yielded cash into her hand, she was immediately persuaded that there were more exciting places to be than the dreary corridors in UCD's campus at Belfield or the cobblestoned quads at Trinity College. A resistance to containment had always pulled on her—an impatient yank on her arm—and while working in an office was a containment of sorts, *she* did not feel constrained therein, because her bank balance had an air of conceit about it, and come the holidays, her spirit, her impulses, were her own to spill, be it on the shores of Lake Titicaca or sleeping with some pigs in a hut in the Pyrenees. Now, instead of a degree, instead of looking for a secure teaching job and a house on a cul-de-sac, she was living in Iraq.

No regrets. None.

And yet something niggled. Her laundry had been left on the end of the bed in a plastic bag. As she put away her pressed and folded clothes, she pinpointed what was bugging her: the women with whom she had celebrated International Women's Day were architects and engineers and project managers. They had skills, real skills (though some weren't much older than Thea), while her professional abilities amounted to typing. And Pitman's Shorthand. A little bookkeeping. According to her last boss, her attention to detail was her real forte.

Attention to detail. Thea shook her head, folded the laundry bag, and went back to the window. How far, in truth, could secretarial work take her? Alia and Najma could design bus shelters that would survive a nuclear attack, but Thea had swapped education for a typewriter: 90 w.p.m. Her great skill: ninety words per minute.

A pink gloom was curling across the town. Perhaps it was in this part of the world, where the evening light was filled with desert dust, that the expression "dusty pink" had been born. The traffic was building now, the bridge lined with buses and pickup trucks, but scattered among the houses, palm trees lifted the city from the touch of time. From this perspective Thea could see, more clearly than had ever been possible from her breakfast café in Dublin, that horizons meant only that you had still farther to go. Her unease about her lack of professional qualifications began to fall away. She must, simply, make good her choices. If she was to live like a cricket, she should learn to fly.

Her contract, carefully managed, would give her the means to emulate Amelia Earhart (leaving out the forever-lost-in-the-ocean bit), and live up to her friends' expectations, perhaps more literally than they had intended. Amelia, no doubt, had carried a stuffed journal or scrapbook as she hopped across the continents. "Yes," Thea said out loud. Yes. That would be a certificate worth having. She would be a flyer and—it came to her as she stood there—she would fly across Australia's red desert. Why not?

A week passed during which her nights, though restless, were undisturbed and her breakfasts were delivered by a parade of waiters, none of whom she suspected. Sachiv, nonetheless, called every evening: he was on night duty and had one eye on the kitchen staff. The harassment had become their courtship. After eleven, when it was quiet at Reception, Thea took to settling on her bed with the phone, no longer awkward, and they talked about their day, their jobs, their lives. Sachiv told her about growing up in Muscat. His father had been a spice trader in Calicut, but during tough times had moved across the Arabian Sea to Oman, where he had established such a successful import business that he was able to send Sachiv to private schools in India. During the summers, while working in the family firm, Sachiv discovered in himself an ease with people and a joy in dealing with everyone from cleaners to buyers. He was not, however, much of a trader, but he thought the hospitality business might suit him.

"Understatement," said Thea.

With a gentle laugh, he went on, "I like to see guests coming to me with their problems or their compliments. If they complain, I will fix it. If they speak kindly, I will pass on their praise to whichever staff member has earned it, and I tell myself every time that whatever they need, I will make it happen. In my job, I can make this person or that person have a much better day."

Not a bad way, she agreed, to spend one's working hours. In turn, she told him that after leaving school, she had taken a secretarial course, found herself a job and a surfer boyfriend, and indulged her sporadic inclinations to shake up her life.

"Like coming to Baghdad?" he asked. "Good career choice, by the way. First-class."

Thea thought that a little flirtatious, but on the other hand—and there was always another hand—the night was long, it was quiet down there, and what else had he to do other than killing the hours by chatting amiably to one of the guests?

But there was no room for doubt a few nights later when he said, as they hung up, "If he phones tonight, call me and I'll be there in two minutes," adding, with that quiet laugh, "I will rush up to protect you."

Zawraa Park was dried out and dusty, and along the sandy rim of the comma-shaped lake, paddleboats lay waiting for more peaceful times. There were a few, a very few, people walking, but it felt to Kim and Thea like a post-apocalyptic place, though the women in the office had said that, during Eid and holidays, the park was always crowded with families enjoying the fairground and lining up for rides on the old Ferris wheel. There was an island in the middle of the lake and pergolas along the shore, but it felt so lonely that Thea much preferred their walks along the riverside or strolling down al-Rasheed Street in the evenings, even though it heaved with men and soldiers.

"I can't wait for summertime," Kim said wistfully, "when we can swim every day at the hotel, go to Lake Habbaniyah, come here and pedal around on the water."

"That's what we think now, but when summer comes we'll probably be hiding indoors, longing for winter, with the air-conditioning on full blast."

"Maybe it's the war that makes everything feel dead. Everyone's afraid to have fun."

Thea glanced at her. "How can they have fun when so many have family at the front?"

The next morning, the suspect waiter delivered breakfast. Thea glanced at his lapel—he wasn't wearing a name tag.

That night, after three, the phone rang. She had no intention of picking it up, but it wouldn't stop. It went on ringing, bullying her, challenging her. More irritated than fearful, she finally grabbed the receiver and barked, "Hello!"

"I want to make sex with you."

"Oh, for God's sake, get your syntax right! You *make* love and *have* sex!" She slammed down the phone. "I've been wanting to say that for weeks."

She made the call. The damsel-in-distress role didn't sit well with her, but she had braved this long enough, dark hour after dark hour. The guy was persistent and might be goaded by her anger, and she never again wanted to hear the harrowing sound of a key sliding into the lock.

Sachiv arrived breathless, saying, as she let him in, "This guy! He knows we're moving you around, but it doesn't stop him!"

"It has to be the one I suspect—he brought breakfast this morning and he seemed surprised when I opened the door. Like he'd found me again. Bingo."

"Describe him."

"Scrawny, thin, a little mustache, curly hair on top."

"I know the one. He's on duty tonight."

Thea sank onto the end of her bed, shaking.

"Are you all right?"

"Yeah. It's just—you never get used to it. The intrusion. The fright. Waking up suddenly and hearing that voice."

"It won't happen again."

"He won't be fired, will he?"

Sachiv sat beside her. "We have to think of other guests. He could do it to someone else."

"But his family—he's probably supporting his parents back home."

"This is not your concern."

"I just want to be able to sleep."

"Now you will. Can I send up something? Some tea?"

She smiled as he stood up. "That will only keep me awake."

He looked thrown, glanced at the wall, and back at her. "Is there anything that would help you to sleep?"

Your voice, she almost said. I would have your voice for camomile.

Action was taken. Thea never again heard, "I want to make sex with you," and woke from sleep only when the dawn light, growing warmer and brighter with the year, slid under her curtain, as morning spilled slowly across her carpet.

The late-night phone calls, however, still came from the office behind Reception.

There was a sniff of spring in the air. They no longer shivered through the days in the office, blowing on their fingers, and Thea began to look forward to plunging into the pool after work when it was warmer. There were two pools—a huge round one and a smaller one—and from her balcony, the turquoise circles of winter-cold water contrasted with the lazy brown Tigris drifting alongside them.

The night-time conversations drifted also, eventually coming to Sachiv's marriage. It had been arranged, he said, and although there had been affection, even love, for a time, these had lifted, then vanished, as his work became more demanding and her life became child-bound. She had understood the demands of his career and conceded that theirs would be a peripatetic lifestyle, but in practice it didn't suit her at all. She was isolated and unhappy in Iraq, and for some time now had been insisting that Sachiv should seek work in a small hotel in India, where they could raise their children among family and where, more importantly, she could play chess.

"Chess?"

"Yes." His wife—he never used her name and Thea never asked, just as they barely mentioned his children—had played chess since her schooldays and was very, very good. A winner. Beyond her children, it was all she cared about. Now, here, she missed her team, missed the opportunities chess would have brought her in India and, above all, she feared that her promise as a regional and even national player was shrinking as she sat in Baghdad, the hours of her day dictated by her husband's schedule, with no known chess players in sight. He suspected he should forsake his own considerable prospects for her considerable gift, yet he could not, he told Thea. He had worked too hard and achieved too much in a few short years, and it would be dangerously premature to ditch his own potential for some regional hotel in India. He had to think of his children's prospects, also, and the life he could give them. Besides, Oman was more home to him than India, and if ever he were to give up the world for a small business, he could do it only in Oman. And so, behind good parenting, conflict raged. "The queens and the kings and the pawns are stacked against me," he said. "Checkmate lies ahead, I fear."

Another Friday, another trip—troglodyte caves in the desert, and this time Sachiv joined them. It was his day off, but Thea had no idea why Reggie had asked him along until, as they left the Baghdad checkpoints behind, she heard her boss say, "So how long will your wife be away?"

"About a month," Sachiv replied. "She's gone to see her mother. It is lonely for her here, with small children and no family support. I work quite long hours."

"'Quite'?" Reggie glanced at him. "You live in that hotel!"

"But wouldn't she prefer to escape the summer heat?" Kim asked.

"She will go then also. July, August. That is when it is worst for the children."

Thea leaned forward. "How bad is it exactly? This heat."

He looked over his shoulder. "It becomes very intense."

"But air-conditioning. . . ."

He dipped his head. "Air-conditioning, yes, but air-conditioners often don't work, and then there are the blackouts."

"August is a nightmare here," said Reggie. "There's no other way of putting it."

"I wanna go home!" Kim wailed.

"It must be worse than hell at the front," he added.

A few hours later they left the tarmac and headed toward an extraordinary square-shouldered sandstone mound, marked by a neat row of openings gouged out of its façade.

"It looks like a prehistoric apartment building," said Kim.

"Or a liner," said Thea.

Reggie pulled up. "Welcome to the al-Tar Caves."

"Can we get up there?"

"If the troglodytes could, we can."

A scramble up gritty, sliding ground led them to the rectangular entrances that opened onto a warren of cold corridors with caves on either side. Thea shivered. "More like graves than homes."

Leaning over to look through one of the low windows, Kim asked, "But what did they live on, stuck up here?"

"It would have been greener back then," said Reggie.

"And it was safe." Sachiv leaned over to look out also. "They could see their enemies coming." His watch, slightly loose, was resting against his wrist bone.

"Let's go up top," said Reggie.

". . . including a perfect rooftop terrace," Geoffrey was saying when Thea and Sachiv, breathless, brought up the rear, "with spectacular views."

"Wow," she said. "I'd gasp if I wasn't gasping already." Pulling her blazer tighter against the breeze, she wandered farther along the ridge. In one direction, a maze of flat-topped sandstone hills, sculpted by the wind, looped around one another, creating spaghetti canyons, and in the other, the great expanse of Lake Razzaza, bare as a bald pate, shimmered. There was no definition, no way of telling desert and water apart, or where the lake met the dusky sky. The wind pushed strands of hair across Thea's open mouth. Before her: infinity.

Then, down there, far off, the air stirred. In the corridor of desert between the caves and the lake, her eyes caught movement. A flutter. It looked at first like a low cloud, a cushion of dust. She stared, focused. . . . *Camels*. Though their shapes were indistinct, their gait was not: the long, graceful strides and the easy speed were undeniably those of camels, a line of them, moving across the plain. Stick figures, barely discernible, walked beside and ahead of them in a kind of mist. It was biblical. Astonishing. Here, everything she had ever sought was delivered: the pale kiss of the earth. The void and the grandeur, the singular and the particular, the stillness set around those camels loping across the flat in single file, conquering whole worlds with each step. All this, nebulous as a mirage, made nonsense of time. Lifting her chin to call the others, Thea thought better of it. She didn't even raise her camera. Better to consign it to memory, this silent tableau, this apotheosis, so that she could savor it later, and often. The silence was peculiar. The herders must have been calling to their beasts and the camels must have been grunting and complaining, but the wind didn't carry any of that. Standing atop a prehistoric sandcastle, she watched the procession, elated. Where had they come from? Where were they going? Was she looking back in time? Or forward?

Because of the chill wind, they ate out of the back of the jeep, using the lowered back seat as a counter. Reggie poured the wine; Thea dispensed rice, lamb, and tomatoes; Sachiv stood outside, twisting about to take in the landscape. He was easy company, good to have around, but Thea was distracted by what she had seen from the hilltop. It would never, she knew, be diluted. The slow march of the camels and the desert rising around them would stay with her forever, always in motion. That caravan would never reach its destination.

"There's so much I want to see," she said, to no one in particular. "The mountains in the north, the Marshes in the south. . . ."

"That we shall do soon," said Reggie, "before the heat and the mosquitos come."

Back in Baghdad, in a traffic jam, they pulled up behind a Toyota pickup carrying two camels, crouched in the back. Unperturbed by the horns and engines, the crush of rush hour, they blinked languidly.

From the sublime, Thea thought, to the ridiculous.

A few days later, Reggie took them to lunch in a local eatery—like a diner, with a few tables and a high counter—by one of the bends in the Tigris. Filtered sunlight brightened their table as they enjoyed the thrill of non-hotel food: proper Iraqi food—kubba, a kind of rice patty stuffed with minced lamb, and a flaky pastry sausage for which Reggie had no word.

"I wish we could get more local dishes in the hotel," said Kim. "There's only so much beefsteak a person can eat."

"This is good, isn't it?" Reggie asked, pushing the last bit of pastry into his mouth. "Love this place!"

"Me too," said Kim, glancing around. "Even if the hygiene is a little casual."

It occurred to Thea, weeks later, that that might have been when it happened.

Sachiv stood by the window, his shirt undone but still tucked into his neat black trousers, his ribcage heaving with the effort of being there, by the window, away from the bed . . . away from her. The right thing. This was the cost of the right thing: arousal that wouldn't subside, skin glistening, guts turning. His lovely wife, his beautiful children. . . . The right thing—what physical wretchedness it wrought, but worse, probably, would be the wretchedness of guilt.

He had arrived only moments before, in the late afternoon, unannounced but expected, muttering that he could lose his job. Kissing and fumbling, they had shuffled, like penguins on ice, to the bed. His jacket was off, already, on the alcove floor; his tie resisted her fingers, his shirt did not, and her straps slipped off her shoulders as if her skin were oiled. It was then, when he was kissing her breast and his hand was deep in the folds of her skirt that his conscience, coming into the room like a sonic boom, found him. It threw him to the floor.

So he stood by the window, panting. Thea knew, or thought she knew, that she could still have him—break him down, if she gave it one more shot. But compassion, not desire, sent her to the window, where she stood behind him, cheek against his damp back, comforting, assuaging, until her hand slipped inside his shirt and brushed along his waist. Palm on bare flesh. His breathing eased, became less frantic. He put his hand over hers. Then he took her wrist and broke out of their embrace, ripping apart their affair before it had even started. She felt sick, and desperate, when his fingers went to his shirt buttons. One by one, he closed them, each button shutting her out.

He remained with his back to her for some minutes more. The first time they had kissed had not been cheap like this—a hurried grope in a hotel room. The setting for that had been a troglodyte cave, with cold walls and a view of caramel canyons—had they noticed.

He turned, like a dancer, and reached for the jacket in a heap on the floor. "I must go."

"At least you leave with a clear conscience."

"Whatever that means."

"It means that when your wife comes back, you can look her in the eye. It means you won't have the shadow of guilt hanging over you every which way you turn."

"The shadow of guilt," he touched her neck, "or the shadow of love. What's the difference? Every morning I will see you come by, in your office clothes, and walk past with maybe a look in my direction, or maybe not, as you sweep through the doors and into your jeep. And then the long day will begin, the hours hanging around me like the summer heat, until the afternoon comes and I will be sure to be at Reception, to see you come in again, passing me, with a glance, or not."

She put her hand on his shirt, where his heart was.

"Worse than having parents with expectations is, of course, having parents with none." Kim smirked at Thea as they wandered by the river in a soft heat that was full of promise, and threat. "Such as mine, who never gave any indication whatsoever that they had even the slightest hopes for my success. Their conviction that the only possibility for my long-term survival was husband-with-job was never rattled, not even mildly! It's a wonder they divorced, given their unshakable faith in their only child's hopelessness."

Thea took her arm, for balance, pulled off her shoe and shook out a pebble. "What's brought this on?"

"A letter from Mom. Says she doesn't get it—why didn't I stay with that nice boy in London? 'Oh, hey, Mom, you mean the guy who stole my keys and let himself into my house during the night? The guy who waited for me on the street any time I went out with friends—*that* guy?'" She shook her head.

"Do you miss him, at all?"

"No. I'm only embarrassed I didn't see the signs. Do you miss Surfer Boy?"

"Not since the day he told me I had no business on a surfboard."

"Was he right?"

"Absolutely. Water's too bloody cold in Ireland. No, I'm going to fly instead. I need to be up in the air. But first I need the little plane." They laughed, but Thea didn't much feel like laughing. Bewildered and overwhelmed by the turn she had taken with Sachiv, she couldn't help blurting, "Kim, this thing with Sach—"

"Isn't a thing. That's how you have to think. He's married. A no-go area, period."

"Nothing's that simple, is it?"

"Come on, Thea. He's cute, no denying, but seriously? Three kids? You don't want to get in the middle of that."

Disaster crept up in an insidious manner. It tapped her on the shoulder, but when she turned—no one there. A flutter of nausea. There. Gone. Had it been there? They were in a line for gasoline. Sitting on some of the wealthiest oil reserves in the world, they were in a long line to buy gas on their way to a St. Patrick's Day party at the house of a German expatriate. Thea thought she felt sick, and dread swept through her as she imagined her evening spoiled: a night spent on the tiles—the bathroom tiles. It passed. They reached the forecourt of the gas station, edging ever closer to the pump. Reggie fiddled with the radio, from the dolorous voice of a newsreader to cheerful Arab tunes and back again.

By the time they drove out with a full tank, there was no doubt: Thea did feel sick. Love, probably. Yes, that was it. Her body was all in a pother.

And it continued to be so at the party, the nausea sliding around inside her like an oil slick until she was eventually forced to retreat to a bedroom, in the stranger's house, where she lay down among a pile of coats. Kim came to check on her. She had probably eaten something, they agreed. Probably a dose of Baghdad belly. They'd been lucky so far. In almost three months neither of them had got sick. It struck

Thea as strange that she didn't feel like throwing up; *that* delight probably lay ahead. When Reggie brought her a glass of whiskey, saying it would settle her stomach, she sipped it, though it was the last thing she felt like, and she did improve enough to join the party, which brought such relief—she was not sick, after all—that she ended up dancing for hours.

In the middle of a small living room, in a slightly shabby house, Reggie took center-stage, swinging about with his hands over his head, and Thea jived away with him, elbowing Germans and Swiss and Scottish engineers out of the way, giddy with relief. Not sick, after all.

The next morning, when they stepped into their office building, the woman who swept the floor, already hunkered down, caught Thea's eye and let out a little cry, then scurried away along the corridor.

When Alia came in behind them, the old woman ranted at her.

"What's she saying?" Thea asked, one foot on the bottom step. "She seemed to take fright when she saw me."

Alia spoke to the woman, glanced at Thea, and went on up, saying, "Don't worry. She is . . . a little crazy."

"No, but, please. Tell me what she said. Have I offended her in some way?"

"No." Alia stopped. "Not at all. Nothing like that."

"What then?" asked Kim, behind her.

"She. . . . It's nothing."

"It's clearly something. She ran away as if I was about to kick her."

Her hand on the banister, Alia glanced from one to the other. "She saw a shadow, that's all. Like a . . ."

"Ghost?"

"Some would call it jinn."

Kim looked nonplussed. "She saw a jinn on Thea?"

"Really, it means nothing."

It meant something. Thea had no sooner sat behind her typewriter than the nausea returned, along with a withering weakness. As the morning went on, she could barely hold herself upright, as if her inner frame had stepped outside her body and gone on a break, leaving her languishing at the desk. Perhaps that was what the old woman had seen—her skeleton taking flight. She hesitated to leave the office: she had only twenty sick days available and those were best saved for whatever nasty surprises the Iraqi summer might deliver. But after several hours of encroaching misery, she conceded defeat and allowed Reggie to drive her back to the hotel.

There, time and days blurred into one immutable image: the dim bedroom, the tossed sheets, loneliness from early morning until mid-afternoon, and long nights. Very long nights.

At some point she had started vomiting—signs of food poisoning at last, or a stomach virus, something that would clean itself out. . . . Except for this other thing—the acute listlessness. And worse than that, worse even than being unable to eat, she was unable to drink. No matter what she ordered from room service—tea, water, juice—she could not swallow it because her stomach didn't want it. Desperate to get well, she became the midnight prankster, calling room service several times a night, ordering whatever seemed palatable, and when it came, so did the inevitable letdown: she could not eat. Nonetheless, the menu obsessed her. Food *would* make her better. This weakness, this jelly-limbed sensation, was the result of having taken no sustenance, so she would look at the menu, day and night, and call the kitchens, asking for chicken and ice cream, salads and cake, yoghurt and toast. . . . In the small hours of morning, the friendly old waiter from Kirkuk would arrive with a veritable cornucopia, leave the tray on the table and take another away. Ever hopeful, Thea would lift the tin lid and stare at the meal, disenfranchised from her own appetite, unable to bargain with it. If she did not eat soon, her health would be dangerously compromised, but more important than that, she needed to drink.

Coke. That was the one drink she craved. She asked for it, repeatedly. "No Coke, madam. Because of the war." There was no Coke in all of Iraq because of the war, as well she knew, but it was the only thing she thought she could swallow. Water was too heavy, tea made her gag.

She longed to phone her mother, but didn't want to alarm them at home, when there was nothing they could do and probably nothing to be worried about, although Reggie was clearly concerned. There were no health facilities he trusted. "Go into hospital here," the saying went, "and you'll come out with something worse." The hotel had a doctor on call, though, and after two days without improvement he was summoned.

He looked like Einstein: white hair, long silver mustache, and a pocket watch. A lovely man, chatty. He had trained in Russia, he told Thea, and spoke four languages, but he didn't know what to make of her symptoms. His diagnosis was unexpected: "You are homesick."

"But I don't want to go home."

"Nausea, no appetite, this is symptomatic of being upset."

"I'm very happy here."

He smiled. "Perhaps you are in love."

Perhaps you're right, she thought, since she was certainly not pining for Dublin's city streets. Her determination to get well was rooted in her dread of being forced to leave Iraq—but love. . . . Love could certainly disable appetite, and romantic turmoil had a habit of lodging itself in the stomach, but why then could she not drink? Einstein had no answer, but prescribed some pills, insisting, still, that the source of her indisposition was emotional, not physical.

So she continued, sick, and becoming more so.

Sachiv called up whenever no one was about, and fussed and flapped, feeling her forehead and urging her to drink water, lots of water. He seemed slightly panicked, as was she.

Unbidden, Kim moved into Thea's room to help her through the dark hours, going with her on the relentless treks to and from the bathroom, where Thea delivered nothing into the bowl. They pondered what was wrong with her and cursed her rotten luck, because with every long, slow, miserable day that passed like this, the risk of being sent home grew stronger. One evening Kim took her for a walk around the pools. The air would help, they told one another. It didn't. Thea felt wretched. Kim's arm linked hers. "I guess the woman who sweeps was right. There *was* a shadow over you, the other day."

They walked back into the hotel slowly, both quiet, both scared.

What the hell *was* this?

Sachiv kept phoning. "Can I send some tea?"

"Coke," she said. "Send up some Coke."

"There is no Coke in—"

"All of Iraq. Yeah, yeah, I know."

On the fourth afternoon, Reggie came. "You know you can be repatriated. You have only to say the word."

"I don't want to go home."

"Okay, but bear in mind that it'll take up to four days to get you an exit visa. And if you're not improving, that's quite a long wait."

"I don't want to leave."

He nodded grimly and left the room.

Sickness and Iraq raged battles over her; Sachiv too was in the mix. And Kim, and the desert, and the Tigris, and the tangerine dawns. . . . *Impossible*. So much more to learn, so much still to do. Too much to do without. Leaving would be as insupportable as nausea, and every time she kneeled over the toilet and threw up the nothing from her gullet, she hoped that this would be the last time, that she was purging the dregs of this mystery disease. It *would* pass. Soon she would feel a change, a turn, and then she would wake, recovered.

Despairing, she longed to be in the office with Kim and the girls, to be anywhere other than this hotel sickroom, especially after another fiasco. Reggie thought he had sent for a doctor from one of the hospitals, but a very young man arrived in Thea's room, claiming he had to examine her. She backed away, told him to get out.

A mere ambulance driver, it turned out, trying his luck—and once again Reggie and Sachiv had cause to hang their heads on Thea's account.

Soon afterward, Reggie stood with his hands in his pockets at the end of her bed. "You should go home, Thea. Get this sorted, whatever it is, and come back in a few weeks."

"No." Orderly palm trees lined along the Euphrates. "I'll be fine." Babylon, where the voices still whispered and the brick foundations of houses lay like skeletons in the earth. The Marshes—*the Marshes*, of which there was no like in the world—the arched mudhif, the women punting through the reeds in their tarada—it all had to be seen, had yet to be seen! And the deserts, where she had once glimpsed in the distance a nomad encampment, with their tents and flocks, and the sand whipping over them. *No*. She could not let it out of her grasp. "I can't go, Reggie."

After he left, Thea lay thinking about the evening they had helped fishermen pull in their catch on the shores of Lake Habbaniyah. The net was so vast that another group of men, pulling at the other end, were so far along the beach that their grunting could barely be heard. The Westerners, quickly exhausted, had soon collapsed on the sand, but Thea had watched and photographed: the men, their eyes glinting, had rolled their skirts above their knees and wrapped the rope many times around their chests, which were protected by bits of cloth, and as they heaved and leaned, their feet slid in the muddy sand. The net stretched to such a distance that it would be hours yet before the catch was in, but the fishermen, hauling their weight against the lake, sang to keep the rhythm flowing, and, weeks later, Thea could still, almost, hear their song.

Good times. Good times in Iraq.

That was the weekend they had spent at a holiday complex full of vacant houses skirting the big, featureless lake. There was an impressive restaurant, designed like a Bedouin tent, which had been all but empty of people and food. They had had to make do with chocolate éclairs for lunch, she remembered, and before going back to Baghdad that evening, they had driven around the surrounding desert looking for Saddam's weekend villa. It had been Thea's mad idea that they should try to catch a glimpse of it, but they had to be careful not to come upon it suddenly, so they drove up and over mounds, skidding sideways down dunes, the music loud, the setting perfect, laughing and looking for Saddam.

And then she thought about her camels, following one another along the shore of Lake Razzaza, searing themselves into her soul. Perhaps she had known, even then, that Iraq would not be hers for long.

In the quiet afternoon lull of the fifth day, tears slipped onto the pillowcase: defeat. Nothing had improved. She had been five days without food or water. Wishful thinking could only do so much.

She called Reggie. "I want to go home."

"Done."

As desperate as she had been to stay, she suddenly became frantic to leave, knowing it could be four days before an exit visa was issued—and how sick would she be by then? Within a few hours, however, Reggie reported that Tariq would rush her application through on the grounds of a medical emergency. With luck, she might be able to leave tomorrow on the British Airways midnight flight—the only flight—to London.

Now there was nothing for her to do but dread the journey ahead. Barely strong enough to walk, she would have to get through Iraqi Immigration and face a long wait because check-in had to take place four hours before every flight—the war, the war—and those four hours worried her more than seven in the air. The airport was basic. How would she manage? And then, at Heathrow, she would have to get across to Terminal One for the Dublin flight. She might collapse, pass out. The fifteen-hour ordeal stretched before her like a long, dark airport tunnel, and she had a whole night and day to contemplate it. Apprehension lay on her, like a person.

Then, in an unexpected turn, word came that her visa had been so swiftly issued that she could travel that very night. Reggie was happy for her, and probably, she suspected, relieved to get her off his hands.

But Sachiv! He was off-duty. No goodbyes, no telling him even that she was leaving! He would come to work the next day and find her gone.

Reggie had a more pressing concern. "You're not fit to travel alone."

"Don't have much choice."

"I'll see if I can find someone going to London who could keep an eye on you. But those flights are block-booked by the government to get the wounded to England for treatment. That flight's a bit of a troop-carrier."

When Kim got in from work, Thea told her that her departure had been brought forward. Quietly Kim started packing a few basics for Thea to take with her. "You'd better get your ass back here," she said, "before I've had time to notice you're gone."

"Try and stop me."

"Why don't you get some air while I tidy up?" Kim suggested, but when she had helped Thea to a chair on the balcony, she gave her a second look. "You know what? Your eyes have gone yellow."

"Huh?"

"The whites of your eyes—they're yellow."

Thea gaped at her.

"You're jaundiced."

"*Jayzuz*. That means it must be hepatitis. I don't bloody believe it!"

"*Shoot*."

The doorbell rang. Kim let Geoffrey in. "Just came to say goodbye," he said. "Lucky you, eh? Getting out of here."

"We've just worked out what's wrong with her," said Kim.

"What?"

"Hepatitis," Thea said. "I don't know much about it, but I know I've got it."

Geoffrey chortled, stuffed his hands deep into the pockets of his cheap trousers, and shook his head. "Thea, if you had hepatitis, you'd be an awful lot sicker than you are now."

"I nearly threw him over the fucking balcony," she told Kim, after he'd gone. "How much sicker does he want me to be?"

Another ring at the door and Reggie came out to the balcony. "Good news! Christ, your eyes are yellow!"

"Yeah. Nobody noticed while I was in my room. Too dim. Hepatitis, anyone?"

"God, yeah. That'd make sense. Wonder where you got it."

"There was a suspect cup of tea about ten days ago—remember, Kim? Silt in the bottom of my cup when I'd finished. Like I'd been drinking pure Tigris."

Reggie looked at Kim. "Oh, no. Not you too?"

She shook her head. "I was on bottled water that day, but I've been wondering about that place you took us, down by the river. Those weird sausages. . . ."

"Dodgy water's more likely."

"What's the good news?" Thea asked. "I need some."

"We've found a guy to take you home. *And* he's Irish. Sachiv found him."

"Sachiv? Isn't he off today?"

"He came in specially to help on this. He knows just about everyone in the hotel and this bloke's a regular here, comes and goes a fair bit. An engineer, apparently. From Dublin. Anyway, he's on his way to a meeting in Stockholm, via London, but he's agreed to fly to Dublin with you instead."

"That's so great!" said Kim. "How did you persuade him to change his plans?"

Reggie chuckled. "Poor sucker was minding his own business, having a bit of lunch. Next thing, Sachiv and I sidled up to him, like a couple of heavies. Sachiv did the rest. Said we had a very sick young lady who needed to get home. He said okay." He smiled at Thea. "So you relax, all right? This time tomorrow you'll be in your own bed."

Tears sprang to her eyes. Reggie had read her anxiety, seen through her bravado.

"What's his name," Kim asked, "her knight in shining boarding card?"

"Alex Cassidy."

"So that's it, then." Thea looked across the city. "I'm as good as gone from here."

And so she was. Quick as a slap, in the turn of her head, Iraq had vanished and Ireland stood in its place. An unfathomable jolt. Disconcerted, she wondered if she had woken from a trance when, less than a week later, she found herself side by side with her father in West Cork, driving the length of the Sheep's Head peninsula, a wild ridge of old red sandstone and white limestone. Dunmanus Bay was inky blue and Atlantic clouds offered a mix of celestial fare—blue, purple, pristine white, slim, flat, tall as pinnacles, puffed-out like a lizard's chest. . . . This long, undulating road led to the end of Europe, where Thea's aunt Brona lived in isolation, surrounded by sloping fields that dropped down to cliffs, which, in turn, dropped into the ocean. To this remote place, far from Dublin, Thea was coming to convalesce.

"This is what you're dealing with," her doctor had said, showing her the size of the liver on a diagram—it took up half a ribcage, which was exactly his point. "It's the biggest organ we've got and yours isn't working. Blood tests will probably confirm you have Hepatitis A, so if you can't get one hundred percent bedrest for a month at least, I'll have to send you to the hospital for infectious diseases."

No, thanks, she thought. A month?

"Hepatitis isn't to be messed with. You're really very ill."

"Of course she'll get total rest," her mother had insisted. "She'll be fine at home."

But Thea was not fine. Her sister Kate was in Cork, her brothers in college, and her parents at work all day, and they seemed to think that leaving a kettle beside the bed, with tea-bags, a mug, and milk, amounted to good care, as if she had no more than a bad cold. So she lay in bed, untended. Getting up to go to the bathroom was as much exertion as she was allowed and as much as she could manage, and since she had to drink gallons every day, she was more out of the bed than in it, either pottering up to the next landing to the bathroom or down to get more water. She was spending half the day on the stairs. It was lonely too, even more so than in that hotel room. At least there she had room service and Sachiv, whom she missed now with every breath she took.

Her spirits were so low as to be underground. When the door slammed every morning, a silence settled in, like some invisible being who took over the house when everyone else went out, but she had neither the energy nor the inclination to see friends. In the evenings, her father sat on her bed and read to her from the newspapers and her mother went on cooking as normal—failing to provide fat-free meals as instructed by their doctor. They simply expected Thea to avoid whatever was bad for her. By eight o'clock they had retreated to the television. Her illness, to them, was a blessing. It had taken her out of a war zone.

It was fortuitous that when Brona called to see how she was doing, Thea answered the phone herself.

"You're not supposed to be out of bed," her aunt cried.

"Everyone's out."

"But you mustn't be rushing down to the phone. The man said one hundred percent bedrest!"

"Sorry. I came down because I wanted to hear a voice." Thea's eyes welled with tears.

"Thea?"

She didn't hold back. Apprised of the details of her recovery, her father's sister said, "This is no way to get well. You must come down here to recuperate."

"Brona, I could get back to Baghdad in less time than it would take me to get to you!" She was easily swayed, though. She adored her aunt, who was also her godmother, and getting away from home, where failure of so many different hues bounced back at her from the bedroom walls, was tempting. Seven hours in the car seemed a small price to pay for a bit of easy company.

The house in West Cork was big and empty, the rooms small and cozy, and Brona was there, bringing Thea fat-free breakfasts and tea on demand. Her blankets were smoothed and a fresh nightie brought every day. It struck Thea as particularly sad that her aunt, who was such a natural carer, had never had children and had been widowed in her forties, yet she lived in that remote place, looking down on the jagged slate-like rocks that protected the coastline like barbed wire. The Atlantic, Brona used to say, was like a husband—sometimes cross, sometimes calm, but always there, solicitous, and wise enough to know when to intrude on her thoughts and her chores, and when not to. "I don't live alone," she said to Thea. "Me and the Atlantic, we're like a snail and an elephant sharing the same garden." Sometimes Thea would come across her standing at the sink, looking out across the bay toward Mizen Head. "I feed off it," she explained one day. "I suck it into my heart and am always the better for it." She turned. "And it'll do the same for you, pet."

Brona played her part too. She read her niece well (though Thea was baffled as to how she managed to be so intuitive, happy hermit that she was): she guessed there was a man and told Thea what to do with him. She scolded her because he was married, but cared for her because she was hurt.

One afternoon, she came up to Thea's bright, sunny room with tea and bread—biscuits were off the menu—and found her lying on her side, staring at the dormer window, her fingers deep in the belly fur of the sleeping cat stretched along her chest. Setting down the mug, then the plate, Brona said, "Would you not read a book or those magazines I got you?"

"No concentration."

"Or concentrating, is it, too much on the one thing? All this pining isn't going to make you better."

"No, it makes me feel even more wasted."

"Ah, darling," she said, "that's no good."

Thea stroked the cat's back. "I didn't even realize I'd fallen so hard, Brona. That this was one of the big ones, one of those love affairs you never quite get over. . . . *He* knew it, though."

"Well, you may be hurting now, pet, but you're only the one person. It could be his wife hurting, through no fault of her own, and their children too. He wasn't yours to have, no matter how bad you feel. And there'll be others."

"There wasn't for you."

Brona narrowed her eyes and gave her an impish look. "You're very sure of that, are you?"

"Brona!"

Her aunt stood up. "That's enough of that. What you have to do, young lady, is get yourself over this man." She tucked in the sheet. "It'll be a lot harder than getting over the illness, granted, but there's nothing else to be done. Sure isn't he taken, and far away, and that's all there is to it."

"But *where* could you have met someone?"

Brona pushed a stray strand of gray hair back over her ear and glanced at the sunlight that was like another person, having leaped in from outdoors and landed on the timber floorboards. And then she came back again, from wherever, whomever, she had gone to. "You have to break the habit of thinking about him. Any habit can be broken."

"And how's that to be done, when I have zilch energy to do anything other than lie around thinking all day?"

"Think about something else. Daydream."

"What?"

Brona nodded. "Fantasize."

"That's what I *am* doing!"

"Yes, but, darling, it's the wrong man you're dreaming about."

"Is there another?"

"That's up to you. Sure, doesn't every one of us have an inner life that's all our own?" Brona's voice was softer than usual. With a glance at the bare crucifix on the wall (Thea steeled herself for a religious rant), she went on, "I couldn't have survived out here on the edge of nowhere without another existence—an imagined one."

Thea disentangled herself from the cat, fixed her pillow to support her lower back and reached for her mug. "*You* daydream?"

"Doesn't everyone?"

"*No*. You know what the nuns always said about daydreamers! 'Time-wasters.' 'Good-for-nothing layabouts.' So tell me! Tell me who you fantasize about."

Brona looked out of her tiny window with her tiny eyes, as if she was about to reveal her hidden life, then did not. Her daydreams were not for the telling.

One fresh, sunny day, as Thea improved, Brona wrapped her up in a great coat, took a cushion and her arm, and led her along the road to a low wall in front of a line of cottages. There they sat, looking down at Brona's leveed field, an exact rectangle delineated by a stone wall.

"You'd never see green like that in Iraq," said Thea. "It's dusty there, juicy here."

"I remember trying to call you and the others up for your tea, during the summers."

"We went up and down this slope like we were going from one room to another." Thea smiled. "Now it looks miles away. I don't think I'll ever get down there again."

"When you've got your strength back."

"I'll go out to the lighthouse. That's my objective."

"That's a long way too."

Thea looked back at the house, sitting on its U-bend, with a view up the road and down it, standing over a lake and an ocean, and hard-hewn fields. A bit grubby, it was like an oversized cottage. She turned to the sea—its rippled surface like crushed silk—and back to the house. "Is it haunted, Brona?"

Brona wrinkled her nose, her eyes still on the awkward fields. "You asked that a lot when you were little."

"Did I? Well, children are very intuitive." It was easier, somehow, to talk about the house outside it. "I've been wondering if that's why you've never left." Thea looked at her. "Is Christie still here?"

"Christie is where God wants him to be: by His side. He didn't call him back so very young just for the sake of leaving him behind with me."

"But there is something, isn't there? I feel it. Sometimes I can hear it. And you—*you* see it, don't you?"

"Get away with that." Brona hunched her shoulders, moved her scarf away from her mouth.

"I lie there all day and . . . I don't know. It has a sense of somewhere else. It feels warm when it's cold, light when it's dark. . . ."

"Time to go on back in, now. Time to go in."

"Why won't you tell me? Don't you want to pass it on to the next generation?"

Brona was on her feet, offering her arm. "It's the quiet, darling. The . . ." she inhaled a great breath of ocean air ". . . enormity of all this. It puts us very deep into our thoughts."

Deep in her thoughts, Thea continued to brood about having lost her job (she had exceeded her twenty days' sick leave in one go), her lover, and her health, but Brona continued to put her back together, like a jigsaw, piece by piece, giving her potions brewed from her own herbs. She was a shaman, Thea decided, some kind of healer, and she was certainly playing mind games with her niece, or something was: the cliffs, the hills, the edge of the ocean—who knew? Because sometimes, when she sat outside wrapped in blankets and looked across Dunmanus Bay, Thea felt a heat, an intense, glaring heat, sliding around her bones which was neither Irish nor spring-like. It made no sense, but she could feel herself heal in its light, and she enjoyed also the comfort of company, even when Brona was gone for hours to shop in Bantry. In this barren place, she never felt alone.

With her energy returning and the flesh coming back to her bones, she was able to take short strolls by the cottages, and always went back indoors to find tea and scones waiting by the stove. Ireland was getting between the ridges, smoothing out the humps and pits that had been so uncomfortable these last weeks. She still missed Kim and Reggie, the women in the office, but calm was spreading. Acceptance. There was no point in arguing with Fate. Hepatitis had taken hold of her and flung her in another direction. Off course. Too far off course ever to get back. Or was she?

Finding work with another firm in Baghdad would possibly be detrimental to her health and her heart, since she doubted her conscience would allow her to mess with Sachiv's family and position again. She had no right to him. It had been short, intense, and although she had been pulled down deep and had known love for the first time, it was a wasted love, good for nothing. Rather than struggle backward down an upward escalator, should she not simply walk on?

One afternoon she decided to go out toward the lighthouse, along the goat tracks between the hills. She promised Brona she would be gone no more than ten minutes, but as she clambered along the ridges, her energy rose to the task. She could feel herself *beating*. The blood was pumping through her and the wind was stinging her face, and the ocean was silver. So she went on, following tracks that went down into dips and up over ridges, until she came past a reedy brown lake, feeling good, almost happy. She sat on a rock, high over the dark, still lake.

Ripples on the water; ripples on her mind.

Sachiv had sat very close to her, on the side of the bed, fiddling with her fingers.

"I should thank you for helping to get me home," she had said, "but I hate you for it."

"We made a mistake."

"Don't be hard on yourself."

"I mean we wasted too much time."

"We'll have more time," she said, "when I'm better."

He looked down at her. "This is a serious thing you have, and Baghdad is no place to be sick. You could not recuperate in the heat. It asks its price, this place."

"So I've discovered."

"You must get well, that is the important thing. But we will see one another again, here or somewhere." He looked at her hands, squeezing her fingers. "Until then, every time the elevator opens—a hundred times a day—I will look for you."

She ran her thumb across his eyelid. "No tears," she said. "I have no tears. Too dehydrated. You'll have to cry for both of us."

Later that evening, the young man who had agreed to travel with her had turned as Reggie and Kim, supporting

Thea—dragging her almost—helped her from the elevator. He was unable to disguise his shock. Christ, he seemed to be thinking, she's *this* weak?

He was jittery, full-on—a good man doing a good thing, who wished he didn't have to—and behind them, near the desk, another good man hovered. They were running late. Like an extra piece of luggage, Thea wasn't even introduced to Alex. They had to get to the airport and, in an awkward jumble, they made straight for the door.

Sachiv went ahead and stood by the jeep. Thea slipped into those eyes one last time. "Don't be surprised," he said, helping her into the car. "Don't be surprised by what I do." He kissed the back of her hand and let her go.

On the way to the airport, Reggie had talked to the stranger in the front seat, while Kim's tight grip on Thea's wrist betrayed her own apprehension. What a lousy, sickly end to their adventure: Kim friendless in Baghdad, while Thea was being pulled from Iraq, like a clam from a rock. The journey was at last under way, but she was scared. The night stretched out, an unlit highway.

Resting her head on the back seat, she lifted her heavy eyelids to catch a last glimpse of Baghdad, but the low white city and the slow river were hidden in darkness. The headlights illuminated only the palm trees. Lines of them, along the roadside, like a guard of honor bidding her farewell.

She too bade farewell, to this strong country and its brave people, to the donkeys and camels, and that blue onion monument, dancing with itself. Images hurried forward, sharp but alluring: the dusty plain between the rivers; old typewriters with heavy keys; women in navy suits; tracer bullets in the night sky. Soldiers and spies. Palms and palaces. White villas and mud houses. Hummus and tabbouleh.

Iraq. Iraq.

I will come back, she thought. I *will*, though she knew, with certainty, that she would not.

III
Meet Me in Muscat

AND THERE SHE STOOD.

Exactly as he had imagined, expected and foretold—he turned, and she was there.

It seemed odd that he hadn't noticed her coming down the long white steps since he was the only other person by the sinkhole, where the slightest sound echoed and sunlight poured in, like tea into a copper urn. The crystalline water, glassy green and still, had dazzled him perhaps. He had been contemplating shattering its mirror-surface by throwing himself in, when his peripheral vision picked her up, right of field.

Her slender fingers lightly holding the hem of her skirt, her shoulders rounded beneath an almost see-through cream shirt, she was staring across the pool, apparently mesmerized by the pitch-perfect reflections of rim upon rim of sandstone curves. She kicked off her sandals and stepped into the water, past clumps of silky seaweed. So familiar, the way she moved. Crouched near the entrance to the cave, where the channel disappeared, like a train into a tunnel, he watched her paddle.

The years had scarcely touched her. Without even turning, she reached into his chest and squeezed his heart so tightly that he let out a grunt.

She had come back, as he had always known she would.

"*Christ*," he whispered. She twisted around and looked up at the rim of the sinkhole high above them, where three tourists stood near the steps, hesitating: it was a long way down and an even longer way up, given the heat.

No doubt feeling his eyes on her back, she glanced over her shoulder, saw him, but carried on paddling. He walked across the stones toward her, stopped a few meters away.

She turned, smiled. "Hello."

"Hello, you."

The intimacy ricocheted. Her smile slipped into confusion; she edged away.

Bringing his voice, his being, up from depths, he managed to say, "What kept you?"

She looked back. "I'm sorry?"

"What kept you so long?"

"I . . . I think you must be mistaking—"

"Not that I'm complaining," he added quickly, moving closer. "It's so great to see you."

"—me for someone else."

Their voices bounced around the buff brown cylinder in which they stood. He put his hands on his waist, smiling. "Oh, come on, I've thickened out a bit, but I haven't changed that much, have I?"

"I'm afraid I don't . . ." Another glance up at the other tourists.

Who was she with? And what was she doing? How could she not recognize him? *Know* him?

"Must be some mistake," she said, and stepped unsteadily away, avoiding the small underwater boulders which stood in her way. Ripples in multiple arcs set off from her shins across the pool, like an eager armada. Distracted, she watched them go all the way to the wall beyond.

A young Omani family was coming down to the water, but their little girl, about six years old, was stranded halfway, too nervous to tackle the vertiginous steps in either direction. She cried, but her parents teased her affectionately and wandered over to the water's edge. Unable to bear her isolation—halfway up, halfway down—he went over to the steps and up to her, offering his hand. After a moment's hesitation, her deep brown eyes considering him, the child held out her little hand and allowed him to lead her down.

As he did so, the woman in the flowing skirt came past them with a cursory nod and made her way up the steps. As soon as the child was safely with her parents, he hurried after her. This required a change of tack, but he didn't mind—the rules had always been fluid. He didn't mind about anything anymore.

The child's father called up to him in English, thanking him for rescuing his daughter. "Not at all," he called back from the top. "She'll be climbing Everest before you know it." The family's laughter burbled up from the pit.

"You're Irish?" The woman had turned on the landscaped path at the sound of his voice.

"Yeah."

"So we possibly *have* met, but I'm afraid I . . ." She gesticulated toward her head, as if it wasn't the one that should have been on her neck. "Must be jetlag—I flew in early this morning. I'm afraid I just can't place you."

Through the dark screens of their shades, his eyes caught hers. She was looking at him sideways, as if playing her life backward and forward through all the people she had known, the places she had worked, in search of him.

"I knew you'd come back."

"Come back? Oh, I've never been to Oman before," she said, with obvious relief that it was he who'd got it wrong, "This is my first time. I gather January is the best month to visit."

If she hadn't been so beautiful still—her auburn hair twisted up in a twirl—and her chin as flawlessly curved, he would have argued, but he was too overcome. "Right," he said, nodding. He'd play it this way, her way, whatever way.

She appeared to be alone. Reaching into her bag for her camera, she leaned over the rim of the sinkhole and photographed the water in a distracted manner. Then she looked at her watch and took a deep breath; a nervous breath.

He tailed her along the path to the parking lot. "Are you . . . here on business?"

"Holiday. With a friend," she added, then veered off to the restrooms with a dismissive "Bye, now."

When she came out, he was leaning against his 4x4, chatting to her taxi driver, who had confirmed that she had arrived that morning—but where had she been in the interim and why was she here now? Long-standing questions were finally, suddenly, within grasp of their answers.

With a glance in his direction, she got into the taxi.

He leaned over and looked in at her. "See you around," he said, because he would.

That afternoon at the Grand Hyatt, thanks to the indiscretion of her taxi driver, he found her in the tea lounge, where she was sitting deep in a couch, staring up at the perplexing centerpiece—a life-size bronze statue of a horseman with a falcon perched on his wrist. Newcomers always stared at it in this way soon after noticing that, every time they looked back at it, another angle of the statue seemed to be facing them. They turned so slowly, the horse and the man and the falcon, that people didn't immediately realize it was revolving.

Taking a seat under one of the canopies, which aped Bedouin tents on either side of the entrance, he watched her, unseen. She kept glancing around the ornate hall—at the cream and gold décor, the broad staircase and the huge stained-glass window—and seemed even more agitated than she had been that morning. Every time people came over from the lobby or up the stairs, her head swung around in jittery expectation.

Who? he wondered. *Who?*

The Vietnamese waitress, wearing a long skirt with a slit right up the side, placed a cup and saucer, napkin and teapot on his table. Around him, men and women did business, their global conversations spreading out in threads, face to face, phone to phone, wireless to wireless. The world at work.

"When are you flying back?"

". . . not organized like a European market . . ."

"And this is Thierry—he's in charge of our after-service."

Omanis. Gulf Arabs. Western women wearing Eastern modesty. Prudence also had dressed with decorum, he noted now, and had changed since that morning into a long-sleeved navy shirt and a straight linen skirt, with big earrings and silver bangles—good look, elegant but funky. She had aged even less than he might have expected. It was so thrilling, so surprising, to see her out in the world that his mouth was dry. He couldn't breathe, quite.

He had always known he would see her again. Even so, he could never have been ready for it.

Her phone beeped. She reached for it, read a text. Her hands were shaking. No longer composed and unflappable, like in the old days. It confused him. All this confused him, but it didn't matter. Nothing mattered, as long as he kept her in his sights.

She held the phone briefly to her chest, before putting it back into her bag.

"Hello again," he said, standing over her.

Her eyes jumped up, but her expression flattened. Disappointment, clear as day.

"May I?" he asked, sitting down.

"No." She stood up. "I'm sorry, I . . . I'm meeting someone." She slipped past him, left the lounge and headed off to the left, in the direction of the ladies' restroom. He followed as far as the lobby, where he collided with a woman who, like him, had her eyes on the flash of Irish skirt disappearing around the corner. "Sorry," she said, and changed direction to follow it.

Back at the office, he stared at the map.

❋

The following afternoon, she sprouted like a porpoise from the deep waters of Wadi Shab, just as he arrived at the pool. Without seeing him, she kicked under again and disappeared. Always her strong suit: disappearing.

His three women, gasping for breath, had collapsed on a rock nearby, and Abid—no better man, he thought—was sitting near the water with an American woman, whose voice droned tonelessly: "The skeleton of a monstrous highway spans the mouth of Wadi Shab, one of Oman's beauty spots, an eyesore, built by Indians for the Chinese."

With one eye on the fluttering water, he wondered why this woman was telling Abid what he already knew, but she went on, "The new colonialism. China is sucking the ores out of Africa and the fish from the Pacific, and here in Oman . . ."

Seeing him arrive, Abid jumped to his feet to greet him, and it was then he noticed that the American was speaking into a palm-sized Dictaphone. She glanced at him—it was the woman who had bumped into him the day before—and went on talking to herself.

His luck was in. He had taken a chance that they would set off on their second day, as most tourists did, including his three charges, Heather, Betty and Sue. Back in Muscat, he had grabbed the trio of Englishwomen like a kid grabbing sweets—he had to be on the road in order to run into her again—and had set off along the standard route, confident of eventually crossing paths. His clients weren't as nifty as he would have liked. It had been slow-going in the wadi, as he led them along a sandy track through a gathering of palm trees, then out into the widening gorge. They had struggled across the stones—he was going too fast—and exhaled relief when they reached the shaded path that ran between the canyon walls. At ground level, the cliffs were smooth as ice, and almost as white, but farther up, beyond the reach of flood waters, they were gnarled and pockmarked with narrow caves. Hetty, as they called Heather, and Betty had rested on a concrete slab under a lip of rock, while Sue, the younger one—at sixty-two—contemplated jumping into the square pool below the path, until he asked how she planned to get out again, given the sheer walls that surrounded it. So they had carried on, dipping their heads to get past overhanging rocks and had finally emerged, hot and sweaty, at this silvery pool, where he had found Abid and the American and everything he was looking for.

The porpoise came up for air, shook her head, wiped her face, and saw him.

"Hello again," he said.

"Hello." She swam toward the stony, crescent-shaped beach.

The American looked up. "You guys know each other?"

"Yes," he said.

"No," she said, squeezing her nose. "We've never met before."

"Now that's just not true," he teased. "We were at Bimmah together yesterday."

Like a basking shark, she hovered above the stones in the shallows. "But not before then."

"If you insist."

"Well, if *you* insist, you'll know my name."

He stiffened. *Caught.*

Abid put a hand on his shoulder. "Let me introduce—this is Thea, and here is Kim. And this is my very good friend, Jibril. Like the angel."

He leaned forward to shake Kim's hand, saying, "Gabriel."

"Pleased to meet you. *Are* you like the angel?"

"My mother clearly hoped so."

"There's a hill in West Cork called Mount Gabriel."

All three looked down at Thea. Yes, he thought. *Thea.*

"I came across it recently when I'd ended up in Schull by mistake," she went on, "and had to complete a loop to get back to Durrus—along the back road that skirts Mount Gabriel."

"Where were you trying to get to?" Gabriel asked.

"The last house before America."

He smiled, transposed, transported already, by that dry gaze.

She lowered her face into the water; let her body float like a corpse. Gabriel noted that she had thickened a bit, like him, around the waist.

He turned to Kim, nodded at her Dictaphone. "Journo?"

"Sure am."

"Special guests of the ministry, then?"

"Well, I'm the guest." Kim jerked her head at Thea. "She's along for the ride."

So why the nervousness, he wondered, at the hotel, when she had looked like a cat on the edge of a highway?

"Thea and I were in Iraq together back in the eighties," Kim explained unprompted, "and haven't seen each other since, so I asked her to meet me here."

Thea lifted her head and said derisively, "*Asked*?"

"Well, *lured*, I guess."

"Lured," Gabriel repeated.

"And it worked!" Kim shaded her eyes to look at Gabriel. "How about you? Doing the guided tour too, huh?"

"Yup."

Thea pulled her knees under her. "Chuck over my towel, would you, Kim?"

Gabriel caught it and handed it to her as she made her way to the nearest rock, where she sat, drying her legs. Her eyes were drawn up, and up, until they found the azure sky. "It's easy to forget, down here, that it's a sunny day up there."

"You forget a lot of things," Gabriel said.

She pulled her towel across her lap. "Excuse me?"

"How can you not remember me?"

"Look, maybe it was my sister you knew. Kate? Where are you from?"

"Cork."

"Well, there you go. My sister went to college in Cork. You possibly did too?"

"I was . . . well, yeah."

"That's it, then."

"I don't know your sister."

"You don't know me either."

"We met in Muscat. Twenty-six years ago."

"As I said yesterday, this is my first time in Oman, so that's simply not possible."

Some things had changed—the swimming, the energy and body tone (her upper arms were strong)—and this directness. He picked up a stone and skimmed it across the pool. It leaped—once, twice, three times—and hit the chalky wall opposite. "You here for long?" he asked Kim.

"Six days. That's all they'd pay for. You?"

He skimmed another pebble. "I live here."

"Oh." She glanced back at the women. "So . . . you're a guide?"

"Sometimes. Tour operator mostly."

"But you do your own driving?"

"He has his own business," Abid interjected. "And he has many drivers, but sometimes he likes to come out with his friends. Isn't that right, Jibril?"

"So you've been in Oman for some time," said Kim.

"A long time," he said, with a slow glance at Thea. "A long time waiting."

It was quiet. No birdsong, even, as they walked back to the vehicles in single file, just the scrape of stones, and that scraping voice: "Cyclone Gonu has done its worst. There are dead trees everywhere. Some appear to have lain right down in the gush of waters that came through this broad wadi, while others have been uprooted whole and carried downstream, where they're bunched up in the shallow, torpid water at the river mouth. It's like walking through a cemetery," Kim went on, "dead palms lying side by side, their root balls—stringy orange strands—exposed, like . . . genitalia. A *Guernica* of date palm." She switched off and said to Gabriel, "You might be quite handy for my article. Mind if I ask a few questions?"

"Fire ahead."

"What makes you so sure you know Thea? She doesn't appear to know you."

He turned to check that his ladies were bringing up the rear. "That has nothing to do with tourism."

Kim shaded her eyes to look around, Dictaphone held to her lips. "A solitary living tree, its foliage starry against the orange cliff, offers a flash of green, a splash of life."

"Oman Tourism will love you."

Thea was standing with her hands on the small of her back, looking up at the mountains pulling away from the wadi floor. "I've always wanted to see a place like this—like those old sepia photos in travel books, where you'd see camels crossing a stony plain."

Abid turned, his gray dishdasha chalky around the hem. "The Bedouin say that if you think of a place, or if it comes into your mind, like that, for no reason, then you must go there, because it has something for you, and you won't know until you get there."

Coming back into the oasis, into the shade of living trees, they passed more damaged ones—some beheaded, their crowns lopped off and dropped beside their trunks; others leaning, like injured soldiers, folding into the ground. It embarrassed Gabriel, as if it was his fault that this place, this jewel of Arabia, had been left in such a state. The damage wrought by Gonu six months earlier was countrywide, but as he glanced at the dead fronds of one of the trees, he saw a shoot of green poking out. Regeneration.

❁

He drove too fast around the U-bends that wound down into Tiwi but, delayed by his trio, he had been forced to watch the other party go ahead, Abid—so portly now, but still smart and neat, his silver sideburns complementing his thick mustache—striding on with Kim and Thea. He hoped to catch up with them at Qalhat.

A curve of bay swept out beyond Tiwi. Beautiful. He reached into his bag for the roll he had made at breakfast and munched it. It was good. Everything was good. This was the *best* day.

The palms that had survived the storm were like a torn population, all along the coast. "This is Qalhat," he explained to the women. "It's one of the most ancient sites in Oman and was an important port in the thirteenth and fourteenth centuries. It was destroyed by an earthquake, and then the Portuguese ransacked it. We'll head up here to Bibi Maryam's tomb."

They stopped near the square pink-brown mausoleum, which enjoyed a panoramic view of the Gulf of Oman. "So who was she," Hetty asked, as they walked up to it, "this Bibi Maryam?"

"She was a Turkish slave who married the Prince of Hormuz and, after he died, she became governor of Qalhat, which was famous for its export of Arabian horses. She built this for herself, and a splendid mosque." The women looked up at the domed roof. "But this is all that remains," he said, looking around, "and a water cistern."

No sign of the others. If they had stopped here, they had made swift work of it. Apprehension and excitement poked him alternately. He would *not* lose her again.

The Bibi's remains were buried in a vault, now covered with the red and green Omani flag, and, taking his clients around the side of the mausoleum, Gabriel showed them what were believed to be the graves of her maids, who killed themselves after she died.

"Like Cleopatra's handmaidens," said Hetty.

Gabriel nodded. "Eastern history is full of determined women."

"Cleopatra," said Betty. "Who else?"

"The Prophet's wife, Khadija," he said, "was a businesswoman—the Prophet was one of her employees. Zenobia of Palmyra. The Queen of Sheba."

"Hardly a handful," said Betty.

Hetty put her hand on the ageless wall. "But how many in Western history, Betty?"

Gabriel looked down the coast. He knew where Abid would take them for lunch.

Right again. When he walked into Abid's favorite Indian restaurant in Sur, their voices came from behind a screen at the back. Kim was saying, "What kind of stories?"

And Thea quipped, "Gin? An alcoholic? That explains a lot," and looked up to see him leading the women to the table next to them. He smirked; she blushed.

"Hello again!" Betty exclaimed.

"Well, hi," said Kim.

Betty maneuvered a roll of belly behind the table.

"Have you come from the boatyard?" Kim asked her.

"Sadly, no. Apparently we didn't have time."

"Such a pity," Sue said primly, "since it *is* one of the highlights of Sur."

"You didn't miss a thing," said Kim. "There's been an inferno. Hardly anything left."

Gabriel looked at Abid. "Madha hadath?"

"Some guy." Abid tapped his head. "A bit mad. Burned it down."

"Instead of a bustling hive of carpenters creating traditional, ocean-going dhows," Kim rattled on, "all we found were the burned-out skeletons of boats and sheds, with a few men working on carved miniature dhows for tourists."

"Quite poignant," said Thea, handing her camera across to them.

Gabriel took it and looked at the screen. She had taken a shot of a charred dhow, its long curved spine reduced to charcoal, everything else gone, but for the detail on its prow.

"So Abid has been entertaining us with stories about jinn." Kim's eyes twinkled at Gabriel. Mid-afternoon light filtered through the door.

"Jinn," said Hetty. "You mean like a genie, from a lamp?"

Oh, how he wanted to lose them!

A longboat, with a crew of twenty, slid along the magenta water, its oars stretching out on either side. From a vantage-point overlooking the creek, Thea and Kim sat on a hump of hill, their arms around their knees.

"This is some coincidence," Thea said.

"How so?"

"I row. I row the Irish equivalent of that boat down there—a traditional currach."

"No way."

"Although ours isn't quite so long and we don't go quite so fast, because there are only four of us."

A few meters away, Abid was trying to engage Gabriel in an argument about which of them had originally found this ideal spot for photo shoots at sunset, but Gabriel needed him to be quiet. His hearing was stretching, leaning out to catch what it could from the conversation to his right. Hetty and Betty were sitting farther along the ridge, their short legs straight, their toes turned up, while Sue filmed the scene below. Much as these women were a hindrance to his pursuit, so too were they facilitators, his excuse for being there, and he had to keep them sweet.

"Darn, but this is beautiful," said Kim. "What a sunset."

Abid took his phone from the deep pocket in his dishdasha and went down the slope to call his wife.

Now Gabriel could eavesdrop, but he kept his gaze on the low white town of Sur, which stretched along a spit of land, and feigned interest in its dhows, lying on the beach below. As the inlet dipped into an orange hue, the mountains in the distance tipped into darkness.

"Remember the sunsets in Baghdad?" Kim asked Thea. "Driving through the city and seeing this great red ball going down?"

"I've done my best to forget."

"Right. Sorry."

"That's why . . . well. Why I didn't keep in touch."

"I figured that."

"I'm so sorry for not writing back. I missed you terribly, but your letters were long and gushy, whereas mine would have been short and flat, and I couldn't bear the comparison. Your life to mine. You, reaching my horizons. And then other stuff happened."

Voices rose from the longboat—the coach driving his team, calling the rhythm, the rowers growling at one another as they slid down the creek.

"But the truth is, I don't even know how long you stayed there."

"Two years."

"Good years?"

The questions were tentative; the answers more so.

"It was fun, yeah," Kim said, looking down at the water, "but it was never quite the same without you. No more belly laughs."

"Glad to hear it," Thea said, and they chuckled.

"You didn't mind my getting in touch now, did you?"

With a warm smile, Thea nudged her. "The best surprise *ever*. And this trip—what a fantastic way to say hello and cancel out that bloody awful goodbye."

"Don't remind me of that night!"

Gabriel took out his phone and pretended to text.

"God, I hated to see you go," said Kim, "I'm afraid to ask how you got through that journey."

"Oh, I managed. The worst bit was waiting at the gate. The airport was heaving with soldiers—passengers, not security. Some were missing limbs, others had eye injuries, but they were mostly the walking-wounded, heading to Britain for treatment. Alex went into overdrive, all fuss and bother. I really, *really* wanted him to leave me alone and let me block it all out, but he was like a mother hen: 'What do you need? What can I get you?' So I asked for the one thing I knew he wouldn't find, Coke, figuring he'd have to go to Syria to get it, but he zipped off, all eager, and I lay back, wishing the hours away. Next thing, he was right there, damn pleased with himself, holding a can of Coke."

"But there was no Coke in—"

"All of Iraq, yeah," said Thea. "Except at the airport apparently. When I asked where on earth he'd got it, he said, 'Umm, the drinks machine.' I knocked it back in about three gulps."

"More than you'd had to drink in days."

"Exactly, and after watching me guzzle it, Alex said, deadpan, 'I might get you another of those,' which was when I started to like him. So I drank that too and, rehydrated and full of sugar, I finally sat up, looked at this guy by my feet and said, 'So what brings you to Iraq?' We talked all night and all the way to London."

"'Reader, I married him.'"

They laughed. "Ridiculous, isn't it?"

"Marrying your Mr. Kool-Aid? I think it's great!"

Not great at all, Gabriel thought.

"Anyway, when we got to Heathrow, I walked through the airport unaided and, get this, ate a fry for breakfast. Worst possible thing. So then of course I started thinking that Einstein, the old doc, had got it right. It was all in my head. I'd gone and left the country for nothing. Not a thing wrong with me, except love."

Love? Gabriel was afraid to move. He was, at that moment, unseen, like a jinn.

"Love?" said Kim. "You mean Sachiv? But I thought that was just a crush. A flirtation."

"Neither."

"You were *in love* with him? But what did you know of him, really?"

"Quite a lot, as it happens. You could even say that his must be the only marriage saved by an infectious disease."

On their way out of town, in tandem, they passed a group of fishermen who were practicing dances on the promenade. Following Abid's lead, Gabriel pulled into the curb and they all stepped out to watch. He wandered over to stand with Thea. A few men were sitting on the low wall that ran along the seafront, playing drums or clapping, while others stood in a line, working out steps, trying different formations.

"Orange T-shirts, brown dishdashas," Kim said into her machine, "hands clapping, movements coordinated, positions secured. The dance acquires shape—a star turning—while the beat gets harder and faster."

By nightfall, they were near the tip of the country and their rendezvous at a maternity ward—the turtle sanctuary at Ras al-Hadd. After a short rest at their hotel, Gabriel drove his group to the beach at midnight, where they stood about in the parking lot behind some dunes, surrounded by vehicles, tourists and guides, all waiting for the sign—a flash of torchlight—which would confirm the presence of laboring leatherback turtles on the beach. An Omani family got out of the car beside them—some women and a man carrying a very small baby. His dishdasha glowed white in the moonlight, while the women's long, slim shadows on the gravel were like well-meaning spirit guides. There was no sign of Abid's party.

When a torchlight flashed on the dunes, Jamil, one of the guides, gathered the crowd of thirty or more around him. "If anyone uses flash, you will be removed from the beach. And do not make noise. Also—there are big craters in the sand, so don't fall into them, okay? Now we can go. He has found a turtle."

With only the moon for light, concentration was necessary to avoid the empty nests that perforated the beach. Hetty grabbed Gabriel's arm. "Heavens!" she said cheerfully, having stumbled into one of the birthing holes. "Twisted ankle, here we come!"

The group gathered in a circle to peer at a turtle digging her nest, skimming her flippers across the sand, pushing it back. Working, digging. It never failed to move Gabriel, the sheer effort involved. Mobile phones were held high, pointed in her direction. Jamil, hunkering behind her, said quietly, "She will lay between eighty and one hundred eggs, but if she thinks the sand is too hot, or too cold, or if she is disturbed, she will go back to the sea and try again later."

"And they always come back to the beach where they were born?" someone asked.

"Yes. They swim for thousands of miles to give birth."

"Like salmon," said another voice.

This turtle failed to deliver. Surrounded, she paused in her work, looked up, thought about it, and scraped her way out of the unfinished depression. People moved back, creating an exit.

"She's had enough," Hetty whispered. "Can't say I blame her."

The turtle forged her way through the gap in the crowd, her sad earnest eyes reflecting the torchlight, and made as tight a U-turn as a turtle could manage, then took her weight across the sand toward the sea, the birth postponed. "Poor thing," said Betty. "Now she'll be in labor even longer."

A flash of light farther along the strand indicated that another warden had found another turtle; the tourists hastened over. Gabriel followed in his own darkness. He knew the beach well. The Milky Way was bristling and the sea breaking in white gushes. He stood on the outskirts of the crowd, beside the young woman from the parking lot, who was handing her bundle of baby back to her husband, and, from somewhere within this group, he heard the low voice that talked to itself: ". . . this organic prehistoric ritual. These great creatures, which move in the sea like paper drifting, are unwieldy, inelegant lumps on land."

People were talking loudly, and Jamil had been set upon by an old woman who kept asking questions about the mating rituals of turtles. "Madam," he said finally, "I am a tourist guide. I do not work here at the sanctuary."

A dedicated tourist, trying to film the ping-pong eggs plopping into the excavated funnel, pushed his way deeper into the huddle, forcing someone else to back out. She stumbled on the rim of a crater. Gabriel reached out and caught her. "Careful."

"Jesus!"

He couldn't see her face, but he knew the feel of her. "Gabriel, actually."

"Yes. Thanks." Thea withdrew her elbow from his grasp.

The surf pounded beside them. He sought her eyes in the shadows of her face. "How is our performing turtle doing in there?"

"She's in full delivery," Thea whispered. "It's mortifying. Nothing like the moving, timeless experience I'd envisaged. It's actually *upsetting* to be disturbing a natural process that has gone on, right on this spot, for millennia."

"People have mixed feelings about it."

"I don't. It's intrusive. Horrible. I feel humiliated on her behalf. They're lifting up her tail!"

"She's in a trance," he said gently. "They go into a kind of trance."

"That doesn't excuse it."

"No."

"Wish I'd been in a trance when I gave birth."

"You have kids?"

"Two boys. Kieran and Marcus."

"Careful!" one of the wardens called.

A baby turtle was rushing between the shifting feet. It scurried over the humpy sand, hampered by its own design, desperate to reach the sea. The warden scooped it up in his palm—it was barely two inches long—and put it down away from the tourist stampede, near Thea. "You see," he said, shining his torch just in front of the hatchling, "see how he follows the light." Patiently, he showed the baby the way to the sea. Its flippers pulled against the grains as it hurried into the beam and after it, until the warden had led it all the way into the breaking waves, safe from those agile predators that fancied the occasional delicacy of baby turtle for breakfast.

"Why does he follow light?" Thea asked. "Don't animals feel safer in the dark?"

"Yes, but they're programed to hatch at dawn," the warden explained, "to follow the sun."

The group was dispersing, moving back toward the parking lot. Two men were trailing Jamil, asking how best to go through the sands.

"You have four-wheel drive, yes?" he asked them.

"Ah, no. Just a car."

"You are crazy, yes?"

"I'd swear no one cares what he says," Hetty declared. "We're all following Jamil just to hear that beautiful enunciation."

"I'm with her," Kim muttered to Thea, then saw Gabriel alongside her. "Gabriel! Hi! Are you stalking us?"

"The tours generally follow the same route," he said.

"I love your accent. Reminds me of Thea."

"Well, it's much diluted. I haven't been to Ireland in over twenty years."

"Really?" Kim was leaning forward to see around Thea. "Not even on a visit? That must be hard."

"Not particularly. I'm not a turtle. I don't need to return to where I started."

"I can't imagine being away from Ireland for more than a few months," Thea said.

"Is that why you went back?" he asked her.

"How do you mean?"

They'd stopped on the last dune before the parking lot. Abid and Kim went ahead.

"Is that why you left Oman?"

"As you can see," she said curtly, "I have not yet left Oman."

"Last time, I meant."

Her breast lit up. Her phone was flashing in the pocket of her shirt. She took it out, saying, "Look, if we're going to keep running into each other, I would ask you to stop speaking to me as if you know me, because you don't."

The whites of her eyes glimmered; he nodded; they walked back to their cars.

"Okay, Abid," Kim was saying, "you can tell *us*—did that hatchling come out of the warden's pocket for effect? They usually hatch at dawn, don't they?"

"Most times, but there are always a few babies on the beach."

"No! Does that mean we might have squished infants in the nursery?"

Thea's phone was throwing a creamy light on her smile, as she leaned against the bonnet reading a text.

"Believe me," said Abid, "many more make it to the ocean than they would if they were not protected."

"Crabs love them," said Gabriel. "And birds."

"Come, come," said Abid, ushering the two women into the jeep. "It is very late now. We will have a long day tomorrow."

❋

Another wadi. Another swim. Another sighting.

This time, Gabriel found Thea in the belly of a canyon. He had led his charges to one of his favorite places—a sliver of water that ran like a crystal snake through a gully, which ended at a turnstile of rocks, above which were more pools and some caves. Stopping on the pebbly shore, the women demurred. Too much clambering, they said. Too much heat. He didn't argue. Thea's bag and towel were on the ground with Kim's, guarded by Khaled, a wiry teenager, and one of his pals.

Sue was wriggling out of her dress, her silver hair up in a tight bun—everything about her was tight, Gabriel thought, while the other two, who complained so much about the heat, refused to swim. He threw off his top and waded in, chatting to the boys, who joined him, and all three allowed the water to carry them around the bend to the end of the narrow channel, where they hoisted themselves up and squeezed through a fissure to the next level.

There, with her back to him, Thea was reclining on a slimy curve of rock, half in, half out of a crescent-shaped pool, her face lifted to the sunlight that had fought its way past the morning's clouds.

"Fuck!"

The sudden grunt and gush of water initially startled her, but then she said languidly, "Oh. Gabriel."

The gold-tinged rocks that dipped into the shallow water were treacherous. He had slipped and crashed down, sliding into the pool some meters from where she lay.

"Be careful. It's deadly."

He grasped his elbow. "Yeah, just figured that out."

"I'd help, but if I move *I* might break something."

The two boys scampered like goats over the ice-smooth boulders, past Kim, who had climbed into a natural jacuzzi one level up and lay with her head on the rocky rim.

"I have a message," he said, rubbing his arm, "from Abid. Lunch will be ready in ten minutes. I hope that information is worth a cracked elbow."

"Not really, no," Thea smiled, "but I am very hungry."

"He's built a fire back at the picnic site. Smells good."

"We bought barracuda straight from the sea. We left the tourist trail this morning and powered along a beach instead. Unbelievable."

He slid closer, like a seal paddling around a curved rock. Such a relief to find her, after the scraping disappointment of waiting fruitlessly over a breakfast of industrial toast and grainy coffee in the hotel restaurant that morning, listening to some American girl at the table behind him talk about her hair, and her mother, and her Visa account.

Thea tilted her face toward the sun. The water fussed around her breasts. "Like an Irish summer's day—trying to catch a few rays between the clouds." She squinted at him. "Or have you forgotten what an Irish summer is like?"

"Even if I hadn't, I'm sure it's different now. Hotter?"

"Wetter. There was talk of vineyards in climate-changed Ireland, but so far all we've had is more rain. Still, you must miss it?"

"Irish rain?"

"Ireland. Both."

"Yeah, I do."

"So why don't you go back?"

"Because it brought out the worst in me."

"Don't you have family in Cork?" she asked.

"My parents, yeah. But they like coming here for the weather." He smiled.

She looked around the rock room in which they lay. "Where are your women?"

Gabriel raised an eyebrow in the direction of the fissure, thinking about the proverbial camel and the eye of the needle, but said only, "Bit too much of a climb for them."

"Why do you do it? Taking clients out, when it's your own business?"

"Actually I run the company for an Omani friend, but I hate paperwork—there's a lot of bureaucracy and schmoozing required to keep government departments happy—and I prefer the open road, so if I get the chance to fill in for a driver, I take it."

"You must like it here, to have stayed so long?"

"Love it. I mean, this is a tough landscape; it doesn't forgive you much, and you have to keep your wits about you—whether it's flash floods or hiking over escarpments—but with the right client, I can take off into the desert and—"

"Oh, I can't wait to see the desert again!"

Closing one eye to shut out the glare reflecting off the water, he said, "*Again?* I thought you'd never been here before?"

"This isn't the only place that has deserts."

"Ah, Iraq."

"Yes." Her gaze drifted off with her thoughts.

Gabriel cleared his throat. "Wahiba Sands tonight, I suppose?"

"Yeah."

"You won't see much desert on the tourist hop, you know."

"Well, it isn't my itinerary. I'm the official travelling companion. All I have to do is get in and out of the jeep at appointed spots and swim. Wonderful."

"It must have been lovely," he said, "meeting Kim again."

She flicked water about with her fingers. "Oh, it was . . . fantastic. I mean, I'd been getting these mysterious postcards from Muscat for months and hadn't a clue—"

"Postcards?"

Thea wrinkled her nose. "Long story."

"Good. Long and mysterious stories go down well in these parts. From the top, please."

"Wherever that is." She turned her face up again, begging the sun to hit on her. "A few months ago, I came downstairs one day and saw the white-rimmed corner of a postcard poking out from the buff dross that had been stuffed through the letterbox. I could just see a narrow slice of aquamarine that screamed holidays. I tried to remember who was away, of our friends, you know—and where?—and pulled it out from the rest of the mail, thinking, a Caribbean beach perhaps, a Himalayan sky. But it was neither. It featured the ridge of a sand dune, its flanks lined with neat grooves mussed only by footprints—two sets, one coming over the crest of the dune and joining another on the other side, continuing together. I didn't turn it over, at first. I was wondering which desert it might be. The Gobi? Namib? Arabia? And when finally I turned the card, the message, written in a sort of childish hand, said, 'Meet me in Muscat.'"

"Sounds like a song."

She nodded mildly, but stayed back there in her hall, or wherever she'd gone to.

"So you jumped on a plane?"

"Of course not. I had no idea who'd sent it. But a few weeks later, another card came, and then they kept coming at regular intervals until—"

"Hang on, back to the second card. I signed up for the long version."

She glanced at him, then back at her toes. "That was delivered in late September. It featured an orange fort with a girth of palm trees and three mountain ridges in the background, stacked one behind the other, each a darker shade of blue than the one before it."

"Nakhal."

"And the message read: 'In January.'"

Gabriel smiled. Thea smiled back. "Someone was messing with my head, but these anonymous nudges were kind of intimate, and I liked the turn of mind of the person who was sending them, even though I couldn't identify them, so I had to operate on a hunch."

"And your hunch said Kim? It would have, to me."

"No, I'm not that bright. Anyway, I thought she'd long since, and with good reason, given up on me. But then another card came, as expected: a gray beach, flat sea, orange cliffs, and a leatherback turtle making her way to the low surf. Message: 'At the Hyatt.'"

"But who was posting them? Doesn't Kim live in the States?"

"Yeah. She asked an Omani friend of hers in Muscat to write them."

Gabriel shook his head, still smiling. "This is wonderful."

Thea looked over at Kim's head, resting on the rim of her jacuzzi. "At that point I started looking up flights. We were due to go to the Rockies this summer, but I started thinking the boys could go without me. White water rafting isn't really my thing—my danger-sports years are long over—and flights to Muscat were equal to the cost of getting to the Rockies. . . . And then those gorgeous postcards and the glassy swimming pools featured on the Omani websites started to do their work. To hell with mysterious meetings, I thought. Just give me that pool, that beach, that desert! The next card read, 'Three o'clock.' That one showed the entrance to a mosque, all blue and white mosaics, and mother-of-pearl."

"So this dribble of details really took effect? I mean, had one card come—'Meet me in Muscat in January at the Hyatt at three o'clock,' would that have worked?"

"Oh, I'd probably have discarded it, but these amuse-bouches made me . . ."

"Crave the main course?"

"Absolutely." She shook her head. "The last one should have given it away: two Bedouin women, swathed in orange and black scarves, holding those leather masks up to their hidden faces. As my niece would say, 'Duh!' But I still didn't think it was Kim. I thought I'd hurt her irredeemably by never replying to any of her letters, after she had looked after me so well, and then we lost track of each other."

"And the final message?"

"It said simply, 'Twelfth.'"

"A date. Irresistible, I'd imagine?"

She paused, her thoughts not for broadcast. Then she lifted her hands from the water. "I stand before you—or, rather, slide around before you—so yes, irresistible, but I genuinely had no idea who was behind it. You mislay a lot of people in the course of an average life."

"Your husband didn't mind?"

"Why would he? He was as curious as I was."

"Could have been an ex."

"He thought it probably *was* an ex, but he has more faith in me than apparently you do. And, besides, he knew I needed . . . a break. Something."

"It must have been nerve-racking," Gabriel said, "waiting."

"Yes. Sorry for dashing off on you that day in the lobby, but I was nervous about who was going to show up. I mean, it could have been my worst nightmare—that horrible teacher I had in fifth class or the awful woman I was in hospital with once. But those cards, those images, created their own story and I wanted to get to the end of it." Behind her shades, her eyes were still; still with disappointment.

She had been expecting someone else, he was sure of it.

"And when it came to it," she went on, "we met up in the Ladies, of all places. You can imagine the screeching."

"I don't have to. I heard it. I was coming out of the Gents." He tried to sit up. His hips wouldn't let him. "Look," he said, slithering about. "I'm sorry for freaking you out with all that talk of, you know, thinking you were someone else. It won't happen again."

"You sure?"

"I can do small talk instead. Honestly. I do it all the time in my job."

"Oh, great. From freaky to chitchat."

She was cheekier than she'd been before; funnier. She had acquired confidence and character. It was a furious turn-on.

"Forget small talk," she said. "Tell me about the woman you thought I was, or am, or . . . should be?"

Gabriel looked up at the white cliff that rose from just beyond their toes. "I don't talk about it."

"You've barely spoken of anything else!"

His shoulder blades were straining with the effort of holding his elbows in place. He looked at her again. Surely she noticed it—the intimacy, the easiness of their exchanges. How could she imagine them to be strangers? "You'll think I'm mad," he said. "Everyone else does."

"Why?"

"Why not?"

"You don't make much sense."

"I never have."

"That's true," she said. "You've made very little sense in our short acquaintance thus far."

Not so short, he wanted to say.

She shivered—he saw it ripple up her arm, like uncertainty. Better, he thought, not to speak of their past here, in the hypnotizing quiet, at the foot of those expressive rock faces, with their mealy-mouthed openings, like angered lips. "What's wrong?"

Thea looked past Kim, along the gully. "It's moody here, isn't it? There's a sort of foreboding or something. I wish I could shake it off."

"You can't. It's embedded in the rocks."

Droplets of water drying on her shoulders were turning white. "I blame Abid," she said. "He's been talking about jinn. Kim keeps pumping him for stories. I don't quite get it, though, how some people see them and others don't."

"Better to say they reveal themselves to some and not to others," Gabriel explained. "Although, strictly speaking, according to the Quran, they can never be seen by humans. Depends what you believe."

"And what do you believe?"

"Call me agnostic."

"I've heard that men can fall in love with them."

Gabriel finally managed to sit up, and leaned over his knees. "All right, all right. Stop beating around the gully. Abid's told you, clearly."

"Told me what?"

"My own personal folklore."

She hooked her big toes together.

"What did he say?" he asked, adding, in spite of himself, "You have nice toes." In truth, although her legs were still slim, her feet had not improved with age.

"He said you're a sad man."

"Ah."

"He said you came to Oman in the eighties to stay with your sister, because the woman you wanted to marry loved someone else."

Gabriel let out an involuntary cough. This still had currency? How effective had been Rolf's myth-making!

"But then you fell in love with a jinn, and that's why you're still here, still alone."

Gabriel nodded.

"So it's true?

"Except the jinn bit. I did fall in love, but she wasn't a jinniya."

"So why did Abid say she was?"

"Because . . ." How, where, to go with this? He sighed. "Because no one else ever saw her, even when they were in the same room."

Thea slid her sunglasses down her nose to look over them. "No wonder they think you're a bit deluded."

"Oh, they don't think I'm mad because I fell in love with her—lots of men fall for jinn and take them as wives. No, they like to tease me because I managed to lose her and haven't replaced her."

"But that was a long time ago, wasn't it?"

He shrugged. "Some things can never be left behind."

Thea pushed her sunglasses back up. "That's true."

A light cloud dimmed the sun, then let it out again.

"And that affair saved me," Gabriel said.

"They call this work." Kim's voice echoed along the gully.

He turned to Thea. "*You* saved me."

She sat up. "Stop doing that."

He reached out, touched her elbow. "I'm sorry. I'm trying, honestly, but I've . . . I'm totally thrown. The resemblance is—"

"The resemblance to *whom*? Your jinn person?"

"You even sound like her."

"Oh, Christ." She turned. "Kim! Lunch is ready!"

Kim twisted around in a slithery spin. "Hi, Gabriel. You been sneaking up on us again?"

"More like arriving with a great splash."

The teenagers clambered over the rocks and came across the stones. Thea gingerly got to her feet. Gabriel offered his hand, but so too did Khaled and she took his instead.

Kim joined them, muttering to Gabriel, "Who's the old guy?"

Thea looked back. "What old guy?"

Kim turned. "Oh. Gone. He was standing on that rock up there, watching us."

"That's the old boy who guards the cave," said Gabriel.

"Where'd he go?" Kim twisted around. "He was leaning on a camel stick, clear as day."

"He didn't go anywhere. He's one of the local jinn."

"No way!"

"Let's get back," said Thea.

"Are you messing with me?" Kim nudged Gabriel.

"If I am, where is he?"

Unable to take her eyes from the cliffs, Kim said, "You mean I've actually seen one? How cool is that? Those years in Iraq, I never got as much as a whisper from the other world."

"We go this way," Khaled said, helping Thea across the nipping gravel to a stream that had forged its own smooth slide into the lower pool. He sat, pushed off, slid away and landed with a *plouf* in the water below. His friend followed.

"Oh, God," said Kim. "I have to do that?"

"Nothing for it," said Gabriel. "It's the only way back."

"Right." Kim seated herself on the rock and slithered down its back, screeching.

Thea insisted Gabriel went ahead of her, but when she dropped underwater right beside him, her hand touched his shoulder and his caught her waist. The fleeting contact gave him a kick, just as her heels kicked her back to the surface. She wouldn't be as easy, this time.

They swam slowly through the corridor of limestone, its smooth white walls curved and soft. Kim reached out to touch the chalky surface. "We're in one of the earth's creases," she said, "deep in the groove of one of its wrinkles. It's like being embedded in our own planet."

Gabriel said, "Pity your tape recorder isn't waterproof."

An Everest-like peak, ice-free, glowed in the evening light as they made their way out of the wadi. On the roadside, women in veils splashed with color walked along the street, their mobile phones gripped to their ears. Gabriel had left the other party behind, feasting on barbecued barracuda under an awning next to a large pool in the evening sun. With difficulty, he had torn himself from her side, leaving her pulling chunks of fish from its bone with her greasy, nimble fingers.

In a small town near the Sands, he let down his tires, watched by six old men sitting in a semicircle on plastic chairs, chewing the cud, their beards as white as their dishdashas, their wise faces relaxed. Then he bought the ladies tea in paper cups, which was sweet and delicious, they said, as they worked their way through a packet of cookies, while rollicking toward the Sands. They were growing on Gabriel. Slow, they might be, but they were earthy and honest, and unreasonably fair to him in view of how badly he was conducting their not inexpensive tour.

The ragged mountain peaks had softened into rusty, rounded dunes, which moved toward them like a welcoming party until they were ahead, behind and all around them. Leaving the road, Gabriel headed into a funnel, a sandy superhighway, broad and track-marked. Bedouin holdings were spotted along the way, with animal enclosures, kids and goats, and an occasional camel.

"Heavens, look," said Betty. "Greenery."

"These are good times in the desert," Gabriel explained. "The cyclone brought rain for the first time in years." At a random spot, he turned off the valley floor and headed right up into the dunes. They were running late for one of the advertised highlights—the desert sunset, so he careered across the sand, throwing the jeep up slopes and over ridges, looking for a spot. Betty squealed, Hetty gripped the handle over her door, repeating, mantra-like, that she was fine because her eyes were shut, and Sue, beside him, put her feet on the dash and sat rigid. It always gave Gabriel a rush, this bit: being in control of people's fear.

They drew to a halt high on a crest, just in time to see a wink of sun slink behind the horizon, which had the outline of a reclining woman. Thanks to his dallying, they had effectively missed the sunset, but the evening sky got him off the hook—its bruise-colored clouds were rimmed with a luminescent, multicolored aura. It darkened here and brightened there, so that the view kept dazzling, and the photos had to be taken again and again, while the desert, with much less ceremony, vanished into darkness.

Down on the flat, a 4x4 rushed by, its headlights beaming and sand spraying up behind it. Abid. The barracuda had cost them this magnificent sky. Pity. Gabriel would have liked Thea to see it.

"Ooh, look," said Betty. "He turned off his headlights!"

"The Bedouin way," Gabriel explained. "They see better in the dark, or so they say."

At the camp, goat-hair tents, randomly spread out and each with its own roofless brick bathroom, surrounded a large communal area, lit by gas lights. Gabriel carried the ladies' bags to their appointed tent, where they were charmed by the heavy timber beds, the dresser, table and chairs. Then he walked back to the restaurant, his eyes scanning the compound until he saw Kim coming out of a tent and stepping across to the bathroom. She didn't appear to see him. He changed direction and did an about loop—it was pitch dark now—which brought him around to the back of their tent, just as Kim came out of the bathroom.

"This is lovely," he heard Thea say to her. "I can lie here on the bed and see that amazing sky through the flap."

"He's proving quite hard to lose, your ex," Kim said.

"My ex?"

"Gabriel."

"Don't you start! So he's here?"

"Uh-huh."

"It's got to the point where I'd be surprised if he wasn't."

"It's a bit like being stalked," Kim went on, "except he's so sweet on the eye that I don't actually mind. Unless you're bothered?"

"I'm getting used to him."

"And I quite like the way he turns up and then vanishes."

Thea chuckled. "Maybe *he*'s the jinn."

Their words were clear, even though their voices were low.

"That guy has a back story, I'm telling you," said Kim. "This jinn woman is about some whole other thing. I'd put money on it."

"Me too."

"Be careful, though."

"Why?"

"He can't take his eyes off you."

"Probably waiting for me to get sucked back into the lamp like the last one."

They giggled again. "I'm not kidding, Thea. He's attractive. Dangerously so."

"And I'm married."

"How married?"

"*Very*."

Gabriel sat down, right there, in the lee of the tent. Even if one of the drivers came past on the way to the drivers' tent, he was well concealed in the shadow, out of the moon's sights.

"I have a terrible confession to make." Thea's voice was close. She was right next to him, separated only by the coarse fabric of the tent.

"Bring it on!"

"Well, my first crush was . . ."

"Was?"

"The Archangel Gabriel!" They hooted with laughter. "*Seriously*," Thea hissed. "When I was little I actually fancied an angel. My little Catholic self was attracted to this shining white knight whom God adored."

"Beware of shining knights," said Kim. "I've had a few of those myself. Ex-husbands, I call them."

"I can't believe you've accumulated two already. You were quite prim when I knew you."

"And should have remained so, clearly!" They laughed again, and Kim said, "Nah, seems I'm not cut out for monogamy."

"Is anyone?"

"You, maybe?"

"I'll let you know at my funeral."

Gabriel ran his fingers through the cold sand, entertained but hungry, and he was about to sneak away to get dinner, when Thea said, "About Gabriel, Kim. There's something else."

"What?"

"He *is* . . . familiar."

A jerking movement. "Are you kidding me?" Kim hissed. "You tell me this now?"

"Shush!"

"So you think you *have* met him?"

"I know I haven't," said Thea. "That's the thing. But it keeps coming at me, this sense of familiarity, but then I look at him and there's no recognition. Nothing."

Gabriel struggled to keep his breathing in check.

"Maybe he looks like someone you know."

"No, that's not it."

A voice called a name, over at the hub, but the camp was otherwise quiet. No music or generators. Gabriel had to be very, very still.

"He actually reminds me of someone I . . . never knew."

"I'm getting a little confused here. You're beginning to sound like him."

Thea sighed. "I should tell you about those months after Baghdad."

"That seems like a very good idea. Kill time before dinner."

Gabriel was aware of Thea moving, rolling onto her side perhaps. "My parents didn't really get it," she began, in a quiet, flat voice. "The low. The disappointment. They were so relieved that I was home safe, they thought I'd be fine alone all day, as long as they left me teabags and Cup-a-Soup."

"Seriously?"

"Yeah. So Dad's sister Brona, a redoubtable old biddy if ever there was one, swept me up and carried me off to the wilderness. . . ."

Her voice, right by his car, almost lulled Gabriel into a trance with her talk of Sheep's Head—a moody, gutsy narrow strip of land poking the ocean—so easily remembered, and even the aunt, living alone on her widow's pension, growing vegetables, might have been one of his own.

"Every day I'd wake up surrounded by mountains and ocean. The sky and the sea changed hour to hour. Brona said the Atlantic would heal me, and it did. The sound of it mostly, at night and in the morning, that roaring, gurgling gush, muted by the walls, though at other times it was as calm as sleep—this vast body of water making not the slightest noise.

"Anyway, I was driving myself mad with thoughts of Sachiv, trying to capture him, brand myself with every detail, every exchange between us, and Brona told me to stop. You know, to stop obsessing about it, and to let Sheep's Head do its work. She even told me to fantasize—seriously. Fantasizing, she insisted, was a form of meditation. 'It's easy,' she said. 'Make up a nice place, a beautiful place, and go there, pretend to live there, until real life needs you back.' Totally barmy."

"Oh, no," Kim said gently. "No, I love that. Isn't it what we all do when we're sad?"

"When another morning came," Thea went on, "with that dragging heartache still in my belly, I decided to give it a go, so I looked around inside my head to see what I might find. After a bit of practice, I discovered a bright, light country within reach. Perhaps it had always been there, waiting for me to push open the door and step in, or perhaps I created it only then. Either way, from then on, during my morning lie-in and my long afternoon nap, I went off to a place that was neither Ireland nor Iraq, but which had an excellent climate and warm seas, and where, for good measure," she added, with a chuckle, "I had a besotted *unmarried* lover, whose eyes and hands were always where I wanted them to be. He was handsome, but not flawless, warm but edgy, giving but impenetrable."

"Sounds like the kind of man *I* need."

"It was amazingly effective. Increasingly, in spite of myself, I'd feel myself tumbling into that nowhere place, into the calm of being with a person who didn't exist and couldn't hurt me. It was the distraction that worked. Not having to think or fret. It stopped me wondering about what you were doing, right then, in Baghdad, or if I'd ever see Sachiv again. In that white, easy place, everything suited *me.* My stranger suffered with love for me, came and went, according to my whim, and, it goes without saying, made passionate love to me on a regular basis. Naturally, I became very attached to him!"

Their shared guffaw made Gabriel smile, but he could barely absorb what he was hearing.

"What you're talking about right there," said Kim, "is creative visualization."

"That makes it sounds less ridiculous, I suppose. Anyway, that's where I hid, what I did, during my convalescence, having pretend sex and pretend love in a pretend place, while my aunt brought me apples and water, and outside the ocean had a busy day, or a temperate one."

Apples and water. Apples and water. Apples and water.

"Sounds good to me."

"But there was something about that house, Kim, and the woman who lived there. Often, I couldn't quite see the sea or feel the cold or smell the damp. There were times when I wasn't there at all, not really—and Brona understood that, but I never did. Never have."

"And you probably shouldn't try to."

"Ha. Says she who is going all out trying to get a handle on jinn."

"What did you call him," Kim asked, "this lover?"

"I can't remember. I'm not even sure he had a name. He didn't need one."

"A virtual lover—long before the internet."

"And so real," Thea said, more quietly, "that I remember him now the way I remember people I knew. Sometimes I even forget that it was *not* an actual relationship that I had way back when. So you could say he *did* exist, because I made him exist."

"Was he not Sachiv, really?"

"That would have defeated the purpose. I can't really say what he looked like, my rebound guy, except that . . . you're going to think me bonkers."

"I already do, hon."

"He had Gabriel's mannerisms, Kim. Gabriel's . . . presence."

Had a prowling leopard come at him at that moment, Gabriel could not have moved.

Inside the tent, with a sudden jerk, Kim seemed to be on her feet. "What are you saying? That Gabriel is, like, imagination made flesh? And isn't that what *he*'s been saying to *you*?"

"I hope not. I hope we're not saying the same thing."

"I mean," Kim was excited, talking fast, "that would be like, well, as if *your* daydream became *his* reality."

"Put that in your Dictaphone and see if it swallows it."

An enclosure fenced off by dead branches housed a small brick kitchen, a room with tables and chairs that looked like a low-grade cafeteria, and a broad dining area with low square tables. Kim and Thea were having dinner there, sitting cross-legged on cushions, when Gabriel headed across to them.

"Is she still alive, your aunt?" Kim was asking, as he approached.

"No."

"You must miss her."

"I do, but we had that time, the two of us. Seven, eight weeks. I arrived thinking my life was over, and when I left, Alex was waiting with a bouquet in one hand and my future in the other."

"Evening, ladies."

Kim, chewing, gave Thea a look, then said to him, "Gabriel. Are you attached to us by an invisible string?"

"They've sent me over to get 'Abid's wives.' There's going to be music and stuff by the fire."

Kim waved her fork around the compound. "Isn't it rather quiet for high season?"

"There's been torrential rain in Muscat. Lots of tours didn't get out."

With a great dash of incongruity, one of the staff came from the kitchen carrying an almost fluorescent cake, with garish orange and pink icing, and placed it before one of the guests, who hooted with surprise, as her friends started singing "Happy Birthday."

"Oh, God," said Thea. "We're in Butlins."

Soon after, carrying coffee and halva, she and Kim joined the circle around the fire, where cake was being handed around on paper plates and a hunched Bedouin woman was offering embroidery for sale. A joint of dead tree was thrown on the flames, as a couple of drivers started singing and clapping, and another played the lute. Gabriel went to the 4x4 to get his own instrument, then sat some way behind Thea. When he started to play, she turned in surprise and for a moment watched his fingers moving along the tiny frets of his ukulele, while its unlikely notes found their place with the clapping and the lute and the rhythms of the desert.

But when Abid came out of the gloom and leaned over Kim's shoulder to speak to her, she and Thea immediately got up and went to the back of the enclosure, where other drivers and guides had gathered around a table.

Compelled to follow, Gabriel elbowed between Thea and Abid. "Was the music that bad?" he asked, taking a tumbler of whiskey from one of the guides.

"Jinn stories," Thea replied, nodding at Kim. "She's very taken with the notion."

Abid was explaining to Kim that Omar, one of the younger guides who was sitting beside her, had been talking about the good jinn who had helped with the family business but had also made him quarrelsome. Kim placed her recorder on the table.

"The jinniya brought him many new customers," Abid went on, "and also a temper. Bad temper."

The others baited and teased poor Omar, who laughed, demonstrating no sign of bad temper.

Over at the fire, guests were retreating in clumps to their tents, but around the gas light on the guides' table, the mood settled and the conversation flourished, plump with stories. Kim's eyes moved from speaker to speaker, soaking it all up.

Jamil, he of the excellent diction, began another oft-told story. "There was a man who had a big date plantation, and one night he was going to water the plantation, when he felt something jumping on his back. A jinniya. And this one, she was very attracted to strong men. He said: 'I hope you can hold on properly or you'll fall down.' When she wouldn't let go, he went to a date tree and rubbed against it. She screamed, 'Stop, stop!'

"But he said, 'I'm not going to stop unless you tell me what caused you to jump on my back.'

"She said, 'I'm in love with you. I want you. I'll do anything for you.'

"He told her, 'If you are like that, you know I'm married.'

"'Yes, I know.'

"'And you know I have kids.'

"'Yes.'

"'Okay,' he said, 'you show me your face,' because jinn," Jamil explained to Kim, "if they want something, they will show themselves as they are. And she did."

"They show themselves if they want something bad enough," she repeated, with a cool glance at Gabriel. "I see."

"That man," Jamil went on, "never had seen a beautiful woman like that ever in his life, so she started telling him, 'My father he brought six jinni for me, but I want to marry a human, a strong man, so I will take you to our world and introduce you to our father. Only problem is fear,' she said. 'If you have fear, you might not make it, but so far you are the bravest man I've ever seen.' So they agreed she would take him there, to see what would happen.

"Then he went home, slept with his wife, washed and all that, and came back to the plantation. When he's going there, to her world, all he feels is a lot of strange people coming close to him. He wonders, what the hell? But they're her brothers, and then he can see a huge light coming through, and it's her.

"She took him deep into the jinn world, where he met her father and it was agreed, so he married her. He have a place for her and he have his wife as well. These jinn, they give him huge wealth and he never had to water his plantation again—it was done for him every day—and they're having a fantastic life, but the problem usually comes when the husband dies. Recognition is a huge problem. But this time his human family, because they had seen great things, like wealth and no one getting sick, they recognized his jinn family and all stayed together in that place."

"Oh, good," said Kim. "I *do* like a happy ending."

Malik, a young driver, then urged Gabriel to tell everyone of his experience, a story Gabriel also knew well. Thea seemed entranced, so he delivered. "Malik," he began, his eyes on hers, "had a bad experience last year. Not long after his grandfather died, he became immobilized. He couldn't move from his bed, and at one point he couldn't even speak. His family tried everything—doctors, medication, but finally they called in a sorcerer, who said his grandfather had had a bad jinn, which had not been able to trouble *him*—"

"Because he was a strong person, his grandfather," Abid explained.

"—but it transferred itself to Malik, where it could do more damage, because he's young and impressionable. But the sorcerer told them what to do to get rid of the evil jinn and," he looked at Malik, "it worked, yeah?"

Malik nodded. "Much better."

"I don't get it," said Kim. "I thought jinn were beings in a parallel world?"

"They can be within as well as without," Gabriel explained. "Some people believe jinn can take over your body, fight over your soul, that kind of thing."

"Who usually wins?"

"Generally, the host will undergo an exorcism, as in Christianity."

"And you believe all this stuff?"

"It isn't for me to say."

"Honestly?" Kim eyeballed him. "You have no view?"

"It's part of my surroundings, and if you live any place long enough, you absorb it and it absorbs you. It's a question of respect. Anytime someone back home told me they'd seen a ghost or that some building was haunted, I respected that. Same here."

"Have you ever seen any jinn yourself?" she asked.

"Not as far as I know."

Abid chortled at his friends, slapping Gabriel across the shoulders.

"So who was she then, your lover?" Kim asked, across the table.

"Kim," said Thea. "That's private."

"It really isn't," he said to her. "Everyone has their own jinn story." He turned back to Kim. "In my view, she was flesh and blood."

"But why does everyone else say she was a jinn?"

"Your driver talks too much," he said, and made an affectionate dig at Abid in Arabic. "She knew how to get into my house and how to leave it unnoticed, that's all."

"Maybe she existed in a parallel universe," Kim said, with a glance at Thea.

"Ah, the dark-matter theory." He nodded. "Yes, jinn do have features in common with that theory."

"What *are* you two on about?" Thea asked.

"The multi-verse concept," Kim said, making space for a solitary South African, who had come to join them. "Your aunt knew about it. She was a woman ahead of her time, because now some scientists believe that ours might not be the only universe, so it isn't unique—therefore not a uni- but a multi-verse, so there could be another universe going on, just here, within a centimeter of us, but because we're restricted to so few dimensions, we can't see what might be there."

"Like jinn," said Abid. "You see? Science has proved it."

"But I have her shirt," Gabriel said, "and that is very much within *this* universe, whether it be multi, twinned or otherwise."

Kim's shoulders sagged. "Really?"

Abid shook his head at Gabriel. "She melted away from you. You told me this."

"What about the shared-consciousness concept?" Kim persisted. "You know, that we own our bodies and brains, but not our minds, which are part of a universal consciousness, and we can dip in and out of it, go anywhere. Maybe you were dipping into your own future."

Gabriel heard Thea groan. No doubt she would have liked her friend to be more subtle in her pursuit of him, but worse than that, Kim had also managed to exclude the drivers, to interrupt the flow of their stories, the catching up and sharing of news that was often their relaxation at the end of a long day's driving.

Somewhat off the point, but to the relief of most, the South African stepped into the lull. "You know Wilfred Thesiger?" he asked, in tight, rigid English.

"Ya, ya, of course," said Jamil. "He was a friend of Oman. In fact, one of the elders from my tribe saved his life when he was in the desert. Some young men wanted to kill Thesiger, but an old man of the tribe, he asked them what would they achieve? And the guys said, 'We will show that we are greater than the Englishman.'

"And the old man replied, 'No, if you kill him—one guy doing no harm—you will show yourselves to be smaller than the Englishman.'"

"But this is in the book!" said the South African, taking a well-worn paperback of *Arabian Sands* from his knapsack. "This very story is in here!"

Jamil shrugged, as if to say, Well, obviously.

Malik asked to see the book.

"Last year," Jamil said to Thea, "I took a TV crew from Brazil across the Empty Quarter, the same way Thesiger went, but even with GPS," he laughed, "we got lost!"

The drivers leaned over the book, discussing the various camels in the photographs, nodding and talking, until an argument broke out about which tribes had escorted Thesiger across the Empty Quarter. Voices were raised; eyes flashed.

"I've no idea what they're on about," Thea said to Gabriel, "but I could listen to this all night. You're so lucky to be able to speak Arabic."

He dipped his chin. "One of the unexpected gifts in my life."

Kim was still where they had left her. "What about human women falling for jinn men? It seems to be the other way around in all the stories."

"A jinn can make a woman fall in love with him," Jamil said wearily, "by taking the face of someone else she fell in love with, and he will adopt that character so that he can get her. He can't marry her, but if there is a child, this child will become powerful, because he will have a human body and jinn magic. He will be able to see in the dark, to make spells. . . ."

"This stuff is bending my mind." Kim made some notes.

The argument about Thesiger rumbled on.

Complaining of sand in her eye, Thea was the first to say goodnight and headed over to her tent alone.

When Gabriel put his head around the open flap, she was sitting at the small table, looking at her phone. "May I?"

"No. Yes."

He stepped in, took the seat opposite her. A gas light glowed between them on the table. She put down her phone. "No signal, which isn't surprising, I suppose, in the clefts of the Wahiba Sands." She looked past him.

Gabriel followed her gaze. Above the dark outline of dunes, the sky was lively.

"I'm out of range," she said.

"Good."

"The ukulele," her eyes came back to him, "that was unexpected, but—lovely."

"Thanks. I was musical once."

"Clearly you still are."

"No. No, I'm a lost musician—a fiddler, a tinkler—whereas once I was tagged as a future concert pianist."

"You're a pianist?"

"Was. Almost."

"Why 'almost'?"

"I made way for my brother."

"There wasn't room for two pianists in one family?"

"Apparently not."

"Ooh," she said. "Bitter."

"Not at all. He was an introspective—"

"Genius?"

He held her eye, across the flickering light. "No," he said. "*I* was the unfulfilled genius. Max was better than that. A worker bee. The kind of man who made things happen for himself, while I made sure nothing much happened for me."

"Why?"

Gabriel shrugged. "Laziness was my default position."

"Again, why?"

So familiar, this questioning. Her simple, direct way of speaking. Hearing it again shook him, but he cleared his throat, regained his composure. He couldn't allow her to wound him again, and yet with these questions she had already undressed him, so that a rush of childhood words came out in a seamless flow of peevishness. "Oh, no doubt I was subliminally trying to get at my parents," he retorted. "In the absence of ineptitude, laziness was my only weapon. They used to preen, you see, get off on my success. My mother in particular. Whenever I won some bloody competition or feis ceoil—she'd be there, wearing that smug, repugnant smile. . . . Don't get me wrong, they're okay parents, but they paraded me like a performing rooster and I've always hated parades." There was no transparency in her white shirt, or in her face; she sat, like an angel at the table, still and glowing. "It was so transparent," he went on, because she hadn't said anything and because he hadn't spoken of this for a long time. "Whenever anyone crossed our threshold, I was made to play, so everyone would know what a clever, clever boy my parents had produced. 'It's a natural instinct,' my mother would say, with her faux-humility. 'Music is his first language!'"

"Parents will always be proud of their kids," Thea said. "My son is studying music—well, he makes sounds, experimental stuff. I don't understand it, but I'm proud of him."

"I very much doubt you're a pushy, overbearing mother."

"God, I hope not. I can't bear those types, and I've met plenty of them!"

"You'll know my mother, then. No tact. No grace." Gabriel looked into the dark corner of the tent, toward her bed. "I was a sensitive kid. I wanted only to play piano, you know, but other kids hated me because I won stuff. I had one friend, Sam, who had cystic fibrosis, and one day we met his mother in town and Mam started on at her about how many hours' practice I had to do, and how tough it was, and how a gift like mine was such a responsibility for the whole family. . . . Gut-shrivelling stuff. The only gift Sam's mum could see in me was health. Later, I tried to point this out to my mother. 'Yes, yes,' she said. 'I know it's hard for him, but you have *real talent*!'"

Thea chuckled at his impersonation, a light screech in the posh tones of Cork's well-to-do. "You're right," she said. "I *do* know this woman—just from her vowels!"

"Maybe I'm too harsh. I mean, the rewards had been great. I loved the applause, the regard of professors and judges, and I liked the way professionals looked at me as if I was a person of consequence, but my life was one long competition and it was like being pressed into a very small tube."

"Until?"

He sighed. "Until one day I realized I'd become like a patient, as much bound to the piano as Sam often was to a hospital bed. So I stopped working. I still sailed through grade eight and into college, but beyond that, I let it go."

"I'm beginning to feel for your mother."

"It's odd, isn't it, how one family gets stuck with a debilitating illness and another with a prodigy? Not," he added quickly, "that I was any kind of prodigy."

"How did your parents take it, when you pulled back?"

"They were devastated, but at least then they started paying attention to Max, whom they'd ignored, more or less, since I'd shown promise—aged about three—and Max had got relegated to 'He plays quite well, too.'"

"Did he begrudge you?"

Gabriel blinked. "It wouldn't have occurred to him."

"And you weren't bitter when the attention turned to him?"

"Bitterness isn't really my thing."

"What is your thing, Jibril?" she asked, with a flicker of a smile that hit him in the groin. "Apart from scaring women with your scary past?"

"Don't you mean women *from* my past?"

"Kim is intrigued."

He grimaced. "Yeah, I picked up on that."

"Don't let her bully you. She's a journalist."

"Don't worry. Multi-verses don't really do it for me. Prudence was as real as you are."

"So how come no one else ever set eyes on her?"

"Because . . ." Gabriel stalled. How to explain it rationally when even he struggled to understand it, especially now, when the very woman whom he had only ever seen within the white-washed walls of his home, and usually between hand-washed sheets, sat with him now asking questions about their affair as if it had never happened? How should he tell her about herself? He had to get into the right gear. He had to play it her way, for now, which meant finding the words and the mindset to disassociate this woman, Thea, from everything he knew of her. He sucked in his breath, and set his eyes on hers to let her know that if she so much as flinched he would see it. "There was something else," he said, "about her."

"Go on."

"We were only ever together in one place—my house. She wouldn't shift from there, though she was pale and wan and craved light. It was as if she had her ear on a wormhole to somewhere else. The jinn world, some would say. And the more I insisted we went out, the less I saw of her. But things were getting pretty weird by then."

"Only by then?" Thea teased.

He dipped his head, conceding her point. "There was other stuff. Noises, in the house."

"Ooh, spooky!" But the jokiness was contrived. He was reeling her in.

"Not spooky, no. Mundane. Irish. Like a radio in the background, and purring—I sometimes heard a cat purring, though there was no cat, and no radio, and no woman in the house who wore stockings."

"Stockings?"

"Yeah, I used to hear that sound—nylons rubbing against each other. That was fairly scary, all right."

The muscles beneath her eyes tightened. She leaned forward to turn up the lamp. "Why did Abid say she *melted* away?"

"Ah, yes," he said, "the punch line—how an *invisible* woman *disappeared*." He spread his fingers across his thighs. "I lost patience one night and I thought . . . I mean, I was fairly sure I picked her up to carry her out of the house, because she was there, but then she wasn't there and I wasn't holding anything, or anyone, and it was as if she had dribbled away to nothing." He raised his hands in a cavalier manner. "Easily explained, in retrospect. I wasn't eating properly at the time and was dehydrated so, obviously, I was hallucinating. She had already left me."

The low murmur of conversation at the top end of the camp lifted into a gush of laughter, then dropped again to near silence.

"How long had it lasted, the affair?"

"Not long. A couple of months, but it has an extended tail—like a comet, gritty and fiery," he turned his head toward the flap, "and I haven't been able to escape the debris. Twenty-six years on, I'm still dust in her wake."

"You must have tried to find her?"

He shrugged. "She wasn't to be found. There wasn't a hint of her anywhere in Muscat. But it comes back at me," he said, dropping the offhand tone, "like a kind of torment. When I least expect it, I'll suddenly feel her in my arms, writhing and thrashing."

Thea ran her hand around the back of her neck. "Sounds very jinn-like to me."

"Sometimes I think," his voice was so low that he wondered if she could hear him, "not that she was a jinn, but that the jinn took her from me. Some kind of punishment."

"But you don't believe in jinn."

"No. No, I don't, but skepticism sometimes comes a cropper on this one."

"And why would they punish you, anyway?"

He thought about kissing her. Instead he said, "One day she'll slip into view, like someone coming in the back door, as she did before."

"Why do you think that?" she asked, with unexpected sharpness. "The past doesn't owe us any favors, you know. We all try to go back. We think we can walk into it, like into a room, and find everything the way we left it, but it isn't there, any of it."

Gabriel leaned forward, then changed his projection and made it part of his upward propulsion as he got to his feet. She wasn't ready yet. "To each our own imaginings," he said, bending over to peck her cheek. "Night."

Kim came in as he went out. He walked around the brick bathroom and came again to the back of the tent.

"Entertaining strange men now, are we?" Kim asked.

"He's certainly strange. Trying to get a handle on him is like trying to make a sculpture—you chip away only to find more stone."

Gabriel heard her move, stand up maybe.

"But I know Gabriel, Kim. He is right about that."

Early the next day, Gabriel was talking to the cook by the door of the brick kitchen when he saw Thea come out of her tent, pulling on a sweater, and head toward the enclosure in jeans and bare feet.

"At last," he said, as she came over. "Sit down. I'll get tea."

She did as she was told. Like a couple, they were—easy together in the ragged morning.

"Sleep well?" he asked, bringing two glasses of tea to the low table.

"A few hours of light oblivion. Oblivion lite, I call it. I haven't had a good night since I arrived. You guys talking late in your tent didn't help."

"Sorry."

"And, come dawn, I was freezing." She sipped the tea, turned her engagement ring around her finger, like Annie did, and looked across the dunes. "You were right about not seeing much desert. It's beautiful here, but these aren't the mountainous dunes I'd hoped for."

"They're farther south."

"I could lie, I suppose. Tell the boys I climbed dunes as high as the Twelve Pins, and pretend my camera wasn't working."

"Two sons, you said? What age?"

Her face softened. "Nineteen and fifteen."

"And the very thought of them makes you smile," he added.

"You should try it. It'd give you something to smile about."

"I have things to smile about."

"It happens to us all, you know," she said, fiddling now with the top button of her shirt, "the big love affair we never want to get over, but the fact is we have to get on, grow up, have families."

"Says who?"

"Our DNA."

"We can't all live the same life. Some of us have to buck the trend. Besides, why do parents always assume that people who don't have kids are missing out?"

"I don't know, now you ask."

He crossed his arms on the edge of the table. "So who was he, the big love affair *you* don't want to get over?"

She looked away, as if, beyond the uneven, clotted cream sand, she saw that other man. Gabriel could almost see his reflection in her eyes. "Ah, yes," he said, "the Indian."

Her eyes swung back. "What?"

"You told me about him."

Thea pushed back from the table. Other people were emerging from the tents and coming toward breakfast. "I never told you any such thing."

"Not now. Last time."

"Have you . . . have you been eavesdropping?"

"No." He shook his head firmly. "No, Thea. You told me about Sachiv."

Abid was hovering on his phone, kicking the sand with his sandals. Word had come from Muscat: the rains had been so heavy, there was concern about flash floods. "There are twenty wadis between here and Nizwa," Gabriel heard him say to Kim. "Any of them could flood when the rain comes from the mountains. We must leave quickly."

Gabriel was delivering the same message to his charges and, not long afterward, in great spits of sand, several 4x4s took off. Now he had a proper excuse to speed, and he took his ladies flying across high dunes on the way back to the sandy superhighway, the vehicle at times perched as if about to somersault, until they reached the broad, track-marked valley that led out of the sands. The pale dunes poured into the dull brown of the valley floor, and as they came past a Bedouin encampment, a herd of children materialized from behind the fences and ran toward them. Betty insisted he stop, and when the children gathered around the window, she handed out cookies. A little girl in a long red dress emerged from the nearest reed hut—no more than three—and came waddling over, as many fingers shoved into her mouth as could fit, and reached up to his window with her other hand. Her eyes were as big as planets. Gabriel gave her a cookie. Thea was right about DNA. He longed to have children, to have a daughter like this.

The drive to Nizwa proved floodless, in spite of purple clouds sitting over the mountains, and they arrived in the old fort town by noon. After checking the women into their hotel rooms, Gabriel went in search of Thea and found her sitting on a lounger in the garden, watching Kim doing laps in the kidney-shaped pool.

"Hello," he said, sitting on the end of the adjacent lounger. "What you up to?"

Thea pushed her hair behind her ear, but didn't look at him. Through her shirt, he could see the outline of bra, the slight bump of nipple. "Not much. Abid says it wouldn't be safe now to go into the mountains."

Gabiel's phone rang. He picked up. "Annie, hi. Can I call you back in ten?"

"No, I'm heading out in a bit," she said, "but it's fine. Just ringing for a chat."

"Everything okay?"

"Yeah, yeah. You?"

He looked across at Thea, caught her eye. "Oh, I'm fine, all right. You'll never believe who I ran into the other day."

"Who?"

"I'll tell you later. Kids all good?"

"Your *adult* nieces and nephew are very well, thank you. Stop calling them kids. They hate it, and so do I."

He chuckled. "Right. Bye, talk soon." He put his phone in his shirt pocket, saying, "Abid's right. The wadis will be unpredictable."

"Which means we'll miss out on Wadi Bani Awf." She looked toward the mountains. "Is it really so spectacular?"

"Do you want me to lie?"

"Yes."

He shrugged. "Seen one wadi, seen 'em all."

"And the truth?"

"Mind-blowing."

"Shit."

"What will you do instead?"

"We had thought Bahla maybe."

"Ah. Jinn-town."

"Apparently. That's why Kim wants to go, but Abid isn't keen. Says his wife wouldn't have him back in the house if he went there."

"People worry about the evil eye," Gabriel explained. "Look, my lot have opted to rest up. They're done in. So I could take you over to Bahla later, if you'd like."

"Kim would like that very much."

"What exactly happens there?" Kim asked, when they were heading out of Nizwa that afternoon. "I mean, why is it called the City of Jinn?"

"It's a tradition," Gabriel said. "If you're lumbered with an evil jinn, Bahla's the place to get rid of it. Lots of wise men and exorcists used to live there and some still do, but not a lot of people pay much attention to that stuff these days. The drivers and guides love to entertain, as you'll have noticed, but the Omani population is highly educated and youngsters are more interested in Facebook than magic, which in some ways is a pity. The wealth of lore that Oman enjoys, the mix of Arab and African myth, is being left behind."

"Same as everywhere else," said Thea.

"All the more reason for me to write about it," said Kim.

He glanced at Thea. "They took me there, you know."

"Who did?"

"Family. When my sister was living here, people got to her, told her to have me exorcized."

Kim leaned forward, her head coming between the seats. "Somebody performed an exorcism on you? To get rid of what's-her-name?"

He shook his head. "It was after Prudence left. Annie thought I could be cured of missing her. As if sadness itself is a bad jinn."

"It surely is," Thea said quietly.

"The way I understand it," Kim said, "almost anything can be put down to jinn—alcoholism, depression, illnesses, bad temper—but a broken heart?"

He glanced in the side mirror. "My broken heart ran deep. I wouldn't go out. Saw no one. Did nothing. I was on the point of vaporizing."

Kim's Dictaphone slid between the seats. "So what happens at these ceremonies?"

"All the usual stuff. Drumming, dancing, unguents and ruqya, chanting, and the sorcerer does his thing, invoking certain suras of the Quran. As in Catholicism, there are two kinds of exorcism. In the official sort, condoned by Islam, there's no messing—they recite *Surat al-Jinn* to banish the evil spirit." He recited what he knew of it, mostly because Thea had already confessed a susceptibility to the bewitchery of Arabic. "Then there's the off-the-record approach, where anything can happen."

"Wasn't it scary?"

"I was scared I'd catch a bad jinn, not be cured of the one I didn't have." He swung his eyes to Thea. "Whatever you believe, it *is* powerful. I've been to a few and there's an atmosphere, for sure. You feel relaxed, lifted. Maybe it's the force of belief, or those pounding rhythms, but you sense a strong sense of something beyond yourself."

Kim leaned toward Thea. "Sounds like your aunt's place."

"What's with your aunt's place?"

"My place. It's mine now."

"It has jinn?"

"Something like that."

Kim's head turned to Gabriel. "Abid said that subjects writhe and gag as the jinn leaves them. Did you?"

"No. I was a very meek subject. Just wanted it over with."

"But have you seen that happen?" Kim persisted. "People struggling and grunting?"

"Often. I've even held a guy down. Their strength can be overwhelming—that much is certainly true."

"So how do you explain it, rationally?"

"I can't. I don't try to."

Bahla, until then a huddle of greenery in the distance, was stretching out to them. An impressive modern mosque, its twin minarets magnificent against the fading blue sky, staked its claim on the outskirts of the town.

"If you're so sure it's all hokum," Thea said, "why did you subject yourself to it?"

"For my sister. She was very caught up in it, for her own reasons. But the truth is, we were both masking something else. We were . . ." he looked in the mirror, pulled out to give room to a man on a donkey ". . . crevés. You know, shattered. We'd had a family tragedy. Double tragedy, you could say, and my crash into self-pity was too much for Annie, so if getting myself exorcized would make her feel better, it was the least I could do."

"Did it help?" Kim asked.

"It helped Annie get pregnant."

"Really?" Thea turned.

"She came to Bahla when she was having trouble conceiving and, voilà, she conceived soon afterwards. The woman told her bad stuff had been preventing her from becoming pregnant. They called it exorcism," he said, with a shrug. "I call it the placebo effect. She believed it would make her feel better, so she did feel better, and that helped her relax. Job done."

"That's rather dismissive," said Kim, "not to say arrogant."

"That's what she said."

"But don't you . . ."

"What?" He glanced at Kim in the mirror.

"Well, it happened to *you*. Stories about the supernatural are always about the friend of a friend of a friend, but you were at the center of it. And you can't explain what happened to you, so you have very little with which to back up your cynicism."

"Except that I've been proved right," he said, jerking his thumb toward Thea. "That's no jinniya."

"That is someone who has never set foot in Oman before," said Kim, "and who, when you were romancing your invisible woman, was flat on her back in the West of Ireland recovering from hepatitis."

Gabriel forced himself to blink. Hepatitis. The sunlit room, her wafting presence. Weak, watery . . . *ill*. It pulled on him. Apples and water. One step, one dip in concentration, and he would be there again with the limpid Prudence. So vague. So thirsty. Absolutely no energy. . . . *Of course*.

The convalescence she had spoken of was not, as he had supposed, in reference merely to her broken heart, but more than that. . . .

Back. Back to the road. He adopted an impassive mien. "Hepatitis, eh? No wonder. You didn't look at all well. I kept telling you so."

"Yeah, well," she said flatly, "being in two places at the one time plays hell with your complexion."

They smiled at one another. Something had changed. No longer angered by his assertions of intimacies past, she now made fun of them. She had taken the power back—he would *not* unsettle her—and was consequently warmer toward him; affectionate almost.

He was getting there. By holding this course, he *would* get to where he intended to be.

"So Bahla worked for your sister, but did it work for *you*?"

Oh, God, he thought, glancing at Kim in the mirror. Is she still here? "They still call me the most miserable man in Oman. Reach your own conclusions."

"You didn't stop missing her, even a little bit?"

"I stopped missing her four days ago."

"The city of sorcerers flickers in the evening light," Kim told her Dictaphone. "A mud-brick wall snakes around the date palms, holding in bits of the town, which has nonetheless spewed out, through gaps, into pockets of homes and yards. Behind it, a soccer match, boys in red and white, and the solitary figure of a man, sitting on the wall, watching. Jebel Akhdar rises on the right, glowing in the sunny areas, but dark on those slopes already in night shade." She clicked it off. "Why they call it the green mountain is anyone's guess. It looks black to me."

"Black gold," said Thea. "Like a pint of Guinness."

"Or the wrapping on an expensive bar of chocolate."

"Eighty-five percent cocoa." Thea smiled over her shoulder.

"Abid told us we mustn't make eye contact with anyone," said Kim, "in case we get the evil eye."

"Look sideways, they say of Bahla," Gabriel agreed, "or you could pick up bad karma in a blink."

"I've never been to a place and not looked at the people," said Thea.

"Pretty town, though, isn't it?" said Kim. "The ramparts are impressive."

"We'll head up to a vantage-point now," said Gabriel, "where you can get a good view of them. The city walls were designed by a woman and once extended for seven kilometers, making Bahla one of the finest walled towns in the world in its day, but I'm afraid the fort is closed for renovations."

"Spot the tour guide," Kim said drily, again lifting the Dictaphone. "The light is perfect—evening, gentle, and Bahloul Mountain glows at its touch. The date palms give Bahla a juicy look, even though it is surrounded by bleak, parched hills, but modernity and normalcy have cast their own features across the town. Like a modern extension on an old house, the refurbished section of the fort, with its perfect turrets, seems to grow out of the yet-to-be-treated ancient wall. Scaffolding conceals much of the edifice but, behind it, the old wall runs up one side of a hill, then down another slope and off into the distance, like a convict taking flight."

After the photo op, Gabriel took them down to the potteries—Bahla's other dying industry—and showed them hive-shaped mud huts, full of clay pots, where pottery was made and stored. Kim took the requisite photographs, but he knew she was looking out for something a camera would never capture, and she soon expressed disappointment at finding no detectable eeriness, no sense of the other. Even the suq was closed. "I'm not much impressed with your capital of spooks," she said. "It's a bit difficult to be creeped out when the sorcerers are keeping such low profiles."

"Don't be fooled." Gabriel walked backward in front of them. "If you wanted to buy a spell and ruin a life, you'd only have to speak too loudly and someone would appear and lead you down one of these alleys."

"D'ya have to haggle?" Kim smiled.

"Of course."

"Would they rid me of *my* unwelcome jinn?" Thea asked him.

"What's that?"

"You."

He grinned. She was flirting now. "You'll never be rid of me," he said.

Back at the hotel, Thea hesitated to get out of the car after Kim had hurtled inside, desperate for the restroom. "I'm sorry to hear about your family," she said.

He jangled the keys, leaning his back against the car door. "Hmm?"

"You mentioned a tragedy."

"Oh."

"What happened?"

"My brother," he said.

The parking lot was quiet and dark. He had drawn up in front of a hedge.

"My talented, hard-working brother was . . ." He braced himself. As in an exorcism, he was about to regurgitate the nastiest of all nasties. "My brother was locked inside a grand piano on his stag night. He nearly died."

Thea's eyes flickered.

"Yes," he replied, "you *can* fit a man inside a piano. A small man and a concert grand, anyway. When Max woke from a drunken stupor and found himself in a coffin made by Steinway, his heart gave out. Turned out he didn't have a very good one. Heart, I mean. He never played another chord and tried to take his own life a few months later."

"My God."

He touched the keys again. They tinkled.

"I'm so sorry."

"Me too."

"And the other? You mentioned another—"

"The other tragedy, for my family, was that I was the one who put him in there."

IV
Out of Range

LOBBY. GARDENS. OUTDOOR PASSAGE. ROOM. MINIBAR.

Thea leaned into the fridge, grabbed a bottle of beer; opened it. There was no sign of Kim. She sat back against her pillows, lifting the bottle to drink. The room was too quiet.

I want to make sex with you.

She jumped up, went to the door to chain-lock it, and turned on the television. Voices, faces. CNN offered good news and bad: a crashed plane with no dead; Gaza strangled; Tom Cruise embarrassed—a Scientology interview leaked, making him seem ever more alien. She paced the narrow space between the beds, one eye on Tom Cruise. Scientologists are the only ones who can really help, he was saying, when they come across a car crash.

We are all mad, Thea thought.

And she thought: Drunken boys, lads. A night out. A prank gone wrong. But from what dark place had come such a plan? She imagined him—this man, Max—imagined him waking, confused, trapped. Boxed in. Blacked-out.

The lid of a grand piano is a heavy thing.

A prank? They weren't schoolboys. They were drunk. To their addled brains, it must have seemed . . . *funny*. A laugh. Harmless, stag-night raucousness. *How*?

The door slammed against its chain. "Thea?"

She hurried over to let Kim in.

"Why the chain?" she asked, coming in with two bottles of water.

Thea went back to sit on her bed, and drank.

"Now you really *do* look like you've picked up a jinn. Please tell me you haven't."

"I wish I could."

"Gabriel, huh?"

"Yup." Thea longed to say more. If it had not yet been spoken about, this fraternal obscenity, it should be.

"Don't beat up on yourself, sweetie. So your eyes have wandered a little. It happens. Doesn't mean you're going to act on it. And even if you did—heck, a shot of infidelity can do the world for a marriage."

"Yeah, like wrecking it."

"Touché."

"I have no intention of being unfaithful—at least not with him."

"Gabriel would be very sorry to hear that." Kim twisted around a little comically. "Is there someone else?"

Thea wobbled her head, slugged back some beer. "Had the postcards come from a delicious Indian we once knew, who knows what might have happened?"

"But I turned up instead. Man, I'm disappointing."

"Not at all. Not one bit."

"Hey, maybe I even saved your marriage."

"It doesn't need saving."

"Good, because we're having dinner with Gabriel tonight."

"*What?*"

"I just ran into him and asked him to join us."

"Kim, no! We can't have dinner with him!"

"Why not?"

Thea pulled her knees closer to her chest. "We shouldn't get involved. This jinn stuff. It's creeping up on us. That old man you saw in the gully, and all these damn stories, we're getting pulled in. Because of Gabriel. He's—"

"Deluded, yes. Haunted, certainly. But you can always see the core of a person in their eyes, Thea, and he has kind eyes."

"I feel exposed around him."

"Well, of course you do, honey. He undresses you every time he looks at you. And you pretty much do the same thing."

"Well. Just because I'm married doesn't mean I can't window-shop."

"Trouble with window-shopping is, it's real easy to buy." Kim puffed up her pillows. "And therein lies the demise of my marriages."

"At least you get to have affairs and a great job and travel all over the place."

Kim looked down at her, hands on her hips. "You make two divorces sound like fun. It wasn't. And no kids either."

"I know—and don't worry, I'm not going to cheat." Thea looked up at her. "Alex is the best. Honestly. And it's lovely, where we are. We've drifted into a mellow life. Wishy-washy warm. Companionable. I value it, I really do . . ."

"Here it comes."

Thea threw up her hands. "It just seems to me that contentment is another word for complacency, and complacent another word for lazy! I'd hate to be lazy in the way I live my life, but I suspect I have been. Lovely kids, adoring husband, comfortable middle-class home and convenient part-time job that pays for our holidays, but allows enough time for my domestic chores. This is my little life, Kim. It's not what I expected."

Kim turned off the television and sighed. "It's true what they say. Women go quietly mad in marriage."

"While children thrive on it, which is why women stay. But we're not birds! We're not naturally monogamous."

"Look, if it's any consolation, I *do* get it. I mean, an attractive guy comes on with this stuff about you being the invisible woman he's been in love with for a quarter of a century, like he's got a screw loose, and makes no apology for it—it's pretty full-on."

"Which is why we're *not* having dinner with him."

Kim looked at her. "He didn't try something, did he, in the car?"

"No."

"So are you going to tell me what has you so rattled?"

Thea got up, started to pace. Gabriel had said, as she got out of the car, "I have never spoken those words, or any variation of them, since the day I set foot in this country, so I would ask that you never repeat them." Fine, but she owed him no such indulgence. He had taken a chance on the discretion of a stranger. How true, she thought, that we can know nothing of strangers. She paced about. "Their family tragedy. He told me about it. I wish he hadn't."

Kim's eyes followed her.

"Turns out his brother nearly died, because . . . because your Gabriel with the kind eyes . . ."

"Go on."

"Put him inside a grand piano."

Kim sniggered. "He what?"

"Funny, isn't it? Gabriel obviously thought so. A great stag-night stunt. Quite a lark, really, but for the fact that when his brother came round, he thought he'd been buried alive and had a heart attack. He's never been right since."

Kim reached for the bed and sat down.

"I don't know how long he was in it, or how he got out or what the hell Gabriel and his mates thought they were doing. All I know is, I feel sick."

"My Lord."

"The cruelty. You wouldn't do it to a dog. I mean—the dark, the cold, the weird moaning of the strings you're lying on, then trying to move and finding . . ." Thea covered her face and sank onto the end of her bed. "*Awful!*"

Her arms taut, hands on her knees, Kim frowned at the carpet. "That's why he came to Oman."

"And why he's never left. He's stuck here, in his own remorse. Can't face the shell of a brother he left behind."

"Yes." Kim nodded. "It's all over him. I can see it now. Shame. Self-loathing."

Thea leaned over her knees.

"That apparition was his bad conscience."

"A bad conscience would never have left him," said Thca, sitting up.

"But she hasn't, has she?"

"No. She's bloody everywhere. Even in this room. I wish we could shake her off."

For several moments Kim didn't seem to move. Then she said tentatively, "Makes you wonder, doesn't it? About the sweeper in Baghdad?"

"The one who said I had a shadow?"

"I think she called it a jinni."

"I call it hepatitis. She must have seen the yellow in my eyes before anyone else did, and thought I was some kind of devil."

"I guess."

Thea looked over. "Are you suggesting that I've been carrying around bad karma since then?"

"No, no, of course not. It's just a little odd, is all."

"If I picked up a Baghdadi jinn, it's been very good to me. I've had a charmed life since I last saw you. That dose of hepatitis gave me everything I have."

"What about that stuff in your aunt's house? Being there but not being there. That feeling of heat . . ."

"Kim, stop! God, you are so suggestible!"

"Just sayin'." Kim raised her hands. "Did you know that three-quarters of Americans believe in angels?"

"Does that include you?"

"Not usually."

"Look. Enough. Let's avoid all spooks and eat here in the room."

"I can't. I have to work—check out the suq, eateries—and besides," Kim swung from one bed to the other, "we can't give up on Gabriel now, right when we're getting to the heart of this thing."

"He said he's never spoken about it before. There's no chance he'll speak to you."

"No, but I *have* to get this story out of him!"

"But it's sordid! He buries his brother in a piano, runs away to Arabia, and starts having sex with an invisible woman!"

"Oh, wow—that's the blurb right there. I can see it on the back of my book."

"Kim. Get a grip."

"But it's fantastic. You could—"

"You *cannot* go writing about this."

"Why not? I'm an investigative journalist."

"You write travel articles!"

"Not for much longer." Kim got up, thinking, thinking.

"It's Gabriel's story to tell. Not yours."

"That's exactly what I intend to do—let him tell his story. Over dinner. He'll say anything to you, with a bit of prompting. I'll be a mildly interested party, tuning in."

"Taking notes, you mean."

"Uh-huh."

Thea shook her head. "You want me to set him up?"

"You were cursing him a minute ago. Now you're protecting him."

Thea's phone beeped. She opened the text from Alex: *All home n having dinner in front of telly. Boys good. Me too. How you? V cold here, so enjoy!* Thea stared at his words. The humdrum of marriage, the predictability, the rituals and routines were dull, dull, dull, perhaps, but also comforting, enhancing; thrilling in their intimacy. And yet, when an unknown person, an undeniably odd person, had crossed her path, she had allowed herself to be sucked in and titillated.

When she looked up again, Kim had taken out her laptop and was hammering away, her fingers like spiders scurrying across the keys. Spiders on a mission.

They wandered, with Abid and Gabriel, through the neat, modern suq of Nizwa, among rust-colored arcades where, in brightly lit shops, they browsed through jewelry and pistols, camel sticks and incense burners. Thea strayed from the others. By remaining aloof, she was punishing Gabriel, unfairly perhaps, but he could hardly have expected sympathy. In one shop, she mindlessly tried on an old ring, so the shopkeeper started bringing out ring after silver ring and placing them on the glass counter. Many were grubby, misshapen; she tried them all.

Gabriel's arm came over her shoulder, offering a ring with a flat, square top. "Found it in a box at the back."

She loved it, wanted it.

"Let me get it for you."

"Absolutely not." She parted with her cash as a warning to him.

"Quite right. Et dona ferentes. Beware Greeks bearing gifts."

"You aren't Greek."

Elsewhere, he pulled out a musket with silver inlay and a long, thin barrel. "And this for your husband, perhaps?"

"Thank you, but he won't ever need such a thing."

They ate somewhere. A spartan place with chicken on the menu and soccer on the television. Kim sat opposite Gabriel, her eyes ablaze. Outwardly, her curiosity seemed no more intrusive than when she had engaged him in banter about the paranormal, but the questions were more incisive, more adroit. She was wasted in travel, Thea thought, and Kim clearly did too.

"So after all this time," she asked him, "you really remain immune to the common folklore?"

Gabriel slid his fingers down his upright fork, flipped it around and did the same again, and again. He never stopped moving, fidgeting. If his hands were still, his knees jigged. "I grew up in Ireland," he said, "and remained immune to our common folklore."

"But in Ireland you never had the kind of experience you've had here."

"Who says?"

"I . . . well," said Kim, "I'm assuming."

"Assumption is dangerous."

Thea stared into the menu. Chicken, chicken. With rice. With roast potatoes. With couscous. On a kebab. In soup. With stuffing.

"I suppose it has already occurred to you that your lover was neither jinniya nor real," Kim went on, "but some illusory creation of your own making?"

"Well," Gabriel rested his elbows on the table, "there's fantasy, and then there's the real thing, if you get my drift."

"I'm not sure that I do."

"Oh, I am."

"Perhaps she was some manifestation of your inner demons?"

The waiter came. They ordered.

"You must have some?" Kim persisted.

"Demons?" Gabriel handed the menus to the waiter. "Absolutely. But my demons are ugly devils, and she was—*is*—very beautiful."

He was enjoying this, Thea realized. Toying with Kim in order to flirt with *her*.

Kim was not the same person Thea had known in Iraq. Neither was she anyone else. It was difficult to transpose her from the eighties in Baghdad to Oman in the twenty-first century, because then they had been young and game, starting out. Now they were slightly worn down and strangers of sorts, but it was lovely to be with Kim again and to like her still. This trip, it transpired, was a journey neither forward nor back. In the moment, they were friends again, and loyal.

On the overhead television some soccer player with dreadlocks scored a goal and leaped about in self-congratulation. "Abid," Thea said, without any warning to herself, "in all your years in tourism, have you ever come across a hotel manager called Sachiv Nair? We knew him in Baghdad, but he grew up in Oman, and he might have come—"

"I knew him," said Gabriel.

Kim's eyes shot to Thea and back to Gabriel.

"You remember him, Abid," he went on. "Worked with the Taj group."

Chewing, with a scrap of bread in hand, Abid raised his eyebrows.

"Is he still here?" Kim's voice was scratchy.

It was as well she interceded because Thea couldn't breathe. It was as if she had imbibed some curious potion and it was rising in her, shading her from the neck up.

Gabriel ripped bread. "Mauritius, last I heard. But that was a few years ago."

"Ah, yeah," said Abid. "Tall guy."

"He set up a hotel in Musandam Province," said Gabriel. "Got married when he was based there."

Oh, isn't he just having a blast of an evening? Thea thought. Kim probing, and now this, for her, a stinging whip of words.

Kim ran her hand around the back of her neck. "He left his first wife?"

Gabriel shook his head. "He was a widower when I first knew him."

Tiredness, melting into the inexplicable, made for a moulded confusion behind Thea's sand-sore eyes. Sleep had not dislodged the dusty particles scraping the lids because there had been no sleep. She had tossed about, as had become the norm, her head buzzing. Sachiv—a widower! His children had lost their mother and the chess champion had probably never reached her potential. So sad, for all of them.

In spite of what she had said so adamantly to Gabriel in the tent, the past was not an empty room. Not at all. Kim's cards, when they had started arriving in the autumn, had thrown her into a reflective, restless mood. Whenever she'd managed to catch a moment's solitude, she had taken to sitting on the bench they had placed between two apple trees on a small hill beside the house, and gazed across the sloping lawn to the wooded valley below. A slow whirring had started up in the back catalogues of her mind, a slipstream of memory pulling her all the way back to Baghdad. And they say you can't go back, she thought, that time is linear, moving only in one direction, but a couple of mysterious cards written in a script that might have been his, and she was as good as there. Time wasn't linear at all.

One by one the postcards had got their toes across the threshold until she went rooting in the cubbyhole, that unexplored hinterland at the back of the house where they dumped everything and found nothing. There were the boxes of baby clothes, the travel cot and a set of drawers, stacked one on top of another, no longer in their chest; there were the rugs and fabrics Alex had bought in Turkey, rolled up and dusty, their swirls of Eastern glory stashed away lest their bright colors brought memories of more exotic times (Alex, after all, had traveled more than Thea); and there too were the boxes of old photos, the ones that had never earned an album, including, in a red Kodak envelope, the few she had taken in Iraq. Few, because she had thought at the time that Iraq lay mostly ahead, and only one image of Sachiv, in which he stood with Kim, in that chilly wind, with Lake Razzaza shimmering behind them.

Sometimes Alex interrupted her musings, looking over her shoulder—"Is that al-Ukhaidir?"—and one day he came in from the garden to present her with a four-breasted berry, fuchsia pink. "A spindleberry from our tree. Isn't it beautiful?" The spindleberry had four bulbs, like their family, and a velvety coat. Holding it between her fingertips, Thea had squeezed to see what would happen, but it was hard, tough, not easily pulped. Still, the temptation to press remained. To squeeze and see what happened.

She had brought that spindleberry to Oman, kept it in the back pocket of her suitcase. This was their first holiday apart, although she and Alex had started out with ambitions of independence, vowing to follow their own interests and take separate trips so that they wouldn't end up as one of those couples who were plastered together like two bricks in a wall and both wearing the same jumpers. They had never worn the same jumpers, but neither had they done much apart because, simply, they enjoyed one another's company. In urging her to go to Muscat, to see who turned up—if only to add a bit of splash to their lives (even their close friends had been delighted with this postal intrigue)—Alex had admitted to his own restlessness. Their children, like all children, had used up much of their parents' energy and intellect, and he wanted to adjust the balance. It had been too long since he had been sailing with his pals. He missed it, and other things too, and now that the boys were more independent, he suggested they should make an effort not to vegetate their middle years away in front of the television.

They watched far too much television.

Recently, he had taken to falling asleep with his hand on her hip. It was lovely, loving, but she asked him to stop. "It's like you're laying claim to me."

"You fall asleep with your toes in my groin."

"Only when my feet are cold. I'm using you, not owning you."

Maybe that was why she couldn't sleep. She was missing the feel of Alex's thighs on the soles of her feet. Frustrated, she threw off the sheet and stood by the window, which looked out onto the parking lot, trying to shake off the jitters in her limbs.

Kim stirred. Not asleep yet either. "Do you believe him?"

"Hmm? Who?"

"Gabriel."

"About Sachiv? Yeah. Why not?"

"He has an agenda. And he's quite the fantasist, let's face it."

"He'd hardly lie about a guy being widowed."

Kim stretched. "Maybe not about that. But Sachiv being available right now would not suit our Gabriel, so don't get too upset over the remarriage bit."

"I'm not upset. Wistful, maybe."

"Did you ever look Sachiv up online?"

"Course I did, and you, and Reggie, but he hasn't left much of a trail, which is odd for a hotelier. Maybe he retired early, to be kept by his new wife."

"If she exists."

"I would have liked to see him again," Thea admitted. "He was such a kind, generous guy—"

"And not unattractive."

"And not unattractive, but I'm not unduly devastated that I missed the bus. These last months I got a bit caught up in the idea of a frantic fling, which brought on a bout of dissatisfaction, and a longing to see him again, but it's unlikely I'd have gone through with anything if I had."

"So what has you staring out of the window?"

"Insomnia." Thea went back to bed.

"You mean the Gabriel Effect?"

"You don't really think he'd tell a barefaced lie about Sachiv just to throw me off?"

Kim was still for a moment. "I think he's capable of lying about a lot of things. Including his brother."

"How so?"

"Maybe the poor guy actually died. At the time, or later. I mean, why has Gabriel never gone back? Not once. Not even for Christmas. Isn't it possible he's got some questions to answer? Charges hanging over him?"

"Fratricide? Really? You said you think he's kind."

"It has nothing to do with kindness. It's about booze. It wouldn't be the first time a groom has inadvertently died at his own bachelor party."

"No," said Thea. "*No*. He would say so. He's admitted everything. If you ask me, he's haunted by the fact that he came extremely close to exactly that outcome. He *nearly* killed Max, and he'll never get away from that."

"I guess."

As her breathing evened out and deepened, Kim made no further contributions. Thea tried again to sleep, but her mind was in a spin. A whirlpool. The Gabriel Effect. Coincidence. Intersections. Supernatural chat. Something about him. About him, *something*. She wanted more of his deluded certainty; to taste again the way he knew her, though he did not. Even though Alex was back home, with her kids, looking after her hearth, her heart, and sending her messages of love and longing, she wanted more of Gabriel.

But the tour was over. The finishing line—Muscat—was in sight. She had arrived with one mystery in her suitcase, those teasing postcards, and would be leaving with quite another. Unless she could get to the core of Gabriel Sherlock, she would be left to wonder forever how it was that he had heard her aunt's nylons brushing against each other.

Most of the now-familiar faces were at breakfast and new ones too—those parties going counter-clockwise.

Ignoring his group and his friends, Gabriel took a seat beside Kim.

"He looks the worse for wear," she said, when the hot-headed Omar went past.

Gabriel stirred his coffee. "There was a row last night."

"About what?"

"The usual thing—details. An alternative route to Dhofar. Abid said he'd gone a particular way, but Omar said that wasn't possible, you couldn't get through that way. In fact, you can—I've done it myself. It goes to the coast north of Salalah and there's a spot, miles from anywhere, a deserted bay, which is great for fishing."

"Fishing in the desert," said Thea. "What a concept."

"Stay a bit longer and I'll take you there."

"She *is* staying longer," Kim said, popping pancake into her mouth. "She doesn't go back till Tuesday. So did it end badly, this argument?"

"Hmm? Oh, umm, yeah, in stalemate. Bedouin hate to lose face, so no one can back down. Omar categorically insisted that Abid could not possibly have done what he certainly did do."

When Kim went to get more coffee, Gabriel raised an eyebrow. "You're staying on? That's great. There are places I'd like to show you."

"You really think I'd go away with you after what you've told me?"

He leaned forward. "Haven't you ever done something nasty you shouldn't have done?"

"Not—"

"Something like, I dunno, seducing a married man and father of three in his place of work?"

Kim trotted behind Thea, as she strode past the gardens to their room. "What *is* wrong?"

"He knows stuff."

"What stuff?"

"About Sachiv. His kids. Everything. Where would he have heard all that?"

"He knew the guy!"

Thea turned to her at their door. "He mentioned Sachiv before I *ever* did—yesterday morning in the camp—and just now he accused me of seducing a married man in his place of work." She shoved the key-card into the slot.

"Guesswork," said Kim, as they went in. "You asked about a hotel manager from years back—it isn't a *huge* leap from there to an affair, *in* a hotel, but he got it wrong. You didn't seduce Sachiv, which proves Gabriel's chancing his arm."

"One problem with that theory."

"What's that?" Kim reached for her nightshirt and started to fold it for packing.

Thea threw her bag onto her bed and turned to Kim, whose expression reflected the contortions of her mind.

"Thea?"

"There were things I didn't tell you about Sachiv."

"For instance?"

"He started coming to my room."

"He what?"

Thea nodded. "After the prank calls."

"But—"

"Yeah, I know, his family, his sweet wife, now dead."

"But you said his marriage was *saved* by your illness. I presumed nothing . . ."

Thea narrowed her lips, raised her eyebrows.

"Oh, Lord. I see."

"Good."

"How did I miss that?"

"I made sure you did. And it was only the once."

"Was he . . ." Kim twisted the nightshirt around her wrist, ". . . was he on duty?"

"*On duty*?"

"I'm thinking about that suit."

"Suit?"

"He looked so damned hot in that uniform. The silver tie . . ."

Thea gaped and laughed at the same time. "You! So disapproving and—"

"Judgmental, yeah. *Well*?"

"Yes! He was on duty."

By lowering herself onto the bed with minimum movement, Kim asked for more.

Thea gave in. "It was very sudden. I came in from work. He watched me pass. We didn't speak, but there was a look of, I suppose, desperation. In my room, I sat in the dimness, thinking this would certainly break me. Every day, every week, seeing him first thing in the morning, last thing at night, knowing there was no escape, no *release*, and then he was there. He'd let himself in—not for the first time. We'd managed to resist once, but the second time we fell to it. Done, before conscience could intervene, before thinking could stop us. Done."

"My God." Eyes lowered, Kim said quietly, "No wonder you thought the cards were from him."

"That's not the point. The point is, how does Gabriel know about any of it?"

They made their way to the Friday market, through a jumble of pickup trucks, men in dishdashas and Bedouin women selling goats. Outside the old gate, traders were selling dried fish in plastic bags and cobblers waited for dusty shoes, but the real trade was happening to one side, where a circle had formed around a parade of livestock and men hunkered down, resting their camel sticks against their shoulders. Beyond, other merchandise, bleating and fretful, pulled on ropes—two beautifully coiffed kids, rusty-red with fluffy white fringes, were tied to low stumps on short leashes and didn't like it.

Leaning toward Thea, Kim said, "They might have known one another better than Gabriel's making out. Sachiv could have told him about you."

"You think? 'Hey, I knew an Irish girl once. A guest in my hotel. Slept with her in one of the rooms during my shift. *Do* bring all your clients to my hotel.'"

"Hmm. Maybe not."

"Besides, Gabriel's mentioned other things that don't add up—or, rather, they *do* add up, and instead of making me wary, it's making me more damn curious. It's turning me into *you*! I want to know more, Kim, but most of all, I want to *see* more. Do more." She turned. "Can't you extend your stay? Then we could take him up on his offer to do another trip. You'll get to find out what you want and I'll get to experience some honest-to-God desert."

"I'm thinking that's what Gabriel might call a crowd. And I have to get back. I have deadlines."

"I'll go alone, then. I can't afford to waste a single minute of this trip. Who knows when I'll get away again?"

Kim stopped among the livestock. "You really think that's a good idea?"

"Yes. Why would I spend three days alone sitting around in Muscat when I could be off in the sands with my own personal driver?"

They wandered on. "Do you think you can trust him?"

"I don't know about trusting him," said Thea, "but I can handle him. I mean, I don't see a string of unresolved murders in this country and Abid clearly thinks highly of him."

"Gabriel doesn't *fancy* Abid."

They stopped beside a solitary camel tied to a tree. Putting her hand on the curve of its neck, Kim looked across at Thea. "Here's the thing. Cynically, the more we find out about 'Jibril,' the better it is for me, but as your friend . . ." she patted the camel's coarse hair ". . . Gabriel's got a jinn on his back of one sort or another and if you mess with him—"

"I wouldn't mess with him."

"You already are, without even trying! And is that fair to Gabriel?"

"I'm just trying to be fair to me." The camel blinked slowly at Thea as she stroked its hump. "I have escaped domesticity, Kim. Last time I escaped the norm, I got to go home yellow and my wings were literally clipped. This is too good an opportunity to pass up. Gabriel can help me fill up my haversack a bit."

"More than you might want him to."

"Stop," Thea said, smiling. "I thought I was going to be Amelia Earhart, remember? Not taking the personal details of people having hip replacements."

"Amelia Earhart died a horrible lonely death in the ocean. You should count your blessings."

"I *do* count my blessings, more than you know, so don't worry."

"It's not only you I'm worried about. Gabriel is already wounded."

"That hasn't stopped *you* hounding him. You're projecting—you want him to be more mysterious than he actually is. I mean, he's flirting his head off with a married woman and teasing you at every opportunity. He's not quite the tragic figure you'd like him to be."

The camel blinked its long lashes again as a large American woman, with big hair and a lime green suit, went past.

"Couldn't agree more," Kim said to it. "Just the kind of person who voted for Bush."

Thea stroked the camel. "You know what her last recorded words were?"

"Who?"

"Amelia. The last thing the radio operator heard her say was 'We're running north and south.' I've often wondered what that means."

Abid strode up, looking disparagingly at the camel. "Only good for meat, this one."

"No!" they wailed together.

As they wandered on, Thea scanned the marketplace. A Bedouin woman wearing the leather burqa was haggling with an old man over her goats; a cow, fussed by the push and shove of the crowd, bucked, sending buyers running; and, off to the side, two young women sat on a wall, one of whom was wearing a flamboyant black and pink scarf and a black facemask.

"Why is one masked and not the other?" she asked Abid.

"If they wear the mask," Abid explained, "it means they are engaged, or married. No mask means they are still virgins."

"You'd swear she's proud to be wearing it," Kim said.

"No different from flashing the engagement ring, I suppose," said Thea.

No sign of Gabriel anywhere. For once, Thea didn't feel watched—a blessing. A blessing and . . . an itch she couldn't scratch. For all her flouncing off and snaps of outrage, those declarations he made, the suave cutting words in which he revealed what he knew of her, were nonetheless seductive and intriguing enough to keep her coming back for more.

They moved through a vegetable market stretched along a street with a great tree at one end. "All locally grown, juicy, fruity veggies, no air miles." Kim flicked the switch on her tape-recorder. "Low baskets, pale green zucchini, bright orange carrots, cabbages as big as heads, scallions the size of leeks. Also . . ." She stopped by a stack of tin containers. "What are these for, Abid?"

He opened one and they peered in at a white greasy substance. "Laban," he said. "A kind of butter."

"Buttermilk," Kim said into her gadget. "Also big bags of tea. Omanis are not traditionally tea drinkers. They once considered it poison. They used dates to sweeten the bitter coffee, so they distrusted tea, which had sugar in it."

Thea looked down the street, with its flecks of vegetable color, men and women shopping and bartering. "While I get to do the weekly shop in a supermarket."

On the way back to Muscat, Kim worked hard. So did Abid.

"Why do you think Gabriel's jinn abandoned him?" she asked him.

"Because he tried to make her live in our world, but jinn cannot do this. He fought with her, so she has never shown herself to him since that time."

"Never *shown* herself? Are you saying she's still around?"

"People say his loneliness is because she is punishing him. That's why he has never found a wife." He glanced at Kim. "You like this story."

"It breaks my heart." Her phone went off. "Hello? . . . Gabriel, hi. Hey, you missed a cue—we didn't run into you at the market." She paused. He talked. "I'm leaving tonight, yeah. . . . About midnight. . . . That's right, I *do* have to eat. . . . We'd love to, thanks. See you then." She clicked off her phone. "He's taking us to dinner tonight, Thea." She looked again at Abid. "So was Gabriel's companion a good'un or a bad'un, so far as jinn go?"

"They say she was good. Good for him, at that time. He could be happy with her even now, if he accepted her, but he should have a human wife too. And kids. What is life without children?"

"Absolutely," said Thea. "A baby crying all night would certainly ground him."

Abid pulled off the highway. "This is nice place for photograph," he said, as they bumped up to another vantage-point, which overlooked a plantation, beyond which the ancient abandoned village of Birkat al-Mawz stood on the mountain's toes.

"Can't believe you'll be gone this time tomorrow," Thea said, clutching Kim's waist as they posed for a photograph together.

"I'm so sorry about the cards. Seemed like such a neat idea. Now it seems irresponsible. Giving you false hope about Sachiv."

"Oh, don't, *please*. I've been an idiot, getting all loved up. It was just something he said when I was leaving that made me suspect him."

Kim squinted at her. "'Don't be surprised. Don't be surprised by what I do.'"

Thea turned. "You heard?"

"Sure did. I was right behind you guys. Couldn't figure it."

"It's been going around my head these last months. Too much time on my hands, clearly. I'm sure I was no more than a fling to him."

"You think?"

"Well, I'll never know."

"*I* know." Kim turned to take in the view. "There's something I haven't told you about Sachiv."

"Oh, God, you slept with him too?"

"I came across him one night, out by the pools, about six weeks after you'd left. I went out for a stretch, quite late, and he was sitting on the end of a lounger, jacket and tie off, his chest sort of concave . . . turned in. When he saw me, he blinked those lovely sad eyes in a hopeless sort of way, and said, 'She will not come back, I suppose.' I said, 'I guess not.' He didn't say anything else, so I walked on by."

"And?"

"He suffered too, is all I'm saying."

"Good," said Thea, as Kim wandered off to take photos. She stared into the thick canopy below her, where houses poked out, laundry fluttered on lines, air-conditioners hummed, and satellite dishes sucked in their programs.

Abid came to her side. "Jibril is a good person. A good man."

"I know."

"We must take care for all people. Whatever they have done."

"Done?" Thea frowned. "Has he done something?"

Abid looked out, hands deep in his pockets.

"You mean his brother?"

A head gesture, approximating a discreet nod.

"I thought no one knew about that."

"His sister told me that story before she went away," he said. "She wanted that I should make sure he is okay."

"And *is* he?"

Abid wobbled his head. "Sometimes."

"And sometimes not?"

"There will be no peace for Jibril. Every time he has a little happiness, meets a nice lady, it is destroyed. She will not allow it. No one else can have him. This, she makes sure."

Thea's hand went to her neck. "She's still with him?"

"I think, yes. She makes him think you look like her."

"Oh, God. He really is cursed."

"But someone like you, a strong person, even if she tried, you would repel her."

"How?"

"Three times, you send her out. You say, 'Leave him,' three times and the jinn will go out. 'Tell them three times to leave,' the Prophet, peace be upon him, says in the Hadith, "and if they don't, we can kill them."

"That didn't work when the exorcist tried it, apparently."

"But you are her rival, and you are stronger than she."

"Abid, I have a family, a husband."

"Yes." He nodded sadly. "This is his punishment."

"And how was your journey?" Fatima asked, when she picked them up not long after their return from Nizwa. "Did you get enough material?"

"Oh, more than," said Kim. "It was a wonderful trip, thank you."

Fatima al-Kindi worked for the Ministry of Tourism and had organized Kim's itinerary. A warm, cheerful woman, she had met Kim at a tourism conference in the States and extended the invitation to visit. They had hit it off and spent some time together—and it was she, it transpired, who had sent the misleading postcards to Thea, according to Kim's instructions. For Kim's last afternoon, she had invited them to join her and her husband, Salim, on their Friday round of family visits.

They drove first to Salim's village, outside Muscat, where his family's large house was buried in its own plantation. While his father entertained them in the yard, his mother and younger sister brought coffee and delicious squidgy dates. Fatima explained to Thea that the Omani way of drinking coffee was to slurp it, but not too much. "When you have had enough, you wobble the cup from side to side, like this."

It was a fresh evening; the sky was pink and, through the tree fronds, Thea glimpsed a sliver of moon. When Fatima and Salim's father went to pray, Salim walked Kim and Thea through the grove, explaining how the dates were harvested and dried, which trees were male and which female. "We have twenty-five different types of palm here. And you have seen the falaj around the country?" He pointed at a cement channel, through which flowed a thin trickle of water. "It is a very ancient irrigation system, but nowadays we use it on a time-share basis. In one oasis, each family will have running water for so many hours, and then the next farm will have it."

Some kids ran about. Family life. Normalcy. A Sunday afternoon, or the equivalent thereof. Thea felt herself dropping onto firm ground, as if parachuted from a height. No roving Gabriel, no talk of jinn. She was reminded of Brona and the stories she told them when they were small. Before bed, they would sit around the fire to hear her tell of fairies, banshees, and the evil pookas; fairies lived under mounds and hills, and in the ring forts dotted about the countryside. They loved music and dancing, and although they could do good magic, like bringing babies to parents who had none, they could also be willful and play tricks if they were angry. This was why, Brona used to say, there was a tradition among rural folk to call, before throwing used tea leaves out of the door, "Uisce Salach! Uisce Salach!"—dirty water—just in case a fairy was passing.

Thea, like her brothers and sister, had longed, but *longed*, to see a fairy, to search the hillocks around Brona's house or visit the nearest ring fort, but their aunt had advised that it was best to leave them to go about their business undisturbed so that they too would leave her undisturbed. After story time, with fresh milk settled in her tummy and the last taste of a custard cream cookie on her lips, Thea would climb up the stairs feeling as if she were coming down. Down to the normal world where there were rules about bedtime and brushing teeth. In the same way now, at Fatima's, she was landing, shifting back to the reasonable after being too long off her feet.

But Kim was not yet done. In the yard, unable to let up, she asked Fatima if it was true that humans could sometimes see jinn.

"Of course not," said Fatima. "It is in the Quran: humans cannot see jinn. They live alongside us, not with us. They are created, like humans, to honor God."

"That's not what we've been hearing."

"If you are going to write about this subject, Kim," Fatima said, a little tartly, "you must take it from a purely Quranic perspective. It is a religious matter."

That drew a line right under the topic, and with a scrape too, but Kim didn't hear it. "How about young people?" she blundered on, turning to Salim's teenage sister. "Do you believe in jinn?"

Thea wished Kim would stop. This was delicate ground, private, a matter of faith. She had gone from being curious to being downright rude.

It was Fatima who took Kim in hand. "Why are you interested in this? It is not tourism."

"We met a man, an Irishman, who apparently fell in love with a jinn lady. I'm trying to understand, that's all."

Fatima ran her finger between her chin and the fabric of her tightly bound scarf. "In love with a jinn?" she said, with a dismissive chuckle. "Jinn feed on bones and feces, and sometimes people leave dead animals, just like that, to decompose, so the jinn can have the bones! I don't think this is very lovable." Everyone laughed. "In the stories, men marry jinn! How handy it would be—one minute your wife could be Madonna, then Posh Spice."

"Because jinn can be whatever you want them to be?" Kim asked. "That would explain some of the strange things that happened to our friend."

"Listen," said Fatima, "this is how it is. If you told someone two hundred years ago that men could get in a great steel bird," she waved her arm in the air, "and be in Tehran two hours later, they would call it magic. If you'd said a hundred years ago that you could write someone a message and they would have it straight away, they would have said, 'Never! Only Allah can do such things!' One day, we will find the answers to strange happenings. What used to be magic is not magic anymore. It is *science*. And in the future we will explain things we cannot explain now." She stood up. "Come, come, we must go to our uncle's."

And so, in another roomy house, more extended family welcomed them.

"Irlanda?" the old uncle said to Thea. "James Joyce!"

"Yes." She smiled.

He spoke; Salim translated. "He says that many young writers try to be like Joyce, but they fail, because they are not true geniuses like him."

Sipping her coffee, Thea tried to remember when last she had been asked about Irish writers and not the country's booming economy. It was a welcome relief.

"He lived in Italy, didn't he?" Salim asked. "*A Portrait of the Artist*—I love this book. He chose exile. Exile from nation, religion, family." He shook his head. "I cannot really understand it. In Oman, family is everything, religion too. This is against everything I believe in, so it is fascinating to me."

"I believe he felt these things restrained him creatively."

The conversation then became a general moan about President Bush, the war in Iraq, and the media in general. The West, the uncle declared, had become empty because it had lost all spirituality.

"There's something in that," Kim agreed.

On the way out to the car, they heard the unusual cry of a bird hidden in the dusk. "What bird is that?" Thea asked.

"Ah," said Salim, "we call that the jinn bird."

"You know," said Fatima, as they drove away, "you should look up 'jinn' in the dictionary. The root of the word—janna—means to hide, conceal, to fall into darkness. Jinaan, that means garden, like a secret place, hidden, Paradise even. Junna . . . protection, like, um, a wall, a shield." The list of words rolled off her tongue in an absent-minded way. Kim pinged her recorder. Thea looked out at the remains of a highway that had been lifted and carried off by the floods. "Janaan for the heart, the soul. Istajanna—to become covered, concealed. Junna—to become possessed, crazy, because that is hidden, also. It is on the inside, you see?"

"Al junoun funoun," said Salim. "Madness shows itself in many different ways."

Gabriel took them to an Indian restaurant, vast and circular, with a panoramic view of the city—car lights filing along highways, minarets glowing under spotlights; suburbs rising and falling over unseen hills, like Chinese lanterns floating on a swell.

It was a curious evening, what with Kim trying to seduce Gabriel into revelations, while he tried to seduce Thea, addressing his answers to her, his arm stretched across the table so that his hand was almost on her elbow.

"So, a successful trip?" he asked Kim.

"Mostly. But I wish we'd got out to see those quicksands."

"Which ones?"

"The ones that eat up flocks of sheep. I asked Abid, but he didn't seem to know what I was talking about. He told us about a European couple getting lost last year and dying in their car, but they didn't sink, so it can't have been the same place."

"They died in their car?" Thea asked, aghast.

"It happens all the time," Gabriel said. "People die from exposure and stupidity."

"Tourists?"

"Ill-prepared tourists and foreign workers. Guys out at the oilfields. They figure they can take a shortcut across the sands because they know where they're going, but they don't consider the monotony of the landscape—the same features for miles around, and they don't have enough water because they think they won't be long."

Thea shuddered. "How much is enough water?"

"Eight liters per person per day," he replied. "Without water, you become confused very quickly and then you make bad decisions, like leaving the car or thinking you'll be able to see something from the top of that dune over there, or the next, and then you turn around and you see a thousand dunes and you don't know which one is hiding the 4x4. It turns out that your only defining landmark doesn't define anything at all, and by then it's too late. Even if you know what to do, which is to stay with the vehicle, but you don't have enough water, you're still fucked, because you won't behave rationally once dehydration sets in. Delirium comes quickly. And if you stay *in* the car, you'll basically cook. It happens every year to some unfortunate wretch."

"What a ghastly way to die."

"Not the way I'd choose," said Kim, "if I had a choice."

"Nor me," said Gabriel.

"What would you choose?" she asked him.

"I wouldn't fry, that's for sure. If I got lost out there, without water, I'd throw the jeep over the rim of a dune. It's pretty easy to roll a 4x4 if you know how."

"You've thought about it, then," said Kim.

"You don't go deep into the desert without thinking about it."

"What if the roll didn't kill you?" Thea asked.

He smiled. "*Then* I'd fry."

"I'd be reaching for the pills," Kim said, with a sigh. "I never really get the way some people can be proactive about killing themselves—throwing themselves in front of a train or off buildings. It'd be like jumping out of a plane without a parachute."

"I understand why people jump," Gabriel said. "Leaping into the void. That makes sense to me."

This man, Thea thought; the grimness of him. When he smiled, flecks of light flickered in his eyes, but mostly he walked about with a dull shadow; and the shadow of the shadow spread to those around him. Kim, for instance: she'd become darker since they'd met him, preoccupied by genies and ghosts, by women who were, and women who weren't, and now, prodding him about death and dying and how best to suicide.

"Have you ever got into difficulty in the Omani wilderness?" she was asking.

"I've got caught in storms, fierce bloody winds blowing up without warning. Zero visibility. A kind of blindness. Scary, but I quite liked it."

"Well, you would," said Kim. "Invisibility again."

Thea looked out. Muscat looked in. Nice town. Easy town. Earlier that afternoon, they had walked through the suq, along modernized alleys under a high roof, where they had bought scarfs and trinkets, and stopped while a boy lit charcoal in a small burner, then broke frankincense and myrrh over it until a faint flicker of aromatic smoke flavored the air.

"I think you mean Umm al-Samim," Gabriel was saying. "The Mother of all Poisons. I don't know about sheep, but cars do sink into it. Although it isn't sand—they're salt flats, a crust of salt, gypsum, and sand on top of mud. Sludge, basically."

"Yes, that's it! That's what I read about."

"Water sometimes flows down from the Hajar, so old hands know you should never drive across it after rain, unless you have ramps in the car, because the water permeates beneath the crispy salt into the gunk underneath—that's the stuff that swallows things, but slowly. It isn't quick."

"Another fun way to die!" Thea quipped. "Stay in the car and wait for the goo to get you."

"Only then you'd die of thirst, as in example A," Gabriel said flatly. "It'd take a jeep several days to go down. Plenty of time to get out. Umm al-Samim prefers to eat 4x4s rather than people."

"Taking back some of its oil, perhaps."

Kim wasn't satisfied. "So much for being sucked into oblivion by whirlpools of dry sand, like in the movies!"

"In Umm al-Samim, it'd be more like drowning. In black ink."

"Jesus," said Thea, "you two really have gone over to the dark side."

"Some people live their entire lives on the dark side," said Gabriel.

"People like you," Kim glanced at her watch, "and all because some lover ditched you. Was she really worth it?"

"My love life interests you a lot," he remarked drily.

"Jinn interest me. Especially since we learned, this evening, that they're partial to bones and feces and live around outhouses."

"And you wonder why I'm so sure my lover was *not* a jinniya?"

"But where did she come from? And, more to the point, where did she go? Because, frankly," Kim said, exasperated, "it isn't credible that you've spent over twenty years mourning a woman you knew for all of two months. There has to be more to it."

"There is."

At just that point, Abid arrived to take Kim to the airport.

"Tell me," she urged him. "Otherwise, I'll have to make it up!"

Instead, Gabriel curved back, twisting slightly to greet Abid over his shoulder. There was something alluring in his every move, Thea thought, even though he wore his past like a carapace.

Kim pressed her Dictaphone into Thea's purse. "Go to the desert," she hissed. "Find out what you can. I'll give you a share of the profits."

Thea grasped her hand. "When am I going to see you again?"

"Let's leave that to the angels. Or the jinn."

They embraced. "I'm so glad you weren't Sachiv."

"Me too. Old lovers," Kim glanced at Gabriel, "only ever disappoint." She leaned toward him to shake hands. "Goodbye, Gabriel."

"I look forward to reading about myself in a supernatural thriller."

Abid said to Thea, "I will come back to take you to your hotel."

"No need." Gabriel said. "I'll take her."

Thea watched Kim go, weaving through the tables to the door, then emerging beyond the vast window, where she turned and waved one last time.

With a deep, satisfied sigh, Gabriel said, "Let's go home."

His house in Muttrah was not far from where the boy had been burning incense earlier that day. He led her into a narrow alley that curved to the left, up some steps, and around to the left again, until he stopped before a low door.

"You've lived here all this time?"

"Yeah. Usually they don't like foreigners to stay more than ten or twelve years at a stretch, no matter who's sponsoring them, but somehow my visa has always been renewed." He clicked his tongue. "It's my Irish charm."

The door to his home opened onto a white sitting room, with a cement bench running along two sides, draped in blue and green cushions. On the far side, an opening led into a kitchen and another onto a dark hall. Thea could feel Gabriel watching, waiting for a reaction, but she was watchful also, prepared to experience some hint of recognition, a flash of déjà vu.

A framed print on the wall behind the seating drew her across the room. "Wow." In the photograph, a beam of blue light was shooting across a vast cave from a sun-bright hole in the roof. "Where *is* that?"

Gabriel leaned against the doorjamb next to the picture. "In the hills behind Qalhat. It was discovered by an American geologist not long after I came to Oman and was thought then to be the second-largest cave in the world, but now it's ranked about fifth. You could park several 747s in there."

Whirls of limestone strata surrounded the gap through which shone the dart of light. "Looks like the eye of a hurricane."

He pointed at a blob hanging in the middle of the light beam. "That's me."

"Seriously?" She looked closer. "You went down there? On a rope?"

"The elevator wasn't working."

She thumped him lightly.

"I'd never climbed before, but when I heard about this, I made it my business to learn. You have to abseil down and then climb back up the rope—which can take an hour. You need to be fit, very strong. There are three openings. One is a narrow slit and you scramble down easily enough through the rocks until suddenly—nothing. Space. Terrifying, the first time. I didn't have enough experience to handle the shock of being so exposed—like being thrown out into the universe—but I had to do it."

"Why?"

"It asked me to."

Thea nodded. "When I was nineteen, my brother took me to Skye and I climbed the Inaccessible Pinnacle for the same reason. Because it asked me to."

"So you've climbed? We should go there." He looked at the photo. "It's called Majlis al-Jinn. Meeting place of the spirits."

She stared at his figure, dangling in the void.

"It's like being inside the earth's womb," he said quietly.

On their way up the stone staircase, Thea could feel his desire coming up behind her, spreading across her shoulders. On a broad landing, the house opened into spaciousness. There were rooms off, bedrooms, probably a bathroom. Wool rugs on the white floor. Recognition stirred. She could smell her own daydream.

"Familiar?" he asked.

"Why would it be?"

He raised an eyebrow.

"You're either very house-proud or you have a housekeeper."

"Wifaq. I've been her personal responsibility for fifteen years. We're growing old together. When I'm sick, she looks after me. When I sleep in, she wakes me. When I can't sleep, she talks to me across the roofs. Come on up."

The roof was a small, walled space, with room only for a table and two chairs.

"It must make for a lonely life, all this waiting?"

Gabriel glanced around the roofs, the aerials and satellite dishes. "I have friends, good friends, but ultimately, yeah, I come back to an empty house. After office hours, I live a somewhat eremitic life."

"Surely you could have moved on by now."

"I did try." He put his hands on the wall behind him. "But every relationship foundered for one reason or another. Prudence is a hard act to follow."

"I'm not surprised, with a name like that."

"But now," he went on, "it seems all my waiting has been worthwhile."

"You'd do better to believe in your own fable than to pin your hopes on me. I am not her. She was not me." And yet this place, this place . . .

"Let's go to the desert," Gabriel said. "You want to go and I want to take you. I'll show you dunes the like of which you'll never forget."

The roar of a plane heading out across the Gulf drew Thea's eyes to its flashing red lights, where the dim yellow line that hinted at its cabin brought her right up, and in, to where the passengers were belted into the flat acceptance of the long hours ahead. Thea felt no longing to be up there, heading home. "You've been so predatory."

"Predatory?"

"Yes." She looked at him.

"Look," he said. "You're married. And whatever I might want, or even long for, I don't inflict harm. Not anymore."

On swirling roads, he lifted her up and dropped her down. On the heights, he perched her on dizzying promontories with a God's-eye view of precipices and canyons and the orange-gray ridges of the eastern Hajar; he pointed out Snake Gorge, a dark, zigzag gash in the gunmetal rock, and stopped by a black hill with bright copper seams winding around it, like tinsel on a Christmas tree. Looping down, she considered the rigid peaks, admired blocky villages nurtured by banana trees in the green pubes of the wadis, and laughed at a football pitch that lay across a road.

Gabriel was a happy man. His business forgotten, his appointments set aside, he delighted in taking her to a wilderness that would kill if you traveled one bottle of water short. Thea was giddy with her own folly—heading into the unknown with an unknown quantity, a man with crazed notions and suspect history. But a man, also, who amused and riveted her, and looked like the archangel of her childhood. She liked to drop her gaze on his wrists and watch him drive. It had been too long since she had been on a mad caper like this. Alex knew she was on a trip with an Irish tour operator and, indeed, had been relieved to know she wouldn't be twiddling her thumbs for three days, alone in Muscat.

Delicious, delightful, was the pool where they swam. Thea lay, floating, happy. Three thousand miles from an Irish January, from open fires and black evenings, she felt not the slightest twinge of homesickness. This was fine, perfect; sun and swimming, and no demands pulling her hither and thither. And this country! Sachiv, during those late-night calls, had spoken a lot of boy-friendly Muscat, where he and his pals had gone fishing in the port in homemade boats, of eating watermelon in its dusty lanes, and of the great mountainous peaks—of rock and sand—that made Oman the country he most loved. He had not overstated its beauty.

She paddled a little to keep afloat, her ears plugged with water. The river was nudging her, as if she were a piece of driftwood caught up in twigs that needed release. It was a relief to go with it, and a relief to have come—for which she was grateful to both Kim and Sachiv since it was they, directly and indirectly, who had got her onto that plane to Muscat. She rolled into swimming. It wasn't too late, it transpired, for her inner grasshopper to find that leather-bound journal.

They made camp by a watercourse somewhere in Wadi Bani Awf when the black night was sinking to earth. While Gabriel lit a fire, Thea stepped away to pee behind a rock, her head clamoring with unwelcome jinn lore, such as their propensity for living in deserted places and their ability to turn into stones, and wolves. In some places, people were afraid to step on jinn—invisible beneath their feet—because they would then be tormented by them. Like chewing gum from the pavement, Thea thought, sticking to your heel. She began to believe. She could feel them watching and suddenly wished herself in Ireland—on a tributary of the Lee, in harmless countryside, where the only sound besides the river would be the moo and munch of cattle behind a hedgerow. . . . But even there the unseen were feared and avoided; she knew of buildings, remote and abandoned, where no one ever set foot because they were reputed to house the walking dead.

Over tea and cookies, they talked of Glandore and Skibbereen, Allihies and Inchydoney. Gabriel asked if the old hotel was still on the headland between the beaches.

"God, no. That was knocked down and replaced by a great big spa hotel. You'd hate it, probably."

"Probably."

"Won't you ever go back?"

He held his plastic mug to his mouth. "Unlikely," he said, and drank.

"Isn't exile a stiff price to pay for a youthful mistake?"

He threw out his chin in a dismissive way, his elbow resting on the rock behind him. "If this is exile, exile is no hard place to be."

"Why did you do it?"

Gabriel flashed his eyes at her, then cleared his throat. He often did so before speaking, as if giving himself a chance to pull back. "No reason. No reason at all."

She waited.

"As best man, I had certain responsibilities."

"Like getting the groom manky drunk?"

A low nod. "A particular challenge in Max's case. Such a sober type. But there were expectations, conventions to be upheld."

Thea sat still, conscious of an unseen audience around them, oval faces outlined in white, like chalk figures on a blackboard, with O-shaped mouths, lines of them, hanging on the next scene. "So get him drunk you did."

"Spectacularly."

The river seemed to slow down, to hush its gurgle.

"Where did you happen upon a grand piano?"

"The School of Music. After the pub, we wandered down that way, about seven of us, drunk as newts, and suddenly Max insisted on going in. 'I have a class,' he kept saying—we were both teaching there at the time—so we all bundled up the steps. The night porter, Frank, let us in. He was fond of Max, so he indulged us, said we looked like we needed coffee and went off to make it. 'I must play,' Max was saying, 'must play,' and we followed him into the hall. The grand was center-stage. Max sat, hanging over the keys, whining about how much he loved his piano, couldn't bear to live without it, wanted to marry it, sleep with it. We said—*I* said—sleeping with it might be difficult, but sleeping *in* it could be arranged. . . . He was sniggering when we got hold of him, but then he slumped—I had him by the armpits—passed out, so we heaved him in, like a sack. Strings snapped and cracked, but even that didn't . . . alert us. We put down the lid and took off."

"Good God. You left the building."

"We left the building."

Even the ghouls were quiet. The invisible audience of open-mouthed specters held their pose.

"Frank saw me leave. He recounted afterwards that I had looked around, like I'd left something behind, and I remember that feeling—was it my wallet? My jacket? My brother, as it transpired."

Thea couldn't speak. For a moment neither could he. Then he said, 'When Max came round, he couldn't lift his head. Couldn't move. Couldn't see.'

Pulling her fleece around her, Thea edged closer to Gabriel, for warmth, or something.

His eyes suddenly brimmed with tears. "He was so cold when Frank found him. It was January, just before that historic freeze hit Ireland, and lying there, with drink taken, he was cold as a corpse, Frank said."

"How long? I mean, when did Frank . . ."

"Hours later. Almost morning. He thought he heard a sort of a cry, somewhere in the building." Gabriel swallowed. "He checked out the upper floors, then heard it again and realized it was coming from the hall, which was odd, because the hall was soundproofed. He went in. Nothing unusual. . . . Said he didn't know what made him get up onto the stage to check the piano or what made him lift the lid. God, he said later, made him open it. There was no other reason to."

"Poor Frank."

"Max was unconscious. Not sleeping. Unconscious, and hypothermic."

Something crackled behind them. Thea swung around. Gabriel put his hand on her knee. "There's nothing here you need worry about."

Only part of his face was lit by the fire; a huge wad of night pressed against Thea's back. "You remember so much."

"I pretend not to, but over the years every bitter little trinket of memory has taken up residence, just to make sure I never forget. Putting him in there wasn't the problem—people have done worse to grooms. The crime was that we forgot to take him out."

The last word went down his throat with a swallow.

"And the wedding?"

"Never happened. Geraldine stayed with it, with him, for a year, but I'd turned him into a lump. Not even a gibbering wreck, just a living lump, and a health hazard. He was traumatized, and in those days there was no rush of counselors to sort him out. The buried-alive thing haunted him. Haunted all of us. And, thanks to me, even though living, to him, was playing, his fingers never again felt the soft slide of ivory, and his feet no longer dance with the pedals."

"And yours neither. What he can't have, you won't have. Even women. Family." The flames warmed her face, but her back was cold.

He pressed his fingers into his forehead, then rubbed his eyes.

"Where did it come from?" she asked quietly. "Such a vile idea."

"From a booze-addled brain."

"But at some level you must have resented him, blamed him for—"

"No. Listen to me." Gabriel turned to her. "I idolized Max, all right? I adored him. When we were kids, I thought he was the best frigging pianist in the whole darn world. I only took up the piano to please *him*, because he wanted to teach me, and my face used to flush with delight whenever he told the parents how clever his little brother was. It made me feel worthy of him. We were so damn proud of each other, but what neither of us noticed, back then, was the light in our parents' eyes when they realized what a little gem they had in *me*. And when I reached the same shitty conclusion—that I was so much better at what Max did best—I wanted to chop off my fingers. Max, of course, encouraged me, coached me, taught me to play more sublimely than he ever would, and had I had the right type of ego—the kind you need to succeed—I might have overcome it. The guilt. I might have handled the conflict in my head and in my hands. But I had to take the baton and run with it, because everyone expected me to, even though that meant leaving Max behind on the track, applauding even while I broke the ribbon. Took all the ribbons.

"Annie saw it. She knew it was only a matter of time before I threw it in, but it was pointless, giving up. Max would never have reached the same heights as I could. He knew it. We all did. But I couldn't go on taking the accolades in his place, not when he kept on *trying*."

"So resentment built up," Thea said, "because he was the reason you stopped."

"I didn't care about that." Gabriel, now, sounded like a different man, his voice gravelly and thick. "I just wanted him to stop punishing himself for not being *me*."

His eyes held back. His loneliness had to be, could only be, as deep as that cave in the photograph. He had not stayed in Oman for love or jinn, she thought. He had stayed in order not to leave. He had thrown everything he could out of his life, even music, except for that tiny ukulele, as if its size made it less of an instrument. *I'm not really playing. This isn't really an instrument. An insignificant not-really-here-at-all thing.*

You'd never fit a man into a ukulele.

"So you live like a monk," she said. "In penitence. Hiding behind a specter." She turned to him. "She was never real, was she? Not even to you."

Without really meaning to, as if he were a child who had scraped his knee, she kissed the back of his hand.

He didn't flinch, but after a time he said, "That's the first real tenderness I've known in twenty-six years."

Later, he played the ukulele, which made a coy, cheeky sound, backed up by the river, gossiping its way across the stones. No rest for rivers, Thea thought. No nighttime.

"My aunt nursed me back to health," she said, "when I was ill."

Gabriel slowed his playing, but didn't stop.

"She wore nylons and had chunky thighs, and a fat cat called Featherweight." In this light, Gabriel's eyes were black, and beautiful. She held them fast. "He purred like a generator."

He didn't blink, but his fingers stopped. She wished he would blink.

"I know," he said.

"I know you know. But how?"

Gabriel put down the ukulele. "I gave up looking for explanations long ago."

"It's as if, somehow, when I was ill, you heard my world and I saw yours."

"Jinn magic can be powerful. She might have used you as an unwitting host."

"I thought you didn't believe in jinn magic?"

"In the best of us," he said, with lowered eyes, "belief fluctuates."

Rigid, Thea lay in the tent, her mind whirring. It wouldn't let her sleep or think or stem her seasick apprehension.

Outside, Gabriel was shuffling around, but he soon went quiet, abandoning her to the night, which took up residence inside the tent. She missed Kim's soft breathing and she needed to pee—she kept needing to pee: that it involved going out among the ifrit and jinn made her bladder fill as soon as she'd emptied it. Gathering her courage and the torch, she crawled out. Gabriel snored quietly on the roof of his jeep. It had been a long, tiring day for him. All that driving around U-bends.

She crouched not far from the camp, not sure where to point the torch, but inclined to hold it over her shoulder so that they might be repulsed by its beam, and wondered if domestic boredom had driven her to wander too far from the school run.

Back in her sleeping bag, she became prey to her own bantering consciousness. Awake, completely. Spectacularly awake, not a wisp of drowsiness within reach. There seemed no safe direction in which she could cast her mind: all led her along unsavory passages. Where there had been certainty—Gabriel was spinning a yarn—now there was doubt. Perhaps he was not? Had she, like him, got too close? With a fragile lengthening of her imagination, she sensed a presence, outside, that was not Gabriel's. An angry jinn such as his could cause havoc where it willed.

But this was not her religion, not her folklore.

Rolling over in her sleeping bag, she felt an ill-placed stone dig into her hip.

The piano—the closed Steinway concert grand—came firmly behind her eyes and would not be nudged aside. She could not have an opinion about Gabriel until she formed one about this. It was, in fact, quite a middle-class story—not a real horror, or even a real tragedy, just a boozy disgusting night gone badly wrong, and a talented family thrown into disarray. Even Gabriel's lover was no longer mysterious. Prudence had been, no doubt, a by-product in the mind of a young man, guilty, perturbed, and vilified. The other lads, no doubt, had got off without much censure; to do it to a friend was one thing, to your brother—unspeakable.

She turned over again. The stones digging into her seemed to be multiplying. Were they *all* jinn?

He had given up a glittering career because he loved his brother so much. On a dark night with drink on board, the poison of that decision had come out, as it was bound to do. Gabriel was the one buried inside a piano.

She had handled it well, his full confession. Come morning, he would be refreshed, a little cured even, having spoken about the events that had exiled him to a place of such deep remorse that he seemed unable to quit it. When a place calls, Abid had said, you should go, because it holds something for you. Perhaps she had been called to help Gabriel, to move him along to brighter things, and this was at the source of their deeply felt connection.

That connection had its paws all over her. Had she not learned? A light flirtation was no stroll in the park: it was a teeter on the rim of Snake Gorge. Pretend it can go nowhere and your flirtation will arrive somewhere else, unhindered, as it had before, and was doing again. Gabriel. Under her skin. Feelers becoming roots. The tingle in her ribcage.

On the back of these thoughts, sleep shimmied toward her.

❃

They were in Eden. Pale sunlight made the water bubble and sparkle; black mountains in the distance were like the Gates of Mordor; and a red goat, standing downriver on a rock, watched Thea emerge from her tent. Gabriel was lying in the shallow water, his head on a rock. How many people, she wondered, loved him?

"Morning," he called.

"Morning." After sending the family a text, describing her surroundings, she paddled over to him. He reached up to take her hand as she hobbled toward a rock and sat down. Still holding her fingers, he said, "What am I to do about you?"

"You could give me back my hand."

He squeezed her fingers. "I wouldn't ask for much."

"Don't ask for anything. You'd only be disappointed again."

"Are you sure?"

She took her hand away.

"That's what I thought," he said.

Gooseflesh across his ribcage; nipples erect in the cold water; red board-shorts flopping about in the current.

"If I could see you, once a year, twice," he said, sitting up, "that would be worth ten lifetimes to me."

He had it all worked out: she would come to Oman for a few weeks every year, or they could meet elsewhere. Damascus. Venice. He didn't care. He didn't want to wreck any marriage—she could hang on to all that, but only come to him enough to help him breathe. "It's you," he said, "or no one."

"Really? What about *her*?"

"Look, I never really thought you were her; more that she was you. Sometimes we see the future before we get there."

"Time in a tombola?"

"Why not? Maybe we were both—"

"Ahead of our time?" she quipped.

"Seems like it."

Her feet and calves were cold. She drew in her breath, let out the prodding night. "You might have killed him."

"Yes."

"Took his music, everything, from him."

"I didn't mean to."

"You're defending it."

Water trickled down his arm. "I don't defend it, ever." His voice was tight, locked in his throat. "Look, with respect, you don't really know—"

"You buried him. That's what I know."

Gabriel's eyes flashed at her.

"What is it?"

"That's what she said. Word for word."

"Who?"

"The other you."

They were almost in the desert when they saw the camel, standing on a ridge, high above the road. They were driving between steep, stark hills, the road curving downward toward the plain, when Thea saw him—a fine figure silhouetted against the sky, his head raised, his posture arrogant, yet searching. He was looking about, across the desert, as if waiting for someone.

"That's very rare," Gabriel said. "Camels don't like hills. They climb only if they have to. They never do it alone."

"So what's he doing up there?"

He glanced up again. "Maybe he's searching for a mate."

"He looks bereft." Thea twisted in her seat to catch a final glimpse of the magnificent, forlorn beast, memories of the caravan by Lake Razzaza soaking through her. No photos, she thought. Not then, not now.

Hours later—many long hours spent crossing an inhospitable landscape that nonetheless attracted her, like an ugly man with charm—Gabriel pulled over to let down the tires and they set off again.

It had been a long day's driving, as he had warned her it would be, and at an apparently arbitrary point he turned off the road and headed fast across the plain until the swell of sands sucked them in, as into the belly folds of a fat white nude. For over an hour the 4x4 strained up and slid down. Gabriel drove, his fingers tapped the steering wheel, as if it were a keyboard; even strapped into a car seat, he jittered. He was wearing a green shirt and faded jeans. Sunglasses.

These dunes were very high, and they came one after another, like waves in a hurricane, relentlessly lashing against them, as they went up and down, and up, and down again. Thea braced her knees and squealed as they tumbled over another sharp crest and saw an almost vertical drop below them.

"Here you are." Gabriel smiled. "Desert proper. The Empty Quarter is bigger than France, and there's more sand here than in the whole of the Sahara, which is fifteen times larger. It's also one of the most beautiful places on earth."

The heat spread into the car, like a swarm of bees, when they stopped and opened the doors. It was late afternoon. Silent, but for a whine of wind, of sand rushing across sand. The view didn't change no matter where Thea turned. She twisted this way and that, loving the ordered disorder; the champagne horizons.

The arc-shaped crest on which they sat was creamy and smooth on the leeside, while the rougher, burnt-orange grain accrued in the dips behind it, creating rippled ridges with rust on the top, cream beneath. Sand flew across the ocher ridges, like a sheet being pulled out, scattering in the wind. In every direction, desert peaks crowded upon one another, like the heads of commuters in a packed train. Alex would have loved it, and so would the boys, but Thea didn't miss them, or want them there. This was hers: the desert, again. This was her return. How often had she thought of it since she and Kim had sat on top of an old ruin, with scruffy children huddled against them and a bare plain floating around them? Emptiness appealed. She wanted to penetrate it, to find something in it or get something back—she wasn't sure which—but all it relinquished was sameness and deadliness. There was nothing to take, apart from the uncompromising look of it. Even its unctuous belly fluids were being drained away. Soon enough, the desert would have nothing left to offer beyond its smart beauty.

"'The desert within the desert,' Thesiger called it," said Gabriel, standing up. "We'll go on a bit before setting up camp."

She loved his hands, the way he flicked his keys around his fingers. Had he been untroubled, she could have loved him. Or perhaps his trouble made her love him a little. Love came in the oddest places. "Where are we going? Not to those salt flats, I hope?"

"No, they're south of here."

"How do you not get lost?"

He tapped the side of his nose. "Instinct." Heading back to the car, he added, "And GPS."

"Can I drive?"

He showed her the rudiments of 4x4 driving and let her take a few dunes. Leaning close to her, he covered her hand with his to help with the gears, coached her and laughed with her. Good times. Good times, in the desert.

It was almost dark when he pitched her tent on the floor of a flat basin, surrounded by sand heaps. Thea went as far as she dared to pee, then hurried back. "I'll bet there are jinn out there and good old Western ghouls."

"You're a believer now?" He was squatting, lighting a fire, but he tipped back and sat, one knee pulled up against him as he prodded burning twigs with a stick.

"I'm beginning to."

"Too many stories this last week. Look, it's a variation on the same theme. In Western tradition, it's the dead wandering around making things happen. We are hardwired to believe—be it in God or the supernatural or shamans. It's on our circuit boards."

"Even yours?"

His eyes barely flickered. "Sometimes," he sighed, "I do wonder about the night in the music school. Some people would explain it—one inexplicable moment of irrational behavior—by saying I was possessed of a bad jinn."

"That could explain all evil acts."

"Exactly." He poked the fire. "Good and evil. Those are the only things that make real sense to me, and I've been to evil and I don't want to go there again."

The remaining rim of light on the horizon pitched itself into night. They ate bread and cheese, made tea and stared at the flames, because the growing cushion of red beneath the burning twigs was the only thing puncturing the black cylinder around them.

Thea hugged her knees. "You should forgive yourself."

"You think?"

She nodded. "I rate forgiveness. It's a good concept."

"I've been waiting for it to come along for years, but no sign of it yet."

"It isn't a bus, Gabriel. You have to go looking for it."

"What would you know?" he said dismissively.

"I know about guilt."

Lying on his side, curved around the fire, he looked up, the whites of his eyes challenging her. "You think?" he said again.

"Yes, I do think."

"So?"

Thea ran her fingers through the cooling sand. "Do you know Sheep's Head?"

"A bleak sort of place, as I remember. Straw-colored and rocky."

"Beautiful and bleak. That's where I went to recuperate after Baghdad."

"Your aunt's place. The one who nursed you."

"Yes. Anyway, one evening when I was feeling better, I went for a walk. My first long walk, towards the marsh near the lighthouse. I hadn't meant to go far, but there's a lake along the way, long and still, so I sat on a rock, looking over it for a while, and I realized, after a bit, that Ireland was reclaiming me. I knew then that I could get on without Iraq. If you have Ireland, you need no other place. So it was good. I felt good. Properly recovered, you could say.

"Then the cold started to seep in—stupid of me, to stay out like that—and it wasn't fair, either, because Brona would be worrying, but when I turned back, my energy store was suddenly empty. I had to take it slowly and rest along the way, even though it was getting dark.

"It was a relief when I saw the black-tiled roof of the house down below. My pace picked up. I scurried through the boggy ground and onto the road, but when I got to the house, Brona wasn't about. The kitchen was empty, but the car was there, so I checked every room—the bathroom, the scullery, the cold rooms we had slept in as children—and I thought, Oh, shit, she's gone looking for me.

"I hurried back outside, calling her. Nothing. Then I went along the road to see if she was down at her veggie patch, but of course she wasn't. Her worrying had driven her out into the dusk in search of me, and with all the different goat tracks, all the humps of rock, it would have been easy for us to miss each other. So I ran back up along the main track and through that narrow grassy valley, shouting her name, over and over again, until eventually I thought I heard her call back, so I stood stock still, wanting the wind to hush. I was right—she *was* calling me from up behind the hillocks. I shouted, 'I'm here. I'm coming. Where are you?' And I stumbled along the high path, across the ridge, but even though I could still hear Brona's voice, it seemed to get ever farther away. I kept shouting that I was coming, that I was almost there, running and slipping, and yelling her name as she was calling mine . . . until I found her."

Gabriel stopped poking the fire.

"She'd fallen off the track, into the ditch, and was lying in the gorse, a tea towel stuck into the pocket of her apron, her face all scratched. Worried that I'd slipped and fallen, she had slipped and fallen. There was so little light left, I almost didn't see her. She was cold. Heavy. Unconscious. I tried to drag her out, but couldn't, so I took off my coat and jumper and put them over her, then struggled through the dark to the house.

"After calling the ambulance, I grabbed a torch and found my way back to her, and I held her and tried to keep her warm. The wind was bitter, screeching like a banshee, or maybe it *was* the banshee, come to take her. . . . I had never been so scared. It took the ambulance nearly an hour to get there—they had to come from Bantry, along that wretched winding road—and I kept stumbling back to see if it had come, until finally it was there, down at the house, and I ran down, screaming. Incoherent. I was shivering so much, they wouldn't let me take them to her. They wrapped me in a foil blanket and put me in the kitchen, while they went to her. For all the good it did."

"She died?"

"She was dead already." Thea's eyes turned back to the fire. "So you could say that I killed her. My self-absorption and selfishness forced her out into the wilderness. She was frailer than we knew. She had your brother's heart."

The desert took a few moments to absorb the story.

"So, you see, I know all about your guilt, Mr. Sherlock. The difference is that I don't inhabit it, I merely live with it, even though the memory of that night, the wind, and the gorges, and me sitting alone in the dark house, frozen, watching the—"

"Blue lights flashing."

She looked over. "Yes."

Gabriel, suddenly, was on his feet.

"But no siren. No sound." Thea pulled her hand around the back of her neck. "Only the beacon, lighting the room with a blue hue, then throwing me back into darkness."

Gabriel stood on the other side of the flames staring at her, arms hanging. "Just as you left, so you come back."

"What?"

"Lights on the wall," he said.

"Huh?"

"I saw the blue lights. On my wall. In Muscat. I saw the ambulance."

"Please don't, Gabriel. Not here."

"And then you were gone and now you're back again, and I can't even see you." His eyes narrowed. "It must be the competition. You don't like it. Twenty-six years isn't enough? You want my whole life?"

"What are you on about?" Thea stood up and gripped his arm—anything to get his eyes off hers. "What competition?"

"A beautiful woman comes into my life and you just have to wreck it, don't you?"

"Who are you talking to? It's me. *Thea.*"

He blinked, finally, and the arm in her grasp relaxed. "I know who it is," he said, sinking cross-legged to the ground. "I know who you are."

She crouched beside him. "I bloody well hope so. You're scaring me."

"You don't understand how devious they can be. If they want you, if they want your love, they'll do what it takes to make sure no one else gets it. They'll even make you mad. She made me mad—"

"No. No, you're just tired."

"And I loved her for it."

"You need to sleep. We should turn in."

Gabriel held her eye. "She's messing with us. Be careful."

"I won't listen to this. I'm turning in. So should you."

❋

Thea bolted upright, woken. Two voices. Beyond the canvas. Gabriel talking to someone. Who? A passing Bedouin in the night? If someone had driven up she would have heard the engine. He spoke quietly, in a low drone, but there had been another voice. That was what had woken her—it had slid into her unconscious and set off an alarm. She couldn't work out what he was saying, but she was aware of motion, of to-ing and fro-ing outside, and Gabriel ranting, tonelessly.

Then, quiet.

The silence pounded. Her ears fretted, thumping in the discomfort of having nothing to do, the pulse of blood through her veins making her agitated. There is no such thing as silence, she thought. The body won't allow it.

There it was again. Light, wispy. A woman, outside.

She pushed off the sleeping bag and crawled toward the flap, but couldn't see anyone until she was half in, half out of the tent, on all fours. The fire was low, all but gone, the night sticky black. She leaned out farther and thought she saw something by the jeep—a darkness against the dark, and Gabriel. A woman? Gabriel took off, walking, talking. Thea's body was vibrating. How long had she been asleep? Stretching farther out of the tent, she tried to follow his trajectory—he went behind the tent, around the other side, around the jeep, then out into the darkness, in measured, regular paces, and still that voice, though Thea couldn't identify words or even the language.

A voice on the wind, the light desert wind. Too scared to cower in the tent, she stood up, and although she knew he was coming, she jumped when Gabriel appeared from the side. She spun around—no sign, no sense, anymore, of anyone else.

"Who's here?"

He stopped. She couldn't see his face. "You."

"Who are you talking to?"

"You," he said again.

"No—there's a woman. Someone. I *heard* her."

"No," he said kindly. "It's just us."

The night air was frigid. Her mouth dry as dust.

"The singing sands, they call it."

"What?"

"It sounds like a voice," he said. "The wind on the sand."

That made sense. She caught her breath, dropped to her haunches. "Oh, thank God."

He walked past her, resuming his trudging.

Thea recoiled into the tent, like a snail into its shell. There was no woman. It was the sands, singing. The only thing now was *his* voice, the rhythmic muttering. Like chanting. Arabic. He was speaking Arabic. She put her hands over her ears. *Christ, Christ, Christ!*

To have come to such a place—what *had* she been thinking? Kim had been right. This was madness. From first sighting, Gabriel had been an unsettling presence and yet she had come away with him, far from all things, alone. What can we know of strangers? What did she think she was doing? Making up for time undone? Adventures lost? Well, here was adventure: Gabriel ranting. She had unleashed his demons, and stood, trapped, between him and them.

Curling up and pulling the sleeping bag about her, Thea willed herself to the safety of her own bed—hers and Alex's—with the sun pouring in across their deep red quilt, and the cat, like a furry hot-water bottle, at her feet, purring when rays of sunshine slipped past clouds and coated him with warmth. So distant; beyond reach. Out of range. She scrabbled for her phone, pressed a button and allowed its light to brighten the inside of the tent. The tiny screen lit up the canvas dome, but there was no signal, no way to contact . . . anyone.

The only person within reach was Gabriel, and he—barely so.

She should sleep, leave him to it. He would sleep, eventually. Dawn would come.

Or . . . he would come in—into the tent. She had gripped his arm, allowed him to touch her. He might come looking for more.

He could be sleepwalking. That was it. He was sleepwalking. Nothing spookier than that. But he might sleepwalk clear out of the camp and disappear over the dunes, in which case—her thoughts stepped carefully from one scenario to another, like feet through a minefield—she would get into the jeep and go for help at first light.

Unless, in his dream delirium, he took the jeep.

A cold flush flooded through her. Where were the keys?

No, she wouldn't need them. He wouldn't go anywhere. Any minute now he'd calm down. Go to sleep.

He kept the keys in his hip pocket.

She peeked through the flap, but could only follow his voice. His pace was no slower, no less rhythmic. He would walk her into a trance with his chanting. This was how they had spoken of jinn—crazy stuff, loss of reason, normalcy yanked away. Love and possession. Perhaps his jinn lover, threatened, had come back to take ownership. Perhaps now she meant business. That must have been what he'd been alluding to when he'd talked of competition—talked *at* her because to him they were interchangeable, she and Prudence. But humans were stronger, Abid had said. Jinn prey only on the weak. Thea let out an involuntary groan. Gabriel was weak, at his core, and weakened further by a new infatuation. His steadiness, the even keel on which he forced himself to live, had made him unsusceptible until this night and its double darkness. Now perhaps the jinn would have their way with him, and so he babbled. Thea listened again, and thought it must be the verses he had recited in Bahla—the ones from the Quran to repulse jinn—that he was reciting again now.

Dry riverbeds. Deserted spots. Exorcisms and potions. Thea believed in it all. The man pacing past the canvas was not familiar. He was neither predictable nor reasonable. He could be made to do anything—like driving off.

If he did, she would die. Eight liters of water per day, or delusion and death.

She needed those keys.

Her legs barely held her. She stepped out onto the sand and stood grasping one of the flaps, thinking of Alex, willing him to her side, though he was sound asleep three thousand miles away. He had no idea that his wife was alone in the Empty Quarter with an unhinged man and vengeful spirits.

Gabriel didn't see her.

"Gabriel."

And around he went again, reciting, invoking Allah.

Thea too prayed, to her own neglected God. Belief fluctuates. When a shot of cold shook her, she called "Gabriel," just as she remembered that it was dangerous to wake sleepwalkers. It had to be done gently; they had to be guided back to bed. . . .

His bed was on top of the jeep.

He came around again. "Please stop," she said.

His step faltered marginally; he stopped talking and the desert near-silence fell around them. She was aware of his shape, some feet away. Her eyes watered. She wanted out. She wanted to run. "You're freaking me out."

"Why?"

"This . . . you're . . . the chanting."

"Who?"

"What are you doing? Have you been drinking?"

"The thing is," he said, his voice normal and his tone cold. "The thing is . . . the thing I didn't mention is, what I did, that was bad. Bad. But you—"

Her tongue, like wafer. "Tell me in the morning, we'll talk tomorrow. You need—"

"You and me, this is something. Something *hot.*"

Bile in her mouth. "You should lie down. You need to sleep."

"Sleep?"

"Yes. Come into the tent."

He twisted on his hips, back and forth. Then he said, "I'm off," and turned toward the jeep.

"No!"

"No, really," he said, still in that casual, devil-may-care manner. "I'd be the death of you, honestly. I do that to people. Kill them and stuff."

"Is that what happened to Prudence? Did you kill *her*?"

Thea froze. Where had that come from? Was that her voice? It didn't sound like it. She looked around. *Who said that?*

"You don't look very dead to me." Gabriel pulled open the door.

Thea lurched, grabbing him. "Don't go!" But which was the greater danger—Gabriel or the desert? What exactly had he been on the point of telling her? Was the bad, bad deed more than what they knew? Was it in fact what Kim had suggested in Nizwa?

He turned slowly, and ran his hand along her arm, over her shoulder to the side of her neck. "I can't stay. I can't . . . hold back."

"I'll come. Wait till I grab my passport."

"You can't come where I'm going."

She couldn't risk breaking their contact. "Gabriel! Stop this. *Please.*"

He stroked the side of her face.

"I'm coming too," she said cautiously, trying to move past him to get into the jeep. To hell with her passport. She'd go without. But he moved in front of her, so that she stepped into him, against him; his breath warmed her neck. His hands fussed around her elbows, then gripped them. They were in the very place where she had seen him moments before with . . . he'd said it. She knew it now. She *was* the woman she'd seen. By the jeep. Near him. Talking.

Time in a tumble.

She pressed closer to him. "I'm cold, Gabriel," she said, her lips on his neck.

"Me too."

Her hand slid down to his belt. A deep sigh, human and recognizable, escaped him. It was working. She was bringing him back. But at what cost? At what pleasure?

With a backward step, she yanked him away from the jeep. Second by second, he was becoming the Gabriel she knew best—earthbound and seducible.

"I won't resist," he said.

Another pull on his buckle and they were near the tent. If he would just lie down, she thought, he might sleep. She kissed his cheek.

"Won't resist," he said, kissing her neck. "Can't."

The back of her fingers felt the bulge of keys in his hip pocket. She crouched at the tent and pulled him toward her; he fell in, landing across her. Squirming beneath him, she found his mouth. He responded. She sucked on his tongue, determined to keep him going until she was safe, until they were both safe. It was easy, though. He pushed up her T-shirt; she pulled his shirt over his head and pressed her hand into his crotch, rubbing, pushing, the keys right there, an odd, jagged shape above her thumb. If she grabbed them too quickly, he might revert, click back. She must not do the stupid thing—be impetuous and hasty, like heroes in bad movies. In the real world, there could be no mistakes. Calm, measured, slow. Slow, like his hand between her thighs and his breath heavy in her ear. So simple. Rambling incoherently moments before, and now a mere man, making the right moves, arousing her. Fear become desire. Focus, she thought. *Focus!* She opened his buckle, his zipper, burrowed into his clothing and curled her fingers around his erection, kissing him again, because she wanted to; had wanted to since, in that intimate way, he had nodded at her by the Bimmah Sinkhole and something warm had shot up from the ground. He moaned. *Get them.* . . . Her knees lifted. *Keys. Jeep. Keys. Safety. Danger.* Kissing so good, so well, and Alex far away, asleep, unconscious, so unconscious that this wasn't even happening.

Gabriel moved down, his mouth on her ribs, her hip. At any moment, he would push off his jeans. Clear thinking was drifting beyond reach. Should she grab them now or were the keys best left in his pocket until he fell asleep? No. If things went wrong, it would be too much of a scramble to get them from his discarded jeans, so she interceded, leaned over to undress him. With a whimper of anticipation, he lay back. . . . She hadn't thought of it, but there it was, right by her cheek, so she took him in, her mouth working so well he wouldn't have known or cared that her hand was searching his pocket. She gripped the keys tight in her fist, her mouth tightening also, too much, because he pulled her off, saying it was too soon, too soon. She moved her arm back, behind her. Nothing to hide them under, nowhere to conceal them, no nook or fold. His tongue flicked her nipple, slid to her navel. *Fuck the keys*, she thought. *Fuck me*. Careful not to let them tinkle, she could feel only bare canvas, as bare as Gabriel's shoulder beneath her palm. If he rattled them in the upheaval, or leaned on them, he might realize that the seduction had been a ploy. There would be no convincing him that it was both ploy and pleasure.

Her legs jerked; he was taking her apart. No one could see them. No one knew where they were. Only the dunes heard her cry out, as the keys dug deep into her palm.

A dome of light. The canvas was beginning to reflect the brightening sky. Gabriel was still sleeping, Thea still awake, failing to adjust to her new status: adulteress. It had gone too far. She had intended to seduce him only to a point, until she got the keys, fully expecting to be overcome with withering remorse even at that. But no remorse had come to halt proceedings, or any real resistance: she had been attracted to him for longer than she had feared him.

Now she understood how Sachiv had felt, when he had skulked out of her hotel bedroom, like a tortured dog.

No. This was different. Alex would have wanted her to do whatever it took to get back to him. Even the thing she did. An unfaithful wife coming home was better than a coffin. She had betrayed him in order not to be lost to him, and she would tell him everything, almost, from luring Gabriel into the tent, to feeling him up and hiding the keys—everything except the sex. And this deceit would be fair, and kinder than hurting Alex for the sake of a clear conscience.

She reached out, quietly, and found the bundle of keys nestling in the corner of the tent, but she no longer sought escape. Gabriel suffered, and his suffering entranced her. He didn't deserve abandonment, of any kind, or the same fate she would have endured had he driven off. She was not a murderess, not cruel enough to run off and leave him in another great vacuum. During the night the jeep had seemed to be the solution, but where would it have taken her, when she knew neither her south, nor her east, nor from which direction they had come? Within half a kilometer she would have been lost, which was the same as being dead. So even now there could be no dawn break. Gabriel was her only way out.

The pale blue of the canvas was visible now, and reassuring. Somehow she slept.

She woke when Gabriel sat up, and crawled, naked, out of the tent. It was cold. She pulled the sleeping-bag around her and put her head through the gap. Sunlight was tiptoeing over the dunes, and the desert, so menacing hours before, had taken on a chummy aspect, its Humpty Dumpty hills marked with jagged shade. Gabriel was standing by a dead branch, a stream of urine giving it a sharp drink. Thea admired him: square shoulders, perfect butt, long legs. What a beauty. What a mess. She retreated into the tent, giddy and weak with relief.

In the creeping daylight, his strange words amounted mostly to those of a haunted man, more disengaged than unhinged. A railway carriage unshackled, left behind, no longer wanted, but still on the tracks. She wondered at what exact point his life had swerved off course. Was it the gift abandoned, like a foundling child, left on a doorstep where no one could pick it up because it belonged to someone else? In abandoning it, he had surely discarded a part of his own soul, which in turn had discarded him.

She heard a sort of roar, a bellow—inhuman. She held her phone away to look at it. Was that where it had come from? The roar of rocks, of space, and Gabriel leaping in. She could see him floating down, arms adrift, like a skydiver. A skydiver without a parachute; a climber without ropes. Another roar came up from the depths of the cave—

She woke, startled. A nightmare. No cave, only canvas. Yet she could hear it still, the gasp of the abyss, as if the earth were inhaling a cherished son. The Majlis al-Jinn was calling him.

Gabriel hadn't returned to the tent. It was deadly quiet outside. Thea swiveled around again to look out. What was he up to? More shamanic circles? She stepped out and straightened up. No sign of him. Her head jerked—left, right, back.

Dunes.

Sand.

Curves.

Jesus. How long had she been asleep?

"Gabriel? . . . *Gabriel*!"

Fuck.

She dived into the tent, grabbed his shirt and scrambled out. Where the hell was he now? She looked inside the jeep and under it, turned around, calling him. The desert mocked her little voice, which didn't echo or carry, but stayed in her throat and in their crater. Her body rattling, she headed for the highest crest and struggled up its flank, feet sinking, sand shifting, as she twisted in every direction looking for any speck of movement. The sands sighed and whimpered. He had wandered off, the bastard, abandoned her to nowhere. Frying. Dying. Family. *Foolish!* Breathless, she came to the top of the rise, her head spinning, but saw only hills and crevasses stretching—

Against the flesh-colored sands, Gabriel was camouflaged, except for his dark hair, which made a black dash over to the left where, in a slight depression, he was crouching, defecating.

Thea turned away and made to go down the slope, but her legs gave up and she sank onto the sand. A sob escaped, and another. Reprieved, again. Safe, again. Tears flowed, until a hand on her shoulder made her yelp.

"What's a man gotta do to get a bit of privacy around here?"

Thea laughed—an involuntary burst of gratitude. He was there. *There*. She would be spared the frying dying and loved him for it.

"Hey," he said, sitting down. "What's the matter?"

Quirky grin, clear eyes—this was Gabriel proper. Tour guide Gabriel. Naked, gorgeous Gabriel.

"I thought you'd wandered off."

He pulled a face. "Wandered off?" He looked down at his body. "I'd be a piece of bacon under a grill."

"I panicked. After last night . . ."

He pulled her close. She yielded. "Last night," he said, "was . . . unexpected."

"It really threw me."

"Me too." With his chin, he pushed back the shirt and kissed her shoulder.

"Are you sure you're all right?"

He glanced at his erection. "What do you think?"

"I mean last night. You scared me."

"I scared myself."

"Why were you reciting those verses? What was that about?"

He stopped kissing her. "Verses?"

"Don't you remember?"

"I remember being seduced."

Her shoulders sagged. "The sex. Of course. You only remember the sex."

"I won't tell." His hand lingered on her knee.

"You were ambling, rambling."

His fingers moved along her leg. "I sleepwalk sometimes." Nibbling her collarbone, he pushed the shirt fully off her. "Terrible bloody sleepwalker."

"You tried to drive off without me!"

"For God's sake, why would I leave you, now that I have you?"

"You almost did!"

"Never." He rubbed his stubble along her shoulder. It was terrible. Terrible, what it was doing to her, what she was allowing him to do. There was no reason for it this time, no excuse. Her breathing deepened. *Stop*, said a weak, unconvincing voice inside her head. *Don't stop*.

"A piece of important advice." Gabriel stood up suddenly, offering his hand. "Never sit arse-naked in the sand. You'll regret it for days." His fingers tightened around hers as he pulled her to her feet. The way he threw her about was dizzying. Self-conscious, she needed to be near him, to wear him almost, like a piece of clothing, so she moved against him, felt his chest on her breast and his arm around her back. Gabriel had never looked so tame, so loving. "Walk," he said, pushing her gently away from his safe skin. "Enjoy the Garden of Eden."

"This? Paradise?"

He nodded. "The day after the apple, God turned Eden into desert."

"And they had to find their way out."

"Without GPS."

It was strange, wonderful, to walk naked along the ridge of a dune, kicking her feet, while the sun, still kind, was rising on her skin, warming her, head to toes, back to front. Her hair was full of sand. Her ears, too. Where did she end and the desert begin?

When she turned around, Gabriel was doing the salute to the sun on a shelf of level ground. All thoughts of flight, of hurrying back to civilization, seemed silly now. Civilization meant accountability. Their affair would be short. Flash in the pan. Dash in the sands. Being there was like being nowhere, and what took place nowhere could not have taken place. To secure escape, she had seduced him; to experience escape, she wanted to do so again. In the pale yellow light, she laid out his shirt and sat on it, to be there when he was done, and watched him extend his limbs in yogic poses on the toasted earth.

It brought on another wave of pity, a pull on her heart. Too close to him now, she had become part of the oddity that was Gabriel. Why else would she pity him, or admire his peculiarity, the way he lived and functioned like any man, yet existed in a realm of his own making? He had no other option. After dismantling his brother, there wasn't much to be done except take cover. And what a job it must be, she thought, waking up every day knowing that while he swanned about in the wadis, Max struggled to get out of bed.

Thea wondered what would become of him when she was gone. Fate might have been kinder by leaving Gabriel in the comfort of his fantasy that Prudence would one day return.

The invitation was quickly read. The salute completed, Gabriel scrambled over and without any fuss—since the seduction was already done—fell back on her and pressed in, there on the flank of the dune, while she opened her eyes at the sky.

"You see how patience pays off," he said, his lips against her ear.

She lifted her knees around his back. No one would ever know.

"Can you feel us?" he whispered, touching her.

Not one—other—person—would know.

"Both of us." Gabriel said. "In you."

"What?"

"Her and me, Prudence. You and her. We're all together now."

Thea yelped, wriggled, pulled away. "Get off!"

"Ow! Fuck!"

"What did you say?"

"'Fuck.'"

Thea stared, panting. There again. Gone again.

"What's got into you?" he gasped, grasping his groin.

She scurried down the dune, like a crab scuttling, her hands and feet beneath her, until she reached the level and ran to the tent, where she rummaged through their clothes. Her phone was in her pocket. Pulling on her own shirt, she collided with Gabriel as she crawled out again, but pushed past him and headed for another dune and ran up it, the sand pulling her, sucking her backward, impeding her, as if someone were gripping her ankles. Gabriel was pulling on his jeans outside the tent.

Her phone, lifted to the heavens, found no signal. "Shit!"

She turned another way, but Gabriel took the phone from her hand, saying, "You're out of range."

"Jesus Christ!" He was dressed already. There already.

"Next time you get a fit of guilt, try not to castrate me, would you? What the hell's come over you?"

"You tell me some jinn lover of yours is *in me*, and you wonder what's wrong?"

"I never said that. I didn't say anything!"

Doubts harassed her. Vacillating so fluidly between fear and desire, she no longer knew if he had spoken at all. "You were down by the tent. Just now, you were down there. How did you get up here?"

"Are you all right?" he asked. "You're babbling."

"Me? Babbling?" She heard hysteria in her voice. "I want to leave now."

"Fine."

There was movement down by the tent. Sand spiralling up. Dust devil. Thea grabbed her phone from him. "The only reason I had sex with you was because you were going to drive off."

"I told you. I will never leave you. And you can't leave me either."

Given their situation, there was a truth in those words that drained her. The sun's early kindness was over. Its warmth had become its heat, and its heat was becoming its deadliness. The aim it took. Like phone signals, clicking onto coordinates. A shard of fire on her scalp. She had yet to drink. She must drink. When did she last drink? "I have to get back to Muscat."

"We'll go to the cave first. I want you to see Majlis al-Jinn."

"No!" That earthly howl echoed plaintively. "No way. The only place I'm going is Muscat! I have a flight to catch."

Gabriel smiled, walking backward. "I'll pack up."

And he did. The scene was so ordinary—a man collapsing a tent, opening the back doors of his 4x4—but the ordinary wouldn't hold. It kept shifting, moving, leaving Thea adrift. She had to phone Abid. Get him to come. Hoping Gabriel's phone would have a stronger signal, she went down to the jeep, reached in and took it from the dashboard. It did have signal, but only marginally better than hers. She went to his contacts and scrolled up for Abid's number—and noticed something.

The soul drained out of her, down her legs, through her feet and into the Omani ground. Love and fear.

Gabriel came over with her sleeping bag. "What are you looking at?"

"There's no . . ."

"Reading my messages now?" He winked, shook out the sleeping bag, scattering sand.

"No Max," she said, "in your Contacts."

Gabriel kneeled down to roll up the bag.

She stared at the names.

"Yeah, well. Max is Max. He doesn't have a phone, just like he doesn't have a life."

"Kim thinks he might actually have died, that that's why—"

"It amounts to the same thing. If you're not really living, you might as well be dead. Now hurry up or we'll never make it to the cave."

"I'm going to Muscat."

He looked up, stood up. "No."

"Take me back to Muscat! I need to go home."

Gently, swiftly, before her very eyes, Gabriel slid into his fretful self—grimacing against the sun, moving back and forth, watching her. In a flicker of sunlight, he became the stranger of the night before—his movements jerky, his words fast. "You don't know where you need to be, Prudence."

Seasick, Thea took on another slope and climbed it, holding Gabriel's phone high, waiting for it to properly find its home, click into its beam and display a stronger signal. A way to the world. . . . Instead, that one bar of signal vanished. There was no way to call Abid, to beg him to come and meet them along the road, to save her from Gabriel and Gabriel from his curse. Her head pounded. Her throat was parched. They needed to drink, both of them, then, somehow, she would persuade Gabriel to drive to the nearest town. Meanwhile, they were alone. Almost.

Thea turned.

There she was.

Down on the flat, Gabriel was talking to her.

To *her*. Same clothes, same hair, same *self.*

"Go away from here." Thea's hand, burning on the hot bonnet of the jeep, was the only thing keeping her upright.

You would repel her.

You are stronger.

They turned. She was holding a bottle. She said, "It's only me," and lifted the bottle to drink. The scraping thirst in Thea's throat eased.

Gabriel stepped toward her. "Thea—"

"Why is she me?" It wasn't like looking in the mirror, or watching a home movie, or being out of body. No. Seeing another person who was her own self was like being in Hell. She managed to speak. "Go away." Three times, Abid had said. *Tell them three times to leave, the Prophet, peace be upon him, says in the Hadith.* "You can't have him anymore. Leave us al—"

"Don't!" Gabriel cried. "Don't say it again."

Double vision. Double perspective. Whose arms were these? Whose eyes? "Get into the jeep, Gabriel. You'll be all right. We're leaving."

Prudence poured water over her face. It wet Thea's hair and cooled her body, as she cried out, "Go from here! Go!"

Someone said, "You can't leave, Thea."

"No? I have the keys. And the water. Get in the car, Gabriel. This is over now."

Not quite. The other, suddenly, lurched at her.

Terrorized, she heard a growl come from deep within her chest and, gathering all her own limbs and with a punch of determination, she pushed past Gabriel, fought him off, clambered into the driving seat.

Ignition. Accelerator. Thrust.

Sand flew out as the wheels took the slope.

Behind, Gabriel was running.

EAST. WEST. NOWHERE. SOMEWHERE. The same, the same, more of the same. White sky. Red dunes. Dunes—too kind a word for the shimmying mountainous fence all around. All around. Arms aching, thighs stiff—gears and grunts, mounds and dips—and the jeep perched on the brim of a high crest. East? West? No idea. And Gabriel, adrift.

Water. Enough to outlast the fuel.

Alex.

Alex.

What have I done? Had to bolt, get out of that crater. Hours ago, now. Her. *Me.* She drank, I drank; she talked, I talked. Her—me—lunging at me, both.

Followed the tracks, lost the tracks. Lost. Went back to find him. . . . Calling. Hollering his name across the Empty Quarter.

Bigger than France.

Quiet as the moon.

Here, no point calling anymore. No means to call, besides. Phone dead. Tears, dry as the word. Chest juddering. And the jeep leaning away from the slope, waiting. It had fought with and against—clutch grinding, wheels sliding, threatening to topple—but purring, now, like a great tomcat.

Alone. He had been all alone, running after the jeep. Side mirror, back mirror: Gabriel, trying to catch up. No one else. No Prudence. Only one man and a collapsed tent. *But I didn't stop.*

Breathe deep. Down, panic, down. "Help will come, stay calm," Alex would say. "They'll find you." And he would say, his own panic rising, "Use the goddamned GPS!"

Can't. Don't understand it. Coordinates blinking, telling me nothing.

No water. He has no water. No shade. Won't last a day. And worse—*oh, God, Alex, much worse*—I'm done for, me too.

Someone should tell his sister. Someone should tell Annie that I killed her Gabriel. Don't know how exactly.

They won't find me.

Air-conditioning guzzling fuel. Decide. *Decide.*

Down the flank, a small depression, a sculpted hole, filling with shade. At last. The day, moving. It would be all right. Easy. Like falling asleep. That's what he said. You fall asleep, don't even know.

Is he sleeping yet, the archangel, back in the folds of emptiness?

Sand scraping, hands shaking. My boys. My darling boys. Kieran. Marcus. The hearts in my heart. *Know that I'm holding you close, and that I'm drinking drop by drop so I might hold you close again.*

The sun sliding. So. The west—that way.

Turn east. Toward the sea. Away from the sand. Keep driving. *I'll keep driving, my loves, as long as there's fuel. I'll keep on going until I find you all again.*

It would be easy. Like coasting toward an unseen runway—ahead, somewhere, an island in the middle of the glittering ocean. Floating, gliding. Like Amelia, searching for Howland in the great blue infinity, tanks emptying into infinity. Running north and south. Coasting into sleep. Real sleep. Oblivion deep.

But not yet.

Thea engaged first gear.

Not yet.

Acknowledgments

THERE IS A SMALL ARMY behind every novel, and I would like to thank mine. I am indebted to Dettia O'Reilly, Honorary Consul of Oman in Ireland; to David Sergeant, Hatim Altaie, Yayha Al Hashmi, and Aziza al Habsi for their guidance, knowledge, and generous hospitality on the ground in Oman; and to Kathleen Hindle, the most amenable of traveling companions, and our driver, Rashid. Warmest thanks and appreciation also to the team at Hoopoe Fiction, especially my wonderful editor, Nadine El-Hadi, for her clarity, conviction, and wisdom; my peerless copyeditor, Hazel Orme; Katie Holland, for her extraordinary patience, and Neil Hewison, for opening the door. It is an honor and a delight to be published by the American University in Cairo Press, not least because the first paragraph of fiction I ever wrote was inspired by Cairo.

I am indebted to the Arts Council of Ireland for the Literature Bursary Award and to Cork County Council Arts Office for the Artists' Bursary Award. The dedicated work of arts administrators—those who keep the arts and artists afloat—often goes unseen, so I would like to acknowledge the support of Sarah Bannan, of the Arts Council of Ireland; Francis Humphrys, of West Cork Music; and, most particularly, Sinead Donnelly, of Cork County Council Library & Arts Service.

Thanks also to Sue Leonard, Elaine Cotter, Bernadette Gallagher, Ahdaf Soueif, and Anita Desai; to Vincent

Woods, for permission to quote from "The Good People"; to Tim Mackintosh-Smith, my guide in all things literary; to Finola Merivale and Tamzin Merivale, for being assiduous, shrewd, and fair readers; and to William Merivale, the writer's perfect companion.

My agent, Jonathan Williams: six books, twenty years; so much learnt, so many thanks.

Finally, Aingeal Ní Murchú, who loved the unseen. Now unseen, but ever here.

Selected Hoopoe Titles

Embrace on Brooklyn Bridge
by Ezzedine C. Fishere, translated by John Peate

The Baghdad Eucharist
by Sinan Antoon, translated by Maia Tabet

The Unexpected Love Objects of Dunya Noor
by Rana Haddad

*

hoopoe is an imprint for engaged, open-minded readers hungry for outstanding fiction that challenges headlines, re-imagines histories, and celebrates original storytelling. Through elegant paperback and digital editions, **hoopoe** champions bold, contemporary writers from across the Middle East alongside some of the finest, groundbreaking authors of earlier generations.

At hoopoefiction.com, curious and adventurous readers from around the world will find new writing, interviews, and criticism from our authors, translators, and editors.